M.N. KINCH

Keepers of Time

Book One of the Keepers of Time Trilogy

First edition

ISBN: 9798869210104

This book was professionally typeset on Reedsy.
Find out more at reedsy.com

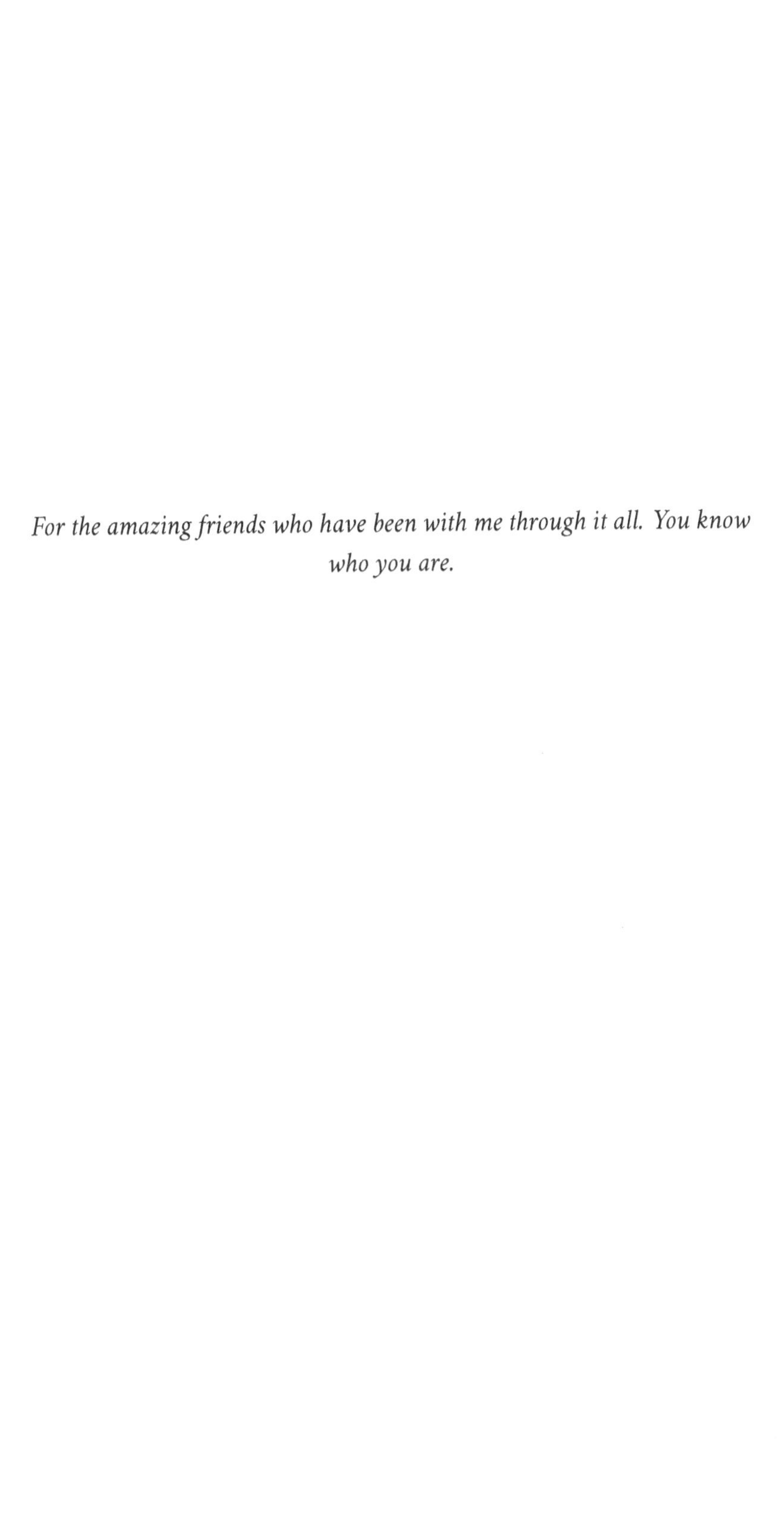

For the amazing friends who have been with me through it all. You know who you are.

1

Joan

Streetlights reflect off the wet pavement, casting glowing stripes of yellow and blue over the road and sidewalk. I jog through the rain, awkwardly clutching my bag under my coat to prevent water from dripping inside and hurting my computer with my precious term projects and internship application on it. No stupid storm will put my master's degree or a summer internship at NASA in jeopardy.

I reach the Clockwork Cafe and Bakery, the place my roommate, Nisha, recommended. I've never been here before, but I need a change of scenery. Something outside of the MIT campus, outside of Cambridge and the typical student cafes full of stressed-out undergrads cramming for finals, where that mood of last-minute panic permeates the air like a gas leak.

So I took a quick bus ride over the river to this quiet street in Back Bay. Sandwiched between a tiny health food store and a bookshop that closes at five p.m., the cafe's wooden sign juts out from the tall brick building, dangling under a working clock. I smell fresh bread and espresso the moment someone opens the door to leave. I grab the door to step inside, push my hood off, and pat my blond pixie cut so I don't get hedgehog hair. I can already feel tufts sticking out on the back and top. I probably look as frazzled as I feel.

A few people sit at the mismatched tables. A skinny dude with giant glasses and a scruffy beard working on a laptop. Two people about my age on what looks like an awkward first date. Some others I don't bother to look at. Antique odds and ends clutter the shelves on the walls: books, toys, teapots, old clocks set to different times. High on the wall behind the register hangs a menu board listing teas and espresso drinks in artistic chalk lettering, accompanied by drawings of coffee mugs and tea bags. Below that, floating shelves of glass jars contain different types of loose tea. Baskets of rolls and muffins under a plastic shield line the counter, separating the seating area from the kitchen. Mumbling voices mingle with the clinking of cups on saucers, spoons in mugs.

Behind the counter is the kitchen—a bright, open room where a tall, slim man with his dark hair in a bun kneads a giant wad of dough. He looks to be in his late twenties or maybe even early thirties. The lines in his forehead and around his eyes don't completely fade when he relaxes his face. His eyebrows knit together, dark eyes glaring as he scans the room.

"Where the hell is Luna?" he says to a petite young woman with chin-length dark hair.

"Probably out watching the rain," the girl says in a dainty, musical voice. She leans against the counter behind him, turning a pink china teacup over in her hand.

The man curses and punches the dough, leaving a fist-shaped indentation. His olive complexion and eyes look just like the girl's. I wonder if they're siblings.

"Just clear the tables, that's all I ask," he grumbles before noticing me. His eyes widen briefly. "Gabby, help her!" he hisses at the girl, jabbing his finger in my direction before turning and storming out the door at the back of the kitchen.

"Oh," Gabby says, looking at me for the first time. A tiny gold star on a chain sparkles in the V-neck of her slightly faded pinstripe dress. Her fine features light up with surprise, like she had no idea there was anyone else in the room. Putting her teacup down, she steps up to the register. "What would you like?" she asks, eyes sparkling.

I scan the menu and rows of tea, debating whether I need a big or small hit of caffeine. "Um, Earl Grey and a lemon scone, please. To stay." Small hit. At least to start.

Gabby presses a few keys on the register. I've counted out exact change and drop the coins in her extended hand. The drawer pops open, but instead of depositing the coins right away, she examines each one before plinking it in the correct slot.

"Oh, this one was minted in 1963," she says, inspecting one of the quarters. "That's quite old for a quarter."

What the actual hell?

She drops it into the register, now scrutinizing a penny. "Oh! This is from the seventies, so it's real copper. Did you know modern pennies are just zinc with a copper coating?"

"I think I've heard that, yeah." I look behind me to make sure a line isn't building up. It isn't.

"I'll start your tea," Gabby finally says, smiling at me. I nod, then grab a plate from the stack, select the biggest scone in the basket, and pick one of the smaller tables to set up my computer.

"I can do this," I whisper to myself as I open my laptop. I click the file "A New Age of Space Travel: Possibilities for Exploration Beyond Mars," by Joan Sanders. I'm supposed to present this project to a panel of NASA reps tomorrow morning, and I'm nowhere near finished. This project is kicking my ass.

It's not like me to leave something to the last minute, but this project has freaked me out from the beginning. After all, I'm only a first-year master's student competing against doctoral candidates with IQs higher than the number on my student loan statement. But that summer internship has my name on it. I knew it the second I saw the announcement on my advisor's door, still warm from the printer.

I need something that'll stand out. If there's anything that's shocked me about MIT, it's how much I *don't* stand out. I sailed through my undergrad, picking everything up easily, but grad school is different. MIT is different. This is where the big kids play. And I'm only finishing up the first semester of my master's program in astrophysics.

I take a deep breath and put my fingers to the keys.

Typing sentence by labored sentence, I nibble at my scone as I flip through my notes. I startle slightly when a pair of hands places a mug of steaming tea on my table, a woman's hands with the same olive skin as the two people behind the counter. I assume it was the girl who was making my tea.

"Oh," I gasp. "Thank you..." I look up and forget what I was about to say.

It's a different girl, mid-twenties maybe, perhaps a year or two younger than me, dripping wet, with silvery hair that falls just past her shoulders. She wears a soaked blue apron over a sleeveless flowered dress that's thin and faded. How is she not freezing? Her lips part slightly, giving her a dazed look. My breath catches in my throat. She has the lightest blue eyes I've ever seen, almost the pale silver color of her hair. They stand out like shining stars against her olive skin. At first I wonder if she's blind, but her eyes focus on me for a split second and she smiles softly before her pupils slide away from mine, looking right past me. Through me. Without a word, the girl turns and drifts away, arms limp at her sides, dripping a trail of water behind her.

This must be Luna, the girl the guy was so grumpy about. I shrug it off and get back to work, taking my time with the tea and scone. The scone is amazing. I look up at the guy in the kitchen, who's wiping down the counters, wondering if he bakes all the cafe's pastries and if they're all as good as this. I could eat here every day.

Gabby, the girl from the register, carries a stack of trays past him and says something that makes him roll his eyes, but he smiles. The corners of his dark eyes crinkle. He hasn't had a shave in a while and his nose is a little pointy, but the effect isn't at all unpleasant.

Stop getting distracted, Joan. Work. NASA. Move it.

I drop my eyes back to my screen and drag out another sentence. My silver charm bracelet clinks on the keyboard, the tiny sun, moon, star, and rocket charms tinkling as I type.

Eventually, I'm the only one left in the cafe. I'm not sure what time they close, but I get the feeling I should pack up. I finish the last sip of now-cold tea, leaving the dregs in the bottom, before closing my laptop and slipping it into my bag.

When I straighten, my heart jumps into my throat. The silver-haired girl stands by my table, holding my plate and empty mug.

"Holy sh—" I exclaim, then stop myself. I hadn't even heard her coming. This girl has a gift for sneaking up on people. "Um, thank you," I mumble, shrugging into my coat and swinging my computer bag over my shoulder. She doesn't answer, but stares down into my mug, frowning. Suddenly, I'm very uncomfortable.

"Thanks," I say again. I stand and move around her to get to the door. I look back just before I step outside. This time, she looks straight at me, eyes wide, gripping the mug so hard her knuckles are white. My stomach churns. I yank on my hood and step into the rain.

Shivering in my coat, I stride down the street to the bus stop, wishing I'd brought gloves. It's almost May. Shouldn't it be warming up soon? I reach into my pocket for my bus pass when I hear the screech of car tires behind me.

I don't have time to turn or scream.

Then, someone slams into me from behind, knocking the wind out of me. We fall to the pavement. Sharp pain shears up my arm, palms, knee, and the side of my face as the sidewalk shaves off my skin. My left wrist snaps and I cry out. Behind me, I hear a crash, the crunch of metal on stone. Rubble rains down on us.

Then, the world is still.

The person on top of me breathes hard. I finally take a gasping inhale. Oddly, I catch a whiff of fresh bread.

"Ow…" I wheeze, too shocked to say anything else.

The person who pushed me scrambles up. "Are you alright?" says a man's voice.

I hiss through my teeth as I roll over, cradling my wrist. A face swims into focus above me—dark hair, cheeks and chin covered in stubble, brown eyes wide with concern. It's the guy from the cafe, still in his white apron. He offers a hand, which I take.

He helps me to my feet. My face and palms sting, but my wrist throbs with white-hot pain. I take a deep breath, pinching my eyes shut.

"You're bleeding," Cafe Guy says, reaching back to untie his apron. He pulls the strap over his head and hands it to me. "Here, use the clean side for your face." He looks grimly over my shoulder.

I turn to see a black Mercedes, half buried in the window of a brownstone boutique. Shattered glass and chunks of brick litter the pavement. A streetlamp flickers above us, illuminating the wisp of steam curling from the front of the car.

A person slumps in the front seat, still.

Cafe Guy approaches the car and I limp along beside him, apron dangling from my hand. "Sir?" I choke as we reach the driver's window.

It's a thin, sandy-haired man in his early twenties, wearing a baseball cap and flannel shirt. He doesn't stir.

"He's not moving," I tell Cafe Guy, scrambling for my cell phone with my good hand. "We need an ambulance." I pat my pockets, but I can't find my phone. It must have come out of my pocket when I fell.

"I'm on it," he says. He pulls out a phone, and his voice fades in my ears as he talks to an operator.

"Sir?" I say again. I touch the driver's shoulder and wiggle it. The man falls limply to the side, light eyes blank and glassy.

"Oh, god."

Cafe Guy hangs up the phone. "They'll be here in five minutes…" His voice trails off as his eyes fall on the man in the car.

I crouch, the impact of the last few minutes finally hitting me. I feel sick and dizzy. Pain blooms in my wrist and I feel it start to swell. I shut my eyes tight, but I still see the man's dead, flat eyes.

A hand grips my shoulder. "Come sit down," Cafe Guy offers. My eyes well with tears of pain and shock. I allow him to guide me to a bench in front of one of the stores a few doors down, where I can't see the man in the car. People across the street stop and stare, whispering to each other. Sirens scream in the distance. My vision swims.

Through the yellowish haze of my sight, I see two figures running toward us—one small and dark-haired, carrying something, and the other taller with silver hair, a step behind her. The girls from the cafe, Gabby and Luna.

"Here," Gabby says, wrapping a blanket around my shoulders.

I'm too nauseous and tired to protest. Luna drapes another blanket over my lap, blank eyes staring straight ahead. I close my eyes.

"Help's coming," Cafe Guy says.

"The driver…"

"We can't do anything for him. The EMTs will take care of it."

I do my best to curl into a ball, letting my head droop until my chin touches my chest. I want to thank him, but I can't think straight.

"I'm Thiago," he says. "Thiago Cardoza. And these are my sisters, Gabby and Luna." I look up at him and he smiles tightly, like he's not used to smiling. I smile back, or try to.

"Joan," I respond. Dizziness overtakes me and I squeeze my eyes shut. Through my eyelids, I see flashing blue and red lights approaching from down the street.

2

Thiago

The EMTs bandage the scrapes on my palms and forearms. They even give me some ointment to dab on the small cuts on the back of my neck from the spray of broken glass. Now I wonder how the hell I'm supposed to knead dough with scabby hands. Disposable gloves, I guess.

I didn't feel the pavement grate off my skin as we fell. I'm sure there's zest of Thiago all over that sidewalk. Zest of Joan too. I feel horrible about banging her up so badly, but at least she's alive.

My heart hasn't quite slowed down yet. Every time I close my eyes, I see her walking and the Mercedes swerving, but I don't remember running. I just remember panic, and suddenly she was under me on the sidewalk.

Gabby and Luna sit on either side of Joan on the bench. Red and blue lights from the squad car, ambulance, and fire truck dance in their eyes. Gabby's eyes sparkle with excitement. For the past fifteen minutes, she's attempted to distract Joan by flipping through a collection of antique photographs she must have had in her dress pocket. Luna, of course, is a million miles away. Joan stares ahead blankly, holding out her wrist for a kind-faced EMT to examine.

"Yup, it's broken," the EMT says matter-of-factly. "You'll need to go to the hospital to get it set, but I don't think it's a severe break. Keep the ice pack on it until you make it to the ER." He moves his hand off the cold pack he's holding on her wrist so she can hold it herself.

Joan nods, dazed. A pang of guilt jabs my gut, but I remind myself that she's alive. What's worse, a broken wrist or getting smeared on the pavement like an insect on a windshield?

"You could ride in the ambulance, or you could call someone to take you in," the EMT continues. "I don't recommend driving yourself."

Joan blinks. I turn to look at what she'd been watching. The other EMTs have removed the driver from the car, zipped him into a body bag, and are now loading him in the back of the ambulance. They move slowly, taking their time. There's no rush when the patient's already dead.

The body doesn't bother me. I've seen my share of death, some of it more gruesome than this. Gabby and Luna barely look at the body—Luna because she's Luna, and Gabby because she's much more interested in showing Joan her collection of photos.

"Do you have someone to drive you or would you like to take the ambulance?" the EMT asks again.

"Oh," Joan says, dragging her eyes from the ambulance. "My phone…" She scans the ground.

I look around the sidewalk where we fell and notice a small, rectangular object at the base of a garbage can. I stride over and pick up the phone. The screen is cracked.

"Here it is," I say, handing it to her. She presses the button a few times, then shakes her head.

"Trashed," she said. "Could I borrow someone's phone to call my roommate?"

Gabby looks at me, her eyes wide, darting sideways at Joan. She's trying to tell me something.

"Here," I offer, holding out my phone.

Gabby rolls her eyes and shakes her head. That was the wrong thing, clearly. I shoot her an exasperated look. How was that wrong?

"Thank you," Joan says, taking the phone and dialing a number. Who still memorizes phone numbers? Other than me and Gabby, of course. It's a useful thing to do, for this very reason. I'm impressed.

Joan holds the phone to her ear and starts talking to someone while Gabby glares at me, still subtly jerking her head toward Joan. I have no idea what she's going on about. I can usually read her better than this, but right now I just can't think straight. Maybe a near-death experience has something to do with it.

Joan finishes her call and hangs up.

"Thanks," she says, handing the phone back to me. "She should be here soon."

I don't say much while we wait. No one does. Even Gabby is quiet.

The EMTs finish their work and leave. After a few minutes, Joan sighs, reaches for her computer bag, and carefully slips out her laptop, opening it on her lap.

The screen doesn't light up. Joan jabs a few keys, runs her finger around the trackpad, and presses the start button several times, but nothing happens.

"Shit," she whispers, her eyes turning glassy. "Shit, shit, *shit*. It's gone. It's all gone."

I didn't think about her computer bag, or what must have happened to it when I tackled her. "What's gone?" I ask tentatively.

"My presentation. My paper. My application. It was all saved on my hard drive." She slaps the computer shut, slides it back into the bag, then leans forward on her elbows, head in her hands, fingers digging into her scalp. "I could probably take it somewhere to get it off the hard drive, but not by tomorrow morning. *Shit.*"

Application for what, I want to ask, but Gabby shoots me another glare. I know what this one means. *Shut up, Thi.*

I watch Joan awkwardly, trying to think of something to say, and my eyes catch a glint of a silver bracelet peeking out of her sleeve. I take a step forward and squint. Charms dangle from the chain; a star, a crescent moon, a sun, and...*a rocket.* My stomach jumps.

She lifts her head again, purple shadows forming under her eyes. The shock is over, but I can tell she's exhausted, and now stressed out about her computer.

Within minutes, a green Accord pulls up, driven by a pretty Southeast Asian girl who doesn't get out of the car as Joan approaches the passenger door.

Joan turns to look at us, at me, and gives a small wave before climbing into the car, her face grave.

She shuts the car door and they drive away. I watch the car disappear down the street. Something stirs deep within me, a feeling both familiar and strange. Gabby's sharp voice cuts through my daze.

"Thiago, you idiot," Gabby snaps. "You were supposed to offer to take her to the emergency room!"

Oh. That's what she'd been trying to tell me. It makes sense now, the obvious thing to do, since I was already here and her roommate wasn't. I just didn't get the feeling Joan wanted me to offer. I thought she'd want to go with someone she knew, not a stranger.

Gabby heaves a sigh, then stands. "I'm going to bed," she announces. She takes Luna's hand and guides her to her feet before they walk down the sidewalk back to the cafe.

A tow truck arrives. I stay for a few more minutes to watch the truck pull the Mercedes out of the storefront before walking back to the cafe.

I make myself some tea before going upstairs to the apartment. The cafe is quiet. After everything, I just want to sit at a table alone in the dark, eat ham on leftover white bread, and drink a steaming mug of some herbal tea blend Gabby invented. So that's what I do. The tea is good, much better than her concoctions usually are.

It now occurs to me that I probably should have gotten Joan's information so I could check on her. But what could I say that wouldn't sound idiotic?

Hey Joan, it's Thiago. The guy from the car incident. How are you?

Huh. That may have worked. But I didn't get her number. I'll probably never see her again. Something inside me deflates. I didn't realize it earlier with all the activity going on, but I do want to see her again. When she was here, though, it just didn't occur to me that I might not.

I drain my mug and leave it in the kitchen before bolting the front door, double-checking the lock, then letting myself out the back door, locking and checking that too. The door to the upstairs apartment is at the back of the building, right next to the kitchen door. I let myself in, then lock the deadbolt, the sliding lock, and the knob lock, double-checking each before climbing the narrow staircase.

At the top of the stairs is a door that leads to the kitchen, and beyond the kitchen is the living room.

Luna sits in the doorway between the kitchen and living room with her cat, Gulliver, curled in her lap. She stares at the door I've just come through, or at least she's pointed in my general direction. Her face is arranged in her usual vacant, staring-right-through-you expression. Gabby is flopped on the couch in the living room, reading an ancient-looking book she probably found in some garbage thrift shop.

"*Pensé que ibas a la cama,*" I say to Gabby.

"I *am* going to bed," she responds in English. "In a few minutes. And we're in the states, Thi. They speak English here."

"Our parents spoke Spanish and so do we," I return in Spanish. "You of all people should appreciate the preservation of culture."

Gabby just blinks, not looking up from her book.

"You both have the morning shift tomorrow, remember?"

"So do you."

"Yes, but I know *I'll* get up on time."

"We couldn't sleep," she says, carefully turning a page. "We had an exciting evening."

My lips press together. I'm partially frustrated at Gabby because I know I'll have to haul them both out of bed in the morning, and partially at myself for not getting Joan's number, not even finding out her last name. The evening *had been* exciting. Far too exciting.

Gulliver slips off Luna's lap to slink around the legs of the dining chairs. He looks up at me with his green eyes, swishing his tail expectantly. I bend down to scratch his ears. As much as I contested Gabby's idea of getting Luna a cat, I enjoy having him around. I try not to let Gabby see that, though. He purrs and arches his neck, pressing his head into my palm.

"Make sure to feed the cat before you go to bed," I say, more to Luna than Gabby, but loud enough that Gabby can hear. If I relied on Luna to keep the cat fed, he'd have starved long ago. I'd feed him myself, but he's Luna's cat and Gabby's idea, and therefore Gabby's responsibility.

Gulliver sashays back to Luna and climbs into her lap, casually licking his paw and swiping it over his ears. With no change of expression, Luna raises a hand to rest on the tabby cat's back, threading her fingers through his thick fur. I smile grimly. Gabby was right; the cat is good for Luna.

I cross the kitchen and squat down to look at Luna.

"You should go to bed," I tell her gently, putting a hand on her shoulder to momentarily coax her out of her trance. She blinks, but her eyes are still glazed. Gabby can do what she wants, but Luna should really be in bed. If anyone needs sleep, it's her. I feel the muscles in her shoulder relax. She pauses, then slowly ambles to her feet. Gulliver calmly slides off her lap.

"That's it," I say. "Time to rest."

I guide her toward the hall.

"Gabby, help Luna get ready for bed." She glares at me. I grin. If she gets Luna ready for bed, she might as well get ready for bed too. She'll be sleepy within minutes. But she's not annoyed about helping Luna. We both love Luna, and we know she gets weird when she doesn't sleep. They both do, actually, Luna and Gabby. Without sleep, Luna is even more listless, Gabby, more distracted, and irritable. And they both...*see* more. I prefer to keep that to a minimum.

I, on the other hand, do fine with little sleep. Eight hours or three hours, I barely notice a difference. I still focus on the task in front of me, the here and now, moving forward and taking care of them, like always. Gabby says I'm a machine. I say I'm the only person in this family with their head on straight.

Gabby rises and catches up to Luna, then leads her down the hall to the bathroom, where she'll help her brush her hair and teeth.

I start cleaning up the mess from breakfast this morning. It looks like Gabby started but got distracted, as usual. Some of the dishes are washed. The leftover muffins are wrapped up, but not put away. Only two of the four kitchen chairs are pushed up to the table.

I hear Gabby and Luna pad back down the hall from the bathroom to their bedroom, and the door clicks shut. When I've cleared most of the breakfast mess, I open the fridge to grab a beer. There aren't many left, but tonight's a night for a drink. I pop off the bottle cap and step into the living room, weave through the narrow space between the coffee table and the old sofa, and collapse into the saggy cushions, resting my head on the even saggier arm. Gabby's book lies on the coffee table. I lean over to read the title: *Moby Dick.* I'm pretty sure that was a book I was supposed to read in high school, but didn't. The cloth on the spine is peeling and the sides of the pages are yellowed and spotted. I'm not sure why she bought this grubby thing when she could have gone to the bookstore next door for a brand new copy. Who knows where it's been?

I sip my beer, letting the bubbles and flavor of the hops dance over my tongue. My mind drifts to Joan again for a moment until my eyes settle on the ornate astronomical clock on the wall across from the couch, right next to the hall. The constant ticking underscores the background noise of our home and pulses in the back of all our minds.

It was my parents' clock, the only one they brought with them from Spain. They made other clocks, of course, had a whole artisan clock shop in Barcelona, but this was the only clock that survived everything.

I remember watching them make that clock, carefully layering the gears inside, painting the housing and peaked roof indigo blue with golden moons and stars. Its face is a nest of golden circles, the smaller ones rolling around in the larger one to track not only hours and minutes, but the positions of the sun, moon, and planets. I have no idea how to read it.

According to the glowing green numbers on the oven clock, however, it's almost midnight. The clock will strike twelve soon. Two tiny doors below the clock face will open, emitting a parade of spinning planets the size of marbles: our solar system. We all sleep through the chiming of the hours. In fact, we'd probably all wake up panicked on the hour if we didn't hear those familiar tones. It isn't until the clock strikes twelve that I go to bed. Almost every night is the same thing; something about the twelve repetitive chimes lulls me to sleep.

I watch the clock, remembering my father's face, my mother's laugh. Why do I always think of them at night? How they used to put us to bed each night, three children in one room. I barely remember Spain, the days before I knew much English, before Gabby was born and when Luna was only a baby—a dark-haired, wide-eyed baby.

I chug the rest of my beer, draining the bottle as the clock strikes twelve.

Gabby hasn't come out of their bedroom. She's probably gone to bed too. I push myself off the couch and place the bottle in the recycling bin in the kitchen, careful not to make a sound and wake my sisters. I pad to the hallway in my bare feet, passing the clock on the way to the bathroom. I brush my teeth, run my fingers through my long hair, and strip off my jeans, walking back to my own room in my tee shirt and boxers.

Mamá used to tell me to watch for signs, though I never knew what those signs were or what they'd mean. I've always watched, though, and I can't shake the creeping feeling that tonight was one of those signs. I think of the charms on Joan's bracelet. The sun, moon, star, and a rocket. I touch the small charm on the chain around my neck.

I climb into bed, roll onto my back, and stare at the ceiling, letting my eyes droop. My muscles are sore. In five and a half hours, I'll get up to bake, like I do every day. Tonight I feel different, like something has ended and something else is beginning.

3

Joan

I swear, they do this just to torture us.

We cluster outside one of the conference rooms of the MIT Edgerton Center, each waiting our turn to present to the department and reps from NASA, all competing for the same internship. The best of the best, all dressed in slacks and pencil skirts, standing up straight like we aren't terrified. No one speaks. Some people pace; some crack their knuckles or nervously fiddle with their hair. The tension makes my skin crawl.

No amount of undereye concealer and coffee can hide the fact that I didn't sleep a wink all night. There was no way to get my project off the ruined hard drive, so after a late-night trip to the ER to get my wrist set, I begged Nisha to let me borrow her laptop, promising up and down that I wouldn't smash it on the sidewalk, that if I were to have another near-death experience, I'd use my body to shield the laptop if necessary.

She just rolled her eyes and said, "Skin grows back. Don't hurt my computer."

Now, I sit on the cold tile floor in my favorite tweed skirt and light pink blouse that usually make me feel like a million bucks, leaning against a floor-to-ceiling window with the computer open on my lap. I cross my ankles demurely so I won't show off my lucky blue underwear to half the astrophysics department. I frantically type anything, *anything* I can remember, struggling with my foggy memory and heavy purple cast on my left wrist.

I'm so tired. One too many all-nighters must be catching up with me.

Words run together on the screen. My eyelids get heavy. My head tips back against the window. I let my eyes close for just a moment before snapping them open again. I fight to focus on the words swimming down the page, but my eyes droop closed again. The MIT hall fades behind the scrim of my eyelashes.

A familiar room forms around me like a developing Polaroid. On some level, I know I'm dreaming. I've had this dream before.

I sit at a rough wooden table in a round room lit by flickering torchlight, a single window looking out into the sparkling night. On the table before me is a massive book, pages rippled and yellowed with age. The leather binding creaks as a hand holding a feather quill pulls across it, writing rows of tiny black lettering in a different language.

Then I realize it's my hand, attached to a body that feels like mine but doesn't look like it. A long golden braid hangs over my shoulder.

Whatever I'm writing is important. I know that much, but nothing else. I don't know why I'm here.

Am I here?

"Joan Sanders? Is she here?"

My head snaps up. All eyes in the hall rest on me. Confused students stare. A few shake their heads, either annoyed or feeling sorry for me. The door to the conference room stands open. My advisor, Dr. Fowler, casts his gaze around until it lands on me.

"Joan, get in here!" he hisses. I sit on the floor in a daze for just a moment until I realize where I am and why I'm here. Panic jolts through me, and I rip the computer cord from the wall, scoop up the laptop, and stand up while struggling to get the strap of the computer bag over my shoulder. The outside zip pocket flops open, spilling notes and pens all over the floor.

"Dammit," I grumble as I bend to gather my things. A girl next to me stoops down to help. "Thanks," I offer breathlessly as I shove everything back into the bag. Dr. Fowler twirls his hand in a "hurry up" motion. His dark skin shines and his eyes are wide. I've never seen him this stressed.

My heart thrums in my chest as I approach the open door, stumbling slightly on my heels. I move to brush past Dr. Fowler into the room, but he grabs my elbow.

"Joan, what the hell happened?" he asks. His brow furrows in concern as he looks over my scraped face and my cast-encased wrist. "Are you all right?"

"I'll explain later," I mutter.

I enter the room and approach the lectern. A half dozen expectant NASA reps in suits and expensive blazers sit around a long table in the center of the room. One or two of them are already writing something in their notes. My stomach leaps, but I take a deep breath.

They're just finishing up their thoughts from the last presentation. They aren't writing about you yet, you dork.

"This is Joan Sanders," Dr. Fowler announces, his voice switching from quiet and concerned to his confident lecture voice.

I try to smile as I open the computer and pull up my presentation to be projected onto the screen behind me. My stomach churns. I've never felt so vulnerable. So unprepared.

"Good morning," I stammer, my voice cracking only slightly. "My name is Joan Sanders. I'm a first-year grad student here at MIT, and I'd like to present you with a project I've been working on, charting unmanned flight trajectories not only to Mars, but…" My throat itches.

I clear it. "To other planets and even..." The room blurs. I blink to bring it back into focus. "...Even bodies beyond our solar...system..." The words sound like a record playing too slowly.

My vision suddenly stretches. The room and people seated around the table fade away, shifting into a new scene. It's like looking down a tunnel or into a telescope. The scene before me changes from an MIT conference room to the living room of my home back in Colorado. I still feel like I'm standing up, but I'm looking down on my mother at her desk. Her long, blond hair is haphazardly caught in a clip at the back of her head, just like it was when I saw her a few months ago. Green leaves flutter on the cottonwood tree outside the window to her left. Her silver watch shines on her wrist and she tips her head onto her other hand. She writes something on a series of stapled forms.

I feel like I'm right there, hovering above her, but at the same time, far away on the other side of the country. I can still feel my feet in my shoes, but I also smell the scents of my home: Mom's citrusy perfume, clean mountain air, old wood, and fresh paper.

My golden retriever, Sammy, trots into the room, his buttery-yellow tail waving behind him, and nudges Mom's elbow with his nose. She straightens, sighs, and scratches his velvet ears.

Mom signs the last form before flipping the entire stack and placing it squarely on the desk, laying the pen over the top in finality.

My stomach sinks. I know what those papers are. I knew this was coming. I've known it for years.

"Joan?" The voice sounds far away.

My sight contracts again, distorting, and I'm backing down the long tunnel until my childhood home disappears.

Suddenly, I'm back in the conference room with seven pairs of eyes on me. A hand grips my shoulder. I turn to see Dr. Fowler, his eyes wide with shock.

"Are you all right?" He asks. One of the women seated at the table holds her phone in front of her, as if she's about to dial a number.

I scan the faces. Wide eyes, several mouths open in alarm.

Oh my god. Did I just black out? In front of everyone? *Now?*

For a moment, there's only stunned silence.

"I'm sorry," I choke, clearing my throat. I look back at the computer screen, trying to remember where I left off.

"Joan…" Dr. Fowler says.

"I'm fine," I tell him quietly, so the others won't hear.

"Joan, I think you should go lie down," Dr. Fowler says firmly, releasing my shoulder.

"No, I've got it," I snap back, louder than I meant to.

"Thank you, dear," says a red-haired woman on my right. She smiles politely. "He's right. You should go get some rest."

"I…I haven't even started," I plead. It can't be over. I can still do this.

"We've seen enough. Thank you, dear."

My skin prickles at the patronizing *dear.* What happened? How long was I standing here like a gaping fish while they all watched me? No. *No.*

I stand still, stunned.

Dr. Fowler clears his throat. "Thank you," he says to the representatives, nudging me. He opens the door to let me out. My stomach drops.

It can't be over.

Shocked, I pick up the computer and slowly approach the door. My stomach feels like a lead weight. I blew it.

"Office. Now," Dr. Fowler hisses as I pass him.

I don't react. I step into the hall and avoid the gazes of the students outside the room. I walk down the hall like a robot, my legs carrying me to my mentor's office on autopilot.

When I get there, I close the door and plop into the seat across the desk from his empty one and rest my head in my hands, taking deep breaths.

I can't believe I tanked. I am so, so very screwed.

A few minutes later, I hear Dr. Fowler approaching in the hall. The door opens. He pauses for a moment in the doorway. I don't look at him. Finally, he crosses behind his desk and sits down, assuming his "mentor" pose, placing his elbows on the desk and leaning in.

"Joan," he says. His voice is more gentle than I was expecting. I stare at his hands to avoid looking into his eyes. "What's going on?"

I don't answer for a few seconds, because I don't know what to say. He waits patiently.

Finally, I clear my throat and force myself to speak. "I don't remember," I stammer. "I was talking and then…" Do I tell him that I went somewhere else for a moment? That I saw my mom and my house like I was really there? No, that would just make things worse. "…then…I don't know, I think I just blacked out."

Dr. Fowler sighs. "I had really high hopes for your presentation, Joan."

A lump forms in my throat. "So did I."

"You've been working on this all semester. You never fudge things like this. What happened? Why now? Does this have anything to do with…" he gestures to my face and arm. "Tell me what happened."

I take a deep breath, then give him a brief overview of how I smashed my laptop on the pavement after almost being hit by a car and was in the ER getting my wrist patched up until two a.m. I leave out the part about procrastinating and finishing my paper at the last minute.

He sighs again, removes his glasses, rubs his eyes, and runs his hand over his short, dark beard before replacing the glasses. "Joan, I know this wasn't your fault. I'd love to tell you that I can get you another chance, but…"

"…it doesn't work that way." I finish for him.

He pauses. I meet his eyes for the first time.

"No," he says, his nut-brown eyes boring into me. "It doesn't. There were some strong presentations today, and even though this wasn't your fault, being unprepared for any reason, and then…zoning out… that doesn't look good to NASA. They're going to think that you don't have the mental fortitude to handle an intense summer internship, let alone a future in the space program. Or that you have medical issues that could interfere with your work. *I* know this isn't like you, but *they* don't."

"No, this isn't like me. I can do this, if I can just talk to them…"

"They don't give second chances, Joan."

I glare at him, but his steady gaze doesn't waver. I know he's right. Even if I could redo my presentation, it won't change their minds. They'll still think I can't do it.

Finally, I nod. My churning stomach threatens to expel the cereal bar I scarfed for breakfast. The weight of my failure settles over me. My eyes sting, brimming with tears that I force back into my head. I will not cry. I won't.

"Joan," Dr. Fowler continues. He picks up a pen, taps it a few times on the desk, and sighs. "I think you need a break."

I look up at him. "A break?"

He nods. "You haven't had a semester off in years. You powered through your undergrad and jumped straight into the master's program. I can understand the smashed laptop and the broken wrist, but blanking out, losing focus even after an all-nighter—that isn't you. Not at all. I think you're overworked." He gives me a sympathetic half-smile. "Take the summer off."

I blink. Take the summer off? I haven't even considered that. A new fear takes hold of me. Now that I'm not spending the summer at NASA, what will I do? I haven't made any arrangements. My dorm lease expires in a few weeks. I haven't applied for financial aid for the summer. I have no money, no job, nothing to do this summer. And I do *not* want to go home.

"I don't need a break," I insist, the timbre of my voice climbing. There's a desperate edge to my words that I don't like. "I can handle it."

He sighs again. "You've done an amazing job here so far, and I want it to stay that way—in the fall, though, after you've had some rest. Don't think this isn't normal. You'd be shocked how many students end up in my office on the verge of a mental breakdown. Everyone needs rest sometimes, Joan."

"I'm not everyone," I snip. "And I'm *not* having a mental breakdown."

He smiles grimly. He knows me too well. "I know you're not," he says kindly. "I know you're smarter and more capable than most, but you're still human. Take the summer off. Read a novel. Sleep in. Make some friends."

The last remark sounds pointed. Make friends. He knows I study alone, work alone, and the only reason I don't live alone is because I can't afford a private dorm or apartment. Studying takes up all my time, which doesn't leave much time for a social life. The extent of my friendships in the last few years have been in passing greetings with Nisha when one of us leaves the dorm, and with Eduardo, the teenaged delivery boy from the pizza place just off campus.

"I'll suspend you if I have to, Joan."

My eyes snap up. He wouldn't. "But my classes..."

"If you have trouble re-enrolling in the fall, I will personally make sure you get into all the classes you need. I've seen students do this to themselves before, and it doesn't end well. I want you to succeed and have a long career in the space program, so I'm telling you to get some rest so you can come back strong in the fall." He pauses. His kind eyes study me from behind his glasses. He then leans forward slightly on his elbows, like he's about to tell me a secret. "I know how hard this is," he says gently. "You don't want to do this. You're scared of dropping the ball. Believe me, I get it. But you won't make it if you burn out." Another pause. I study my hands in my lap. Finally, he stands. "I have to get back. Hang out as long as you need to. You have my email, and I'll see you in September. Have a nice summer, Joan."

With that, he gives me a nod and lets himself out, leaving me alone in his office.

I stare at the wood grain of his desk, letting my eyes slip out of focus. Take the summer off. Rest. Make friends.

I have no summer internship. No summer classes. No job, no money, no friends. What the hell am I going to do?

After a few minutes, I stand and leave the room, then exit the building that will forever bring back memories of the day I zoned out in front of a group of NASA recruiters. I don't want to go back to my quiet, empty dorm. I don't want to be alone, but I don't feel like talking to anyone.

I barely pay attention as my feet carry me to the bus stop at the edge of campus. I watch the Charles go by as the bus ambles over the bridge to Back Bay.

4

Joan

I hobble down the street to the Clockwork Cafe, just like I did last night. Only now I'm wearing a bright purple cast. I used to be jealous of kids in elementary school who got to wear candy-colored casts that their friends could write and doodle on. They always had daring stories of how they sustained their injuries, stories that grew taller by the day, but I've never broken a bone. I hardly ever got a scraped knee or even a sunburn. I always stayed inside to read, play the piano, and do homework. I didn't have many people who would want to sign a cast anyway, for a lot of the same reasons.

I smile bleakly and wince as the scrapes on my face stretch. It hurts to smile and I'm sore as hell, but at least I'm alive. I suppose leaving half my skin on the pavement is better than winding up as roadkill.

As grateful as I am to be alive, I feel like shit.

I bombed the presentation. I know it wasn't my fault that I was in the ER until the wee hours of the morning and had to cobble something together at the last minute. It wasn't my fault that I blacked out—or whatever that was—during the presentation, but it doesn't matter. I blew it. I don't blame NASA for not wanting me. I wouldn't have given me the internship either.

Blacking out during the presentation and seeing my mom—I have no idea where that came from. Maybe I should go back to the doctor and get my head checked too.

I reach the spot where the car had jumped the curb and nearly ran me down. There's still a gaping hole covered by a tarp in the front of the boutique. Tire marks mar the sidewalk right where I'd been half a second before the car shot over the curb. I'd be in the morgue right now with the poor driver if Cafe Guy—no, Thiago, his name was Thiago—hadn't knocked me out of the way.

I never thanked him. Maybe that's why I got on the bus to come back here.

I open the door of the cafe. A delicious cloud of fresh bread smell nearly blows my short hair back. I breathe in the earthy aroma of coffee. My stomach dances a jig at the thought of a warm muffin and a cappuccino. I borrowed a cereal bar from Nisha for breakfast—I'll pay her back, I swear—but I'm starving now.

Only two people sit at the tables in the cafe—a man reading a newspaper and sipping an espresso, and a middle-aged woman working on a laptop with headphones in. Thiago stands at the counter in the kitchen, slicing a long loaf of bread, pulling his knife through the crust in smooth, practiced strokes. His stubbled jaw is set in concentration. A wavy tendril has escaped his messy man bun and he impatiently brushes it behind his ear. His sisters are nowhere in sight.

Something dings, and he looks over his shoulder at one of the industrial-sized ovens, then startles slightly when he sees me. I don't know if he's surprised to see me or just shocked by the crusty red scrapes wrapping up the left side of my face.

I attempt a half-smile to spare my cheek. "Hi," I say.

"Hey," he says back, putting down the knife and approaching the front counter. His coffee-colored eyes watch me from beneath dark brows, between which are two deeply carved frown lines.

"I realized I didn't thank you last night," I continue. "I wasn't thinking clearly."

"Oh," he says, looking embarrassed. He shoves his hands in his pockets. "That's all right; you had every right to be distracted. Almost being mown down by a car can do that to a person."

I chuckle, but he doesn't. I didn't notice last night, but he speaks with crisp consonants and long vowels, the ghost of a Spanish accent greatly softened over time.

"Thank you," I offer.

He nods in response. "I'm sorry about your wrist. And your…" he gestures to his face.

I smirk. "You're right, you should have tackled me a little more carefully. I don't know what you were thinking."

"Oh," he says again, confused. The lines between his eyebrows deepen.

"I'm joking," I say quickly. "That car would have clobbered me. You saved my life. I don't know why you look so sheepish."

If anything, he looks even more sheepish, chewing the inside of his lip. His Adam's apple bobs as he swallows. "You're welcome," he says, finally.

This is clearly a man who's not used to being thanked, or maybe being spoken to at all by anyone other than his sisters. He shifts his weight and presses his lips together, glancing away. I clear my throat.

A chair scrapes loudly on the kitchen floor. I hadn't noticed Gabby come in. She scoots a chair in front of the tea wall and steps up onto it, humming absentmindedly as she brushes a feather duster over the jars. Her jeans are covered in tiny embroidered flowers. I wonder if she found them that way or decorated them herself. Thiago rolls his eyes.

"They don't need dusting again, Gabby."

"I like to dust," she says without turning around.

"Then try dusting all the trash you bring into my cafe," Thiago snaps, gesturing wildly to the shelves crammed with antique odds and ends.

"They aren't dusty. You just don't like my things," Gabby snips back, stepping down from the chair, looking over at me. She smiles, satisfied, like she knew I'd come back. "Hello Joan," she croons. Thiago looks from her back to me, exasperated.

Gabby snatches a terra cotta mug from below the tea shelves. "Would you like some tea?" she asks. "Or coffee maybe? On the house." She grins elfishly. "I just remembered how fun it is to say 'on the house.'"

A smile tugs at my lips and I grimace as my cheek stings. "I'd love coffee, thank you."

"Oh good," Gabby says, grinning. "Do you like lattes? I'm teaching myself latte art. I'm not very good, but it usually looks like something if you're creative enough."

"A latte would be perfect."

Gabby grins and turns to the industrial coffee grinder.

Thiago watches all of this with his eyebrows knit together and mouth slightly open. He turns back to me, shaking his head.

"Well, hell, would you like a muffin too? I just made a batch of cranberry-orange. They go well with the coffee."

My stomach rumbles. "Yes, please." He nods and gestures for me to take a seat while he grabs a plate and starts pulling fresh muffins out of the tin. I sit at the table nearest to the counter and watch Gabby shift her weight from foot to foot in a strange dance as she pulls a shot of espresso, steams a small pitcher of milk, and then carefully pours them into the mug, her face screwed up in concentration as she wiggles the pitcher back and forth. She peers into the mug and frowns, then shrugs and carries it out to me.

"Well, it's not my best work," she said, "but it'll taste good." She places the latte on the table in front of me. White and soft brown swirls form a sort of squished spiral with a frill. "I was going for a spider, but it didn't work very well, did it?"

"I like it," I tell her. "It looks like a galaxy." She looks into the cup and her eyebrows lift.

"It does!" she says, her face lighting up. "Oh, I know!" She scampers to the cream and sugar station and comes back with a shaker. "Do you mind?" I shake my head. She sprinkles a delicate dusting of cinnamon over the milk foam, sending tiny brown speckles across the arms of the galaxy in my cup.

"Stars," she says softly. "Hey, it's a Milky Way made of milk!"

I laugh for the first time all day. Even Thiago gives an amused chuckle from the kitchen. "It's beautiful," I tell her. I really mean it.

Thiago circles around the counter carrying a plate with a beautiful golden muffin that he places next to my coffee. "Gabby makes a good latte," he sighs.

Gabby beams. "I'll make you one too," she says to him, practically skipping back around the counter.

"Don't waste the espresso," Thiago says.

"Oh shush, you could use some coffee." She gets busy with the espresso machine again. I pick up my latte and take a sip. It's full and rich, the perfect temperature. "It's fantastic," I say.

"Thank you!" Gabby calls from behind the counter.

Thiago grins. "You can sit down, you know," I tell him.

His smile falls off his face and his eyes dart briefly around the room. Finally, he carefully pulls out the chair across from me and sits.

I take another sip of the latte and tear off a small bite of the muffin. Thiago was right. It's delicious with the coffee.

"It's my mother's recipe," he says. "Base recipe, anyway. I like to play around with it."

"She must be an amazing baker," I say through a bite of muffin.

"Yes, she was."

Was? Oh, damn. Why can't I not be an awkward clod for two minutes? I swallow a little too hard.

"I'm sorry," I say quickly. "I just don't think sometimes…"

"It's fine," he says stiffly. "It was twenty years ago."

My social graces are nothing to brag about, but I usually know better than to ask nosy, personal questions before I've even gotten past the small talk stage. I sidestep and instead ask something I've been wondering about for the past fourteen hours.

"By the way," I say casually. "I wanted to ask you about last night. How did you get to me so fast? You just appeared out of nowhere. How did you even see what was happening?"

Thiago shifts in his seat, resting his clasped hands on the table. "I was locking up outside and I saw the car," he says tonelessly. "It was swerving, and I saw you walking, so I ran as fast as I could."

"You outran the car?"

"It wasn't going very fast."

"But faster than a person can run, right?" *Shut up, Joan.* "I'm sorry," I say, shaking my head. "It's rude of me to interrogate the guy who saved my life."

"It was just one of those adrenaline things," he shrugs, his eyes not quite meeting mine. "I don't know how I ran so fast. I just saw what was happening and I didn't think." There's something robotic about his words, like he's rehearsed this story. He smiles blithely, and I smile back, tapping my finger on the side of my mug before raising it to my lips. I don't look away from him as I sip.

Behind the counter, there's a tinkling of broken ceramic. "Oops!" Gabby yelps. Thiago's shoulders drop and he closes his eyes, his jaw stiff. "It's okay, Thi," Gabby calls. "It was that Bugs Bunny mug you hated. Too bad. It belonged to a little boy who lived with his mother in the seventies. He used it every day—"

"I'll get the broom." Thiago stands up so quickly that his chair falls over backward. His olive skin blooms pink and he rights the chair before striding behind the counter to the espresso machine. Gabby bends over to pick up the pieces. Thiago squats down beside her, telling her something I can't understand. I look away when he glances back at me. Then she follows him out the back door, her cupped hands full of ceramic shards.

That was weird. Is he really chewing her out for breaking a mug? Somehow, I think there's more to it than that.

I finish my latte and muffin, then I place my dishes in the bus bucket below the cream and sugar station and linger, examining the antiques lining the shelves while I watch the door. Teacups, clocks, a sock monkey with a red scarf, an old telephone. From the sound of it, Thiago doesn't like these things, but I think they add to the cafe's quirky charm. Everywhere you look, there's something interesting to see.

I reach out to pick up a tarnished silver sugar bowl when I hear Thiago's raised voice outside. I can't understand what he's saying, but he sounds pissed. Then I realize he's yelling in Spanish. Gabby yells something back, her voice shrill and angry.

I look around at the other cafe patrons. The man with the espresso has left, and the woman with the headphones doesn't seem to notice anything going on around her. I inch closer to the counter, straining to grasp recognizable words, but I don't dare go into the kitchen in case they come back. I took a few years of Spanish in high school, but I've never used it for anything more than ordering food.

Gabby clearly did something Thiago didn't like, but I'm confused. She just said the broken mug once belonged to a little boy, which was strange, but from what I know of Gabby, she says strange things often.

I do wonder how she knows about the mug's history, but there are plenty of explanations for that. She could have gotten it from the previous owner, or maybe it was part of the eBay description, or perhaps the owner of the antique shop told her. What's the big deal?

Thiago's voice booms behind the door, and I catch one distinct word: *secreto*.

Secret.

I'm rusty, and much better at reading Spanish than speaking or listening. They speak quickly, voices crossing over one another. My brain sluggishly grasps the familiar words. Something about parents—*Mamá y Papá*—death, and that word again: *secreto*.

Now I'm even more curious.

Then the back door bursts open, the doorway framing Thiago with his squared shoulders and those lines between his eyebrows, frowning. I jump and try to pretend I was looking at the baked goods in the baskets all along, but his eyes fall on me. I can tell, he isn't fooled.

He stomps across the kitchen until he's directly across the counter. I stand my ground.

"I save your life, give you a free muffin, and this is how you repay me?" His voice is hard and steady, dark eyes boring into mine. "By eavesdropping?" His vowels are getting longer, like his old accent is slipping in.

Gabby appears behind him. Her face is set in a hard frown and she holds her chin high, defiant. Her eyes flick to Thiago and me. She catches my eye, rolling her eyes and shaking her head. *Don't worry about him*, her face seems to say.

Thiago glares at me. His face is red and his bearded jaw is tight. I automatically want to glare back, but I force my face to soften.

"Um, how much is a loaf of sunflower bread?" I ask, avoiding his very accurate accusation. Would I rather he think I'm stupid or a snoop? I know which one is true.

He shakes his head, then turns back to the counter to resume slicing bread. "Just take it," he says. "We need to get ready for the lunch rush."

Gabby shoots me another apologetic look. I give her one of my own.

"Okay," I say. "I'll see you around then." Thiago waves without looking up, and I turn to leave. The heavy door bangs shut behind me.

I stuff my hands into my pocket and scowl at my feet as I stride back down the sidewalk. This Thiago guy is just a grouch. Yes, he saved me, but he sure has his panties in a wad over something. I don't understand what Gabby did wrong, and he was a dick for yelling at her.

I brush muffin crumbs off my jacket, knowing I'll be back for answers. Besides being a jerk to his sister, Thiago's explanation for how he knew to follow me last night was terrible. I've seen more convincing soap opera performances.

I don't know what's going on with these people and I don't know why Thiago is constantly at odds with his sisters, but I do know when I'm being lied to.

5

Gabby

I stomp up the stairs to the apartment, more for show than from actual anger. Thiago will feel better if he believes he's gotten to me, that his brotherly warnings have sunk deep.

I don't understand what all his fuss is about. I didn't let anything important slip. I'm sure Joan wouldn't have noticed anything unusual if he hadn't behaved like such a child and drawn attention to it.

Don't use your abilities. Just pretend to be normal. Protect our secret.

As if I can just turn it off so easily. Or that Luna could.

He guards this family like a trained doberman. It's annoying, but I can't be too upset with him. Without him, I don't know where Luna and I would be. He kept us together while we were shuffled around foster homes. He created this life for us—the cafe, the apartment above it, our jobs. He's worked hard to keep us—and our secret—safe.

The apartment is messy, though slightly less messy than I remember it from the last time I was up here at breakfast. Luna must have cleaned up a little, though she chose strange things to clean. Bowls still sit in the sink with soggy cereal pooled in the bottoms, but clean dish towels hang from the oven door handle instead of the slightly dirty ones that were there this morning. Books, papers, empty beer bottles, and coffee mugs still cover the coffee table in the living room, but she neatly arranged the throw pillows on the couch. I brush it off. Luna does strange things.

Where is she, anyway?

I open our bedroom door directly across the hall from Thiago's room. No Luna. Her bed is made. The quilt is pulled up across the twin mattress. Gulliver is curved into a fluffy cinnamon roll shape on her pillow, his tabby stripes twisting into an optical illusion that spirals down his spine and meets at his closed eyes. I scratch his ears where he likes it. He purrs and stretches his front legs before curling into a tighter ball.

Luna's half of the room is much neater than mine, but only because she has fewer things. Luna's side has a bed, a small nightstand I found at a thrift store, a lamp, and a wall full of random images she's pulled from magazines and newspapers. Pictures and articles from National Geographic. A two-page spread of the northern lights, a picture of Big Ben, and lots of snowy landscapes.

My bed, on the other hand, is unmade. Clothes pile on the floor, though I know exactly which ones are clean and which aren't. My red ukulele peeks out from under my comforter. Old books stack high on my own nightstand, topped with my favorite antique teacup and saucer. Dregs of chamomile and lavender coat the bottom of the cup.

Oh, that shouldn't be on the books. I pick it up.

My eyes fall on the framed picture next to the books of us with our parents at a beach, the last photo taken of all of us before they died. Papá has Thiago's long nose and holds me as a baby in the crook of his arm. Mamá smiles at the camera with her dark hair in a ponytail, her arms brown and lean in her summer tank top, almond eyes shaped like mine and Luna's. Thiago, nine or ten in the photo, stands on Mamá's side. He half-hides behind her, squinting into the sunlight with his hair falling in his eyes. Knobbly knees poke out the bottoms of his swim shorts. Luna stands between my parents, four or five years old when her hair and eyes were dark and we were all normal children, or as normal as the children of Spanish immigrant clockmakers can be.

I take my teacup to the kitchen and carefully rinse it in the sink. I see movement out of the corner of my eye and lean to see into the living room.

Luna straightens a picture on the wall, one of my framed collages. When she's satisfied, she moves onto another, straightening it carefully, though I don't think it needed straightening in the first place.

"What are you doing, Lune?"

Without looking at me, she smiles and moves onto a framed photo of herself and Gulliver as a kitten the day we got him.

As I said, Thiago and I are used to Luna doing strange things, but she's never straightened pictures before. I step into the living room and take a closer look.

Among the mess on the coffee table, she's set out the ceramic coasters she and I decorated at a pottery painting place last year for my birthday. We've never used them because we never use coasters. There's a drinking glass containing a handful of drooping pansies that she probably stole from a planter on the street.

I sigh. I should have watched her better.

Luna continues to straighten pictures, and I realize what she's doing.

She's sprucing the place up, though endearingly not noticing the mess in the kitchen or on the coffee table. Why? Is she expecting company? We never have guests.

Then I get an idea of where she was a minute ago when I first came up, the only place in the apartment I didn't look. I go back into the hall and open Thiago's door.

As neurotic as Thiago can be, he never makes his bed. But there it is, sheets and comforter pulled up neatly, pillows nice and straight. She's even added a lacy throw pillow from her own bed. It clashes strangely with Thiago's black and blue blanket. Another glass of flowers sits on his nightstand.

Luna shuffles to my side.

"Luna," I say, my eyes on the flowers, "who are you expecting?"

She won't answer, of course. At least not out loud. I turn to watch her. Her eyes focus for a brief moment, indicating she's understood me. After a moment, she raises a hand to her head and rakes her fingers through her silver tresses, but just near her scalp. I lift my own hand to my hair and mimic her, running hair through my fingers.

The girl with the short hair.

"Joan?" I ask. "From last night?"

The corners of Luna's lips twitch, breaking her usually serene expression.

I know better than to press Luna for specifics. Having told me all she can, she drifts back into the living room to resume straightening pictures.

So Joan's coming over. Luna fancied up Thiago's room. It doesn't take a genius to see why. If she's going to be in our home, in Thiago's *room*, there's a reason.

My mind flicks back to a letter tucked away in Thiago's room. The one he thinks I don't know about.

Watch for signs, it says. Could this be a sign?

Maybe Joan is supposed to know about us. And Thiago just chased her away.

I close the door and cross the tiny apartment to go down to the cafe. I need to talk to Thiago.

He's serving a customer, no doubt seething because I wasn't there to do it. One of our other employees, Tanya, has come in for the afternoon. Maybe I should stick around and silently do my job for a while before I approach him, but I don't have the patience. I wait till the customer finally chooses a muffin from the basket and sits down.

Thiago turns to the espresso machine and starts pressing grounds into the handle. I realize I don't know what that thing is actually called, but I brush it off and carefully approach him.

"What?" he snips, not looking at me.

"*Lo siento,*" I tell him.

"Uh-huh. What do you want?"

"Nothing," I reply in Spanish. "I was careless and I know you're just trying to protect us. It won't happen again."

"Right. What do you want?"

"Well, I was just upstairs with Luna…"

"Instead of working, yes."

"…and I think you should invite Joan to Luna's birthday. It'll make Luna really happy."

Luna's birthday is in two weeks. For such a cranky guy, Thiago loves birthdays because it's an excuse to cook something special. I'm sure he'd love to show off to someone new.

"The girl with the boy hair?"

A smile twitches at the corner of my mouth. He pretends he doesn't care, but I saw how he looked at her. He doesn't want me to know, because he doesn't even want to admit it to himself. I know my brother.

"It's called a pixie cut, doofus."

"Whatever. Are you kidding? She walks in here, nearly gets herself killed, then eavesdrops on our conversation after you go off blabbing…"

"It'll make Luna happy," I repeat.

His eyes narrow in suspicion before rising to the ceiling right under the living room, where Luna is probably still walking around, pointlessly straightening the pictures with Gulliver at her heels.

"Luna?" he says, still looking up.

I nod, smiling despite a twinge of frustration. He doesn't get as upset when Luna uses her abilities because she can't help it. He only gets mad at me.

He sighs. "I don't even know where to find her."

"You don't have to," I say. "You just will. That's all there is to it. You know that." He shakes his head again, scowling. "She's a student at MIT," I go on. "So she probably lives in Cambridge. That's a start."

"I'm not running around Cambridge to find one girl."

"You won't need to. If you go, I think she'll find you."

He shoves the espresso handle into the machine, places the cup underneath, and turns on the water. "Luna really wants her there? Did she tell you that?"

Of course she didn't *tell* me that. She hasn't told anyone anything in decades. But it's not a lie. I'm just setting the inevitable into motion.

"Luna likes her. She's never had a friend besides us."

Thiago groans, dumps the espresso into the mug, and starts steaming milk.

"I knew you didn't come down to work."

I playfully touch my cheek to his shoulder, smiling sweetly. "I'll start wiping counters."

He only grunts in response, but I can tell he's calmed down.

The milk steamer squeals as I tie on my apron. When the milk is done, he holds the pitcher out to me. "Do you want to make this latte pretty?"

I grin. I knew he appreciated my talents. I take the pitcher and set to work making a flower that ends up looking more like a melted snowman.

The oven beeps and Thiago grabs hot pads, opens the oven, yanks out the cookie sheets, and clacks them on the counters a bit rougher than usual. He hates it when I win.

I didn't have to tell him to find Joan. It would have happened anyway. But I do like to help things along.

It's not that we're not in control. We act the way we act, and sometimes we need someone to give us the idea. Luna just stands at the window and watches from above, dropping breadcrumbs to lead us along a path only she can see.

6

Joan

I knew my summer at NASA was already up in smoke, but it didn't make the rejection email any easier.

Dr. Fowler had been right. They didn't think I had the mental fortitude to deal with the rigor of the internship. They even suggested I seek help from a medical professional and wished me the best on my journey back to health. I almost printed the email just so I could tear it into teeny, tiny pieces and flush it down the toilet.

That crucial line on my resume, gone. Poof. Maybe I shouldn't have banked on it so hard, but that's how I do things. I make up my mind and I work hard, never looking back until I reach my goal. That's how I pulled straight A's from kindergarten to my first semester of grad school. That's how I got into MIT. That's how I won every piano competition from junior high onward, placed in every science fair, and how I knew I'd get that damned internship.

Now my dorm lease is expiring and there's nothing I can do about it. I only have a few weeks to find an apartment and a job to afford it. And at the moment, I'm too bummed out to do either.

Then that asshole Thiago kicked me out of the Clockwork Cafe two days ago. I don't know why that's still bothering me. Maybe I'm just in the mood to be bothered.

So there's only one thing to do.

The smart part of my brain knows eating my feelings won't help, but the part of my brain that's in charge decided it was time for ice cream, and lots of it, saddlebags be damned. I've never quite gotten rid of the freshman fifteen from seven years ago, but screw it. I'll allow myself tonight to wallow in my misery before coming up with a plan to get my summer back on track.

I'm surprised the Toscanini's staff doesn't know me by name, but I'm certainly not the only student or out-of-towner who keeps this place humming. Voices of customers and workers echo off the tile floors and exposed brick walls. There's not an empty seat in the house, but I'm planning to leave and find someplace quiet anyway.

My eyes burn as I scan the list of today's flavors. The chalk writing blurs, and I reach up to wipe my eyes, forcing the tears back into my head where they belong. I'm not prone to weepiness, and I refuse to make a scene in a room full of people.

"Another rough day?" says a familiar male voice behind me, with just a tinge of a Spanish accent.

Oh no. I sigh before looking over my shoulder.

Thiago stands in line behind me, in his usual white tee shirt and jeans, minus the apron. He smiles at me, a mischievous twinkle in his eye.

"Running into you sure doesn't help," I snap, turning back to face the front. "What are you doing in Cambridge?"

"Shopping. There's a gourmet grocery store around the corner," he says, holding out a paper grocery sack to the side where I can see it. "Special baking ingredients. I always stop in here before I head home."

"Aren't there enough swanky grocery stores in Back Bay or Beacon Hill? You really have to come all the way over here?"

"It's just over the river."

I don't answer. Now that I can finally see the stupid menu board, I start debating flavors.

He sighs. "Look, I'm sorry about the other day. I didn't mean to dismiss you so…dismissively."

"Uh-huh. I don't know how else you'd dismiss someone, but yes, you were quite dismissive."

"You were being nosy."

I turn around to glare at him. "It's not my fault you were talking so loud. Anyone with functioning ears would have overheard you whether they wanted to or not."

I can almost hear his brain whirring for a snappy retort. I glance down, peering into the shopping bag dangling at his side. A bottle of vinegar or red wine, three cans, a jar of what I think is peanut butter and one of jelly, and a bag of carrots. "Interesting assortment you've got there," I tell him.

"You keep your nose out of my assortment, blondie." He says the word 'blondie' like a foreign word, with a little too much emphasis on the _o_.

"You came all the way to your precious gourmet store for that?" I say, raising my eyebrows. "Strange for someone with your culinary prowess to buy canned soup and pb and j."

He stands up a little straighter. My goodness, he's tall. I'm five ten and only come up to his eyes.

"We're short on good help right now," he says. His eyes flick away from mine for just a moment. "I don't have time to cook anything that's not for the cafe. We eat the breads and muffins that don't sell, but we like to mix it up." He jostles the bag sarcastically.

That still doesn't explain why he's in Cambridge. I roll my eyes and turn to face the counter. Thankfully, I've made it to the front of the line without collapsing into hysterics or blowing up at Thiago.

"Three scoops," I tell the guy behind the counter, a burly young man with blond hair and acne scars. "Salty caramel, Earl Grey, and Roxbury Puddingstone." The guy goes to work on my order. Thiago steps up and orders a single dainty scoop of honey orange saffron. I shake my head in disgust.

"What?" he says, noticing my expression.

"Are you this pretentious on purpose?"

"Absolutely," he replies with a smug smile. For the first time, I notice how long his eyelashes are, perfectly framing his chocolatey-brown eyes.

Oh god, Joan. Don't start. That is the LAST thing I need right now.

The guy hands me my towering cup of ice cream, which, luckily, is easy to hold with my hand in a cast so I can wield a spoon with the other. I step up to the register, preparing to blow a third of this week's grocery money. I'm afraid to check the balance in the empty, echoing cavern that is my bank account, but if I'm going to spend the afternoon wallowing in my sorrow and obvious ineptitude as an astrophysicist, I may as well do it right.

"I'll get hers," Thiago tells the girl behind the register as another worker hands him his ice cream.

My cheeks get hot. "I didn't ask you to do that."

"Consider it a peace offering," he answers as he awkwardly tries to fish his wallet out of his pocket with both hands full.

I sigh, taking the grocery bag from him, accidentally brushing his warm fingers with my own and cursing the tiny sparkle in my stomach. He nods in appreciation and pays for our ice cream.

"Do you want to eat at the river park?" I say, nodding to the front door. He looks at me with a subtle lift of an eyebrow. A puzzled look, not unfriendly. "Unless you have to get back home. That canned soup won't microwave itself."

He smirks. "No, I'm okay for a while. Gabby's running things. There may be a crater where the cafe used to be when I get back, but it's probably okay."

We exit onto the tight street and skitter across the crosswalk to the alley that cuts to the next street over. As we walk, I stab my spoon into the scoop of Roxbury Puddingstone, everything Rocky Road ever dreamed of being, and immediately, I divine a giant chocolate chunk. Thiago watches as I dig the spoon underneath to unearth it and pop it into my mouth.

"What?" I say, my voice gummy and thick as the bittersweet chocolate melts in my mouth.

He chuckles and shakes his head before taking a small bite of his own scoop. We walk in oddly comfortable silence for a few moments until we reach the riverside park. The small, grassy area looks out over the Charles, which is surprisingly calm today. A bird with a long white neck stalks through the shallow water near the shore, poking his pointy beak into the rivulets for fish or insects. A few boats dot the gray-blue expanse. The tall buildings of downtown rise on the far bank like sentinels.

We find a shady bench under a tree and I plop down. Thiago takes a seat just inches from me, and to my surprise, I don't scoot away. I take a bite of salty caramel and let the cold sweet and saltiness overtake the bitter disappointment, the stress of wondering what the hell I'm going to do with my life now. I don't want to go home. And much as I hate to admit it...I don't think I want a lab job right now. My brain is fried from all-nighters of physics equations and theorems and numbers running down the page like washed-out ink.

Then it hits me. What I need is a different kind of job. Something that will let me rest while allowing me to stay in Boston.

"Thiago," I start, then pause, realizing it's the first time I've said his name out loud. I think I like saying it; it feels dark and exotic. A smile tugs at my mouth before I continue. "Did you say you need to hire more help?"

"I did," he says, poking his spoon back into his cup.

"Well," I go on, casually raking my spoon over the crest of salty caramel, "I'm on this current ice cream bender because I didn't get an internship I worked really hard for. I was thinking I'd stick around for the summer, though, so what do you think of me working for you?"

"The girl who snoops?"

I choose not to take that personally. "I'm a professional. I'd never snoop through my employer's business."

"But some guy you just met, sure."

"Wouldn't you? If he was interesting and obviously hiding something?"

Shut up, Joan. Do you want to get hired or not?

Thiago shakes his head. "I've hired too many students. Their work ethic is terrible. They use it all up on school and leave nothing for a job."

I take another bite, leaving the spoon in my mouth a moment longer, taking my time. "I had a steady job all through high school, even with a full load of AP classes, and I still made sterling scholar and valedictorian."

"What the hell's a sterling scholar?"

"I've worked full time every summer of college, even after two semesters of a full course load. Also straight A's."

"Good for you. So why didn't you get the internship then?"

A bolt of anger shoots through me. My eyes snap to his. "Because my computer didn't survive the other night, remember?" That's not the whole reason, of course, but if it weren't for the accident, if I had my presentation done and if I'd gotten sleep that night, things might have gone differently. But I don't tell him that.

His eyes soften. "Oh, that was the project you were upset about." He turns toward me slightly. "I didn't realize...I'm sorry. I didn't mean to be rude."

I shake my head and smile briefly. Two apologies from Thiago in one day. My fingers tighten around the ice cream cup and I take a deep breath. "I might not have gotten it anyway though," I admit. I didn't realize I was even thinking that until I said it out loud. "This is MIT. We all had straight A's. No one's impressed with my report cards or my valedictorian sash, or my honors cord from my undergrad. We all have them. Seriously. Every one of us."

Another white bird joins the first, and together, they wade along the shore, their long legs carrying them forward in graceful strides, necks extending and folding back on themselves like ballerinas' arms.

"I'm sorry," I say.

"For what?" Thiago says, eyebrows drawing together with curiosity.

"I know how I probably look to you. Poor privileged princess, the perfect student who suddenly isn't the best anymore."

"How do you know how you look to me?"

Something lights up in my chest. I bite the inside of my lip to keep from smiling.

A few beats of silence, then Thiago says, "Do you do latte art?"

"No. I'm not as talented as Gabby."

"Good. You can start tomorrow."

The light in my chest gets brighter. My stomach tingles. I didn't realize my shoulders were tense, but they suddenly release. "That would be great," I respond, trying not to sound like someone who's about to pass out from relief.

He smiles. The late-afternoon sunlight illuminates his eyes, highlighting flecks of amber in the smooth brown. "Come by around four p.m. It'll be slower then and we can train you. We'll see how you do."

"Okay," I say, elated. Then I laugh, one sharp guffaw. "That was the easiest job interview ever."

"Can I ask you a question?" Thiago says suddenly.

"Can I ask you one afterward?"

"Sure."

"Then yes, ask away."

"Why does a smart girl like you want to work in a coffee shop?" he asks. "Even if you didn't get the internship, there must be a lab or some science place where you can work."

I shrug. I've thought of that, but something about working at the cafe just feels…right. "I need a job," I start, "and a change. I want to spend the summer somewhere with windows where I'll get to see the sun go down, where I won't be squinting at tiny numbers on a page or stars on a chart all day. I love that stuff, but…I've worked my ass off for years on my degree, and I think I just need to rest. And even if I had gotten the internship, I'd probably spend the summer serving coffee anyway." I think of fragrant streams of espresso running into tiny mugs, of talking to actual people as I serve them scones and tea, of wearing a tee shirt and apron instead of a lab coat or business casuals, of knowing exactly what time of day it is just by the quality of light streaming in through the large front windows of the Clockwork Cafe. Such a change from fluorescent lab lighting and air conditioning turned up too high.

I notice Thiago watching me with…is that sympathy?

We just look at each other for a moment. He's surprisingly easy to be with, easy to talk to. A grouch sometimes maybe, a bad liar, but…it's comfortable. Like I've known him for years.

"Now I get to ask you a question," I tell him.

He purses his lips. "I think I can guess."

"What were you yelling at Gabby about?"

"None of your business, that's what."

"Hey!" I say, turning toward him on the bench. "You said I could ask you a question."

"I didn't say I'd answer."

I roll my eyes. There's that dickishness shining through. Whatever.

I'll find out one way or the other. I don't tell him this, though I'd really love to, just to show him that I don't quit that easily. But the man just offered me a job on the grounds that I won't be a snoop. This would be a bad time to confirm his suspicions that I'll probably snoop anyway. I don't mean to be nosy. I'm just…curious.

I scrape the last bits of ice cream out of the corners of my cup. Thiago watches the two white birds. My brain buzzes a little bit from all the sugar, but I do feel better. For now. And I have a job, a buoy to carry me through the summer until the New England leaves burn gold and fall semester starts, bringing a new parade of classes, professors, and students fighting over opportunities like hyenas on raw meat.

I sigh and shake my head. When did I become so disillusioned with academia?

The sun sinks lower, lighting the wispy clouds on fire and casting gold sparks over the river. We say nothing until Thiago reaches for my empty cup, stacks it in his, then gets up to toss them in a nearby trash can. I stand, picking up his groceries to hand to him when he returns. His warm fingers brush mine again. My hand tingles.

"Make sure to wear comfortable shoes tomorrow," he says with a small half smile. "You'll be on your feet a lot. Usually, I tell girls to tie up their hair, but…" he eyes my pixie cut.

I chuckle. "You set a good example for your employees. We wouldn't want your loose tresses flying around the beignets, now would we?"

He smiles and pats his man bun proudly. "Keep up that sass and you'll be wearing a hairnet."

We linger for a moment, then Thiago clears his throat. "I need to get back to the cafe before Gabby burns it down," he says. "Are you close?"

"My dorm's just a few blocks away," I say. I shift my weight awkwardly on my feet.

"Can I walk with you?" he asks. "I don't get out much. I could use a short walk."

Warmth spreads in my stomach. "Sure," I say. I start walking in the direction of my dorm and he walks beside me. I feel my hand twitch toward his, which surprises me. I barely know him, but reaching out to take his hand would feel like the most natural thing in the world.

It makes sense now. I don't just need a job this summer. I need friends.

To keep my hand busy, I instead fiddle with the charm bracelet on my other, unbroken wrist.

I realize Thiago's looking at the bracelet, his blank expression unreadable.

"You were wearing that the other night," he says.

I run my thumb over the star charm. "I wear it every day." Why is he so fascinated? His eyes lock on it. "My grandpa gave it to me when I was ten. I hardly ever take it off."

His shoulders have gone stiff, his arms halting their casual sway. "Oh," he says awkwardly. "It's very pretty." His t's are crisp and he nearly stumbles over the word. He turns his head to face forward. As fixated as he was on the bracelet just a moment ago, now he's purposely not looking at it. What the hell?

I fold my arms across my chest, tucking the hand with the bracelet into my opposite elbow. "You're into charm bracelets?" I say pointedly. "You just get more and more interesting."

He stuffs his free hand into his pocket, now watching the sidewalk as he walks. "My sisters have charms just like that," he says. "A moon and a star." He reaches up to a thin chain around his neck that's tucked into the front of his tee shirt. Hanging from the chain is a tiny gold cross and a silver sun charm, exactly like the one on my bracelet. "And I have the sun."

I examine the charms on my bracelet. A sun, a moon, a star, and a rocket. All purchased at different times in different places, but the sun is just like the one on Thiago's chain. I make a mental note to peek at Gabby and Luna's charms when I start work tomorrow. Something itches in the back of my brain, but I try to ignore it.

"I just thought it was interesting," he says, shrugging.

From the look on his face, his stiff jaw fighting to look casual, and his tightly squared shoulders, he thinks it's more than just interesting.

It's a coincidence. Nothing more.

We walk in silence for about a block. I observe him out of the corner of my eye. He relaxes slightly and we fall back into that strange, contented silence.

Finally, we reach the edge of the MIT campus, just outside my dorm building.

"I guess I'll see you tomorrow at four," I say, turning to face him.

He smiles stiffly, but it's still a smile. "Try to avoid getting run over by anything until then."

He jerks his arms as if he wants to hug me before leaving, but he thinks better of it and turns away to walk up the street.

I watch him for a moment before going inside. I hadn't been happy to see him at first, but I'm surprised at how much I'm looking forward to tomorrow afternoon. Anticipation mixed with nervousness. I flick the rocket charm on my bracelet with my thumb.

He's hiding something. I know it.

First, he appears out of nowhere to rescue me from a rogue car, now he somehow bumps into me and offers me the one thing I need this summer, and then his weird fascination with the bracelet. Come to think of it, I think I remember him staring at it the night I met him, too.

What's so special about my bracelet? What's he hiding?

A normal person would probably think this was sketchy as hell and avoid him. I know he's hiding something, but I sense no danger. I'm as fascinated with him as he seems to be with me.

Yes, I'm looking forward to tomorrow very, very much.

54

7

Thiago

"You've wiped down the counters twice already," Gabby says in Spanish as she restocks the muffin baskets. She's trying to butter me up for something if she's speaking Spanish.

"I knead dough on these counters."

"You just want them to be spotless and impressive."

"Impressive?"

"It's almost four o'clock," she says with a sly smile.

I roll my eyes. Joan should be here any minute. I shake my head and turn back to what I'm doing, wiping down the wood surface mottled by countless knives slicing bread over the years.

I work silently while Gabby piles the muffins into pyramids, exactly like I've told her not to do because it looks ridiculous.

"Just put them in the damn basket," I hiss. She ignores me and keeps stacking.

Luna stands around in the back of the kitchen. I watch her out of the corner of my eye. I always do. I never know when she'll decide to disappear back upstairs, out the back door, or, worse, out the front door to wander into traffic.

A group of customers leaves their dishes in the bus bucket and files out the door, chattering about something mundane. Joan would want to hear every word, I'm sure, just to pester them about it later.

The door closes behind the group only to spring open again, and Joan walks through. Gabby subtly catches my eye with a devilish smile. I shoot her a warning look.

Sunlight from the front windows lights Joan from behind, setting her short blond hair aglow. Her eyes fall on me immediately. She wears jeans and a soft pink tee shirt, nothing special, but I can't help but notice the shape of her hips in her jeans. Something catches in my chest and for a second, I don't know what to do. I look back at her and attempt a smile.

Luna appears at my side with a clean white apron dangling off her outstretched hand. Joan approaches the counter, smiling, and reaches over the register to take the apron. Luna beams before turning back to me. Her silver eyes focus on me ever so briefly before slipping out of focus again.

I glance at one of the few working clocks on the wall, though I know perfectly well what time it is. Five minutes early. Joan smiles, her pink lips forming an elegant curve, before tying the apron around her slim waist. I watch her slender arms working, notice how her pale collarbone slides from her collar when she moves her shoulders.

"I wore comfy shoes," she says.

"Good," I say, dropping the washrag in the basket below the counter and wiping my hands on my apron. "I'll show you around."

I turn to look at my kitchen, my happy place, wondering where to start. I want to look professional, like someone who knows what he's doing instead of flying through each day by the seat of his pants.

She circles around the counter to the kitchen, finishing off the bow on her apron.

"Okay, what do I need to know?"

"The kitchen," I say hoarsely. I clear my throat and turn away so she can't see my cheeks flush. "Um, ovens. I do the cooking, so you don't really need to worry about those. I may ask you to get something out from time to time if I'm busy, so the hot pads are just there," I say, motioning to a drawer labeled *hot pads.*

"Got it," she says.

Luna approaches Joan from behind. Seeing her shadow, Joan checks over her shoulder, startling slightly.

"Oh god. Hi, Luna," she says, placing a hand over her heart. "We might need to stick a bell on you."

Luna smiles vacantly.

"Over here," I say, and both girls follow me to the fridge near the espresso machine. I watch Luna curiously. Gabby's dark eyes glance at Luna, and then at me, eyebrows raised in question. I shrug. It's not like Luna to hover. She's usually more into drifting around aimlessly. She must really like Joan.

Now that Joan knows Luna's there, she doesn't seem to mind. Meanwhile, I'm about two seconds from having yet another fruitless discussion with Luna about personal space.

"I love your necklace, Luna," Joan says, indicating the crescent moon charm on the chain around Luna's neck. Luna smiles, looking right through Joan.

My eyes dart to the bracelet on Joan's unbroken wrist, the crescent moon charm exactly like Luna's. I shouldn't have said anything about it yesterday. I kick myself inwardly.

I open the fridge, glad for the rush of cold air. "Milks for coffee and tea. Everything's labeled. Whole on top, skim under that, soy and almond milk on the bottom for the non-dairy weirdos. I'll have Gabby show you the espresso machine in a minute."

Joan nods, her eyes sweeping over my (thankfully) organized fridge, her mind cataloging each bit of information. I can almost see words and numbers flying behind her eyes into her mental files. The color of her eyes reminds me of the dark local honey I buy for baking. I clear my throat again and point to the cream and sugar counter in the seating area. "Check the jugs every hour or so, more if it's busy. And you know, top them off." I close the fridge and immediately start sweating without the cold, dry air pouring onto me.

"Milks are organized, fill the jugs at least every hour," she repeats.

I nod in approval, then look around the kitchen again.

"Is there somewhere I can clock in?" she prompts.

"Oh! Yes," I say. I curl my finger in a "follow me" gesture and lead her to the back door where a clipboard hangs from a nail.

"I haven't invested in a fancy clock-in system or anything like that, so just sign in and out. Honor system."

Joan eyes the battered clipboard, the hastily printed-out table with names and times scribbled in, the ballpoint pen hanging from a string. I can't tell what she's thinking, but I suddenly wish I had a computer or something more professional than a damn clipboard.

"Okay," she says.

Luna touches my arm lightly, then looks in the direction of the espresso machine just as it lets out a high squeal. Gabby, who was pouring a customer's iced coffee, jumps and yelps before adjusting something on the machine.

I steal a glance at Joan's face. She raises an eyebrow, eyes moving from the machine back to Luna.

"I really need to get that fixed," I say quickly and move on. "The register. Being a science major and everything, I'm sure you're familiar with numbers, so that shouldn't be too hard. Questions?"

"Is the schedule posted somewhere?" Joan asks.

"Um, not at the moment," I answer. "I can write it down for you…" I grab a napkin from a package under the counter, and suddenly Luna's holding out the pen from the clock-in clipboard, severed string dangling. I didn't even notice she'd gone.

"Thanks Lune," I say quietly. I flatten the napkin on the counter and carefully write out the shifts I'd like Joan to work for the rest of the week, making sure to not rip the thin paper.

"It's good to see you again, Luna," I hear Joan say. "Thanks for helping me the other night. I really appreciate it." My stomach warms up. I can imagine Luna with her absent smile and somehow believe she understood.

There isn't much left to show. "Gabby's better at the espresso machine than I am," I tell Joan. "So she can teach you. Let one of us know if you have questions, all right?"

Joan nods and reaches back to tighten her apron strings. "I will. Thanks again for the job, by the way." In the tight space between counters in the back of the kitchen, she stands closer to me than she ever has before. For the first time, I noticed the faint freckles scattered across her nose.

"You're welcome," I say gruffly. "It'll be nice to have someone around that I don't have to babysit."

Gabby throws a dirty look over her shoulder and I widen my eyes, daring her to deny it. Joan chuckles.

"Thanks for showing me around." She turns and saunters to the espresso machine, long legs and ass working in her jeans. I look up and realize Gabby's watching me. She wiggles her eyebrows at me before turning to help Joan. My face heats.

I feel Luna hovering behind me. "Luna, go bring dishes back or something, will you?" I snip. She does nothing. I start to say something, then I see Gabby's pale face, looking over my shoulder. Joan stands behind her, eyes wide and cheeks white.

I whirl around to face Luna. She's stiff, her eyes pinched shut, pale as milk. I've seen that posture so many times.

Joan and Gabby appear on either side of me. "Luna," Gabby says softly, gripping her shoulder. Joan reaches for her pocket.

"Don't call anyone," I say sharply. Her hand stops. "It'll be over in a minute."

"What's happening? Is she having a seizure?"

"Yes," I lie. "They come and go. Take care of the customers." I look at the register. No one's standing in line. The few late-afternoon diners are scattered at tables. No one seems to notice anything happening in the back of the kitchen. They can't hear us over the Frank Sinatra Gabby chose today. "Just go, Joan."

Looking hurt, Joan quickly straightens and turns to weave around the counters and to the register, where she starts straightening tea containers, throwing a quick glance over her shoulder.

"Luna," I whisper. Her eyes twitch beneath her closed eyelids. I wait, just in case she tries to communicate. In case things aren't normal when it's over. Gabby holds Luna's shoulder, ready to spring into action if necessary.

A few seconds later, Luna's muscles relax. Her shoulders drop from her ears and the sinews in her neck settle back into her skin, which is returning to its normal golden color. Her eyes flutter open, staring straight through me, a soft smile on her face.

I exhale. Everything is fine. Gabby sighs.

"Are you okay?" Gabby says, rubbing Luna's arm. Luna, of course, doesn't answer, but walks between us to approach the seating area. Gabby and I watch her drift out to the tables, collect someone's mug, and carry it back to the sink. Joan looks over her shoulder at Luna, then back at me, questioning.

"I'm glad it's never like that for me," Gabby says under her breath. "It looks so scary to black out like that." She watches Luna, then her eyes shift to Joan. "She was just trying to help."

Guilt hits me like a kick to the stomach. She's right. For that reason alone I don't want to go over there. Suddenly, I just want to knock back a few shots, then take a long nap. Gabby reads my face and rolls her eyes. "Don't be such an ass. Just go say you're sorry."

"She'll just ask more questions."

"So answer them. Tell her Luna has absence seizures sometimes and that they're nothing to worry about."

"She's not going to believe that."

Gabby nods to Luna, who's out looking for more dishes. "She can see that Luna's fine now. Just tell her something so she at least feels like she knows what's going on."

I sigh. Fine.

I approach Joan, who's tactfully pretending nothing happened. She doesn't acknowledge me until I clear my throat. When she's finished straightening the last jar, she turns around, her jaw set.

"I'm sorry," I say stiffly. "I didn't mean to snap."

"Does this happen a lot?" she asks, ignoring the apology. "What if that happens when you and Gabby aren't here? I'd like to know what to do."

"It's not a big deal," I insist, scrambling. "She has absence seizures sometimes, but they pass and everything's fine. Nothing to worry about. Just ignore them."

I hear Gabby behind me, pretending to rearrange dishes so she can listen. I turn to her and frown, jerking my head toward the back door, telling her to leave us alone. She glares back, sassing me with her eyes. I don't know who I want to strangle more—my sister or Joan, who's getting more under my skin every moment.

Gabby kicks the back of my leg. I spin around, wanting more than anything to give her the world's worst wet willy, but I take a deep breath before turning back to Joan.

"How about this," I begin. "If it happens when Gabby and I aren't here, text me, and I'll be right there."

"What if you're at the store or something and can't get back right away?"

"Don't worry. I'm never too far away."

Her lips press together. She's not buying it.

"Just…" I say, measuring my breaths. "Just wait for it to pass. Say her name calmly. Stay with her until it's over to make sure she doesn't fall or something. It only takes a few moments, but I promise it will pass and she'll be fine. Look at her now. It's like nothing happened."

Joan looks at Luna, who's rearranging some of Gabby's antiques, then back at me, eyes narrowed. She doesn't completely believe me, but I can tell she's as sick of talking about it as I am. "Fine," she says.

"I really am sorry," I repeat.

"It's fine. I'll just let you handle it next time." She waves a hand dismissively.

I can't tell if she's mad at me or if she's really dropped the subject. She clearly has a handle on the register and the iced mochas she's making, so I go back to the counter, brushing past Gabby on the way.

"Well done," she hisses sarcastically.

"What was I supposed to do? Tell the truth?"

"Of course not," she snaps, clanging a pan in the sink. "But you could tell her how to handle it without being rude. Did you consider that? Or are you just so nervous about having her around that you can't help but be a jerk?"

My neck and shoulders feel tight. Gabby never knew our mother, but right now she looks so much like her, with her hands on her hips and her eyebrows arched irritably. I feel a little sick, both from seeing Mamá's ghost in my sister and because she's right, like she often is.

Saying nothing, I return to my work.

The rest of the shift passes in peace, though I keep a close eye on Luna. Gabby does the same. Joan helps the customers, brings dirty dishes back and washes them, keeps the baskets full. She's already better than most of the other employees I've had in the past year. If only she weren't so nosy.

I mix batter and knead dough for the last batches of the day and get them in the oven just as the evening rush hits. Joan handles it with grace, patiently helping customer after customer, even the fussy ones with long, complicated orders. I watch her, still annoyed, but admiring her efficiency as well.

Soon, it's closing time. We haven't spoken in hours.

"Gabs," I say as my sister passes with a load of dirty dishes. "Show her how to close, will you?"

Gabby sighs theatrically. "Darn, you know what? I just have too many dishes to wash," she says. "I simply couldn't. Can you show her?" She dumps the dishes into the sink. Joan looks over her shoulder at the noise.

"*Dios ayúdame*," I mutter. These women will be the death of me, I swear.

Joan takes croissants out of the baskets with tongs, neatly laying them on baking sheets lined with parchment paper. I like how she arranges them in perfect rows and not in stupid designs or piles like I've told Gabby not to do. I like the contrast of her messy short hair with the precision of her actions, the neatness of her tiny pearl earrings, and her perfectly smooth skin.

"Joan?" She looks up at me, her face stony. "Let me show you how to close out the register."

She drops the tongs on the tray, letting them clang on purpose, then strolls to my side, arms crossed over her chest. "What do I do?" she asks flatly.

God, she and Gabby are a nightmare. I make a mental note to avoid scheduling them on the same shift in the future, lest their hard-headedness feed off each other.

"First, you open it," I say, pushing the button to pop open the drawer.

"I figured."

I show her how to close out. She nods along, arms still crossed, not looking at me. "I can finish," she says finally, reaching for the pile of bills. She starts counting, swiping them from one hand to the other, pink lips moving slightly as she counts to herself. She's already faster than me or Gabby, so I leave her to it and slink off to finish putting things away.

While Joan finishes, I stack a selection of muffins and scones on a plate, the ones she's ordered before and a few new ones, then cover them with plastic wrap.

When she's done, she turns back to me

"Anything else?" she says curtly.

Stomach churning, I scoot the plate toward her. "You should take these home."

Her lips press together. She looks up at me, eyes soft. I didn't realize my shoulders were so tense, but I feel them relax when she smiles.

"Thank you," she says, picking up the plate and turning to leave.

"Joan," I say suddenly. She turns back to me. "Great job today. I mean it."

"I had a good time," she says. "I mean, it could have been better, but it was pretty good."

I roll my eyes, but I smile too.

She hangs her apron and signs out on the clipboard. On her way out of the kitchen, she crosses behind me and gently nudges my arm with her elbow. "See you tomorrow," she says, her mouth curved into a slight grin. I try to smile back, but I'm pretty sure it just comes off as a grimace. My arm tingles where she touched me.

I watch as she rounds the counter. My stomach jolts when she looks back and catches my eye before leaving.

Of course, Gabby was watching the whole thing from the sink where she'd been washing the same saucer over and over.

"She was flirting," she singsongs, a satisfied smile plastered on her face. "I guess you didn't make a complete mess of things."

I look away so Gabby can't see me smile. "Shut up, Gabs."

Gabby claps her hands and giggles like an idiot. She finishes the dishes, takes Luna's hand, then winks at me before they disappear through the back door to go upstairs, leaving me alone in the cafe to enjoy a cup of tea before going up to wait for our parents' clock to strike twelve.

8

Gabby

After helping Luna get to bed, I lay on the couch and watch the interlocking circles move on the face of my parents' clock. It's meditative to watch the seconds pass, the hands in their tireless journey around and around. How many nights have I lain awake, listening to its soothing rhythm? I don't remember my parents, but the ticking of their clock is like a lullaby preserved in gears and wires.

When the clock strikes eleven, the little suns and moons parade out, spinning in front of the face. Stars twirl, sparkling in the low evening light. *Mi Estrella*, Mamá used to call me. I watch these stars all the time, hoping for insight.

I sit up to finish my tea, then leave the mug on the coffee table and go to my room. Luna sleeps on her side under her comforter, snoring quietly with Gulliver tucked behind the bend of her legs. She doesn't stir, but Gulliver opens his sleepy green eyes to look at me before shutting them again and curling his fluffy tail over his face. I reach out to scratch his ears before sitting on the floor to examine the stack of books on my nightstand.

If Thiago had his way, I'd know nothing of our past. Our parents' lives would be a mystery. In his perfect world, I would have graduated high school with straight A's and finished nursing school instead of dropping out to work in the cafe.

But Thiago doesn't get his way. I just let him think he does.

Of all the weird objects I bring home, he tolerates books best. He's not much of a reader unless it's cookbooks. (I do keep an eye out for old-fashioned cookbooks, because he appreciates those.) He doesn't know about the carved-out book on my nightstand, camouflaged against other books that look just as old. I found it in a thrift store and had to have it—a book for hiding my own secrets.

He doesn't know about the items inside: Papá's glasses, Mamá's favorite pen, and the tiny note that came with the star pendent on the chain around my neck on my first Christmas.

Para Gabriela, Mi Estrella

Mamá

That's all the note says, but I treasure it.

I may not remember my parents, but I know them well. I carefully lift Papá's glasses from the cavity of the hollow book. Thin wire rims. Inexpensive, well-used. Fingerprints smudge the lenses. I know most of them are mine, but I'd like to think that some of Papá's fingerprints still cling to the thin glass discs.

I run my thumb over the silver arms folded neatly behind the lenses and close my eyes.

Like looking out the window of a speeding train, images fly by before I can get a good look. I will them to slow. It's not always this easy. I can only control this vision because I've Seen it many times. I know exactly where I'm going.

The images stop and, finally, I see Papá's hands as if I were looking through his eyes, his glasses. He paints the housing of the beautiful astronomical clock that hangs in our living room. Papá's hands dip a horsehair brush into a pot of midnight blue, then carefully paint the back of the clock in long, careful strokes.

Papá loved making clocks. I can feel it.

The vision changes. Papá now sits on a worn sofa with a baby in his lap, dressed in a tiny blue dress and lacy bonnet. I can't see the smile on his face, but I feel his joy. The baby smiles, opening her toothless mouth and wrinkling her tiny mushroom nose.

"Mi Gabriela," Papá says. *"Mi linda Gabriela."* He reaches out to hold the baby's feet. The baby smiles and squirms as he makes her feet dance. He sings "Yellow Submarine" in a flat and tuneless voice, bouncing her along to the beat. He sounds so much like Thiago.

The images fade. A small headache burns behind my eyes.

I open my eyes and carefully replace the glasses in the book before picking up Mamá's pen. This one always has a lot more to say. She had this pen for longer than Papá had his glasses.

She loved to write. I only know this from looking back with the pen, because we have very little of her writing. None of her stories or poetry. I wish Thiago had saved some, but I can't fault him. He saved what he could, what he thought was important. He saved the items in my book. He saved the clock. He saved Luna and me.

I grip the pen tightly.

I hear Mamá singing before I see her. Mamá and Papá both loved to sing, but unlike Papá, Mamá could sing well. Her voice drifts through the recesses of my mind, either in my own memory or in the haze of the vision that forms before my mind's eye.

I know this song. "A Thousand Years", released in 2011. I used to think it was a lullaby until I heard it on the radio as a new hit in middle school and I realized Mamá used to sing me a song that wouldn't exist for at least another decade. The thought gives me excited goose bumps.

Mamá's face swims into view. I take in her wide, dark eyes, her bright red lipstick, her thick, wavy hair that falls nearly to her elbows.

She looks like me, with full lips and a heart-shaped face, but she's much more beautiful. Luna inherited our mother's gorgeous hair, but I sure didn't. My own bob-cut hair is thin and fine, more like Papá's.

Near the sunny window of a small, sparse apartment, Mamá holds me as a baby. She sways, singing. I coo and wave my arms to her song, and she laughs. Her laugh is just as musical as her song.

"Mi Estrella," she says. *"Mi niña pequeña fuerte."* My star. My strong little girl.

Outside the window, I see the Charles River. We've already moved to Boston. My parents won't be alive much longer.

I think Mamá knew.

In the vision, four-year-old Luna shuffles into the room. Her wavy, dark hair already falls halfway down her back. She tugs on the bottom of Mamá's blouse.

"Mamá," she says. Her voice is thick, unsure. "Hungy," she whines. It's strange to hear Luna's voice, back when she spoke. Not that she spoke often, from what I've Seen.

Mamá looks down at Luna, nothing but love on her beautiful face. "I know you're hungry, Luna," she says in Spanish. "I'll make lunch soon."

Luna's young, round face crumples into a frown. "Hungy," she insists, with great effort. "Hungy *now.*"

The vision fades. I exhale. I wish I could sustain the visions longer. I try to practice, but it's hard when I'm always half-listening for Thiago's footsteps in the hall.

I place the pen back in the book. Each time I let it go, it's like saying good-bye. I never got to say good-bye to them. I barely got to say hello, at least while they were both alive. I wonder if Mamá watched me in the future like I watch her in the past, if she got to know us that way because she knew she wouldn't be there to watch us grow up.

Mi Estrella.

Almost always, I start with the happy visions. Something pleasant to stall what always comes next.

It's a compulsion. I don't know why I do it. It kills me every time, but some part of me needs to know what happened and why.

The first time, I actually had to talk myself into it. I didn't want to See it, but I wanted to know what happened because Thiago wouldn't tell me. He stopped trying to make sense of it, but I felt like there was more to know.

Maybe we could find the man who did it. Maybe we could find clues about the task Mamá mentioned in her letter to Thiago that he thinks I don't know about.

Thiago stopped trying, so I took up the burden.

There's another object in the hollowed-out book. I lift the small white handkerchief with trembling hands and unfold it in my lap, examining the familiar constellation of rusty blood spots. Mamá's blood.

I wrap the tainted material around my hands and close my eyes.

The vision starts with a slight buzzing sensation behind my eyes and a dull throb deep in my skull.

A one-bedroom apartment where the five of us lived. The living room doubled as a bedroom for Thiago and Luna, while I slept in a crib in my parents' room.

We're in the kitchen, all of us but Thiago, who should be on his way home from school. Mamá wears a light blue collared dress, her uniform for her job at a bakery where she works the night shift. She stands at the stove, stirring a large pot and humming. Papá sits at the table across from tiny Luna and me in my high chair. I kick my chubby legs while he spoon feeds me mashed banana from a bowl. My dark hair swirls on top of my head like a soft-serve ice cream cone.

It's mid afternoon, that one precious hour between my parents' opposite shifts around the same time Thiago got home from school, when we can all be home together. Slanted yellow sunlight from the window casts a glowing rectangle on the opposite wall. A portrait of a happy family, minus my brother.

Someone knocks on the front door, a precise series of three long knocks followed by several short ones. Thiago's signal that he's home and coming into the house. I hear the door open in the living room and shut.

The moment the door clicks shut, Mamá whips her head around, dropping the sauce-coated spoon to the floor. Panic flashes across her dark eyes as they dart to the door to the living room. She knows we can't run; we wouldn't make it out in time.

Papá leaps to his feet as Mamá scoops up Luna and me with startling strength and shoves us into the cleaning closet in the corner of the room.

Luna's eyes are wide and terrified. She doesn't make a sound. The door shuts silently.

It happens so fast—from happy family to disaster within seconds. Mamá grabs a chopping knife from the block on the counter and hurls it at the doorway just as a large man steps into the room. He notices and dodges just in time as the knife flies into the living room.

He turns back to my mother and smiles. The man wears a black wool pea coat that's almost too tight over his powerful shoulders and looks to be in his mid to late thirties, with short, dark hair and tanned skin. A light layer of stubble coats his cheeks and chin. Dark circles ring his eyes.

The man takes another step. Papá lunges, but the man's hand flies out and suddenly, a knife lodges in Papá's stomach. The stranger is so fast, I didn't even see him draw the knife. Neither did Papá. Papá's eyes bulge with shock and pain. The man keeps his eyes trained on Mamá as he jerks the knife, slicing through Papá's gut. Blood spills over his hand and onto the floor.

Papá falls. Mamá screams.

There's no sound from the closet. Not a peep.

Mamá grabs another knife and slices at the stranger's head. He casually swipes Mamá's hand away, twists the knife from her grip, and places it on the counter, out of her reach. She aims a kick at his groin, but he's too fast. His large hand grabs her foot and with a quick twist of his hand, Mamá's leg snaps and she crumples to the floor.

Mamá kicks her good leg at the man's ankles, but he simply takes a step back. Her face is shiny with sweat. Her foot faces the wrong way.

"Where is it, Inés?" the man asks in a deep voice tinged with a British accent.

My mother spits, her face red with fury and terror.

The man ignores the spittle that's just spotted his shoe. He reaches down to grab her hair, lifting her head and shoulders off the floor. "*¿Dónde está?*" he growls. "*¿Dónde?*"

"Gone," she hisses in English between her gritted teeth. "It's been gone for years."

The man twirls his dripping knife in his fingers. "I don't believe you," he says softly.

The throb in my head turns to a sharp, stabbing pain. I cry out, my eyes flying open. The vision ends.

My face is slick with tears. An aching hole forms in my chest. *Mamá. Papá.*

Sometimes I can See further than that, to ten-year-old Thiago arriving home to a ransacked apartment and his parents dead, the murderer nowhere to be found. To when Thiago found Luna and me huddled in the closet, miraculously alive, but both of us changed. Luna changed so profoundly that she's nearly unrecognizable as the child she once was. How Luna clutched me tightly and stared straight ahead with blank, faded eyes. Her ghostly pale lips parted in silent shock. Even her hair looked lighter, though that could have been the bright afternoon sun streaming into the closet when he opened the door.

I keep hoping to uncover a clue, something I hadn't noticed before, but there's nothing.

But I know the man was looking for something my parents had at some point, something that had been gone for years before their murders. Also, this man knew my mother's name, so this couldn't have been the first time they'd met.

What on earth was he looking for, and how did they know each other? After years of revisiting my parents' deaths, I still don't know.

It always ends like this. With them on the floor bleeding and me on the floor crying. There's something I need to know. I'm sure of it. But I can't find it. I just watch their deaths over and over again, shouldering a burden that was never meant to be mine.

9

Joan

I sit at a table, clutching my feather quill with the massive, open book before me. Fresh ink shines on the page. My hand moves again, trailing letters across the parchment in a language that I don't quite understand, but feel like I could if I looked at it long enough. I pause, stretching my cramping hand. So much writing.

A man clears his throat.

I look up to see a man seated across from me at the large wooden table. Wavy dark hair spills over his eyes, obscuring his face as he watches me. His dark, unkempt beard indicates that we've probably been in this room for a while.

I've seen this man before, I realize. Many times, but only in dreams. He's powerfully built, dressed in an old-fashioned black shirt and coat. Wind howls against the outside walls, whistling through cracks in the small window.

The man looks up at me, bright green eyes peering through strands of hair. A feeling stirs, one that doesn't make sense and doesn't seem to come from my own body.

Terror.

My eyes snap open and I immediately squeeze them shut again

when I'm assaulted with bright sunlight. My heart pounds a panicked drumline in my chest. I'm lying on the twin bed in my tiny room, cheerful morning sunshine streaming through the window.

I lie there for a few minutes in a daze before pushing myself up on the creaky mattress and resting my heavy head in my hands.

I don't believe in dream interpretation or that dreams are anything but our minds filing away information from the day, but these dreams feel different. That man is always there, though I'm almost positive I've never seen him in my life. Maybe I saw him in a crowd when I was a kid, just long enough for my brain to take a snapshot and make him the subject of recurring dreams.

These dreams used to be infrequent, an every-once-in-a-while thing, but they're happening more often, increasing steadily from once every few months to once or twice a month. The images are clearer.

He's always there, sitting in the room with me while I write in a massive book, and I'm always awakened by a sharp feeling of terror. It doesn't make sense. He never does anything to frighten me in the dreams, but still I wake up with my lungs in a vise and my heart pounding in my chest.

What does this mean? I've had two of these dreams in less than two weeks, sharper than ever. What's changed?

I had a near death experience recently. That could certainly rattle a few things in my head. I lost a chance at the internship of my dreams and started a new job I wasn't expecting.

I've started hanging out with three very strange people. Am I just disoriented from the abrupt change of plans for my summer? Is my imagination running amok because I feel like there's something different about them that they're trying to hide?

Whatever the cause, something's changed the dreams. I can't help but feel like I'm changing too, slowly, from the inside out. My cells are being replaced one by one with something different, something familiar.

I check the clock. It's after noon.

Holy crap, I never sleep this late. *Ever.* No wonder it's so bright in this room, and of course the dorm is empty. Nisha would have left hours ago.

I jump out of bed, get dressed, and take off for my shift at the Clockwork Cafe.

***

There's something soothing about making tea and coffee. Maybe it's being around the hot water, slowing down to pay attention to what you're doing even if there's a line out the door. You can go fast, but at some point you have to wait for the espresso to finish draining into the little cup, wait until the milk is fully frothed and the tea finishes steeping.

"Haste and impatience make bad coffee," Thiago tells me, "and there's never an excuse for bad coffee."

I shake my head, smirking, because this is clearly the only situation in which Thiago exhibits patience.

Thiago works silently, as stoic as the day I came back to thank him for saving my life. At first, I thought he was irritated with me or just a grouch, but then I just realized that's how he is, focused on the task at hand. He concentrates on kneading dough, rolling croissants, mixing muffin batter, batch after batch. He's like a machine, turning out beautiful pastries every time with perfect precision.

I watch him scoop ingredients into a mixing bowl without measuring, just shoveling in flour and sugar with a plastic scoop, adding pinches of salt and baking soda, sometimes stopping to stare into the bowl for a moment before dribbling in a smidge more vanilla. Yesterday, he grated lemon zest into the muffin batter. Today, he adds a small handful of something orange from a smaller bowl.

"What's that?" I ask him.

"Candied orange peel," he says. "I made it last night."

"*Late* last night," Gabby adds as she passes with a tub of dirty dishes. "I could hear you banging around down here until after midnight."

I inch closer and peer into the bowl. "Do you make a different recipe every day?"

"It's not really a recipe," he answers. "I mostly bake the same base every day and add whatever sounds good. Different fruit, chocolate, sometimes I'll make a savory batch. I'm thinking of trying orange and lavender later this week."

"I keep trying to talk him into adding some of my Earl Grey," Gabby says from the sink. "But he won't."

"That's a terrible idea," Thiago says, catching my eye. "Actually," he says quietly, leaning closer to me, "it's a great idea, but I don't want her to know that."

"I heard that, dumbass," Gabby snaps. I can see she's smiling.

I chuckle and shake my head. Thiago plucks a spoon from a jar on the counter, dips it into the muffin batter, and offers it to me. He smells like orange and bread dough. I inhale deeply, tiny champagne bubbles tingling down my arms.

"Tell me what you think," he says. "If you're not scared of raw batter."

"I've eaten way too much cookie dough in my life to be scared of raw batter," I say before placing the spoon in my mouth.

My first thought is *wow*. The batter is light, smooth, with a bright pop of orange followed by a more subtle, darker vanilla flavor. "Holy shit," I say. "That's amazing."

"You like the Mexican vanilla?"

"I love it. It's…" I can't quite place it. I wish there were an equation or number to explain it, because words fail me.

"Sexy, right?" he says.

A smudge of flour streaks his cheek and nose from when he rubbed his face with the back of his wrist.

"Definitely," I answer. "That's a good word for it."

Thiago smiles to himself and nods, satisfied, before turning to get the muffin tins out of the slotted shelf. "Good," he says. "I think this one's a winner."

He starts spooning the batter into the tins while I cross behind him to put my spoon in the sink. I can't resist sticking my elbow out just a little to brush the back of his tee shirt.

God, I'm acting like a boy-crazy teenager.

Gabby takes the register, which gives me a chance to master the espresso machine. We work smoothly, her taking orders and writing them on Post Its that she sticks to the mugs lined up next to me. Large quad shot mocha. Small vanilla skim latte. Iced Americano. It's fun, putting each drink together like a puzzle. It's equal parts art and science.

I get better at making elegant lattes. I learn to hold and move the tin of milk just right so that a beautiful leaf or heart forms on the surface.

"I love making lattes," Gabby tells me. "It's like looking at clouds. You can find so many pictures in them, and it's so easy to turn them into art. You just put a stirrer in there and swirl things around a bit..." she demonstrates, adding whiskers to what I think is a cat face. "...and it's art!" She beams, proud of herself. I can't help but smile.

"I don't ever think about turning things into art," I tell her as I take the latte. "When I make lattes, I think about surface tension. And the different densities of the milk and espresso."

"Really?" Gabby says, her eyes sparkling. "That's fascinating. I don't think I've thought about that stuff since high school science class."

"At least you've taken science," I say. "I've never taken an art class in my life." I place the mug on a saucer. Out of nowhere, Luna appears to take it from me. She smiles dreamily as I carefully hand her the mug. Somehow, she always gets the orders to the right people. I don't know how she does it. "I took choir for my fine arts credits in high school, and music classes in college. No art. You know how some people look at abstract paintings and say, 'Oh, my toddler could do that'? Yeah, I'm not even that good."

Gabby shakes her head. "Abstract art isn't as easy as it looks. But you don't have to be 'good' at art to make art. No one gets to decide whether it's good or bad. It doesn't have to hang in a museum and no one has to like it. It can just be for you. And that's exactly what I tell Thiago when he doesn't like my collages." She shoots a glare in his direction. He looks over his shoulder and gives her a devilish smile. Gabby smirks and rolls her eyes. They tease, but there's friendliness there too.

The longer I work, the more I realize how much I love being in the cafe. This summer isn't going anywhere near how I'd planned, but I think I'm okay with it. I meet Thiago's eyes over the counter as I pass. I smile at him and he smiles back, pausing for a few moments before I move on and he returns to his work.

That's when I realize we're friends. Me, them, him. We're together in this now, whatever *this* is. Connected. This is exactly where I want to be this summer. With this strange man, these three weird siblings, with their quirks and eccentricities and mysteries.

But if I'm one of them, why do I still feel like they aren't telling me something, that Thiago seems to listen when Gabby talks to me, and like he's scrambling to cover up whenever Luna does something strange? Maybe that's why I wanted the job. Maybe that's why I came back. To get a closer look at these fascinating people and their secret, whatever it is.

A clatter of metal snaps me out of my thoughts.

"Sorry! Sorry," Gabby says, picking up the tray she just dropped. Thiago blinks, then returns to his croissants, shaking his head.

My phone vibrates in my pocket. I pull it out. My mom's number and a photo of her with my golden retriever, Sammy, flashes on the screen.

My jaw tightens, and I shove the phone back in my pocket, not relaxing until the vibrations end.

I breathe a sigh of relief before the phone vibrates again. I pull the phone out again, dread bubbling inside me. She wouldn't call twice in a row if it weren't important, but I know what she's going to say. I don't want to hear it, but I know I can't avoid it any longer.

No customers stand in line at the register. I glance at Thiago and hold up my phone, pointing to the back door. Understanding, he nods. I answer the phone and push out the door to the alley behind the restaurant.

"Hey, Mom," I say.

"Hi, Sweet Pea," she starts. "Do you have a minute?"

I know that tone. My whole body tenses up and I brace myself. "What?"

"I'll just get to it. I've been putting off telling you this, it's hard to say, but…I signed the divorce papers. It's final now."

I draw in a shaky gulp of air, for two reasons.

One, it's happened. The reason I didn't want to go home this summer.

Two, I know she signed them, because I saw it. That day I blacked out during my presentation, I saw her sign them like I was floating above her. It felt so real, like I was really there. My heart pounds.

"I'm sorry, honey," she goes on, quickly mowing over my silence. "We've been trying to make it work for years, but it just…isn't."

My stomach turns to lead. I think of my brother Josh, finishing up the school year across the country at UCLA, our parents halfway between us in Denver. "Does Josh know?"

"Not yet," she breathes. "I think your father wants to tell him. He's closer to him than I am, just like you and I are closer." My jaw tightens. "Close" is a generous term for what we are, but yes, I suppose I'm closer to her than Josh. I don't recall us ever having long heart-to-heart talks or going on mother-daughter dates, but she did come to every piano recital and science fair. She always knew when I was sad and would bring home my favorite cookies from the bakery next to her work. "I'm so sorry."

I shake my head. I don't know what to feel. They were never happy during my childhood. I suppose this is for the best, but it's so…final. The last splinters holding my family together just snapped.

"Sammy's staying with me," she offers. My sweet old dog, my golden boy, my best friend throughout my teenage years. My stomach twists, wishing I could bury my face in his thick fur like I did growing up when I needed to cry. Which was often.

"So how's school, honey?" she says, a fruitless attempt to patch the conversation back together. I roll my eyes. That's my family, always dodging the painful topics to talk about school, work, achievement. "Have you found out about the internship?"

A sharp pain pricks between my eyes. I pinch the bridge of my nose. I haven't told her about the internship, or that I almost got hit by a truck and that my wrist is currently in a cast.

"They canceled it," I tell her hoarsely, weighing my words carefully. I can't tell her I didn't make it, or that I blacked out during my presentation. She'll either scold me or worry, and I really don't want to deal with either. "They're not taking interns this year after all, so I'm working at a lab in Boston until fall semester."

"Oh," she says. "Okay. Next summer maybe. You'll have an even better shot after another year of school. What are you doing in the lab?"

"Um…" I mumble, glancing toward the cafe door. "Recording atmospheric data, mostly. I'm sorry, Mom, but I really have to go."

"Oh, okay…"

I hang up the phone and bury my face in my hands. My mind spins.

Divorce. Separate Christmases and Thanksgivings. Mom alone. Dad alone. Me, Josh, stuck in the middle.

A few minutes later, the back door opens. Thiago steps out with a bag of trash.

"Don't mind me, just pretend I'm not..." I meet his gaze, my eyes suddenly swimming. I force the tears back in my head, stand, and brush off my apron.

Thiago lets the door close behind him. "Are you okay?"

"I'm fine," I say quickly, blinking moisture from my eyes. Thiago's eyes narrow, like he knows I'm lying. He folds his arms, head tilted.

"You can take a minute if you need to," he says in a gentle tone I've never heard before. "It's not time for the lunch rush yet."

I press my lips together and breathe in sharply through my nose, opening my eyes wide so they'll stay dry. My chest tightens like someone's sitting on it. My fingers start to tingle. Suddenly without conscious thought, I step forward and throw my arms around Thiago, pressing my face into his shoulder.

"Oh," he grunts, his body stiffening. Then, I feel him soften and his arms wrap around me, gingerly at first, but then tighter until it's an actual embrace. I feel him press his cheek into the side of my head.

Slowly, the urge to cry lessens. My muscles relax and I just let him hold me. His neck feels warm against my face. I feel his steady breathing, his chest expanding and contracting beneath his tee shirt, his dark hair tickling my cheek.

When we break apart, I wipe my fingers beneath my eyes in case my mascara got smeared. "I am so sorry," I say, suddenly embarrassed that I practically pounced on my boss. "That was so unprofessional, I don't know what I was thinking."

He shakes his head. "Don't be sorry," he says, fumbling for his pockets. "You look like you just got some bad news."

I nod. "My parents are getting divorced. For real this time," I say.

"It could be a lot worse news, I guess, but…it's not great."

He nods wisely, like he's heard all this before. "That sucks."

I cross my arms over my chest and stare very deliberately at a brick on the ground to keep my eyes from welling up again.

To my surprise, he puts a comforting hand on my shoulder.

I realize I want to be held. I want warmth and comfort and all the things I don't usually allow myself, and I find myself stepping closer to him.

He wraps his arms around me again, no awkwardness this time. I tip my head onto his shoulder and just breathe for a moment, closing my eyes. I feel his cheek on the back of my head in a full-bodied hug and his hands on my back, holding me firmly. It's the best hug I've ever had.

Something inside me aches in a way I've never felt before. It's like a part of me has been numb for so long I forgot it was there, and it's now coming back to life, painfully.

Finally, I pull away. "We'd better get back inside," I say hoarsely. "Thank you." I approach the door, yank it open, and step back into the cafe.

10

Joan

When I open the door to go back into the cafe, my heart leaps into my throat as I nearly run into Luna, who stands a few feet from the doorway, facing the door and holding a mug of tea. Like she was expecting us.

I curse under my breath and jump again as Thiago's chest bumps against my shoulder blades. His hands dart to my shoulders to steady himself. My cheeks suddenly burn, and my stomach feels warm.

He doesn't remove his hands right away. I know my pounding heart isn't entirely because of Luna.

Luna's dreamy smile doesn't falter. Staring right through me, she holds out the steaming mug.

"Oh," I say, taking it. The vapor rises and fills my nose. Earl Grey, my favorite. "Thank you, Luna."

She smiles softly, then turns away to straighten Thiago's impeccable stacks of baking trays. I smile and shake my head, wondering if she realizes they don't need straightening and whether she's just lingering so she can listen. She really is Gabby's sister.

Thiago's hands linger for a moment longer, then they slide away. "She must have been listening at the door," he says, answering the question I was about to ask.

The hot mug feels good in my hands. I hold it close to my chest, letting it warm my heart. Steam rises and curls around my neck like a scarf.

Thiago brushes past me, giving me a small smile before returning to his work. I place the tea on the counter near the register, sipping occasionally between customers. The tea is exactly what I need to calm my mind.

For the next three hours, I focus on work. I don't speak to anyone but the customers. A few times, I feel Thiago's eyes on me, but he says nothing. Even Gabby gives me space, which I appreciate.

The only one who doesn't is Luna. She continues to hover, finding unnecessary tasks to do nearby, though I never catch her watching me like Thiago does. Surprisingly, I enjoy her silent presence. She's just there, like a handrail if I need it.

When the line dies down, I feel a hand on my shoulder. I turn to see Luna, standing a little too close and holding out a perfectly golden muffin dotted with blueberries.

"Thank you," I say, taking the muffin, grinning at the sweet gesture. She smiles and drifts away. I look down at the muffin and my stomach rumbles violently. I hadn't even realized I was hungry. It's like she knew before I did.

Things start slowing down for the night and I pick at the muffin, knowing full well it will probably be my dinner.

At closing time, I close out the register while Gabby and Thiago clear the pastry trays. Gabby places a croissant on a plate and gives it to Luna, sending her to the seating area. It occurs to me that I've never seen Luna eat. She probably doesn't unless someone reminds her.

When I finish closing a few minutes later, Luna sits at the table, croissant forgotten on her plate, a few crumbs dusting the front of her flowered tee shirt. It had taken me a few days to get used to the constant faraway look in her silver eyes. I found it unsettling at first, how she always looks like something hit her hard in the head, but now it's just a part of her. Like Thiago's incredible concentration or Gabby's tendency to go off on tangents. Luna also doesn't mind when I stare. At first I worried I was being rude, but Luna doesn't seem to care or even notice.

I slide into the seat across from her with a lemon bar on a plate. She doesn't show any sign that she's noticed my presence. In fact, she seems to look straight through me.

"Can I join you?" I ask. I don't expect her to answer. She blinks slowly, and a small smile appears on her face. I'll take that as a sign that she heard me and doesn't object.

I pick at my lemon bar with my fork for a few moments, not sure what to say, or if I even need to say anything.

"I love your name, Luna," I finally tell her. She doesn't show any sign that she's heard me. I take another bite. "I love anything to do with the moon. It was the first celestial body I ever got to see through a telescope. That's when I knew I wanted to be an astrophysicist. The moon inspired me first."

Luna blinks again. Maybe that means she's listening. I like her company. She doesn't expect anything from me, and I don't expect answers from her either. Ironically, that makes me want to talk to her, because I know I don't have to.

"I was six," I go on, feeling more and more at ease. "It was my grandpa's telescope. He was a retired NASA engineer and had a house in the mountains, and he told me he could show me the craters on the moon. I didn't believe him, so he set up his telescope outside and let me look. I saw the craters and the actual texture of the surface. It was like being in space."

Why am I telling her all this? I think I've been in a reflective mood lately, and that phone call hasn't helped. I go on, just because talking feels good. "He taught me the names of the constellations, how some are visible only during certain times of the year, and he told stories of missions he worked on and famous astronauts he met. He gave me this for my birthday." I jingle my charm bracelet. "It just had the rocket charm on it then, and I collected the others over the years." I look closer at the bracelet. It's a bit tarnished and dull even though I've taken good care of it. "I always wear it so that when school gets hard or when I feel like giving up or getting distracted, I remember why I wanted to explore space in the first place."

The corners of Luna's lips twitch in what might be a smile. I have no idea if she can understand me, but it feels good to talk, like unloading a backpack full of rocks that I didn't even know I was carrying. I never talk to anyone about feelings, or memories. I haven't talked about my grandpa in years. Not even to my mom.

"You know," I go on, "I really like spending time with you guys. You and Gabby, even your grumpy brother." I smile. A warm drop of light blooms inside me. "You're a good listener, Luna."

Luna's eyes focus on something. I follow her gaze to my bracelet. She reaches out and touches the crescent moon charm dangling from the chain.

"It's the moon, just like you," I tell her with a smile. Her lips part slightly as she reaches for her neck. Her fingers thread through a fine silver chain around her neck, and she fishes something out of her collar. She holds it out, and I see it's a crescent moon pendant.

"That's right, you have one too," I say, leaning in to examine it. It looks exactly like mine, though maybe a touch older. I'm sure it's the same manufacturer, which is weird, because it's a small company and I'm pretty sure they went out of business. I tried to order more charms from them once. What a strange coincidence.

Luna smiles and lets the charm fall to her chest, outside her shirt this time.

I see a shape in my periphery and turn to see Thiago standing in the kitchen, holding a bottle of beer. He leans with his elbow on the counter, casually. I meet his eyes and he smiles. I realize I love his smile. It's a little uneven and goofy, but genuine. His eyes soften and the lines between his brows nearly disappear. That wonderful heat flares in my chest again. I smile back.

I stay with Luna until I finish my lemon bar, then take my plate back to the sink to wash it. Thiago approaches, his warmth preceding him. Or maybe that's just me.

"I've been meaning to ask you," he begins. "We're celebrating Luna's birthday on Saturday night. It's usually just the three of us for birthdays, but I think Luna would be happy if you came. She likes you."

"Of course," I say, grinning. "That'll be perfect actually. Beats the hell out of spending the evening on my couch eating a whole roll of cookie dough."

Thiago smiles and shakes his head in disgust at the mention of store-bought cookie dough. "She'll be thrilled," he says. "Gabby too. I'm shooting for dinner at eight. Text one of us when you get here. If we don't answer, just chuck something at the window." I can't tell if he's kidding or not. He takes a swig of beer, eyeing me while I towel off my plate.

"Are you going to be okay?" he asks. "I know you had a rough day..."

"I'll be fine," I cut him off, my lips flicking up in a quick, insincere smile.

He watches me with suspicion. "Let me drive you home," he says, plunking the half-finished bottle on the counter. "You don't have to ride the bus."

My first instinct is to protest, but the truth is, I would love a ride home. The last thing I feel like doing is spending the next forty-five minutes on a bus trying to avoid eye contact with a bunch of strangers.

"Thank you," I say quietly. "I'd like that."

He nods, reaching back to untie his apron, then holds out a hand for my apron, which I give him. My fingers brush his. They're warm and extremely soft from kneading dough all day, every day. He hangs both aprons by the back door and plucks a wad of keys from another hook, twirling them around his long index finger.

"I'm parked up the street," he says.

I follow him out the front door and we turn right. Immediately, my eyes dart to the tire-marked sidewalk like they always do when I pass this spot, the piece of sidewalk where Thiago tackled me. They've almost finished patching up the hole in the front of the boutique.

Today, a woman stands by the light post.

She's tall, middle-aged, with shiny, dark hair falling to her waist, dressed in a tank top and brightly patterned skirt. Her smooth, tanned arms cross over her chest and she stares out into the street, full lips pressed together.

Her head turns to me as we approach. She looks like she hasn't slept in days. Silver rims her large, dark eyes.

I slow my steps. So does Thiago, following my lead. "Are you all right?" I ask her.

Her lips press together as she looks at the hole in the storefront. "There was an accident here," she says in a thin voice.

"I know," I respond, holding up my cast. "I was there." Her eyes dart from my cast to my face. Recognition washes over her beautiful face. "Oh my god," she says, jaw going slack. "You're the girl he almost hit, aren't you?"

I stop. My fingers fidget. "Yeah," I say stupidly, because I can't think of anything else. The woman extends a hand to shake mine, and I take it. Her grip is firm. Her fine-boned hands are smooth and cool.

"Marlene," she says. "I'm Jeremy's mother. The driver."

"Oh," I say, my stomach dropping to my feet. "Joan Sanders. I…I'm so sorry. I didn't mean to be insensitive. I can't imagine how you must feel."

She looks down at the sidewalk and nods. "No, I'm sorry," she says. "I just came back to…I don't know why I'm here, actually. I just keep seeing him in my mind again and again, and I had to come back. To see that it wasn't just a bad dream."

I follow her gaze to the patched storefront. I sweep my eyes across the sidewalk, which still sparkles slightly with glass dust.

"It's my fault," she says. "He wasn't supposed to be driving. I wasn't paying attention, and he slipped away with the car."

I want to ask why, but for once, I keep my mouth shut.

Marlene crosses her arms over her chest again and looks at her sandaled feet. "I'm sorry for your injuries," she continues, raising her head to look at me again. This time, her eyes are dry. "I'm happy to pay for any medical bills you've had." Her eyes move to my cast, then up to my healing face.

"Oh," I say, shifting my weight uncomfortably. "It's okay. Really, you don't have to do that."

She eyes my MIT shirt and beat-up sneakers. "You're a student at MIT?" she asks.

I nod. "Astrophysics."

She nods, attempting a small smile. "I remember being a student, eating oatmeal two or three meals a day. A hospital bill is the last thing you need. Let me help." She swings her shoulder bag around to her front and opens it, digging inside for a moment before pulling out a business card, which she hands to me.

I take it. *Marlene Cole, historical romance author of The Thread of Gold series.*

"My phone number and address," she says. "Please call me when you get an invoice, or have them forward the bills."

"Oh…okay," I say, uncomfortable but extremely grateful. "Thank you."

Marlene nods, smiling. Her eyes fill with tears again. "I'm sure I'll be seeing you again, Joan." She sweeps by me to walk down the street, her long skirt brushing my leg.

Thiago and I look at each other, exchanging puzzled expressions before we continue down the sidewalk to his car.

As if my parents' finalized divorce wasn't enough. I didn't need a reminder that I narrowly escaped death just a few weeks ago, and the driver didn't.

"That was so weird," I say. We walk slower than before. "That was really generous of her, but I don't know if I can accept her help."

"Why not?" Thiago says. "She offered. It's okay to accept help, you know."

I sigh, remembering that I almost turned Thiago down when he offered a ride home, for no reason other than I just wasn't used to saying yes when someone offers to help me.

"Do you have the money to pay for your ER bill?" he asks.

I shake my head. "No," I say, conceding. "I don't."

"So let her help. She obviously feels horrible about what happened."

We reach Thiago's car. He opens the passenger door for me. I climb in, my cheeks heating. He closes the door behind me and circles around to the driver's side.

"You know," he begins. "I've never seen Luna warm up to someone like she's warmed up to you."

"I really like Luna," I tell him. "I think we're actually becoming friends."

"I think so too. She usually makes people uncomfortable…" He clears his throat. "It caused a lot of problems with foster parents and school and stuff, but you're great with her."

This surprises me. Sure, she has a tendency to pop up out of nowhere. Her demeanor can take some getting used to. But problems?

"Does she really bother people that much?" I ask. "I would have thought *you'd* be the one to make people uncomfortable." He rolls his eyes. I grin wickedly. Poking fun at Thiago always boosts my mood.

"Thanks, smartass," he says, but he's smiling too. "But yes. She does bother people." He chews the inside of his cheek and stares straight ahead. After a brief pause, he shoves the key in the ignition, starts the car, and jerks out of the parking space and onto the road.

"I didn't mean to hit a nerve," I tell him. He blinks and takes his foot off the gas to let the car slow down.

"Sorry, I just floored it a little hard," he says. He glances sideways at me before returning his eyes to the road. "Thanks for being her friend. And Gabby's friend, and…" He clears his throat, but I think I know what he was going to say. *My friend.* "They've never had friends," he finishes.

"Have you?" I ask.

"No," he says bluntly.

"Huh," I say, watching the white lines in the road disappear under the car. "Me neither, I guess. I spent all my time studying, doing homework, taking extra classes and extracurriculars, and playing piano. I spent the night of my prom studying for my AP tests. Every boyfriend I've ever had has dumped me because I was too busy. I haven't been to a single college social event."

I look at Thiago while he watches the road. There's loneliness behind his eyes. It's like looking into a mirror.

"How long were you in foster homes?" I ask. I don't know why. Maybe it's to take the focus off myself, but I really do want to understand him better.

"Eight years," he says, looking forward at the road. "From ten until I was eighteen, when I could move out and be my sisters' legal guardian."

"Your parents died when you were ten?" I say incredulously. So young. I can't imagine.

He seems to mull something over before speaking again. "They were murdered."

My breath catches in my chest. Suddenly I'm very sorry I asked, but also intrigued.

He turns a corner and goes on. "Gabby was just a baby and Luna was four, maybe five. I got home right after it happened. I didn't see it. But the girls did."

"Oh my god," I breathe.

"Luna was hiding in a closet with Gabby. My mother and father were dead on the floor. Stabbed."

My jaw hangs slightly open. "Gabby and Luna saw your parents die?"

"I think so," he says. He stares straight ahead, his eyes cloudy. "Luna's never been the same."

"Is that why she…" I don't know how to say it politely, why she is the way she is, but Thiago nods in understanding.

"That's part of it."

My eyebrows rise to my hairline. I shake my head, making sense of what I'm hearing. "What happened to the person who did it?"

He turns another corner sharply. "Nothing," he says darkly. He clears his throat again. His face goes white. "The apartment was trashed when I got there, but they never found him. There was no sign of a break-in. No murder weapon or prints. Honestly, I don't think they tried that hard."

I listen, horrified. "What about Luna?" I say. "She saw what happened."

"She wasn't able to tell us. Luna hasn't spoken a word since that day."

I think of her handing me my apron on my first day, always greeting me with a dazed smile. God, Luna. I had no idea.

"I'm so sorry," I tell him. I don't know what else to say. My chest aches for him, for his family, ravaged by tragedy and still holding together after two decades.

He waves off my apology, color returning to his face. "The important thing is, we're still together. We have the cafe and a place to live. It's better than bouncing around foster homes. Life is good." He turns to me and smiles, though his eyes don't crinkle.

We say nothing for the rest of the drive. When we pull onto the familiar streets of the MIT campus, I realize I don't want to go home just yet. Not to my lonely student apartment, not to my dark, empty bedroom.

The car slows as we wind into the student housing complex, but Thiago drives even slower than he needs to. The car stops in front of my dorm, but I don't move to unlatch my seatbelt or open the door. I don't move at all.

With the car running, we sit in silence for a few more moments. It's like we're inside a glass bubble, so fragile that a word or a look could shatter it. It feels safe. Companionable in our mutual loneliness that feels a little less lonely at the moment.

Slowly, as if trying to avoid frightening a skittish bird, I slide my hand to where Thiago's rests on the shifter and lay it over the top of his. He doesn't move away. He's still, like he's holding his breath, before he turns his hand over and twines his long fingers through mine.

We stay like that for a moment, holding hands in comfortable silence because we know we don't need to say anything. I watch our hands together, the look of his golden skin against my pale ivory, the perfection of our fingers woven together. It feels natural. Not like it felt with other guys I'd been on dates with, where their hand felt foreign and ill-fitting. It doesn't feel like the first time I've held his hand.

My eyes flick to his face. He gazes at our interlocked hands, his eyes soft, but with those lines between his eyebrows slightly deeper than usual. I wonder if he's thinking the same thing.

95

11

Joan

The azure sky is starting to pale, but it won't be dark for another hour at least. I love long summer evenings.

I arrive outside the cafe clutching a scented candle topped with a stick-on bow. About an hour ago, it occurred to me that I should bring a gift to a birthday party, so I spent twenty minutes tearing my room apart until I found something unused, suitable for someone I don't know very well. Everyone likes maple-scented candles, right?

I stand on the sidewalk, inhaling the floral scent of the dusk. It's hard to believe that just two weeks ago, this street was washed in a torrent of cold rain. Now I stand outside comfortably in a tee shirt and cutoffs.

Finally, I go inside and look around for Thiago, Gabby, or Luna. Tanya and Karl, Thiago's other employees, run the register and espresso machine. There's a line and several people seated at the tables. No sign of the Cardozas. I texted Thiago a few minutes ago, but no answer. Gabby didn't answer either. Luna, of course, doesn't have a phone.

I remember what Thiago said when he invited me: *Just chuck something at the window.*

He wasn't serious, was he? Tanya and Karl both look frazzled. A parade of mugs lines the counter, waiting to be filled. I don't want to bother them, so I slip back outside, find a quarter in my pocket, and look up at the windows above the cafe. The lights are on, sheer curtains wide open. I turn the quarter in my fingers, thinking about my angle to the window and briefly forgetting I can't throw worth a damn. I take careful aim and throw my quarter as hard as I can.

Miraculously, the quarter pings off the glass. I look around to see if anyone's watching. Luckily, this side of the street isn't crowded and I'm partially hidden from the other side by a small tree. I pick up the quarter for round two when one of the windows slides open. Gabby's face appears, smiling.

"Hi!" she calls down. "I'm sorry, I didn't have my phone on me. I'll be right down." She disappears in a flutter of curtains. I stand below the window stupidly, feeling like I should be holding a boombox blasting Peter Gabriel above my head.

A minute later, Gabby trots around the corner of the brick building. "Come around back," she says, motioning for me to join her. I follow her down the alley between the cafe and the health food store next door, past the dumpster, and to a door in the back. She opens it to reveal a steep flight of stairs. She runs up, taking the steps two at a time. I follow, easily taking two steps at once with my giraffe legs. Steamy, tomato and garlic-scented clouds waft down the stairwell. I inhale deeply.

"That smells amazing."

"You'll love paella," Gabby says over her shoulder. I love the way she says "paella," how the *ah* drifts upward to the *ay* far back in her mouth. I mouth the word silently to myself, trying out the feel of it.

I hear familiar music. My mind casts around for a moment until I recognize it and laugh.

"Is that Backstreet Boys?"

"Luna chose it," Gabby replies with a grin.

The top of the staircase opens up to a small, bright kitchen. Thiago stands at the stove, stirring a giant cast iron skillet full of rice, animatedly humming something that has nothing to do with the music playing. Past the kitchen is a living room with a sofa and coffee table. Luna sits on the floor, using the coffee table as a desk, carefully cutting pictures out of a magazine and littering the space around her with paper scraps. She bobs her head out of time with the music.

Gabby slaps Thiago on the shoulder. He turns and smiles at me as he pulls an earbud out of his ear. My stomach backflips. "Sorry, I didn't realize what time it was," he says. "Time flies when you're stirring rice."

"It's fine," I return his smile. "I just threw stuff at the window, like you said." I expect some sort of reprimand, but he smirks and invites me to make myself at home.

Luna is cutting out a picture of a snowy landscape from a magazine with a pair of safety scissors.

"Happy birthday, Luna," I tell her, sinking into a cross-legged position beside her. Luna's eyes flick to me and her lips curve into a smile, but she keeps cutting. I've never seen her so focused. "What are you making?"

I don't expect an answer, and I don't get one. At least not from Luna.

"She likes to decorate the wall by her bed," Gabby tells me from the kitchen, where she's setting the table. "It's her favorite thing. I usually work on my collages while she cuts out pictures. It's kind of a thing we do."

I look around the room and notice several framed collages made from various magazine cuttings, ticket stubs, receipts, notes, and old photographs. They're chaotic-looking, but oddly beautiful. Somehow, the different images and materials make sense together in a way I'd never be able to replicate.

"Are these all yours?" I ask Gabby.

"Yup," she says, beaming. "I'll have a gallery someday. I'd hang them down in the cafe if Thi would let me…" She shoots him a glare that he doesn't notice. "But they look nice up here for now."

"This will be done in a few minutes," Thiago grunts, ignoring her. "Wine?" he offers, pointing to a dark corked bottle on the counter. The label says *Garnacha*, a wine I've never had before. "If you aren't into red, we have a pinot grigio somewhere," he continues. "Or beer, water, juice…"

"The red would be amazing."

He grabs a corkscrew from a drawer. I watch as he expertly twists the screw down into the cork and pulls it out smoothly. I'm impressed. I can't open a bottle of wine in under two minutes, and I'm more of a Franzia girl anyway. He then selects a wine glass from the cupboard and carefully fills it halfway. He hands me the glass and I nod my appreciation before sitting at the table.

Gabby pours herself a glass and joins me. Thiago replaces his earbud and bobs his head out of time with the Backstreet Boys emanating from a dusty CD player on the coffee table.

"I take it he doesn't agree with Luna's musical tastes?" I ask Gabby. I sip the crimson wine, holding it in my mouth a moment to taste it. It tastes like red wine to me. I hope it wasn't expensive.

"He doesn't agree with anyone's musical tastes," Gabby smirks. "If it's not the Beatles, it's not music."

"Not true," Thiago interjects. "Lennon has some good solo stuff."

Gabby snorts and shakes her head.

Now that I listen more closely, I realize he's humming "Norwegian Wood," though he's completely tone-deaf. My eyes wander to Luna in the living room. She's given up on the magazines and stares out the front window.

"So, are you the youngest?" I ask Gabby, then realize I'm probably being presumptuous again. I never know if people are self-conscious about age, or anything really. Gabby is the smallest and looks like she just graduated from high school, though somehow she gives the air of being older. Especially with a glass of wine in her hand.

She nods, following my gaze to Luna. "Thiago's the oldest," she says. "Luna's twenty-five today, and I'm the baby. I turned twenty-one in October."

I sip my wine again. I was right, Luna is close to my age—just a year younger. There's more I want to ask about Luna, but I don't know how to do it without sounding like a jerk.

"Dinner's ready," Thiago announces, pulling a set of trivets from a drawer.

"Is there anything I can help with?" I ask him.

"Nope. You're our guest. Have some more wine." He winks at me, and I pause with my glass an inch from my lips. Thiago, winking? I grin and pour myself another ounce or two.

Gabby tries unsuccessfully to get Luna's attention to come to the kitchen. Luna is now absentmindedly tearing up magazine scraps while she gazes out the window. Bits of paper scatter around her like snow.

Finally, Gabby gets up to lead her to the kitchen, and Luna slides into the chair next to me, smiling vacantly. Moments later, we're all seated at the table around the giant pan of paella, wine glasses refilled. Cranberry juice for Luna.

"Let's say grace," Thiago says.

Gabby rolls her eyes. "When do we *ever* say grace…"

Thiago ignores her and tips his head, holding out his hands to me and Gabby. I take his large, warm hand, and Luna allows me to take her hand. Gabby sighs and takes Thiago and Luna's other hands so that we're all linked around the small round table. I bow my head, feeling awkward, because I've never prayed in my life. My hand that holds Thiago's tingles. My heart beats faster.

Thiago clears his throat. "'Bless us, O Lord, and these, Thy gifts, which we are about to receive from Thy bounty. Through Christ, our Lord. Amen.'"

"Amen," Gabby echoes sarcastically as she drops Thiago and Luna's hands. She reaches for the serving spoon to shovel a heaping pile of rice on my plate. Mussel shells curl around the pan like flower petals. Thiago holds my hand for just a half second longer. I think of two nights before, sitting in his car, our hands intertwined. Our eyes meet briefly and I can tell he's thinking the same thing. When he finally lets go, I wish he hadn't.

Gabby serves Luna, Thiago, then herself, and tops off her wine before beginning to eat. I take a bite of the paella. A kaleidoscope of flavors explodes in my mouth. Tangy, garlicky, savory, salty, smoky. I shovel in another bite.

"This is delicious," I tell Thiago through a mouthful of rice. A piece falls out of my mouth and onto my plate. My cheeks heat, and he smiles like he's trying not to laugh. I swallow what didn't fly out of my stupid trap before I start laughing. "It's really amazing," I add.

Thiago tips his wineglass in appreciation and drinks deeply, the corners of his mouth still upturned in an amused, but not unkind, smirk.

While we eat, Gabby chatters about her people-watching adventures in the cafe, her favorite thrift stores within walking distance, and whether I would like to go antiquing with her soon.

I nod, careful not to let any more rice fall out of my gob.

"We should go tomorrow morning," she says, turning to Thiago. "Could you put us both on the evening shift?"

Thiago rolls his eyes and twirls his fork in a defeated gesture that says, "If I must."

"Perfect!" says Gabby, tinkling her fork to her plate excitedly. "I'll take you to the Music Box down the street. It's got all kinds of old clocks and books and sheet music, and I love the furniture, but Thiago won't let me bring any of it home, way too big…"

She goes on, and I wonder how she manages to talk and eat without spraying the entire table with debris, as I'm sure I would if I were talking and eating at that rate. Luna picks at her food, taking a bite or two or even three before she stops to stare at something. Gabby eats daintily between comments, taking small bites punctuated with sips from her wine glass. Thiago eats in silence, pushing his food around his plate before selecting the perfect place from which to scoop a bite. After he finishes off the first bottle of red wine, he brings out another. I enjoy the meal, taking seconds of the paella and a taste of the second bottle of wine. I can tell this one is different from the first, though I can't pinpoint how. I'm hopeless at wines.

"I've made a cake, so save room," Thiago says when we all slow down. We've barely finished half the pan, and I'm stuffed.

"Oh, I forgot about the cake!" Gabby exclaims, putting a hand to her stomach. "Did you know the Japanese have a word for the separate stomach that's only for dessert? They call it *betsubara*. I suppose I have room for cake…"

Thiago stands to move the paella pan back to the stove. I get up to take my dishes to the sink, knocking my elbow into my empty wine glass.

My stomach lurches. Before I can grab it, the glass topples off the table. I brace myself for the sound of breaking glass, but it doesn't come.

The kitchen grows quiet. I blink. Thiago and Gabby have turned to look.

Luna's outstretched hand clutches the wine glass by the stem. I didn't even see her move. She looks at the glass in her hand curiously, like she's just noticing what happened. I turn to Thiago for an explanation, but he avoids my gaze, which I'm sure isn't accidental.

"Thank you, Luna," he says quietly, gently taking the glass from her and placing it on the table.

Gabby stops talking to gather the rest of the wine glasses and lines them up by the sink. Luna studies the woodgrain of the tabletop, paying no attention to us or the fact that she just snatched a falling glass from midair with superhuman reflexes.

"Nice catch, Luna," I say, hoping to prompt some acknowledgement from Gabby or Thiago.

No one speaks while Thiago sets out dessert plates and lifts an enormous chocolate cake from on top of the fridge. Gabby adds mismatched, used candles, runs out at twenty-one, then shrugs. "She won't count them," she says under her breath to me. Luna doesn't appear to notice.

Thiago lights the candles. We sing "Happy Birthday," Thiago's flat voice underscoring mine and Gabby's. Luna smiles and hums vaguely before blowing out her candles, though Gabby has to blow out the last three for her because she's staring into space.

Thiago starts cutting the cake into large slices.

"So…" I try again, "is Luna secretly a superhero?"

Thiago slices the cake and dumps a huge wedge on a plate that he hands to me. "I hope you like it," he says. "Sour cream in the batter. That's the secret."

I take a bite. It's the most amazing chocolate cake I've ever had and for a moment, I forget all about the wine glass. "Wow," I say. "This is incredible."

"Thank you," Thiago says before taking a swig from yet another glass of wine. I can't believe how steady his hands are. After almost a whole bottle, I'd be on the floor. Only two glasses in, I wouldn't trust myself with sharp objects at the moment, but he serves the cake like it's nothing.

Gradually, Gabby starts up her chatter again until she's moving along at a steady clip.

"Has Thiago told you he can juggle?" she suddenly asks me.

I shoot a wicked smile at Thiago, swirling my wine in my glass playfully. "No, he has not," I say.

I expect him to glare or balk, but he grins back, his face rosy. "Just one of my many talents," he says.

"Show us!" Gabby says a little too loudly. The wine's getting to her too.

Thiago tosses his head back and drains his glass, then stands, very steadily, and picks three tangerines from a fruit bowl on the counter.

"Prepare to be amazed," he says, also loudly, before the tangerines start flying between his hands in a perfect cascade, then he reverses and the fruit starts flowing the opposite direction. I'm genuinely impressed.

"Is this what they teach you in chef school?" I laugh.

He chuckles. The pattern of the tangerines changes again, with one appearing to pop back and forth like a tennis ball before he catches them all in one hand and takes a deep bow.

Gabby and I clap. Even Luna raises her hands to bring them softly together, just once.

He returns the fruit to the bowl and sits back down to pour himself another glass of wine.

I'm still stuffed from dinner, but I somehow manage to finish my cake. Then we all move to the couch so Luna can open the small pile of presents on the coffee table. By now, the sky is velvety blue and stars twinkle out the window. Gabby helps Luna open her presents by pretty much opening them for her. There's a vintage flowered dress from herself, socks and a blue sweater from Thiago, and my candle. Gabby unscrews the lid and holds the open candle to Luna's face. Luna hasn't acknowledged any of her gifts until now, but she inhales and smiles, her eyes focusing on the room for half a second before slipping back into her usual dazed expression.

"I think she likes it," says Gabby, placing the candle on the table. She folds the dress and sweater and stacks them neatly with the pack of socks on her lap before standing up. "I'd better get Luna to bed," she says. "She's getting tired."

I look at Luna, puzzled. She looks like she always does, dazed and content. I wonder how Gabby can tell she's tired.

Gabby takes Luna by the hand, helps her up from the couch, and leads her to the bathroom. I watch her open a drawer, put toothpaste on a toothbrush, and put it in Luna's hand. Luna brushes for a few seconds before stopping, and Gabby reminds her to keep going. This happens a few times until Gabby coaxes her into spitting the toothpaste in the sink. Gabby then leads her to the bedroom, leaving me alone with Thiago on the couch.

"Is Luna…" I start, vaguely wondering if I'm being rude, but feeling bold after the wine. "Is it autism?"

Thiago pauses, glass inches from his lips. "No," he says finally, taking a sip and not looking at me. I hear soft ukulele music from the girls' bedroom and raise my eyebrows, turning to Thiago.

"Gabby plays for her at bedtime," he shrugs. "It helps her get to sleep."

"Oh." My head floats and my limbs feel heavy. Thiago reaches for his dessert plate on the coffee table to finish his last few bites of cake, arm brushing mine. His skin is cool. Veins twine across his hands and forearms. As he leans forward, I notice the tiny cross glittering on the thin chain around his neck, right next to the sun pendant that's exactly like mine. I think of the prayer at dinner, how Gabby said "When do we ever say grace…" I never pegged him as the religious type, and honestly, I'm still not sure he is. Then again, there's a lot I don't know about him.

"Thiago," I say, feeling bold again. "I still want to know…"

He shoves the last of his cake into his mouth.

"…how did you know to follow me the night you saved me?" I wait, hoping the wine and glow of the evening will loosen his tongue like they've clearly loosened mine.

He sighs, chewing thoughtfully.

"I mean, you were just there," I continue. "I'm grateful, but it doesn't make any sense." I swallow hard. "There's something different about you. You and your sisters. I don't know what, but it has to do with that, doesn't it? You saving me the other night."

Thiago sighs again and curses in Spanish.

"It has to do with Luna, doesn't it? She knew I was going to knock my glass off the table. She knew about the truck too, didn't she?"

Thiago turns to look at me, eyes stony. He chews his lip, like he's trying to make up his mind.

"I won't tell anyone," I add.

He smirks and shakes his head. "Of course you won't. No one would believe you."

12

Joan

My heart races. "I want to know," I say, holding my voice steady.

Thiago sits back on the couch, turning his body toward me. He chews his lip, thinking hard.

"You're right," he says finally, eyes lifting briefly to meet mine. "I followed you because of Luna." He looks nervous, even scared. His eyes drop back down and fog over as he speaks. "Luna knew you were in danger." He opens and closes his mouth a few more times, fidgeting as if he's overcoming some internal hurdle to get the words out. Finally, he finishes "...because she can See the future."

Suddenly, the fuzziness from the wine evaporates and the room around me sharpens. Did I hear him correctly?

"Luna can...See the future?"

He nods.

"What...how? Is that what those 'absence seizures' actually are? She's Seeing the future?"

"It's not just when she freezes up," he says. I can almost see his heart pounding through his shirt. "Always. She's never *not* Seeing the future, we think. That's why she's always so..." He waves his hands around the sides of his head, indicating Luna's aloofness. "She can't focus on the present for more than a few seconds at a time, tops. But sometimes, she has very strong visions. Clear ones. Like the other day when I told you she had a seizure. And the night of the accident. I think she Saw it in your teacup when she cleared your table. Sometimes objects, like the cup you drank from, can trigger a vision." He looks sideways at me, throat bobbing.

Is he scared that he told me? Afraid of what I'm thinking? Honestly, I don't know what I'm thinking. I'm somewhere between wanting to know everything there ever was to know about them and peeing myself in fear, because I'm clearly in the presence of a very unstable person.

I sit straight up with my hands on my knees, part of me wanting to leave, part of me wanting to stay. This is what I've wanted to know since I met them, and I want to hear the rest, but it's insane. My head spins.

The weirdest part is, it's like a story I've heard before.

No. This is crazy. It makes no sense on a logical level. It defies everything I believe in as a scientist, everything I trust in the universe. It spits in the face of natural law.

On the other hand, I'm not surprised. Was I expecting this?

"Luna grabbed my wine glass when I knocked it over at dinner. She knew it would fall."

He nods. "That happens sometimes. She snaps back just for a second, stopping some annoyance or catastrophe before it happens. Sometimes it's helpful. She put an umbrella in Gabby's bag once on a perfectly clear day that turned stormy, against all weather predictions. Last year, she dialed the police five minutes before the cafe was robbed, and they walked in right as the thief stepped up to the register and told Gabby to open it. It doesn't happen often, but sometimes."

The ukulele music stops. I hear Gabby's voice, soft Spanish

consonants emanating through the walls.

"Gabby sings her to sleep every night," Thiago says, watching the bedroom door. "If she has constant visions when she's awake, I can only imagine what her dreams are like."

A beautiful astronomical clock hanging near the window strikes ten, sounding a clear bell.

"Has she always Seen the future?" I ask.

"No. Just since our parents died." He fingers the cross absentmindedly. "Before then, she was a normal child. She was only five when she was hit with that first vision. It changed her. Her hair turned white, her eyes lost their color. She stopped speaking. The worst part is, I have no idea what she Saw, or what she ever Sees. She just floats around in a different world." He exhales sharply. "I shouldn't be telling you this."

"Well, I did ask."

Thiago sighs. Now that he's talking, he seems relieved, like he's been waiting to get this off his chest. "There's more. It's not just Luna."

My insides twist, either from excitement or nerves. I follow his gaze to the closed bedroom door. He looks tired, suddenly. Weary. His eyes are bloodshot and perspiration beads at his hairline.

"Gabby?" I say. "Gabby Sees the future too?"

"No. Gabby Sees the past."

Now *that* I didn't expect. But when I think about it, it makes sense.

"She has visions?" I say, "but she seems…." I almost say "normal," but that isn't quite accurate. I think of the mug she broke when I came back to thank Thiago for saving my life. *This mug belonged to a little boy in the seventies…*

"She has visions sometimes," he continues, "but not as often as Luna. She needs an object to trigger her visions, and not all objects work."

"Is that why she collects antiques?" I scan the room, the ornate clock on the wall, framed antique photos and book pages, an old rocking chair in the corner that doesn't look like it could support a toddler. "She collects objects that spark visions?"

Thiago nods again. "She's kind of a junkie, but don't tell her I said that."

I still have so many questions. "So if Luna Sees the future and Gabby Sees the past," I say, "what about you? Do you have visions?"

"Well," he says. "If Gabby is the past and Luna is the future, I suppose I'm the present."

"You suppose?"

"I don't have visions. Or maybe I choose not to. I'm just here. All the time. I think that's why I'm the only one who can focus for more than ten seconds and get anything done around here." He rolls his eyes and smirks, though his forehead still shines.

He casts another weary glance to the girls' bedroom. I can't hear Gabby anymore. I have a feeling she's listening behind the door.

I sigh. This is impossible. I've spent my life studying science and the universe and this flies in the face of everything I know. We as humans know so little. So much of the universe is still unexplained, but this…this is impossible.

"You don't believe me, do you?"

I meet his gaze, still sitting up straight with my hands on my knees. His hand twitches toward mine, like he wants to hold it, but he thinks better of it and folds his arms in his lap. He's fidgeting again.

"I shouldn't believe you," I say, more harshly than I mean to. His forehead wrinkles and he chews the inside of his lip. "I can't," I continue. "Visions don't exist. People can't See the past, or the future, or the present. Psychics are hoaxes. I don't know what's going on with you guys, but it can't be this. It's just not possible."

But then I remember: during my presentation to NASA, I somehow saw my mom signing divorce papers, like I was actually in the room with her. That certainly sounds like a vision.

No. That was different. Just a mental glitch caused by stress and possibly a head injury from the accident. Visions don't exist.

"You wanted the truth," he says.

"I still want the truth," I snap. "I don't believe in stuff like this."

He smirks and nods to himself. "That's right. You're a scientist." He says it like a dirty word. I feel a pang of irritation. "You've seen evidence, though. How else would I have known to save you? How would Luna have grabbed that glass?"

"Lucky coincidences."

"You weren't willing to accept that explanation two weeks ago. I tried, remember?"

He did try. He told me he was stepping out to lock up when he saw the car swerving down the street.

"Yeah, and I might have believed you if you were a better liar."

The line between his eyebrows deepens. I may be seconds away from losing my job and what I hoped might be new friendships, but I can't seem to shut up. Fear and anger run wild in my chest.

"You want more proof then?" he says, standing up. "You want to see it for yourself?"

"That would be great, actually," I snip, but my voice cracks. What am I agreeing to?

He glares for a moment before crossing the living room to the closed bedroom door. He knocks softly, then opens the door and pokes his head in, mutters something I can't hear. He turns back to me. Gabby tiptoes out behind him before shutting the door quietly. Her dark eyes flick to me for a split second and I know: she's heard everything.

Thiago returns to the couch, then leans forward on his elbows. "Gabby," he says. "Show Joan what you can do."

She eyes him suspiciously, as if waiting for him to change his mind. Then her shoulders square as she approaches me. Her eyes settle on my hands resting atop my knees.

"Can I see that bracelet?" she asks, pointing to my charm bracelet. I hesitate, then carefully unlatch it and hand it to her. My wrist feels naked without it.

Gabby sits on the floor before me, holding the bracelet in her open palm. She closes her fingers around it. Her eyes slide out of focus, then start twitching from side to side as if she were watching a movie or reading rapidly.

"You and your grandfather used to talk about space and the stars," she says. "He would take you up into the mountains with his telescope. He showed you the craters on the moon, the rising of Mars and Venus. Saturn's rings. You wanted to see farther than the planets in our solar system. He gave you this bracelet for your birthday the year before he died, and you always wear it." Her eyes stop twitching and refocus on me. I'm frozen in my seat, lips parted in surprise. "You told him Saturn's rings looked like hula hoops, and he laughed. He wore a lot of plaid."

My throat clenches. She holds out the bracelet, and I reach out to take it, looking at it in my hand, coiled up like a tiny silver snake.

I don't know what to say. No one says anything while I carefully fasten the bracelet around my wrist.

"I know it's hard to believe," Gabby ventures. "But I think you're supposed to know. About us."

I swallow hard. I don't believe in "supposed to." I don't believe in fate, magic, psychic powers, metaphysical woohooery, or anything else that can't be measured or proven.

But how else would Gabby have known about my grandpa? Or me telling him Saturn's rings looked like hula hoops? I've never told anyone that before. I haven't thought about it in years.

I toy with the old chain. This can't be true, because if it is, what else is true? Are werewolves real? Is magic real? Were the monsters I imagined hiding in my childhood closet real after all?

I shouldn't believe it, but…I do. And that scares me.

"I need to go," I croak, standing.

Gabby and Thiago exchange glances, and Thiago stands. "I'll walk you out."

Silently, he follows me across the apartment, down the creaky staircase, around the alley, and out to the quiet street, where fireflies buzz around the streetlights.

There has to be an explanation. Maybe the Cardozas are spies or weirdo stalkers who have gone through my stuff or found out about my life in some other way. But there's not much to go through. I've never kept a journal. I don't talk about Grandpa much. That memory exists only in my mind. And now Gabby's, I suppose.

"I'm sorry," Thiago says suddenly.

"For what?"

"You probably think we're insane."

I examine my pink-painted toes in my flip-flops. He's not wrong.

But as much as I don't want to, as much as it defies everything I believe about how the world and the universe works, I know he's telling the truth. Not just because I've seen what these siblings can do, but because I think some part of me knew already.

That was the part that kept looking for the truth even when he gave me perfectly reasonable explanations. On top of that, something about this story feels familiar, like a story I heard when I was small and forgot about until now. Of course, I might just be seeking emotional confirmation of something I want to be true, but for the first time in a long time, I feel like I'm exactly where I need to be. This thought rings like a bell in my heart, vibrating through my entire body, drowning out all rational thought until it's nothing but a buzz in the background.

"What does it mean?" I ask.

"What does what mean?" Thiago asks softly, his eyes searching my face. I wonder what he sees there.

My throat tightens. "The visions. Your powers. Why do you have them?"

He shrugs. "I wish I knew. Our parents had the gifts. My mother Saw the future, my father Saw the past. Gabby and Luna received those powers when our parents died. We don't know why."

"Your powers are inherited?"

Thiago nods and swallows. "Passed through death."

A chill trickles down my spine. Thiago looks away, up at the full moon casting silvery light over the tops of the buildings in the surrounding city. The quiet of the street is eerie. Goose bumps erupt on my arms.

Suddenly, I'm very aware of the weight and cool metal of my bracelet on my skin, and the memories that come with it.

"Well," he chokes. "I'd offer to drive you home, but…" he bobs his head from side to side. I understand. I saw how much wine he put away. "But I'll wait with you. If you want me to."

I smile. "I'd like that." He must have been scared to offer, because he suddenly looks relieved.

I start walking toward the bus stop and he follows, walking slower than normal. I slow my pace to match his, hoping I have some time until the next bus.

"I'm really glad you came," he says. "I think Luna had a nice evening."

I smile, a little drop of warmth slipping into my stomach. "So did I. Considering."

It's true. Sitting around the table with them, eating, drinking. It felt natural. Normal. I haven't had that in years, being so busy with school while my high school friends partied, while my college roommates hid in their own rooms with their own homework and their own problems. I never realized how lonely I was.

We reach the bus stop and I sit on the bench, leaving room for Thiago to sit next to me. He sits beside me, heat radiating off his body, drawing me in like a magnet. I want to curl into that warmth, to sidle up next to him and just be still for a moment while I process everything that happened tonight. But I don't. I keep an inch of space between us on the bench while I breathe deeply, thoughts zooming around my head too quickly for me to catch and examine any of them.

Within a minute, the bus rounds the corner down the street and ambles toward us.

"I understand if you don't believe me," Thiago says. "I wouldn't believe me either."

I hesitate, my eyes on the bus as it groans up the street. "It just doesn't make any sense," I tell him, shrugging. "I like you guys, but…I just don't know what to think."

He nods, understanding, his eyes sad and resigned. As the bus gets closer, I stand. Thiago follows, rising next to me with his hands in his pockets.

"Well, I guess I'll see you tomorrow afternoon." he says, shoulders slumped. "Good-night." His face is shadowed, his eyes sad. I fiddle with my bracelet.

"Good-night," I echo. He looks exhausted, clammy and pale, his hair sticking to the back of his neck.

The bus screeches to a stop in front of us, and the doors slide open. No one gets off. We've already said good-bye, so I give Thiago a quick smile and climb on, quickly swinging into the nearest seat. Thiago waves as the doors close. I wave back.

The bus heaves itself away from the stop. Thiago watches the bus pull away, not turning to walk back home until right before the bus turns around the next block. Before he disappears, he rubs his hand on his face and over his hair.

It took a lot for him to tell me this. He trusts me, and he did save my life. I can't bring myself to be upset with him, or Gabby, or to think badly of them. I'm tired too, though. All I want is to get home, take one of the Ambien I keep around for finals week, and sleep on this.

As I travel over the river, looking back on the lights of Back Bay, I think over the evening. I think of what he told me. I think of the eerie feeling of Gabby looking back into my life, at details she couldn't have known, that I hadn't told anyone, written anywhere, or even thought of in years. And I can't shake the odd feeling of rightness.

As I cross over the bridge to Cambridge, something reforms inside me. I feel my accepted truths shuffle around in my brain like books on a shelf to make room for something new.

13

Thiago

I wake up before dawn like I always do. A dull ache throbs behind my eyes, and my mouth tastes sour from drinking way too much red wine last night. While last night got a little fuzzy after the first bottle, I remember what I did. I remember what I told Joan. Yet, that fear, that expected panic never sets in. I feel…strangely light.

I haul myself out of bed, my limbs sluggish and weightless at the same time. I pause to stretch out my stiff shoulders, twist to pop a kink out of my back. I pull on jeans and a clean tee shirt and twist my tangled hair back into a bun. Then I shuffle down the hall, brush my teeth, step into my shoes and stumble down to the cafe, leaning on the handrail to keep my footing on the narrow stairs.

Why don't I feel afraid?

I've kept our secret my entire life to protect my sisters from the power that got our parents killed—the power that now lives in them. I dreaded the consequences of letting that precious secret slip to anyone. I thought I'd be terrified and that our lives would come crashing down immediately, but I don't feel that way.

Maybe I would if it were anyone else.

I told Joan everything. I'd tell her again if given the chance. Maybe

I always wanted her to know.

Did I do the right thing? It threw her for a loop. I don't think she believes me—and I don't blame her—but she didn't call me crazy. But what if she doesn't come back today? What if I scared her off for good?

The smell of last night's espresso lingers in the dark cafe. I switch on the lights, start the drip coffeemaker, tie on my apron, and start my morning routine.

It's a good thing I could mix muffin batter in my sleep because I pay almost no attention as I dump ingredients into a bowl and fill the muffin tins before lining them up in the oven. I replay last night over and over in my mind. Joan's face as the gears turned in her mind, trying to make sense of what she just learned. Her wide eyes when Gabby Saw her past. The curiosity she couldn't quite hide in her voice when I walked her to the bus stop.

Or was it fear?

I peel plastic wrap off rows of the perfectly risen croissants I started last night. Those go in the second oven.

Blue-tinged morning light streams into the cafe through the front windows, growing warmer and brighter each minute as the sun rises. Tanya and Karl should be here in half an hour. I love opening in the summer because I get a few quiet minutes of this morning light before my staff shows up and we let the customers in.

The first oven beeps. I grab a hot pad, pull the muffins out, and line the trays in neat rows on the counter.

A knock on the door almost sends me jumping out of my skin. I whip my head around to see Joan standing outside, backlit by the morning sun.

She smiles. Something inside me warms at the sight of her, but my stomach jolts with nerves. Why is she here so early on a Sunday when she's not scheduled and she isn't supposed to go antiquing with

Gabby for at least another hour or two? What does she have to say? She watches me through the window, her expression unreadable. I'm pretty sure my nausea has nothing to do with all the wine I drank last night.

I wipe my floured hands on my apron and cross the seating area to let her in. The fresh morning smell rushes in when she steps inside; the scent of the river, blooming flowers, and just a hint of smoke. Somewhere underneath it, I catch the subtle scent of Joan's rose perfume.

The door closes behind her. She pauses. We stand still for a moment or two, a few feet apart, while each of us searches for words.

Finally, she meets my eyes and speaks.

"I just wanted you to know…" she says, shifting her weight. "That I'm not going anywhere. It doesn't make any damn sense and I can't believe I'm saying this, but I believe you."

For a second, my knees wobble. Tension runs out of my muscles like water. She knows all about us, and she's still here. I don't have to keep our secret alone anymore. Someone else can carry it with me. I've never wanted to embrace someone so badly in my life.

I stick my hands in my pockets and shift my weight, mirroring her. What could I say that could possibly express the unfamiliar lightness in my heart?

"Thank you," I say, just above a whisper. A smile flickers behind her caramel-colored eyes but doesn't quite show on her face. I know she understands what I mean, why I'm grateful. I clear my throat.

"Would you like to have breakfast with me?" I ask.

Her smile finally rises to the surface. Morning sunlight dances across her face. "Okay," she says, grinning.

We don't have much time before opening, so I whip up a pair of lattes—two percent milk for me, whole for Joan, the way I know she likes it—and put two hot muffins on a plate. Joan sits at a table, gazing out the window at the rising sun. Once or twice, I almost forget what I'm doing and watch the way the sun lights up her short, golden hair like a dandelion in a field.

I hold a mug on a saucer in each hand and balance the muffin plate on my forearm as I carry them to our table and slide into the chair across from her. Still looking out the window, she picks up her mug and raises it to her lips.

"Penny for your thoughts?" I say as I peel the wrapper off my muffin. One of Mamá's favorite English expressions, though I can hear Gabby's voice in my head: *Nobody says that anymore. I would know.*

It's not like Joan to be so quiet. She doesn't answer right away but takes another deep sip of her coffee.

"It'll cost you a lot more than that. My thoughts are a dollar each," she smiles, but it fades quickly. "And I have a lot of them right now."

I fiddle with the handle of my mug, approaching the subject carefully. "While I appreciate your belief, I know it's a lot. I didn't mean to freak you out last night."

"You didn't. It's just…it's like learning that unicorns are real or that magic exists…because this is basically magic."

Magic. I never thought of it that way. A curse, perhaps. A disease. But not magic. Nothing as fantastical as that.

"It's like my whole worldview blew up. I'm just watching the dust settle."

"That makes sense."

After all, I grew up with the knowledge that some people can See the past and future. I can't imagine how it must feel to have to fit that into a completely different belief system.

I finally take a sip of my latte and make a face. It's not bad, but Gabby's are better. I won't tell Gabby that though. It will go straight to her head. I anxiously watch Joan drink deeply from the mug, showing no sign she notices.

"What was it like?" Joan asks, leaning forward on her elbows and cradling her mug in one hand. "When your parents had powers like that? And when you and your sisters grew up with those powers?"

I shove a huge bite of muffin in my mouth, just to give myself a moment to think. I chew thoughtfully, scrambling for words.

"No one's ever asked me that before," I admit. "I don't know, I never knew anything else. Someone around me could always See the past or the future. Papá loved history, of course, because he didn't just read about it in books. He told lots of stories. He'd meditate to See the past clearly. He didn't have to touch objects to See it, like Gabby, but it took him a long time to focus on a single point. Sometimes he found what he wanted and sometimes he got lost."

I take another sip. Joan watches me intently, her eyes sparkling with curiosity. I only ever see her look like that when she rambles on about some astrophysics concept I don't understand. I never thought she'd look at me that way, but I like how it feels.

"Mamá…" I go on. "Her visions were unpredictable. And powerful. They struck at unexpected times. She wouldn't drive a car in case a vision hit while she was behind the wheel. She sang songs that wouldn't be on the radio for years. Sometimes she canceled plans for the day because she Saw us getting caught in the rain. And sometimes she Saw events that took place many years in the future. She didn't tell us much about those, but I think they troubled her. It's hard to say how much she knew, but…" I clear my throat again. "She knew she was going to die." My hand tightens around my mug. "Maybe not when or how, but she knew she and Papá wouldn't see us grow up."

Joan watches me quietly, not with a look of pity, but of compassion. Her lips part like she wants to say something, but she closes them again.

I lean on my elbows with my hands clasped together and keep going.

"Gabby was a baby when the ability transferred to her, so she doesn't remember *not* Seeing the past." I shift in my seat. I feel Joan's eyes on me, and I have no idea what she's thinking. "It was a few months before her powers started to manifest, but I noticed that sometimes she touched things and then started laughing or crying, or she just stared off into space. It took me a long time to figure out how her powers worked. Because she was so young, she couldn't tell me yet.

"Luna, though, she changed immediately. I think she was hit with a powerful, horrible vision the moment the power passed to her. She didn't speak much before she received the power, but she never said a word after that day. She wouldn't look me in the eye. For a while, I thought she was just traumatized, but she started reacting to things before they happened. I realized she wasn't just in her own invisible world, she was Seeing the future constantly. We were in foster care at the time, so I had to keep them under control so they wouldn't give anything away. Constantly telling Gabby that normal people didn't have visions and to stay quiet about hers. Making excuses for why Luna always knew things before they happened." I pause to swallow. Those were rough years. "I didn't want my parents' killer to find us. I also didn't want to get kicked out of our foster homes and separated. That was my youth. Covering for my sisters before Gabby learned to control herself and could help me with Luna. We got shuffled around a lot. Luna made people uncomfortable. Gabby too, though she tried not to. Luna was placed in a special ed program at school, but the teachers weren't sure what to do with her because she was practically catatonic."

For the first time, I glance up at Joan. She sits still and straight in her chair, hands cupped around her coffee. The corners of her lips tilt upward and her eyes are soft. Her gentle gaze warms me. I keep going.

"We were all bullied at some point. Luna especially, though I don't think she noticed much. Gabby and I already got heat for being weird foster kids, but also for being Luna's sister. For standing up for her."

I tighten my grip on my mug and grind my teeth together. The memory rekindles old rage I haven't thought about in years.

"That's awful. Why would anyone bully Luna?"

"Because she's different, and kids are assholes," I grumble. "They'd push her around, steal her things, even write awful things on her arms or face in Sharpie because she wouldn't do anything about it. Not even blink. Most of the time, they found that hilarious. But sometimes," I pause, chewing my lip. "Just a couple times, she did stop them. She knew they were coming. She'd catch something they threw at her, or grab their hand just before they touched her. I think they were afraid of her..." I swallow. "But not afraid enough to leave her the hell alone. Those were the times I worried we'd be discovered. Gabby and I tried to protect her. We got in a lot of fights back then."

Joan presses her lips together and shakes her head. "I'm sorry," she says. "I...I can't believe anyone would do that to her."

I wave my hand dismissively. "It happened, and it's over. Gabby and I remember, but I don't think it made any difference to Luna."

I sip my drink, letting the warm liquid soothe me from the inside out, extinguishing the old anger.

"It got better after junior high. I started working in restaurants, and I pushed Gabby to study and get good grades so she could go to college and take care of herself. Gabby even went to a year of nursing school before she dropped out. But it works. She helps me run the cafe, and we both take care of Luna."

Joan's head tilts, her eyes soft and mouth quirked into an expression of grim compassion. The other opening employees should be here any minute, but I'm not ready yet. I just want to stay here a little longer. I never talk to anyone about my childhood. Not even Gabby.

Joan watches me with soft eyes and a gentle smile. The sun grows brighter, bathing the cafe in warm light. Her pale skin glows and a dainty pearl hangs from a thin chain that sparkles around her neck. Suddenly, I want to run a finger over her smooth shoulders and collarbones, her throat, just to see if her creamy skin is as soft as it looks.

"You're a good brother," she says. "Gabby and Luna are lucky to have you. You three are lucky to have each other."

I sigh. "I know."

Her hand moves across the table. She hesitates before sliding it over mine. Her thumb runs over my knuckles, sending ripples of warmth up my arm.

She opens her mouth to speak when the back door opens. Gabby steps into the kitchen, humming to herself, then freezes mid-step when she sees Joan and me.

Without thinking, I pull my hand away, but it's too late. Gabby will ask me about it later and I'll never hear the end of it. Never.

Gabby looks from me to Joan and smiles.

14

Gabby

After what we told Joan last night, I didn't think she'd show up the next morning. But when I go down to the cafe to get coffee, there she is, sitting across from Thiago at one of the tables. I notice their hands on the tabletop, inches apart.

Not only is she here, she showed up early. To have an intimate talk with Thiago, by the looks of it.

For a split second before they turn to look at me, I notice their expressions. They look at each other warmly, like they're sharing a secret. I can't stop myself from smiling.

"Oh," I say when I walk in, freezing in place. "Am I interrupting something?" Thiago chews his lip, looking slightly annoyed. Joan shakes her head *no* and smiles.

"Are we still on for antiquing this morning?" she asks.

I hesitate. I was so convinced that we'd scared her off that I completely forgot about our plans this morning. "Oh…" I say stupidly. "Yeah! Let me get some coffee and we can head out."

I make myself an iced mocha to go, all the while watching Joan and Thiago out of the corner of my eye. They don't speak, but they exchange little smiles as they finish their drinks. I try to hide my

125

smirk. Something is definitely happening over there. I knew it.

Joan gives Thiago a conspiratorial grin before she gets up to follow me outside. I swear his cheeks flush. I've never seen such a genuine smile on my brother's face. It looks good on him.

Joan and I stand on the sunny street, its residents just stirring on a Sunday morning. A young couple strides down the sidewalk, hand in hand. A tiny, elderly woman walks her Shih Tzu, her lips caked in messy pink lipstick that clashes spectacularly with her bright red sunglasses.

"The Music Box is just six blocks down," I tell Joan. "So we can walk."

I start walking and Joan falls into step beside me. I get the feeling she's walking a lot slower than normal, taking only one step for every two of mine.

"So," Joan says. "I guess I understand why you like antiques now."

I smile. "It's not just antiques," I answer. "It can be anything. Garbage on the street. Someone's mug after I clear tables. Anything. Antiques are just more consistent."

I steal a glance at Joan. Her lip press together, hands shoved in her pockets. I get the feeling this is hard for her, that she's struggling to comprehend this new knowledge without freaking out. It's normal for me, but I can see how learning that some people have visions of other times might be strange for someone who only lives in one time and doesn't See flits of the past as she brushes past everyday objects.

"What's it like?" she asks. "Seeing the past?" I can't see her eyes behind her sunglasses. I can't tell if she's genuinely curious or just trying to make conversation.

"It's like…" I've haven't actually spoken much about it. Luna wouldn't hear me anyway and Thiago doesn't want to hear. "It's like riding a train," I say finally. "You're in your own world inside the train, where things move with you and feel normal, but you occasionally glance out the window and catch a snip of something else like a house or a landscape or a person, though you can't focus on anything because it's gone as soon as it appears. But sometimes, the train stops and you can observe for longer."

Joan chews the corner of her lip, mulling something over. "Do you ever get off the train?"

I scrunch my eyebrows together. I've never thought about that. "No," I say finally. "I just stay in and look out the window. I guess getting off the train would be like…time travel."

"Right," she says, surprising me. Was this where she wanted the conversation to go all along?

I laugh, but stop quickly in case I've hurt her feelings. "We can't time travel," I say, corking this idea immediately. "We can only See glimpses. I suppose Luna Sees a bit more, but we stay rooted in the present. Our bodies can't leave. Just our minds." Sometimes I wonder if Luna's experience is like mine, if she Sees the future the way I See the past. I look over at Joan. Even though I can't see her eyes, I swear I see gears moving in her head.

"Do you think time travel is possible?" I ask.

She shrugs. "There are theories that confirm it," she says. "But it requires speeds way beyond human technology, and even then it would be very limited. At best, we could maybe go a few seconds into the future. I just thought…"

"Maybe there is a way?" I offer.

"I guess," she hesitates. "I know it sounds impossible, but only last night I thought what you and Luna can do was impossible too. I'm sure there's a scientific explanation for it. Something beyond our current understanding, but still within the realm of possibility. So if that's possible, I just wondered…what else is possible?"

I can understand that, how one hole in your beliefs, one small glimpse of possibility can open doors you'd never considered.

We reach the antique shop. Its hanging wooden sign creaks on rusty chains outside the door. The bell on the door tinkles when we enter. A plump, middle-aged woman with red hair looks up at me from behind the cash register and smiles. I smile back. We know each other by face, though not by name.

Joan immediately discovers a box of old sheet music and stops to examine each page.

I continue toward the back, brushing my fingers over the aged surfaces of the antiques as I glide through the shop. Floorboards creak under my feet with each step.

Images flash in my peripheral vision as I touch each object. Unclear, undefined. A sunny day and a blossoming tree as the skirt of a yellowing lace wedding dress slides through my fingers. I smell grass and motor oil when I touch the sleeve of a soft leather jacket. A burst of orange sunset and a creaking sound from a polished wood rocking chair that's losing its sheen. A baby's giggle from a worn, one-eyed teddy bear. Muffled sounds echo in my mind, buried under layers of centuries like surface sounds heard from under the ocean. I inhale deeply, pulling the past into my lungs, instantly feeling calmer.

Thiago thinks I'm ridiculous for visiting antique shops and thrift stores, but I can't help it. Every time I return to the cafe with a new treasure, he rolls his eyes and returns to whatever he's cooking. He says I'm addicted to my visions. Am I? Maybe. I line the walls of the cafe with the objects I love the most, that prompt the most beautiful sounds, the loveliest days. I love teacups especially because they mean glimpses into happy moments like beautiful spring afternoons shared with friends. If Thiago had his way, the cafe would be stocked with simple white mugs purchased in bulk, sterile and devoid of memory. Empty shells. But I want to serve our tea in beautiful vessels with a story to tell, even if I'm the only one who can hear them.

Clocks cover the wall and shelves in the back of the shop. My second favorite. Cuckoo clocks, vinyl wall clocks from the fifties, a grandfather clock standing stoic in the corner. A box of watches and old alarm clocks. Some of them work, emitting ticks of various pitches and volumes like strange instruments. Some sit silently, their hands stationary on their tarnished faces, frozen in time. I pick through the watches and smaller clocks on the shelves, pausing to hold each one in my hand like most people would select fruit at a farmer's market, letting its story flit through my mind's eye. Not every object shows me something, of course. Most of them are quiet enough to ignore if I want to.

My eyes fall on a fat pocket watch, lid shut tight, as big as an apricot. I pick it up. It's heavy for its size.

I squint to look closer at a symbol etched into the lid; a small circle inside a larger one with a line cutting through the center of both. I've never seen it before, and can't even begin to guess what it might mean. I run my thumb over the etching and then dig my nail into the groove and carefully pry the lid open. The hands are stationary inside. I take a breath and suddenly, the minute hand twitches.

The watch ticks. The train stops.

All air is sucked out of my lungs, then the vision opens.

A barren field; tall, yellow grass rippling in the wind under a blue shell sky. The sound of cloth flapping in the breeze. No, it's the edge of a dark coat. The image shifts to a young woman with long, blond hair, her face painted with fury. The picture shifts again. I hear a woman humming, a song I've never heard before. The woman crouches on a stone floor in a puddle, her hair a sopping tangle around her face. Faster and faster the images fly at me. Shreds of sounds flit through my mind before I can identify them. Laughter, piano music, ticks of a large clock. I See a massive clock tower at night, framed by moonlit clouds. A man's tortured scream. A blinding white light and unbearable heat.

A rotting, gnarled hand protrudes from a fold of tattered red cloth, reaching for me. I try to scream, but I don't exist yet. Images change like a film on fast-forward, then like a flipbook, nights and days, seasons and years, different times and places.

Then a brief flash of my mother's terrified face.

Terror wrenches my gut. I only caught a glimpse, but I know it was her. There's no mistaking those wide, dark eyes and small nose that's just like mine.

Mamá! My heart seizes in my chest. She's terrified and I can't help her. I feel my eyes twitch, my hands shake. I want to reach for her, but I can't reach across time.

I hear a faraway scream and the images stop.

I snap the lid shut.

Joan stands next to me, her hand about to touch my shoulder. I flinch, holding the watch to my chest.

How long had I been standing there? "I'm sorry," I say, knowing how I must look to her. I glance at the woman behind the counter. She's looking this way too. It's certainly not the first time I've had a vision in this store, but never that vivid.

My mother came in contact with this watch and its owner, and she was terrified. Who owned this watch? What did they have to do with my family? I try to remember what else I Saw, to make some sense of it, but I see no connection.

This watch has a long, twisted history. I need to See more.

The woman at the counter looks concerned, but says nothing as she turns back to whatever she was doing. Joan stares at the watch in my hand, then looks at me.

"Are you okay?" she asks, quietly so the woman doesn't hear. I nod, gazing down at the watch. "Was it bad?"

I nod. "Sometimes it's bad." We both look at the watch in my hand. It's silent, still, innocent.

"Are you going to get it?"

I turn it over to check the price.

Damn. I don't have anywhere nearly enough. "No."

Joan nods, disappointed. "I'll be over here," she says, drifting back to the box of sheet music near the front of the store.

I place the watch back on the counter, but don't let go of it. I can't. I'm sure it will show me more, but I'm afraid to open it again while I'm in the store.

But I Saw my mother; somewhere along the way, she and the owner of this watch crossed paths. I heard her scream. I want to know why. I *need* to know.

I need this watch.

My mind spins, touching on every possibility, anything I could sell or trade, anything I could tell Thiago, how much money we keep in the register and how furious Thiago would be if I raided it.

I open my hand and look at the watch, feeling its weight and taking in its dull bronze finish. My heart pounds. The veins in my hand pulse until it almost feels like the watch is ticking again.

I pick up the watch and mosey around the back of the store, pretending to look at the vintage toys and books on the shelves. When I pass behind an old vanity where Joan and the lady at the counter can't see, I slip the watch into my purse. My heart thunders so loud I'm afraid they'll hear it.

A few minutes later, Joan approaches the counter to buy a slim volume of sheet music. Slowly, casually, I work my way to the front of the store without so much as a flush in my cheeks. The bell on the door tinkles innocently as we leave.

My purse is already full of odds and ends, but it feels so much heavier on my shoulder while we walk home.

Joan flips through the book she bought. I glance at the cover. Beethoven's grumpy face leers back at me. "Do you play?" I ask.

She nods, smiling absentmindedly as she turns the pages. "Since I was four. Beethoven's my favorite."

I nod. "He's pretty good," I say lamely.

I watch the sidewalk in front of my feet, my cheeks finally turning hot and my eyes stinging. I've never stolen before. Dread roils in my stomach. I won't be going to that store again, that's for sure. I doubt I'll get caught, but the wrongness, the dirtiness I feel is horrible. Maybe when the watch has revealed all it has, I'll sneak it back to the store. Maybe I'll find a way to make up for it, slip the store owner the money somehow when she's not paying attention. But for now, I need it.

"Are you okay?" Joan asks. My heart leaps, then I realize she probably thinks I'm upset about what I Saw. I suck the tears back into my head and nod.

"Do you need to talk about it?"

I smile bravely and shake my head. "It happens sometimes," I say, trying to sound casual. "You just have to shake it off."

"Do you See bad things often?" Joan asks, then she blushes. "Sorry, that was probably pushy. It's just, human history is kind of a mess. I'd imagine you'd See at least as much bad as good."

I watch my shoes on the sidewalk. She's right. I've Seen unspeakable things I've never told Thiago about or written in my journal. Things I've carried with me for years, sometimes releasing the horror into my collages or my nightmares. But I let them go.

Nothing has made me feel the way this watch does. It has something to show me. *Me.* I'm not just a casual observer in its story. My mind spins through the images again. I'm afraid to open the watch, but I know it'll reveal secrets I've spent the last twenty years unraveling. I might have found the final piece of the puzzle.

15

Arial

Centuries alone can change a man. Especially a man who's done what I've done.

I appreciate New York City and its eccentricities, though I liked it better when it was newer. Cars are faster, but I think it took less time to get around in horse-drawn carriages. Now, shiny automobiles fill the streets, honking and spewing smoke into the air, banishing pedestrians to even more crowded sidewalks. I don't mind the crowds, however. They make it easy to disappear in, like a tree blending into a forest. Everyone is in a hurry and not paying a speck of attention to one another. At least, until they believe you're in their way.

As I flow down the sidewalk with the usual wave of foot traffic, a middle-aged (what a strange term) woman slams into me from the side and treads on my foot. I don't bother to look at her.

"You could walk faster, you know," she quips. Her bony elbow stabs my arm as she pushes around me, into my line of vision and for a moment, I stop breathing.

A cascade of wheat-colored hair falls around her pale face in honeyed waves. She slithers through the crowd and disappears down the stairs into the subway station. Voices around me protest as I freeze in place.

Can it be her? After all these years?

I follow her.

She's fast. I scan for her as I descend the stairs to the subway and notice her rounding a corner, a mobile phone pressed to her face. A briefcase dangles from her other hand. Despite her dark gray pantsuit, she wears athletic sneakers, as is the custom for professional New York women who walk to work with their high-heeled shoes in their bags.

I struggle to catch up to the woman, eliciting irritated grunts and exasperated hisses from commuters as I bump into them. The blond woman passes through the turnstile and I fumble for my metro card. Finally, I find the card, swipe it, and follow, far behind.

Should I call to her? I need to see her face. I need to look into her eyes.

Katherine. It's been so long since I last saw her. She'd have a completely different face now, but I think I'd know if I saw her. But would she want to see me? Would she remember? Do I *want* her to remember? I've pondered these questions for centuries, and I still don't know the answers.

I weave around passersby to get closer to the blond woman. Thankfully, she stops to wait for a train. I work my way through the crowd, edging forward until I can see her face through the curtain of familiar, flowing hair.

Finally, she catches me watching her. The woman's eyes widen with fear. She knows I followed her. I don't blame her for being afraid. Her eyes dart around nervously until the train stops. The doors squeal open and she rushes inside, not bothering to wait for passengers to exit first.

My heart sinks into my stomach. It's a very different face from the one I remember. Flat, dark eyes instead of sharp blue ones. An angular face instead of rounded. Most importantly, a completely different soul dances behind that unfamiliar face.

It's not her. Even if I look past the face to the demeanor beneath it, it can't be her. Katherine wouldn't be afraid to find a strange man following her. She'd be furious. This woman lacks Katherine's sharpness, steadiness, shrewdness—traits I can't imagine her losing, for then she'd cease to be Katherine.

A river of people flows off the train, then another river flows in. I catch a glimpse of the blond woman through the window, still watching me with fearful eyes. The train starts to move, slowly screeching away into the tunnel, taking another painful disappointment with it.

How many women have I followed and frightened, hoping they were her? Too many. Hundreds, probably.

I exit the station. As I climb the stairs, I look down at my shoes and notice the rubber soles peeling off the toes. The dull black leather is beginning to crack. I've had these shoes re-heeled many times. It's time for a new pair, one of many I've worn through over the centuries. I could use something more in line with the current fashion anyway.

People pass me as I make my way down the sidewalk, but I don't look at any of them, especially the women. I can't take another one. I wish I had a photograph of Katherine, that cameras existed before she slipped away. I don't even have a drawing. Sometimes I wonder if I've forgotten what she looked like. Perhaps my memory of her is inaccurate, clouded and reshaped by time and perhaps a touch of insanity. I haven't ruled it out, but I remember what she felt like, being with her. I remember who she was, even if her face has faded.

I find a men's shoe shop on 7th Avenue and go inside to browse the aisles and select a pair of brown leather loafers, surprisingly similar to the worn-out black pair on my feet. Perhaps fashion hasn't progressed as quickly as I thought. I purchase them with one of my fraudulent credit cards without speaking to the young man at the counter. He doesn't speak to me either. This is the other reason why I enjoy New York. Social niceties like small talk are rarely observed.

Before stepping outside, I sit on a bench near the front of the shop to switch my old pair for the new. I feel the young man's eyes on me, most likely puzzled that a man who'd bother to buy such high-quality shoes would allow his old pair to fall into such a state. When I've finished putting them on, I stand and step back outside into the noise, then deposit the old shoes in a rubbish bin next to a stand selling hats and tee shirts to tourists.

This pair should last for several years, if I continue to live that long and have them repaired a few times. I sincerely hope this will be my last pair. I learned long ago to purchase quality clothing. That's one thing I've realized in my long, long life: nothing lasts, but some things last longer than others. Even when you live forever, aching feet are difficult to endure.

I flow with the crowd down the sidewalk like a leaf in a stream with nowhere to go.

Suddenly, I feel like my heart has exploded.

Sharp pain rips through my chest. My vision goes black. My ears fill with a sound I haven't heard in decades.

The thunderous, bone-rattling tick of the Clock Tower.

Each tick digs deeper into my skull, boring through my brain like termites. *Tock. Tock. TOCK.*

After a few minutes, hours, years—they're all the same to me now— light streaks across my vision, and the ticks quiet to the gentle clicking of the watch.

My old pocket watch.

I open my eyes to see the outline of the sky framed by New York skyscrapers, but also another changing scene showing through it, like a double-exposed photograph.

A quaint city street, old-fashioned, perhaps the historic district of a larger city. For a moment, I see a young woman's face, dark eyes with dark hair cropped to her chin. The watch sits in her outstretched hand, a forgotten iced coffee drink in her other hand. She seems to be standing in a secondhand shop, surrounded by knickknacks and old furniture. Though she appears to be looking at the watch, her eyes aren't focused. Her pupils twitch as if she were watching a film.

I exhale, my eyes wide. I haven't had a vision in so many years. I nearly forgot the sensation of almost leaving your body as images force their way into your mind. Until now, I never realized how much I missed it.

The scene fades, giving way to the jagged skyline and concerned faces of a crowd of New Yorkers looking down at me.

"Give him some room, will ya?" A man's voice barks. "Are you okay, buddy?"

I'm lying on my back on the sidewalk. A pair of hands holds my head. A man with startlingly light eyes and a gray mustache looks down at me.

Immediately, I push myself back to standing. I sway slightly, but regain my footing before ambling down the sidewalk.

"Hey fella, you need a doctor!" the man calls after me. I don't answer or turn around. I need to get to a train station. Now.

The ticking of my heart. The ticking of the watch. The ticking of the Clock Tower. They're one and the same.

It's been so long since I felt the tick of the watch, of the Clock Tower, any shred of power at all. I lost the watch long ago—or rather, it was stolen from me—and the last scraps of my power with it, but I still hear its tick sometimes, still feel it pulsing in my bones and organs. It's closer than it's been in decades, though it's hard to tell where, exactly. It's like following a soft, persistent sound to find out where it's coming from, only to realize it's moving around.

As much as I'd love to savor the feeling, I need to find that watch. I duck into a deserted alley and crouch behind a dumpster, close my eyes, and slow my breathing. I need to think for a moment. To feel.

I feel the beating of my heart, the ticking of the watch. I crane my head, turning it from side to side, straining to locate the watch.

Finally, I notice the ticking is stronger when my head turns to my left. Northeast. So I'll go northeast.

There was a time when I could travel hundreds of miles in seconds, but that was centuries ago. Now that power is bound to the watch, so I'll have to go by train, which might prove to be useful. As inconvenient and slow as train travel is, it will be much easier to pinpoint the watch's location. I pause to close my eyes and breathe in the city air, tune into the ticking of my heart. *Tick. Tick. Tick.*

I stand and leave the alley and do not stop until I reach Penn Station, where I purchase a ticket on the next train going north, which will get me as far as Bridgeport. I'll go from there.

A fire I haven't felt in decades rekindles in my chest. For the first time in too long, I feel hope. My step quickens as I approach the train, my new shoes slapping the pavement. My palms sweat.

I hope I will have to spill no blood in my search for the Clock Tower, but I will if I must. I've done it before. I can certainly do it again. The weight of the knives tucked into my coat presses on me. I think of the times I've used them. The feel of the blades sinking into flesh. The shock on the victims' faces when they realize they're about to die, right before the pain hits, if it hits at all.

I casually reach in my coat to run my finger along the hilt of a knife I've come to call *Amica*. My first knife, nearly as old as I am, and a far more faithful and true friend than any human companion, though I haven't used it in nearly twenty years.

It was a couple in a small apartment in Boston. They'd fled to the states from Spain with their children, carrying the watch with them. By the time I found them, it was too late. The watch was gone.

Boston is northeast of New York, I realize. Maybe the watch never left Boston after all. I graze the leather-wrapped knife handle with my thumb. *You may become useful again, old friend.*

I board the northbound train and settle into a seat near the window. Soon, I will have the watch, and I will stop the clock. I absentmindedly run my thumb along *Amica's* handle as the train lurches from the station and twines north, the ticking in my chest leading me like a magnet.

Tick. Tick. Tick.

16

Joan

At closing time a strip of night sky glows above the buildings across the street, faded gray from light pollution. Somewhere out there, billions of stars burn even though the city lights wash them out.

My feet hurt. It's been a while since I've been on my feet for hours at a time, but they'll toughen up over the next few weeks. I'm having too much fun at the Clockwork Cafe to care.

I watch Thiago turn down the lights and lock the door, flipping the sign on the front window to *closed*. I smile. He's methodical, doing everything the same way each time. Lock the door, test the lock, flip the sign, check the lock again.

Gabby finishes the dishes, says goodnight, and disappears up the stairs after shooting me a sly sideways glance. I look away. I know what she's doing. That crafty little sneak.

Thiago and I are alone in the cafe. The large space feels surprisingly small with just the two of us, like the room is shrinking, driving us closer together. Small, and suddenly a lot warmer. My stomach dances and tiny bubbles tingle in my arms. My face heats.

Thiago stacks muffin trays in the kitchen while I gather the leftover muffins and scones into a tray for breakfast before my morning shift, which starts in eight hours. I don't mind back to back evening and morning shifts, but I wonder if I should ask to crash on their couch tonight.

Is that really why you want to spend the night? says a voice in the back of my head. I refuse to explore that thought further.

I cover the tray of leftovers with plastic and place it on the back counter where Thiago's placing his stack of clean trays. Our elbows brush. He glances sideways at me.

"Have a cup of tea with me?" he asks.

My stomach tingles. I nod.

He smiles at me, then fills two white mugs with hot water and pulls two infusers from the drawer, filling one of them with ginger tea for himself. He looks over his shoulder at me, holding up the other.

"Rooibos," I tell him.

He nods and fills the infuser with red tea before dipping it into my mug. He carries both out to the seating area to a two-person table and I follow, scooting into the chair opposite him. He stirs the infuser around his cup absentmindedly, his long fingers lightly pinching the handle.

"How do you like the job so far?"

"It's great," I say automatically, and I mean it. "It's a nice change."

He nods again. "Not too boring? I could give you some equations to do between customers."

I roll my eyes, grinning. "It's a different kind of thinking." A crimson cloud of tea spreads through my mug. I let my eyes relax as I watch the color deepen and the steam rise in delicate coils that swirl when I exhale. "It's just nice to look at muffins and antiques and windows instead of black and white equations in a windowless lab. I love physics and studying. It's usually my happy place," I go on, "but sometimes you need a break, you know?"

"Everybody needs a change sometimes," he says wisely, running his finger over the handle of his mug.

"Says the guy who hates change," I tease.

He blows a raspberry. "I didn't say change is fun, I just said we need it sometimes." He shakes his head, but he smiles. "So what do you do when you aren't stuck in a windowless lab?"

"Oh my," I say, feigning flattery. "Thiago Cardoza, making conversation just for the hell of it?"

"Don't tell anyone."

I snort, then bite my lip, thinking. What do I do for fun these days?

"I love music," I finally tell him. "Classical mostly. I love Mozart and Beethoven. I listen to them while I study."

"That actually works?"

"It helps me concentrate. And relax."

He takes a tentative sip of his tea, winces slightly and sets the mug back down. I don't bother to try mine yet; I know it's too hot.

"I play piano too," I continue, "but all I have at my apartment is a little Cassio keyboard. I have a real piano, but I only get to play it in the summer when I go home."

"But you're not going home this year," he observes.

I swallow and shake my head. "No." Bitter thoughts of divorce drift through my mind, and I realize I didn't even think to ask Mom what will happen to my piano. I hope she doesn't sell it. Please, let her hang onto it until I can take it to a home of my own. Though I have no idea when that may be.

Fully aware of his studying gaze, I take the infuser out of my tea and wrap it in a napkin. We're silent for a few moments.

"What do you like to do?" I ask, desperate to change the subject and stop thinking about my future.

He shrugs. "I cook. I bake. I work so much, that's really all I do. But I love it, so it's good." He tries another sip of tea, this time not wincing. Following his lead, I try mine. Still too hot for me. "I wish I had more time to cook for fun," he continues. "Baking is a science. There's plenty of room for creativity, but not as much as just throwing things in a frying pan and seeing how it turns out. I put as much art into my baking as I can, but I'd love to play with other dishes."

"Like what?" I ask, leaning forward on my elbows. I can tell he's warming up for one of his rare monologues. The ones I love to listen to, savoring them like a hot drink.

"Well," he says, "I really like messing with vegetables. I wouldn't mind having a garden sometime either, growing stuff for the shop, trying out some weird new varieties…"

My eyebrows lift as I listen. I must look surprised, because he trails off. "What?"

"Nothing," I say. "I just never figured you for a veggie guy."

"Why not?"

"Maybe because I'm so used to seeing you work with dough…" My cheeks flush. I don't want to admit how much I like watching him knead dough. "Vegetables are so different."

"Just wait till you see me chop a butternut squash. Or dice an onion. You'll be moved to tears."

I facepalm. "That was the worst joke I've ever heard," I groan. "You should be ashamed."

He shrugs. "But we never got vegetables much growing up, so it was a treat when we had a nice fresh salad."

I think I see a flicker of something like pain behind his eyes, but it's gone before I can be sure.

"Where did you learn to cook?" I ask. "Did you go to school?"

He shakes his head, absentmindedly running his finger over the rim of his saucer. "No, no school. In our foster homes, sometimes the kids and foster parents took turns cooking dinner, and I realized I liked it. I started trading away my other chores so I could cook more and vacuum less, but nobody minded because I got so good at it."

I prop my elbow on the table, resting my chin on my hand as I listen. I like listening to him.

"I started with simple stuff from scratch because money was really tight. Homemade pasta, fresh bread and soup, anything I could learn from cookbooks I found lying around. Soon I was baking bread and cookies for everyone's sack lunches." I smile, picturing a young Thiago packing lunches for everyone. He smiles too, but his smile falters. That strange shadow passes behind his eyes again before he snaps back to the present. I wonder what he's remembering. I want to reach out and touch him, comfort him. Would he move away from my touch? I stay still.

"Cooking for everyone made things better." He pauses to drink deeply from his mug, then sets it back on the table with a soft tap. He looks around at the dark cafe. "I started working here in high school, trying to save enough to support my sisters and me when I graduated and I could be their legal guardian. I rode the bus from Eastie to work before and after school, cleaning and even baking."

"All the way from East Boston?" That bus ride could easily take an hour.

He nodded. "I loved it here. And the owner liked me. He rented the upstairs apartment to us when I graduated, and a few years ago, he retired and he sold me the business even though I barely had any money. I think he really believed in me. It's everything I wanted, but it's a lot of work."

I smile. I don't want him to stop. "Well, now that I'm here, maybe you can have more time for other things."

He smirks. "I might still need more help before I can even think about taking time off."

"Maybe you just need to let other people help more."

He gives me a look something like a glare, but it softens so quickly

I'm not sure it ever was. "That too," he says. "Seven days a week is too much."

"You don't take days off?"

"Not really."

"What about Gabby and Luna?"

"Theoretically, they have days off, but they usually end up helping a bit here and there, which is fine because they both seem to disappear during their regular shifts anyway." He takes another sip of tea. I try mine again. The honeyed flavor shines through the hot water, now the perfect temperature.

We sip in silence, Thiago looking out the window sometimes. I look out too. The lights are off in the cafe, and we can see the velvety gray sky outside, the glowing moon rising from the roof of the deli across the street. The stars are there somewhere, twinkling behind the shroud of light pollution.

We finish our tea and Thiago rises to take our mugs back to the kitchen. "You haven't played a piano since you were home?"

I shake my head. "Nope."

He assesses this, nodding as if listening to a conversation only he can hear. "Come with me," he says, crossing to the front door.

"Where are we going?"

"For a walk."

I rise and follow him to the door, which he unlocks and holds open for me, then relocks it after himself, checking the lock twice before starting down the sidewalk. We pass the spot where he slammed me to the pavement. I touch my cheek, still a little raw, but mostly healed.

I'm surprised the streets are so empty, but it's after eleven on a Thursday night. It's strange when the city shuts down. Thiago turns and I follow down a street I've never been on. Surprising, given how often I'm in this part of town lately. It looks like the street where the cafe is, with lots of old buildings, bike racks, and trees growing out of breaks in the sidewalk.

I watch the sky, sometimes making out a bright star here or there. Thiago glances at me, looking up to see what I'm looking at. "Something up there?"

"Everything's up there," I say. "We just can't see it very well with all the city lights." I point to a faint white dot shining through the haze. "Orion should be right there," I say. "Rigel and Betelgeuse are barely visible."

"Beetlejuice, Beetlejuice, Beetlejuice?"

"Yeah, not the dead guy in the striped pants. Betelgeuse is one of the brightest stars in the Orion constellation." I squint, then point to a faint star to the lower right. "That's Sirius, Orion's dog."

"That's a weird name for a dog. And who the hell's Orion?"

I chuckle. "He was a hunter in Greek mythology, placed among the stars by Zeus. Most constellations have roots in ancient Greek or Roman myths. It's amazing how those stars and shapes have been there for millions or billions of years, and humans have always fit them into their own stories. It makes us feel bigger and smaller at the same time."

"Huh," Thiago says, looking up. "I've never understood constellations. It's the worst dot to dot picture ever. People say 'oh look, it's the twins' or 'look there, it's a chimpanzee riding a unicorn,' but I don't see it. I just see dots."

I chuckle. "We see what we want to see in order to make sense of what we don't understand. Didn't you ever see shapes in the clouds as a kid?"

"Sure," he says. "When I bothered to look."

I don't even notice where we're going until Thiago gently places a hand on my arm to stop me and points at an upright piano. Right on the sidewalk on this empty street in the middle of the city. I step toward it and see that it's painted in blue and yellow swirls and dots.

Van Gogh's *The Starry Night*.

"What's it doing here?" I ask.

"Some art installation thing. There are a few of them around here, but I thought you'd like this one. Stars."

I lift the wooden cover off the keys and sit on the bench. "Can I play it?"

"That's why I brought you here. Play me something."

I lift my hands and hover my bent fingers over the keys. I hope I can play with my stupid cast on. "Any requests?"

"Whatever you feel like playing. Whatever you've wanted to play all year but haven't."

I look around at the empty street, the moon, the fuzzy gray sky, and this artful piano that appeared out of nowhere, and begin a slow melody, rising and falling as my foot rises and falls on the sustain pedal. My hand feels clumsy in my cast, but I can still move enough to play a simple lower hand.

Thiago tilts his head. "I've heard this," he says.

"Beethoven's piano sonata number fourteen in C sharp minor," I tell him. "Better known as 'Moonlight Sonata.' " I lean into the keys and the melody builds.

Thiago looks up at the sky. "Fitting," he says. He leans on the piano with his elbows on top and rests his chin on his arms. My eyes dart to the inch of skin above his waistband as his arms lift, but I concentrate on what I'm doing.

The song resonates in the deserted street. It's been so long since I've played. I close my eyes and galaxies turn in my head. When I finish the first movement, I look up to Thiago. He smiles, his eyes softer than I've ever seen them. "Play another one."

I smile and put my fingers to the keys again. I hesitate, then fall into a new melody, a rising and falling bass clef, a lilting treble clef.

When I finish, Thiago looks over my head, thinking. "I don't know that one," he says. "I like it."

I press middle C. Even the sides of the keys are painted with blue and yellow dots. "It's mine," I say.

"Really? You write songs?"

I nod. "Well, I wrote that one. I haven't composed since high school. I haven't had the time. Or the inspiration."

"It was beautiful."

"Thank you."

I look around the dark street, wondering if I've woken anyone up, but this is clearly a business area. The Cardozas are probably the only ones who actually live here.

"I've never played a piano in my life," Thiago says. "Not even 'Chopsticks.' "

"What? Everyone's played 'Chopsticks.' "

"Not me."

I scoot on the bench and pat the open space beside me. "Sit," I order. "I'll show you a few things. Not 'Chopsticks.' "

Thiago squeezes on the bench beside me. Our arms and hips press together. His skin is warm against my arm. My heart flutters as I breathe in his bread and espresso scent, underscored with something floral. Tea maybe. It's a beautiful smell.

"This is middle C," I tell him, pressing down the key. The note rings in the night air. "The D is between the two black keys, see? C is right next to it." I press the D. "So A starts here, and it goes all the way to G." I press down the A key with my thumb, then slowly climb the scale up to G.

I drop my hands to my lap, inviting him to try. He lifts his fingers tentatively to the keys.

"This is D," he says, gingerly pressing the key between the two black keys. "So this is middle C." He presses the C with his thumb, slightly louder.

"Right," I say, resisting the urge to tip my head onto his shoulder. He works his way up the scale, slowly, his fingers tangling when he has to shift his hand upward. "Like this," I tell him, reaching to guide his thumb to the D key. Then I demonstrate again on a higher octave. The corners of his mouth flick upward. We play the scale again a few more times, him on the lower octave and me on the higher.

Then I teach him "Twinkle Twinkle Little Star," which he manages on his second try, though the timing is off and his fingers move clumsily. "See?" I tell him. "You're picking it up."

"Doesn't quite set the mood like 'Moonlight Sonata' though, does it?"

"'The mood,' huh?" I tease, though heat flares behind my navel, in my lower belly. He glances sideways, briefly meeting my eyes, though I can't read what's behind them. He returns his gaze to the keyboard and slowly brushes the edge of my hand. I curl my fingers to twine between his. He wraps his large, smooth hand around mine, giving me a sly sideways glance before turning to look forward with a grin. My body fills with tiny bubbles like a bottle of champagne.

"Thank you for bringing me here."

"You're welcome," he says, meeting my eyes again. He smiles warmly, a smile I've only seen on his face a few times when we're alone. A smile just for me. "It was great to hear you play."

He looks down at our clasped hands again as if admiring how they look together, then he raises his face to the faint stars. "We should get out of the city sometime," he says. "Somewhere we can see the stars. You could make up more constellations for me."

"I didn't make them up," I laugh.

He shakes his head, the corners of his mouth turning upward. "I'd never know the difference. It would be fun to go, though."

I look to the moon. "I'd like that."

We sit silently for a moment, looking up at the sky together, hand in hand.

I can't believe how much has changed in just a few weeks before such an odd series of events brought us to this piano bench on a quiet street in Back Bay, looking up at the stars together. Weeks ago, I didn't believe in magic. I'm not sure if I do now, but I can't shake the feeling that Thiago, his sisters, my strange dreams, are leading me to something bigger. I always thought I was in control of my life, but now I'm not so sure.

I'm not sure how long we sit together on that bench. Time almost stops for a while, and I'm glad to be here.

Then, Thiago squeezes my hand. His arm burns hot against mine, and my heart starts to pound. We look at each other just long enough for me to notice a strange starlight burning behind his eyes and an expression I've never seen before, like he's asking a question he isn't sure how to articulate.

My hands tingle. My neck burns. Suddenly, I can't take my eyes off his face, his chocolate-brown eyes framed by long lashes, his high cheekbones, his full lips quirked into that smile that inexplicably drives me mad.

We draw together as if pulled by a gravitational force, like an asteroid pulled into a planet's orbit. I take his stubbled face in my hands, tip my chin up, and kiss him, answering his question with a silent *yes*.

His arms wrap around my waist, pulling me in, kissing me back as if he knew what I was thinking all along. I move an inch across the piano bench and slide my hands to the back of his neck, slipping my fingers into the soft curls at the base of his skull. His lips move with mine and I open my mouth just a little, tasting him, detecting just a hint of ginger tea.

When we break apart, I keep my hands on his cheeks, running my thumbs over his cheekbones before trailing my hands down his chest. His heart thuds beneath my hands. My heart races to match it.

I never break his gaze. With his arms around me and his hands pressing into my back, he smiles. Such a beautiful, strange thing to see him smile. It's genuine and awkward all at once, like he's still learning how.

Then he kisses me again.

On that piano bench in the empty street, I feel deep inside that something's changing, not just between me and this man I've known for such a short time, but in my life. In my whole universe. A star has just exploded to reform into something new.

17

Gabby

I dash up the stairs after my shift ends. All afternoon and evening I've struggled to focus on work while my mind drifted upstairs to the pocket watch in my nightstand. I haven't touched it since I brought it home this morning, after I'd *stolen* it from the antique store. I didn't dare sneak upstairs on a break. Thiago can't know about the watch, or that I stole it. Even though I usually have no problem going upstairs for breaks, I couldn't risk him barging in to tell me to get back to work.

Joan lingered after they closed the cafe and Thiago stayed with her. Normally, I'd be curious, asking him questions that he'd swat away like annoying flies, but I left them alone. If he stays downstairs with Joan to do…whatever, that'll buy me time to work with the watch.

Luna sits cross-legged on the floor by the coffee table cutting pictures from a magazine. Paper scraps litter the table and floor around her, which I'll have to clean up later.

"Luna, it's time for bed."

She doesn't acknowledge me but keeps cutting with her safety scissors. This is the only time she appears remotely focused and grounded, when she's cutting pictures. I approach her and tilt my head to see what she's cutting. It's a picture of a barn owl taking flight, her clumsy scissor work leaving plenty of space around the owl.

"Finish that up, and I'll help you put it on the wall," I tell her. She shows no sign that she hears me, but a few seconds later, she places the scissors on the coffee table, holding the cutout in her hand.

I help her to her feet before leading her to the bedroom. We stop before the massive collage on the wall above her bed. She allows me to take the picture, grab a piece of tape from the dispenser on the nightstand, roll it into a small loop, and stick it on the back of the cutout.

"Where do you want it, Lune?"

She pauses, silver eyes sweeping over the wall. I hold the paper out to her. She takes it, then carefully climbs onto the bed to stand. My heart quickens as I watch for any sign of her losing her balance. There's no way I could catch her, but maybe I could cushion her fall somehow.

Standing steady, Luna sticks the owl at the top middle of the collage near the ceiling.

"Good job, Lune. Now come down."

She bends her legs to sit and turns back to me. No problem. I sigh with relief. I help her change into pajamas, brush her teeth and hair, then climb into bed where I sing her a quick lullaby on the ukulele. "Sea of Love," the Cat Power version. One of my favorites.

When Luna's eyes drift closed, I put down the ukulele and crack the door so I can listen for Thiago, just in case. I slowly pull open my nightstand drawer and fish out the watch, which I had stuffed into a sock. My heart pounds as I feel the weight of the watch and carefully work it out of the sock like toothpaste from a tube. Finally, the heavy brass watch plunks into my hand. I examine it, poking my thumbnail into the symbols scratched into the body, fiddling with the tarnished chain. It's silent; I don't feel it ticking under the lid. I close my hand around it, breathe deep, and shut my eyes.

For a moment, nothing happens.

Then slowly, light blooms beneath my eyelids.

The vision doesn't focus. It's like adjusting a camera lens but never getting it quite right.

Finally, I See the blurred image of a woman's face, lit by flickering candlelight. I can't make out her features clearly, or her surroundings, but she's pale, young, with light eyes and long, wavy blond hair falling around her face. She wears an old-fashioned tunic shirt, her pale collarbones exposed above the loose neckline.

Is it the same woman I Saw in my vision in the antique shop? I think so, only now she's looking right at me. She looks oddly familiar, like someone I saw when I was young and forgot about long ago.

But she can't be looking at me. She's looking at whoever's holding the watch, isn't she? That's usually how it works. Goose bumps erupt over my arms. I feel like she Sees me across worlds and centuries, just like I'm looking back at her across time.

She smiles. Her wide eyes shine with…is that fear? What is she afraid of? "I know who you are," she says in a slight Scottish brogue just above a whisper.

Holy shit.

She *knows.* She knows I can See her.

"Do not be afraid," she says. "I know that you're watching. I've been watching you as well."

A small soft cry, from somewhere, in some time. A shiver passes through me and I realize the cry was me, far away in my bedroom, my mind split between centuries. A dull ache throbs behind my eyes. I'm not used to watching one thing for this long. I struggle to concentrate, but the woman's face grows even more fuzzy.

"Listen to me. You need to practice," she says, her voice ringing with urgency. Her eyes grow wider. "You need to learn to control your visions. Control them as well as you control your conscious thoughts. You must learn to use your visions so you can fix the clock."

Fix the clock?

Even through the blur, I See terror on her face. Her lips keep moving but I can't hear anymore. My head pounds and the vision fades. The colors of her face bleed into each other until I only see dull gray nothing.

My eyes snap open. For some reason, I'm staring at the ceiling. Vertigo washes through me when I realize I'm not sitting up anymore, but lying on the floor on my back. I try to move, but the room twirls around me. Bile rises in the back of my throat. My ears ring and my head throbs like I'd just been to a rock concert. I shiver; my hair and shirt are damp with rapidly cooling sweat. Something soft touches my foot and I jerk, but it's only Gulliver. He steps onto my leg, walks up the length of my body, then settles on my chest in a heavy, purring mound.

Luna's face appears above me, framed by her icy white hair. Her silver eyes focus on the watch in my hand.

"What are you doing awake?" I say, pushing myself into a sitting position while Gulliver leaps off me, meowing irritably. My stomach churns, and I throw out a hand to steady myself against the side of the bed before I hastily shove the watch underneath with the intention to move it the second Luna goes back to sleep. "Come on, back to bed." My head spins as I stand. I grip Luna's shoulder for balance. Her skin is burning hot, so I hold my palm to her forehead. She's warm, but I don't think she has a fever. I make a mental note to check on her before I go to sleep, which may not be for a while. Luna's eyes stay focused on the bedskirt where I put the watch.

I guide her back into bed and pull the covers over her. Thankfully, her eyes slip out of focus again and it seems she's forgotten all about the watch.

"How about another song?" I pick up my ukulele again for a quick round of "Somewhere Over the Rainbow." I know the song so well that my mind drifts off as I play and sing, though I'm pretty sure I skip a verse in there somewhere. Luna won't notice.

All my life, I've watched people in the past, but it never occurred that these people might be watching *me*.

Maybe this woman in the past could See the future, like Luna. Maybe she was like us. The thought that we might not be alone, that this might be part of something much, much bigger both terrifies and thrills me. It makes sense though. We know the gifts are passed through death, that Luna inherited her power from our mother and I got mine from my father. Their gifts had to come from somewhere, and whoever came before them had to receive their gifts from someone as well.

Which makes me wonder: where did it all start?

Learn to use your visions so you can fix the clock. I think back on the vision from the antique store when I opened the watch, the flash of a gigantic clock tower. Something stirs in my memory, and I remember where I've heard something about a clock tower.

I tiptoe across the hall to Thiago's room, taking care to step over the creaky spots in the floor. Slowly, I open Thiago's door.

I take it in at first, the unmade bed, the jeans tossed carelessly in the corner. Luna's tidying up sure didn't last. I step inside, careful not to move anything on the floor, and go to the dresser.

I know where he keeps the letter from our mother. I first found it when I was ten, hidden in one of her books that he always kept during our adventures in foster care, but I haven't read it in years. Thiago thinks I don't know about it. There are a few books stacked casually (or appearing so) on his dresser, so I start there.

There's our mother's copy of *Gulliver's Travels*, her favorite book. I carefully pull it out from the stack and open the worn cover. My heart catches at the sight of my mother's handwriting, so much like mine. *Property of Inés Rivera Portillo* in faded pencil, almost too light to read. I thumb the aged paper and turn the page. There, tucked between the cover and the title page, is a piece of lined paper, soft and yellowed, the creases worn and starting to pull apart. I pull it out, set the book back on the stack, and open the letter.

Now that I look at it, I think I modeled my own handwriting after hers, at least when I write in Spanish. I've adopted the accents so small they're almost dots and her quick slash through the Z's per the Spanish custom. I haven't read the letter in years, but it comes back to me as I read the Spanish words.

Thiago,

I wish I could tell you this in person, but you will need these words long after I am gone. Your father and I will not be with you forever, but there are things you need to know and remember.

First, take care of your sisters. You are the oldest and their brother, and they will need you when their parents are no longer with them. Protect them and above that, trust them. Listen to them.

I snort and roll my eyes. Evidently, he's chosen to ignore this part.

Second, you will need to watch for signs. I cannot See everything that will happen to you, but I do know this: you will need to find what we have been seeking for years. Somewhere in time and space, there is a tower with a clock built into it that our ancestors helped build that is tied to our abilities by the thinnest threads. This clock is the linchpin that holds time together. It ensures that time keeps moving steadily, in one direction. For decades now, we've been aware that it is slowing down, deteriorating.

You need to understand, the clock CANNOT stop. It must be fixed, and the Keepers of Time must do it. No one else can.

This is our role: to protect the flow of time. If that clock stops, time stops. Everything stops.

You also need to know that we are not the only ones looking for the clock. There is another who was part of the clock's conception and construction. He intends to stop this clock. You must not let this happen.

My heart thunders in my chest. I knew I'd heard about the Clock Tower before. This had to be the clock the woman in my vision was talking about, the clock I Saw when I first touched the watch. The Clock Tower, the watch, the woman in my vision, the Keepers of Time. We're all a part of this.

I know this from my visions, but they only take me so far.

You and your sisters have a hard life ahead of you. I See that I am not in it. You three are alone, but you can read the signs.

The Clock Tower is slowing down, but it is safe until the signs begin.

First, you will save a life and see that she is one of you. That is when the search for the Clock Tower must begin, because the tower will be close, and the other who seeks the clock grows closer. My visions of this future are hazy at best, but you will feel a call to move when the clock is near.

Then you must move.

This is the mission of the Keepers of Time. This is the responsibility written into your cells and passed to you through the blood of generations before you. This is your future.

Trust your sisters, and trust the present. They're all you have.

Until we meet again,

Mamá

I scan part of the letter again. *The other who seeks the clock is growing closer.*

This part always scared me, and now a lump the size of a lemon sits hard in my throat. Mamá was afraid of this man, this unnamed *he*. I'm afraid too.

Could he be the previous owner of the watch?

I should probably get rid of the watch, but I can't. The watch is everything we need to know. I'll have to learn everything it has to tell me, and quickly. The watch has history; a long, violent one, and somehow my parents were wrapped up in it. We—Thiago, Luna, me, and Joan too—are wrapped up in it by extension.

Joan. She has a part in this too. I'm sure of it. *You will save a life and see that she is one of you.* I think back to the night we met Joan, how Luna went rigid when she picked up Joan's cup and how Thiago darted out of the cafe door just in time to save her from being crushed by a car. She's the only person we've ever trusted enough to share our secret with, and she believed us. She wears a bracelet with all our charms on it—the sun, moon, and stars—plus a charm of her own: a rocket. It means something, though I'm not sure what just yet. I can only See the past.

My ears perk up when soft piano music drifts in through the window. "Moonlight Sonata." Someone must be playing one of the art pianos in the street nearby. Could it be Joan? Thiago must have taken Joan to play it. I refold the letter and replace it in the book before leaving Thiago's room and closing the door.

I go to the living room and open the window, letting the music drift in. I feel like I've just run a marathon. My limbs shake and my head pulses dully. The music is soothing, and I close my eyes and let it wrap around me.

Then the song ends and another begins. My eyes snap open. I recognize this song. I've only heard it once before, in the antique shop when I first opened the watch. What is it? I try to tell myself it's just an obscure classical piece that was written centuries ago and Joan just picked it up somewhere, but it still raises goose bumps on my skin.

It's a beautiful song, but unsettling, how I've now heard it twice in two days when I've never heard it before.

What is that song, and how does Joan know it?

Luna was right; Joan is a part of our future, maybe an even bigger part than I thought. She has a place in all of this too.

18

Thiago

abby's never going to let me hear the end of this. Never. Thank god her bedroom door is closed when I get back up to the apartment, which saves me a few hours of torment from her excitement that's equal parts endearing and irritating. She'll find out about me and Joan tomorrow, whether I tell her or not. She'll read it in the way I move and in the tone of my voice when I ask Joan to grab the muffins out of the oven for me. Gabby always knows.

I think about how I'll act tomorrow, how Joan will look while she takes orders and makes drinks. I imagine the smooth slope of her neck as she tips her head down to pull a shot of espresso, her slim arms bent gracefully, her skin just as pale as the porcelain mug in her hands, and the light catching the golden shine in her short hair.

Of course Gabby will notice. And I won't care.

In the dark and quiet apartment, I open the fridge, take out a beer, and pop off the cap before striding into the living room to settle into the couch. My parents' clock ticks on the wall: two minutes to midnight.

I sip my beer and look out the window at the stars, though it's even harder to see them from in here. Orion. Serious. Beetlejuice. I've never paid much attention to the stars, partially because I've always lived in a city, but also because I just don't bother to look up. I focus on what is right in front of me and try not to look too far ahead or behind. I certainly don't look up, at least until now.

One minute to midnight.

Before Joan got on the bus, I asked her to text me when she gets home, just to make sure she's safe. I keep one ear trained on the clock, like always. The other listens for my phone, waiting for the text tone.

Something feels different. I think hard, straining to remember the last time I kissed someone I cared about, whose first and last names I knew, and who I looked forward to seeing in the morning. I can't.

The clock strikes midnight. My mind counts the reassuring chimes. We all made it through another day, and it's a new day tomorrow.

When the chimes finish, I sip my beer and stay put.

A few minutes later, a text message dings. The small screen lights up the dark room. Joan's name flashes.

I'm home. I'll see you in a few hours. :)

I grin. For a second, I feel bad for putting her on a back-to-back night and morning shift. I'll be down there again myself in four or five hours, and she should be back in six. I should have offered her a couch or something. Would that be weird? Maybe I should ask Gabby if it's weird, but that would prompt some awkward questions and a lot of winks and suggestive smiles. I text back.

See you then :)

I've never texted a smiley face in my life, but I hit send before I can erase it. I smile. I smile a lot these days. I drain my beer, plunk the glass bottle on the coffee table, and stand. I've never looked forward to the morning shift so much.

***

I steal a glance at Joan while she stacks clean mugs beside the espresso machine. She pauses to watch the front window from behind the counter, squinting into the morning sun. A group of students—at least they look like students—push something heavy-looking, rolling it to a stop in front of the cafe.

"What's that?" she asks, craning her neck to see out the window over the morning customers' heads.

I slap the dough I was kneading on the counter and wipe my hands on my apron. "Whatever it is, I don't want it parked in front of my cafe." I stride through the kitchen, intending to burst out there and tell them to dump their garbage somewhere else. Then I pause.

It's a painted piano like the one I took Joan to see last night. The morning sun washes out the colors like an overexposed photograph, so I can't quite see the design, but it's definitely an old upright piano. I look at Joan. Her face lights up. My irritation evaporates.

She glances at me. The morning rush has died down, so I gesture to the front door, in a *go ahead* motion. Joan rounds the counter to dash across the seating area and out the door, where the students have plunked a bench in front of the piano. Joan lands on the bench the moment all four feet touch the sidewalk, then flips open the lid to examine the keys and plink out a few chords, talking and laughing with the other students like they've been friends for years.

Some tall, tattooed guy with sunglasses leans on the piano, smiling at Joan. I can't see where his eyes are going, but I can imagine where, if she's leaning forward just right.

"Gabs, watch the line. I'll be right back."

Gabby looks up from where she was arranging cookies into a smiley face shape on a tray, then looks out the window. "Ooh, another one?" she says. "I want to see—"

"In a minute," I grunt as I pass. "Watch the cafe."

I burst out the front door as casually as possible, still wearing my apron. Joan launches into some upbeat, fast, classical music song I don't recognize.

"Oh, look at this," I say gruffly to whoever might be listening, trying and failing to sound cheerful. "What a lovely paint job." For the first time, I actually look at the paint. It's a landscape, a cottage nestled on a small island in the middle of a lake with misty purple mountains in the background. It actually does look great.

"Thanks," says the bearded guy who was looking at Joan. I'm just a little taller than him. "I painted it myself."

"Nice," I say. "Did you paint the Van Gogh one two blocks over too? I think I like that one better."

The guy looks taken aback. "No, that wasn't me…"

"Oh, sorry," I say, raising my voice over the music. Joan slams down the keys in an impressive run, shooting me a sly smile. I should relax.

"What a lovely tarantella," says a deep, crisp voice behind me.

I turn to come face to face with some guy I've never seen before, tall and broad with short dark hair peeking out from under a Mets cap. He wears sunglasses so dark I can barely see his eyes behind them. A well-shaped dark beard coats his cheeks. Despite my alarming straightness, I can tell he's a good-looking guy, just a few years older than me. He tucks his hands casually into the pockets of his canvas jacket.

"Thank you," Joan says, continuing to play without looking up. "I'm rusty."

The man smiles, pulls out a wallet, and fishes out a twenty-dollar bill, which he places on top of the piano. Joan's eyes dart up and her eyebrows jump, but she doesn't miss a note.

"Oh, I'm not playing for money," she says, blushing. "You don't have to do that."

"I know," says the man. I note his slight accent. I want to say British, but that's not quite it. "I want to. Skill like yours should be appreciated. But you really should have a tip jar. You wouldn't want your earnings to blow away." He taps the bill with his finger and turns to enter the cafe. Through the glass, I see Gabby watching us from behind the counter.

Before the man enters the cafe, he holds the door open for Luna, eyeing her curiously, which sets my teeth on edge. It's not a predatory look, but something is…off. When Luna's outside, he turns away and steps into the cafe, letting the door close behind him.

Luna carries a large jar that I'm pretty sure contained tea until a moment ago. I hope Gabby helped her and that Luna didn't just dump all the tea on the floor or something. Luna floats to the piano and places the jar right on top of the bill. I smile, shake my head, and pick up the jar before dropping the bill inside and replacing it on top of the piano. I pull a crumpled five from my pocket and slip it in.

"Play as long as you want," I tell Joan with a smile. "You sound wonderful."

She smiles back. The morning sun lights up the gold flecks in her brown eyes. "Are you sure? I should be working."

"You are working," I say. "Bringing people in. I'll come get you if there's a rush, but keep playing. This street could use some good music."

"Well, it's not the Beatles," she teases with a half-smile.

I snort. "Anything you play is good."

She smiles again and looks down at her fingers, ending the tarantula or whatever, and transitioning smoothly into a familiar tune, leaning into her arms as she plays the intro of "Let It Be."

"You can sing along if you want," she says.

I shake my head vigorously. "Not if I ever want another customer to come near this place." Luna sways to the music, her head lolling dreamily on her shoulders. I put my arm around her and gently lead her back inside.

A small crowd gathers around Joan and the colorful piano. Even from my place in the kitchen, I see the tip jar filling up. To my delight, the music does seem to draw people into the cafe because an hour later, there are more people than usual. Gabby and I manage, so I let Joan stay out at the piano. Through gaps in the group bunched around the piano, I see her face as she plays, laughing and talking easily with her audience while she lets out song after song, some fast and upbeat, others slower and soothing. All from memory.

I'm impressed. If she didn't want to be an astrophysicist, she could probably play professionally. She already sounds like a professional. She has the personality for it, to draw people into the song with her. No one passes by her without stopping for at least a few moments, and almost everyone deposits a few coins or a bill into the jar.

During a lull, I head back outside to listen, finding an open spot directly behind her where I can stand. She starts playing the song she played for me the night before, the one she wrote. It sounds even better today. Maybe because it's a newer piano, or maybe it means more to me today because I know she wrote it. The melody rises and falls, the higher hand following the lower, the two melodies calling back to one another. That's when I realize I haven't really listened to music before. Like, really listened. Music has always been background noise for something else, but rarely the center of my attention. I've certainly never just listened to a piano, relegating it to the category of "boring" instruments in my head along with the giant stand-up violin thing and most of what you'd find in the woodwind section of an orchestra. I've never heard an instrument hold its own like this without a bass guitar or drum to back it up.

The man with the Mets cap walks back out and stands beside me to listen. I happen to glance at his face and realize it's gone white. I can't see his eyes, but I can tell they're wide behind his glasses.

I wonder if I should ask if he's okay, but he doesn't appear to be experiencing a medical crisis. I steal sideways glances at him while I watch Joan, prepared to spring into action if he collapses or something.

He watches Joan with a pained expression I don't like. My shoulders tighten, and my hands slowly roll into fists. Just in case.

When Joan finishes her song, the small crowd applauds and a few people deposit bills into the jar before disappearing into the cafe. I turn to go back inside to help Gabby, but pause as the man in the cap approaches Joan.

"That was lovely," he tells her hoarsely. "Is it an original?"

Joan peers up at him, squinting in the sun. I can tell from her stiff smile that she's uneasy. "It is," she answers. "How did you know?"

"I've just never heard it before. It's beautiful." He reaches into his pocket, pulls out another twenty, and stuffs it into the full jar before nodding to her and turning to walk away. I watch him retreat with his hands in the pockets of his jacket, not looking back.

"Do you know that guy?" I ask Joan, still watching the man. He reaches the far end of the block and turns around the corner. Did he look back before he disappeared? I can't tell.

"Nope," Joan says as she stands. "He seemed nice, but..." Her jaw and shoulders stiffen. She's just as weirded out as I am.

"He was awfully complimentary," I say.

Joan shrugs. "Maybe he's just an awkward guy. That doesn't mean he's a bad person."

I chew the inside of my lip so I don't say something rude. Joan's tendency to see good in everyone, to give everyone the benefit of the doubt, is something I admire about her. After all, she gave me a chance after a shaky first (and second) impression. I can see how that trait might come back to bite her in the ass, though. What if someone doesn't deserve that doubt?

Carefully, she closes the lid over the keys and picks up the full tip jar. "This is by far the most tips we've ever gotten."

"'We?'" I echo. "What are you talking about? That money's yours."

She shakes her head. "I made this money on the clock. It's for all of us."

"You brought a ton of people into the cafe. You should keep it."

I hold the door open for her. She walks in, crosses behind the counter, and empties the jar into the cafe tip jar by the register in a clatter of coins and flutter of bills. My breath catches when she looks up at me. Suddenly, I want to kiss her again.

But I feel uneasy thinking about the man who left the twenties. Some weird pent-up energy from the last several weeks is building up inside and making my head spin. I get back into the kitchen and we work over the top of each other without speaking, reaching plates of pastries across Gabby, who seems only mildly annoyed, sometimes throwing small, secret smiles at each other across the kitchen.

The wave dies down and there are no customers in line. I put a load of dishes in the dishwasher and take a quick breather to watch Joan's elegant wrists as she empties the bucket of espresso grinds into a plastic bag. She passes by me on her way to the back door. I decide it's a great time to empty the kitchen garbage and follow her out a few moments later.

Just as I thought, she's waiting for me without looking like she's waiting for me. Still with that strange, hungry look, she immediately steps closer, takes my face in her hands, and kisses me. The bag drops from my hand.

For a second, I'm suspended in space and find my hands wrapping around her waist, creeping down to the roundness of her ass. She doesn't stop me, but kisses back harder. She backs me up against the brick wall and presses against me. Ivy tickles the back of my neck. She smells like bread from the cafe, but it smells different on her somehow, with an edge of something floral. I get the brief idea to try edible flowers in a batch of scones soon, but that thought evaporates as her tongue slips into my mouth, which surprises me. I like it.

Her fingers thread through my hair. I feel the elastic holding my hair come loose and my hair falls around our faces. She pauses to pull back and look at me, and I realize she's never seen me with my hair down. She smiles and kisses me again, her soft chest pressing on mine.

The pent-up energy inside me releases like water from a dam. I briefly try to remember the last time I did this anywhere outside a dive bar or the apartment of some girl I went home with whom I'd known for an hour or two, tops.

This is better. So much better.

***

I stand back in my old building in Eastie where I lived with my parents in front of the horrible, familiar apartment door. I know this is a dream, but I still dread what I'll find behind that door when I inevitably open it.

My hands shake. Even in a dream, my heart thunders in my chest. I don't want to do it, but I know I will.

Finally, I reach out to turn the knob and step into my old apartment.

Decades-old grief claws at my chest when I see my parents on the floor at my feet. Papá's face presses into the carpet. Mamá lies on her side in an expanding pool of her own blood, eyes open and blank. My pounding heart becomes a black hole in my chest, sucking in all the air around me.

Somehow in the vacuum of shock and grief, a panicked thought rises in my mind. *Where are Gabby and Luna?* A new dread builds in my stomach. My eyes dart around the kitchen, even though a part of me already knows exactly where they are. My terror smothers the thought. *My sisters. Where are my sisters?*

I listen. Silence.

At once, I feel like two minds. My panicked, dreaming child-mind and the part of me who has lived this scene again and again. Even though I know what happens and where my sisters are, the raw panic and pain still burn like a fresh wound. I'm alone. My life has changed forever, along with my sisters' lives. Somewhere beneath the shock, I have a vague sense that I've just been shoved into a role I'm not ready for. This is what my mother meant in her letter. It happened. She would not be there to live our futures with us.

There's only one place in this room to hide. I lunge to the closet and throw open the door. Little Luna huddles among the mop and cleaning supplies, clutching a tiny bundle. Gabby. Luna is washed out and pale, *different*. Even her dark brown hair and eyes appear paler than usual. She won't speak. She won't look at me. Her mouth opens and closes soundlessly as her pupils dart back and forth, following something I can't see. She clutches Gabby tightly to her chest so firmly I worry she'll hurt her. Gabby squirms, but stays silent. I carefully pry her away and place a hand on Luna's arm. Her eyes don't focus on me, or on anything. She looks like Mamá did during strong visions, in another time and place.

We are alone. Completely alone.

I jerk awake. Alone. Nothing but the sound of my ragged breathing.

Sheets tangle around my legs in twisted ropes. Once I've kicked them off, I haul myself into a sitting position and place my head in my hands, my fingers twining through my unbound, sweaty hair. *Just the dream,* I tell myself. *We're safe.* I take a deep breath.

These nightmares have haunted me for nearly twenty years. How many times have I awakened just like this, in my bed in a foster home or in this apartment, the terror as fresh as it was that day?

I scoot off the bed and put on the jeans I wore the previous day, then quietly open my door and stagger into the hall and to the bathroom, where I splash my face with a few handfuls of cold water.

The water calms me down. I dry my face with the towel on the rack. My heart still thuds dully in my chest as I pad down the hall. Before stepping into the living room, I silently crack open Gabby and

Luna's bedroom door to make sure they're all right. To make sure they're alive. I always wake from those dreams terrified to find them murdered in their beds. I make out their sleeping forms in the dark. Luna lays on her side, facing Gabby's bed, and Gabby faces the wall, curled in the exact same position. I listen, relieved to hear their steady breathing, then close the door.

The coolness of the tiled kitchen floor soothes my hot, bare feet. I weave around the table and open the fridge, squinting slightly as the bright, silvery light illuminates the kitchen. I pull out one of the last beers and crack it open to take a long, deep swig before I've even closed the fridge.

Then I hear a noise.

I pause, lower the bottle, and listen.

A clicking, almost rattling noise coming from the alley below.

Slowly, I step to the kitchen window and press my forehead against the glass to peer down at the alley by the cafe's back door.

A man stands at the back door wearing dark gray clothes and a knit hat. He bends to examine the knob and then tests it. Trying to get in.

A man is trying to break into the apartment. Ice shoots through my veins.

I look down the dark stairway leading to the alley. The only way out of the apartment is that door or the fire escape in full view of where he's standing. If we try to escape, he'll see us.

A potent mixture of fear and rage brews in my chest. I tiptoe back to fumble for the baseball bat I keep next to the fridge and wish I owned a more suitable weapon. The bat feels like a useless chunk of wood in my hands. Who knows what kind of weapon the man might carry.

The door rattles again. Hot adrenaline tears through my veins. I force my breathing to slow, to stay steady, as I press my back to the wall by the top of the staircase and tighten my grip on the bat. If he gets in and comes up the stairs, he won't know I'm there until he gets a face full of Louisville Slugger. One good swing should break a few bones and hopefully send him tumbling backward down the stairs. If not, the blow will stun him enough for me to give him a good shove. I hope. Either way, I won't let that son of a bitch near my sisters.

I wait for another minute, gripping the Slugger so tightly that my hands ache. I haven't heard a sound in at least twenty seconds. Thirty. Nearly a minute.

Finally, I go back to the window and look down.

The man is gone.

19

Gabby

I wish I could have gone outside to hear Joan play, but Thiago and I were so busy with customers that I didn't even get a bathroom break until well after lunch. Then after my shift, I remembered it was my turn to do laundry, so I spent the evening at the Wash 'n' Run, sitting on a dryer trying to read an ancient copy of Ovid's *Metamorphoses* that I found at a flea market, but of course, I could only think about the watch.

When I finally make it home, I jog up the stairs to the apartment with the laundry bag slung over my shoulder like Santa's bag of toys, my mind on the pocket watch. I need to see if I can talk to the blond woman again and figure out what the hell we're supposed to do.

The apartment is dark, and I deposit the laundry bag on the dining table for now. When my eyes adjust, I see Luna framed by the window and cast in moonlight. Something moves on the windowsill.

"Luna?" I say, my stomach jumping. What *is* that? The thing on the sill moves again. As I approach, I see a smooth and silvery shape perched outside on the windowsill—an animal. Then I realize it's a barn owl, watching Luna just as intently as she watches it.

"What the hell…"

Luna doesn't move. She gazes at the owl standing on the sill, her fingers lightly brushing the glass between them. The owl looks up at her with round, liquid black eyes, nipping lightly at the glass where her fingers touch, almost affectionately. A small smile plays across Luna's face as the owl fluffs its feathers and shakes like a small dog shaking water from its fur.

"Luna, what are you doing?" I touch her shoulder. She doesn't react, but the owl's head swivels toward me. I swear I see its black eyes widen in surprise before it spreads its large, milky wings and tips off the sill, gliding away into the night.

Luna watches it go, smiling. Her silver eyes are focused.

"Come on," I say, unsettled. I gently take her arm to lead her away from the window. "Let's go to bed." She keeps her eyes on the window as we step away. I throw one last glance out into the darkness where the owl disappeared.

Luna does strange things sometimes, but what on earth was that? Did that owl just randomly show up on its own? I shake my head. It's nighttime, and barn owls live everywhere. That one just decided to hang out by our window for some reason, maybe watching for mice in the street below. Animals have always been drawn to Luna. Stray cats follow us on the street, barking dogs fall silent and wag their tails when she's around, and birds and butterflies frequently land near and even on her. It makes sense that an owl, out for its nightly hunt, would do the same.

I help Luna brush her teeth and change into her pajamas. Then I brush her hair and sing her a quick verse of "Rainbow Connection" on the ukulele, forgetting half the words because my mind wanders to the watch in my nightstand. When Luna's eyes drift close, I put down the ukulele and open the drawer.

The watch sits in the bottom of the drawer, nestled in my socks like a fat brown toad. It's strange to be so intrigued and attached to something I hate so much.

I use one of the socks to grab the watch, then climb into bed and pull the covers over my head like I used to when I'd read past my bedtime with a flashlight and try to hide it from Thiago and our foster parents. Now, I have a much worse secret to keep.

I curl into the fetal position, cradling the watch in the sock. I can barely see it in the darkness beneath my comforter. Finally, I let my bare thumb touch the lid.

Images fly by like I'm looking out the window of a speeding train. A wisp of wavy blond hair. The flash of colliding daggers. Sandy stone walls lined with flickering torches in sconces. The man in the scarlet cloak, his face hidden beneath his hood.

Then, a massive clock tower made of rough black stone. Its pointed roof juts into a sky of glittering stars like a single rotting tooth. I See it just long enough to notice the hands sluggishly jerking between Roman numerals.

Something is wrong with it. It moves too slowly. Time drags out between ticks.

I only See it for a moment, but I'm positive it's the Clock Tower Mamá mentioned in her letter.

I push further and further back into the watch's history, searching for the blond woman who could See me in the future as I looked back at her in the past. I need to talk to her. Maybe she can tell me what I need to know about this watch. Maybe she can help me make sense of it and tell me what I'm actually supposed to *do*.

Learn to use your visions so you can fix the clock.

I push further, like flipping through a book to find my place after the bookmark has fallen out. A familiar ache thrums behind my eyes.

"I See you."

Finally, I hear a woman's voice with a slight Scottish accent. A sharp pain twangs in my head. I struggle to focus on her face, but like the first time, the vision blurs like I'm watching something out of my periphery.

It's her. The young blond woman I spoke with before. The one who can See the future. She sounds relieved to See me, and it occurs to me that maybe she's searched for me in the future just as I search for her in the past.

Last time, I only Saw her for a few seconds before the vision broke and she faded away. I won't let her drift away this time. I'll hold onto it until I find out what I need to know. But how do I speak to her? Can I speak out loud?

"I See you too," I whisper in the space under my blankets.

Through the blur, I See the woman smile, though her eyes are strangely sad. "I hear you," she says. "Listen carefully, Gabby. The watch you're holding is important. It leads to the Clock Tower because it's made from parts of the tower. They're connected. Keep it safe."

Goose bumps prickle over my skin. It's like learning a fairy tale you heard in your childhood is real. "The Clock Tower that keeps time running," I whisper out loud. "The one we have to fix."

The woman nods. "Yes. Listen closely. The Clock Tower is no ordinary structure. It holds time together, but the tower itself does not stay in one place. The tower travels through time and space, appearing in the past, present, and future in different locations in the universe. It is impossible to find without the watch."

My grip tightens on the watch. I don't know if I feel the ticking or my quickening pulse beating in my head.

"Even I can't See where or when it will be for sure. The watch has started to tick again, which means the Clock Tower will appear somewhere on earth soon, in your time. You need to find it and fix it, or time will stop." Her eyes widen, and I See that they're strikingly blue. "*Everything* will stop."

My stomach roils. I grip the watch tighter. "Mamá said someone else is after this watch."

The woman nods, her eyes narrowing. "Yes. He made it, and he wants it. He knows you have it."

My head throbs, tinging the edges of the visions with red. I can barely hear her.

"He killed Mamá and Papá?"

Her face turns grave. "Yes."

I let the gravity of that message sink in. It fits with everything I've Seen from the watch, from Mamá and Papá's things, and from Mamá's letter. They had this watch, and that man killed them for it.

Somehow, through luck or fate, the watch found its way back to my family. To me. There's more to know, but I can't hold the vision much longer. My eyes sting and my temples ache.

"Who are you?" I ask, for no other reason than curiosity. Maybe knowing her name will help me find her again.

The woman smiles sadly. "My name is Katherine."

The vision swims. A red hue washes over the images as they melt into themselves. My eyes snap open to darkness. The pounding behind my eyes is so bad, I feel like they're going to explode. Something drips onto my hand. I touch my nose and feel sticky wet warmth. The back of my throat tastes like copper.

I push off the covers and turn over to get out of bed and deal with my bloody nose. But first, I shove the watch under my pillow.

My heart leaps when I see Luna's eyes shining in the darkness. She lies on her side, facing me, with the covers pulled up to her nose. Her eyes are wide open, focused on me, shining in the dim light.

"Luna, go back to sleep," I tell her, my voice wavering. I can't remember the last time I felt so unsettled around her, but the way she looks at me is...troubling. That blank expression and uncharacteristic focus. She doesn't move. She looks more aware than I've ever seen her. Does she know what I was doing? Could she sense it somehow?

I rip a few tissues out of the box on the nightstand and hold them to my nose. My temples pound. "Go to sleep," I repeat.

Then I hear footsteps in the living room, trailing into the kitchen. I hear the fridge opening and the unmistakable plink of a twist-top bottle. Thiago must be awake. I sigh, pinching the skin between my eyebrows to stem the flow from my nose. I know he has nightmares. He must have had another one if he's drinking a beer in the middle of the night.

Suddenly, Luna bolts upright in bed. My heart leaps into my throat at the sudden movement.

Her eyes go wide.

I hear a slight rattle coming from the alley below. Slowly, I tiptoe to the window, part the blinds with my fingers, and look down.

A man stands by the back door, fiddling with the lock. I can't see his face.

"Oh, shit," I breathe. Behind me, Luna is as still as death. I listen. No footsteps in the kitchen. Did Thiago hear that too? Is he standing by the kitchen window, watching and listening? I know he keeps a baseball bat in the kitchen. I wouldn't be surprised if he's waiting at the top of the stairs right now with our only weapon. My heart pounds, outrunning the pounding in my head.

I turn to look at Luna. She sits upright, staring straight ahead, then her head slowly turns downward and to the side, pointed right where the man stands in the alley. Her eyes are unfocused again, her lips parted.

My mind whirs. We can't use the fire escape, because the man would see us. All we can do is pray he doesn't get inside, or if he does, that Thiago can take him down before he gets to Luna.

Protect Luna.

I dart across the room and grab Luna's arms to pull her off the bed. "Come on, Luna. Move." She obediently shifts her legs to hold her weight as I pull her off the mattress, help her lie down on the floor, and push her under the bed. It's a terrible plan, but the best idea I have at the moment.

Hiding saved our lives once.

"Under the bed, come on…" I push until Luna slithers under her bed and lies quietly on her stomach, eyes wide open.

I return to the window, part the blinds, and look down.

The man is gone. I breathe a heavy sigh of relief.

For several minutes, I wait by the window, checking every few seconds to make sure the alley is still empty. Maybe I should go talk to Thiago to see if he saw what I saw, but I can't move.

No footsteps in the hall. No noise outside the bedroom door at all. Thiago hasn't moved from the kitchen. I'll bet he's still watching the alley below just like I am.

Neither of us will sleep tonight.

20

Arial

When I arrive in Boston in the evening, I follow the ticking from the Back Bay Station to a quaint street lined with illuminated street lamps and planter boxes jutting out from the brownstone buildings. The scene is only marred by a storefront covered with plywood to hide a massive hole. Faded tire marks streak across the sidewalk. Clearly, some fool ran off the road and into the storefront, tearing a hole in this otherwise lovely street.

I follow the ticking to a small cafe. The sign out front reads *Clockwork Cafe and Bakery*, complete with a working clock. Just when I almost stopped believing in signs and fate.

The ticking of the watch beats in my chest next to my old heart, like a second pulse pumping magic through my veins, just under my skin. My watch is here.

If I had my old powers, I'd simply tear into that building and take it now, but in my current state, I'll have to do things the old fashioned way, as they say (though at this point, I can't think of anything more old fashioned than magic). I buy a sandwich at the deli across the street and choose an outdoor table, where I pretend to read a newspaper while I observe the cafe and activity through the windows of the space above it. If my years have taught me anything, it's patience. Watch before you leap, or however the expression goes. So I watch. I wait to see if the watch moves, but the ticking never leaves the cafe.

After a quarter of an hour, I stand, cross the street, and approach the door. A bell on the door tinkles behind me when I step inside. I take in the antiques lining the walls as I wait in line for espresso. Clocks, everywhere. Old toys, many of which I remember seeing children play with when they weren't considered antiques. I watch the dark-haired man rolling dough in the kitchen, his hair tied in a knot at the back of his head. A petite young woman works the espresso machine, also dark-haired. *Gabby*, says the strip of masking tape on her blouse.

I say nothing to Karl, the uninteresting young man at the register, beyond the necessary exchange and never look anyone in the eye. The first rule of invisibility is to avoid eye contact without being direct about it. If you make eye contact, they *see* you. They remember you. I prefer not to be remembered.

I feel the watch ticking, almost hear it in my inner ear. I tilt my head, trying to locate the sound. Is the watch here? I scan the shelves on the wall, hoping to catch a glimpse of its familiar bronze casing. It's so small, it could easily be tucked behind something. Or does one of the cafe patrons have it?

I reach into my coat to run my thumb along the hilt of *Amica*. If that watch leaves this cafe, I'll follow.

I select a table and stay for about half an hour until all the patrons have turned over, nursing my espresso and pretending to read a magazine. The ticking never fades.

It's in the building then. Or with one of the employees.

A silver-haired young woman carries a mug on a saucer back to the sink. Blind, I assume, from the way her glassy, pale eyes never focus. She weaves around the counters in the kitchen mechanically, never bumping into them, as if she has them memorized. Interesting.

The dark-haired girl snaps something at the young man and smiles when he retorts. Barbed, yet loving. Siblings? The man gently touches the silver-haired girl's arm and points her toward the back door. Perhaps she is related as well. A family-owned cafe?

I finish my espresso and rise to deposit the cup into the plastic bucket, tilting my head.

That's when I realize the ticking isn't coming from the cafe itself, but above it. The space above the cafe looked like a flat. There were potted plants in the windows. Perhaps the siblings run the cafe and live above it.

Siblings.

The man with the bun says something in Spanish to Gabby, and that's when I place where I know them. They're the proper age to be the children of that Spanish couple who had the watch all those years ago. The last time I used *Amica*.

They stole the watch, or rather, one of their friends did. It was a dark-haired little bitch with eyes like flints, whose fire reminded me of Katherine. I don't remember the actual moment it was taken or even have proof that it was her, but I'm sure it was. There were enough of them to keep me occupied, and she was the only one who came close enough. I've caught many thieves picking my pockets because I used to be one myself. I know the tricks.

But I never felt the watch leave my skin. I only realized it was gone when she was gone. I never found her again, no matter how hard I looked.

Sometimes in the following decades, I felt the watch ticking. I followed it like a predator follows the small, appetizing sounds of its prey. But the watch always moved. It was like I was purposely being lured around and away because before I could truly determine where the ticking was, it was gone. It was a game. Sometimes I wondered why the Keepers didn't simply try to destroy it to keep it from me forever, but the fact is, they needed it as badly as I did.

I managed to find them five years later, this time in East Boston. When I visited them in that squalid flat twenty years ago, Inés told me they no longer had it. I didn't sense the watch anywhere nearby, so I believed her. And I killed them anyway. I might even regret it, but it's impossible to tell. It's been so long since I've felt anything.

Now here it is, calling to me from the flat above the cafe, in the possession of the next generation of Keepers. Could it be that they've had it all this time? Why hasn't it called to me before now? Or is it possible that they've only recently acquired it again, that fate somehow delivered it into their hands once more?

I'm not sure, and it doesn't matter. The watch is here, now.

But I must be patient. I can't afford to muck this up.

I'll come back tonight while they're asleep, take a look at the locks, the entrance and exit, and see what I'm dealing with.

21

Joan

Thiago puzzles me. I'm enjoying the process of collecting his oddly shaped pieces and fitting them together one by one.

Over the past weeks, a new picture has started to form. I see a man entirely different from the one I first took him to be. Kinder, much more gentle than he'd care for anyone else to know.

My favorite puzzle pieces are those rare moments when he's alone in his world of contentment. Those are the days when the food tastes best because it's infused with his happiness and creativity. Once those puzzle pieces of joy fall into place, I feel like I see him clearly. Everything else is background. That joy is the center of who he is when he's not afraid.

Sometimes he steps out of the cafe during the afternoon lull and returns with small paper bags from obscure stores and excitedly pulls out tiny jars of ingredients I've never heard of, like a child lovingly showing off each of his new toys. Vanilla bean paste. Black garlic. Whole nutmeg like tiny stones. Curls of fresh cinnamon. Strange fruits that smell of other worlds. Sometimes he stays up late turning these magical ingredients into sweet breads dotted with exotic fruits and sparkling with subtle, unexpected flavors. He makes savory tarts in daring combinations, topped with sliced vegetables arranged in colorful constellations of herbs and spices. He offers them to us to taste, eagerly asking for notes and opinions.

"Is it overpowering? The tea?" he asks as Gabby chews a sample of green tea-infused scone. I look down at the scone in my newly cast-free hand and carefully break off a piece. Yellow flecks of lemon zest dot the fluffy inside. I smell just a hint of tea through the bright lemon scent as I take a bite.

"Green tea should be subtle," Thiago adds.

"I just don't like green tea," Gabby says simply through a mouthful. "It tastes like hay. But…everything else is good."

"I like the lemon peel," I add once I've swallowed. "It's a bright flavor up front, and the tea comes later. It's perfect."

He smiles that rare, boyish smile I've come to love. Heat rises in my belly.

"Should I put these out? You think people would like them?"

Gabby and I both nod because our mouths are full. Thiago stacks the scones on the serving tray and covers them with plastic wrap before turning to slide the baking tray into the industrial-sized dishwasher. Gabby walks away to finish refilling tea jars. I take another bite of scone, watching Thiago move around the kitchen. His back and shoulders flex under his shirt, his large hands and muscle-corded forearms working as he wipes down the counter, rubbing the cloth over the wood. My mind starts to wander to some interesting places and my palms tingle with the urge to slide up his shirt and run over that back and shoulders, well-developed from hauling flour sacks and kneading stubborn piles of dough. I glance at the clock to see if we have a few minutes before opening to slip out to the alley and make out like teenagers.

Gabby passes in front of the door, and I look away. I know she knows about us. For the first week after we kissed, she'd wink at him or wiggle her eyebrows at me when she noticed we'd both been missing for a few minutes. One day she rolled her eyes and handed Thiago a napkin to wipe a smear of my lip stain off his neck. I'd never seen him blush like that, and I realized how much I love it when he blushes.

I appreciate that Gabby seems all too happy to give us alone time. Just as I'm about to catch Thiago's eye and glance toward the back door, he catches mine first. Instead of the signaling back-door glance, he says, "Do you want to go stargazing tonight?"

The question catches me off-guard. For a second I don't say anything.

"I know a place outside of town where we could see the stars better," he adds. "Less light pollution, more open space. We can bring food and have a picnic."

My smile starts in my stomach, then rises up my body until it appears on my face. I feel like a champagne bottle full of bubbles, about to pop with joy. "That would be amazing. I could bring my telescope! I haven't used it since I moved out here."

"I've never looked through a telescope," he says. "I'd really like that." His dark eyes flick to Gabby's back, and he leans forward for a quick kiss, right there in the kitchen, lifting my chin with his finger. It's brief, but it leaves me momentarily stunned when he pulls away to walk the scones to the serving counter. He's not usually a PDA kind of guy. I blink once, then realize that we open in one minute, so I turn to retrieve my apron from the hook near the back door.

Thiago Cardoza. Always a fascinating puzzle.

The morning rush keeps us both busy. We barely look at each other as we work, but the air sparks between us. I feel him walk behind me while I pour a shot of espresso, and I pause.

He asked me to go stargazing. He wants to see my joy too.

***

Our shift ends at six. After a quick greeting to the evening staff, Thiago disappears upstairs while I finish my work. He reappears a few minutes later with a folded quilt under one arm and the strap of a small cooler over his shoulder. After he catches my eye, he cocks his head toward the back door. I hang my apron by the door, sign out, and follow him.

The second the door closes behind us, he sets the cooler and blanket on the ground and his lips are on mine. I curl my fingers through the folds of his tee shirt and pull him closer until our stomachs and hips press together, lighting a scorching fire behind my navel. We've perfected this dance over the past few weeks, signaling each other to step outside for a quick makeout session with one of us backed against our favorite spot on the brick wall, but we don't often get a chance on busy days like today.

He trails kisses along my jaw and nips my earlobe, sending shivers down my neck. The back of my tee shirt rides up and I shiver with delight as I feel his warm palm on my bare skin.

Eventually, we make it to his car in the tiny lot on the other side of the building, hand in hand.

I chuckle as he opens the door for me.

"What?" he says, his mouth quivering with a mischievous grin.

"We've come a long way in a few weeks, haven't we?" I say. "A month and a half ago, you could barely stand to be in the same room with me."

He shrugs, and I climb in. "That was before I knew you were a good kisser."

I snort, but my heart stutters. We're disgusting. We're everything I can't stand about newly dating couples.

Wait. *Are* we dating? Is this our first official date? Are we a *couple*? I hadn't thought about it until now. I'm not usually into labels.

Just enjoy it, Joan. Just shut up and enjoy it. This is already better than all my past relationships put together.

Thiago climbs in and buckles his seat belt.

"Can we stop by my place and grab my telescope?" I ask.

"I was planning on it," he responds. He starts the car, pulls onto the road, and drives toward the bridge to Cambridge, the Beatles playing on the CD player.

"CDs, huh?" I tease. "And Gabby's the one stuck in the past?"

"They work," he says simply, but he smirks. "Besides, until four years ago I was still using a tape deck."

"I guess that works when all your music is at least thirty years old," I return. "Michelle" plays over the slightly static speakers. I sing along quietly, leaning on my elbow out the open window. I catch glances of Thiago watching me out of the corner of his eye, a soft smile on his face. I fight not to mirror his smile on my own.

When we make it to my apartment, I grab my telescope while Thiago keeps the car running in a red zone.

"So where are we going?" I ask when I slide back into the passenger seat.

Thiago grins. "It's a surprise."

We get back on the road and head north out of the city. Soon the concrete and cars give way to thick trees that block our view in every direction. Late-afternoon sunlight dapples the road, and I roll down the windows to let the New England summer air wash over me.

We alternate between singing along to Beatles songs and chatting comfortably about music, cooking, and school. I don't recognize him as the clammed up, stoic grump I met almost two months ago. The more I learn about him, the more I want to know.

And still, that nagging question tugs on my mind. What are we? And why do I care so much?

"What do you want more than anything?" I blurt out. I want to know. And anything to distract me from the whirring questions in my brain.

For a moment, the car is silent except for the sleepy sitars of "Norwegian Wood."

"That's a really big question, sorry," I say immediately, my cheeks heating.

He runs his thumbs over the worn steering wheel, chewing on his lip. "I want to stop being afraid."

I watch him as he watches the road, my mouth pulling into a tight line.

Somehow, I'm not surprised. I know exactly what he's talking about. He doesn't elaborate, and he doesn't have to. He fears for his family— for their financial security, their futures, and most of all, their safety. I feel that fear when we touch, when I kiss him, that faint tension that prevents him from completely letting go. The hesitation. The fear, the constant upkeep of his fortress, the burden he feels. The more time I spend with him, the more this longing builds, the flavor of it more and more prominent.

"You're afraid because you love them," I say quietly. "That's how you know you love someone, right?" I feel that weird feeling I always get when I'm about to say something stupid. It's like watching a car crash in slow motion. "When you're afraid for their safety. But you want the best for them too."

He nods again. "Yeah. It's…it's always on my mind."

"It affects everything you do. You feel like it's all on you."

Another nod.

That fear drives everything he does from the way he crafts his pastries with so much care to how he carefully locks the doors of the cafe each night, double-checking each one before repeating the ritual on the doors and windows of the upstairs apartment. It drives the way he works: relentlessly, constantly, as if he knew that if he stopped for a moment, the change of momentum would upset the balance of everything he carries and bring it crashing down around them.

His throat bobs as he swallows and looks at me, brows tilted in an expression that says very clearly: *thank you for seeing me.*

I return with a small smile that says *thank you for letting me.*

Then I shake my head as he turns back to the road. Now what's this silent communication thing we have going on?

Suddenly, we burst out of the trees onto open, rocky grassland with the ocean spread wide beside us. Salty ocean air blasts my face through the open window, and I inhale deeply.

We drive until Thiago turns off the main road onto a winding dirt stretch. In the distance, I see a porcelain-white lighthouse perched on the rocky coast like a sentinel.

My breath hitches. I've lived in New England for years and I've never actually seen a lighthouse. I've barely left the city at all.

"What is this place?"

"I come here sometimes when I just need a break from everything," he responds.

"You take breaks?"

"Only in dire emergencies. Like when Gabby's driving me crazy."

I chuckle. "That's the norm, isn't it?"

My favorite boyish smile spreads on his face. He slows and turns the car into a dirt overview by the side of the road and turns off the ignition. With the car off, I can hear waves crashing on the other side of the hill.

I leap out of the car and breathe in a lungful of salty air. Cool ocean breeze rustles my hair and plays with my loose tee shirt. I hear the car door behind me as Thiago gets out and grabs our picnic out of the trunk before I listen to his footsteps approaching me from behind. When I can feel his heat just inches behind me, his arm slides around my waist and I feel his lips on the back of my neck, methodically kissing each bump of my spine. My knees nearly buckle as waves of heat ripple down my legs.

"The view's better on the other side," he says against my skin. He nips my neck and releases me to stride toward the ocean, motioning for me to follow him over the grassy hill.

It's pleasantly warm outside and smells fresh, not quite as briny as I'd expect right by the sea. Boulders dot the hills. After a few minutes, I look behind me and realize I can't see the car anymore. All I see is Thiago, the sea, and the lighthouse, far away. Not another soul around.

Thiago stops near a clump of boulders on a lookout cliff over the wide, open ocean and spreads out the picnic blanket, carefully smoothing the wrinkles before sitting down. I sit cross-legged across from him on the soft quilt as he unpacks the picnic basket.

We eat avocado sandwiches on Thiago's signature white bread and a strawberry-topped slice of homemade chocolate cake in a takeout container from the cafe. I slip off my sandals and dig my toes into the velvety grass. The sun sinks behind us. Stars come out one by one until familiar constellations form.

"That bright one is Jupiter," I say, pointing at a bright, constant spot of light in the sky. A breeze blows toward me and I smell fresh bread and a hint of cologne. I smile. He wore cologne for tonight. I've never known him to wear cologne.

I carefully set up my telescope. It's small, but powerful, and probably the most important thing I own. The black case is worn, but I've kept the actual telescope in pristine condition.

"Where'd you get this?" he asks, tapping the case with his finger.

"It was my grandpa's," I say as I steady the tripod. "He left it to me when he died."

"You used to stargaze with him," he says. "Isn't that what Gabby said? When she Saw your past?"

I pause. I had forgotten all about that. We haven't spoken of that night since it happened. It just felt normal that I knew about them now. "He's the one who taught me about space," I say. "He worked for NASA on the Apollo missions. I used to visit him in Florida and he'd take me to launches sometimes. The Kennedy Space Center was my Disney World. I thought space was this magical realm, and I wanted to explore it more than anything."

I peer through the eyepiece of my telescope and adjust the focus. Butterflies dance in my stomach, the same ones I feel anytime I view the expanse of space through a telescope.

"Take a peek," I tell him.

He leans forward and shuts one eye to look through the eyepiece. A smile spreads across his face. The butterflies in my stomach suddenly multiply.

"Wow," he breathes. "I can't believe this little tube can see that far. It's like magic."

"It's a complicated collection of mirrors and glass and…"

"So…magic," he insists, grinning slyly. I poke his leg with my foot.

"Everything's magic," I counter. I gaze up to the starry wilderness, greeting the constellations like familiar friends, tracing their imaginary lines with my eyes. I haven't seen a proper night sky in months. "There are billions of stars out there, many of them bigger than our own sun, and so far away that they're just little dots of light to us. Even billions and billions more beyond those that we can't see at all, constantly exploding and dying and reforming in this crazy cycle. Nebulas and quasars and planets and rocks flying through space and spinning around each other like balls on a pool table. Only, a lot more organized than that. It's the most magical thing I've ever heard of." I sigh as I gaze up. The mystery of a night sky never fails to astound me.

"I've never thought about it like that," Thiago says, leaning back on his hands and looking up. One of his hands slides over so that his fingers brush mine, and soon they're entwined. We hold hands on a blanket on a cliff above the ocean under the brilliant night sky and sounds of rolling waves. I can't think of anything more perfect. And I realize that I've never gone stargazing with a guy before. Not once. And I'd certainly never let a date look through my telescope.

Why not? Was I afraid to let anyone see me this way, completely enraptured and at home under a night sky, rambling about the mysteries of the universe? At most, I've gone off on tangents about the life cycle of stars or physical theories over dinner in some restaurant I don't actually care about but seemed appropriate for a date.

No. Something about this is different.

Suddenly, the lighthouse ignites, shining its beam of light out to see without drowning out the stars. My arms and legs tingle with magic.

"We're made of stardust, you know," I say. "Nearly every atom in our bodies was once a part of a star, millions of years ago. We all started there." I nod to the sky. "And we'll be stars again someday, after the earth is gone. Nothing's really ever created or destroyed, it just changes."

This is usually the part where the guy usually checks the time, asks for the check, or suddenly remembers dry cleaning he has to pick up at eleven at night.

Thiago's eyes sweep over the vast, shimmering sky. "Maybe that's why you like the stars so much," he says. "Maybe some part of you remembers being one."

Heat flares in my chest and trickles into my stomach, a bright spot of affection blooming inside me.

"I never thought of that," I say quietly.

"I mean, while we're talking about magic."

I give a small smile. My eyes follow the curve of his neck down to his smooth collarbones, disappearing into his tee shirt. I feel his hand in mine, the gentle pulse in his long fingers. I find myself leaning closer until our arms touch. Electricity sparks under my skin. I want to touch the soft skin on the inside of his arms, to run my finger down the front of his throat, his chest, his stomach.

Without letting go of my hand, he eases onto his back with his other hand bracing his head. His shirt rides up an inch and the two peaks of his hip bones slide out of his jeans. I swallow hard. My skin is on fire.

"Thank you for bringing me here," I tell him.

"You're welcome," he says. "I never paid much attention to the stars."

"You've always lived in the city. You can't see them there."

"We should come out here more often, then."

Electricity buzzes under my skin. I bite the inside of my lips and reach out, raking my fingers across his warm, smooth skin. He shudders as I slide the tips of my fingers just under the waistband of his boxers, stroking from hip bone to hip bone.

I change directions and slide my hand up to his chest, beneath his tee shirt, then lean over to kiss him. His lips are warm and soft. I can taste the echo of the chocolate cake we just shared. When I pull away, he looks over at me, a strange blaze in his eyes. He reaches for me, cupping my face in his hands and guiding me back to him, kissing me again. Before I know it, he's pulling me on top of him. My toes rake the tops of his. My shirt rides up and our bare stomachs press together.

His back arches, pressing himself against me. I push myself up, straddling him, and he sits up so I can grab the hem of his shirt to yank it up over his head. I run my hands over the burning hot skin of his torso and lean down to kiss him.

We're moving quickly. And somehow, I'm okay with it.

"This is what you want?" he breathes into my mouth.

I know he's not just talking about what's about to happen on this picnic blanket.

I nip his bottom lip. "Yes," I answer without a shred of hesitation.

It's true. I do. I want all of it. This night and whatever comes after.

He kisses my mouth, my face, my neck as his hands slip into my shorts, gripping my bare hips, my ass, exploring the sensitive skin between my thighs.

A soft moan escapes me. I sit back to reach down and pull my shirt over my head. He watches me with clouded eyes as I reach back to unclasp my bra, then toss it aside with my shirt. I pause, resting my hands on his chest. His eyes drift downward, lingering on the small peaks of my breasts, then he meets my gaze, smiling softly. I lean down to kiss him again, twining my fingers in his hair.

"I swear this isn't why I brought you here," he says, his eyes twinkling.

I chuckle against his stubbled cheek. "Liar."

"I mean, I'm not complaining…"

"Uh-huh." I kiss the tip of his nose before touching my forehead to his.

"…but I didn't plan this."

"You mean you didn't drive me to this remote location and this particularly private group of boulders where we wouldn't be disturbed?"

"Do you really think I have that much forethought?"

I plant a soft kiss on his lips. "Well, I'm not complaining either."

He looks at me for a moment, his expression unreadable. It's the way he looked at me the night I played piano for him. Then he kisses me again.

Heat blisters me from the inside out as his mouth travels from my mouth to my neck down to my chest. We help each other shed our pants and pause only briefly when we bonk heads and giggle together, the mood not lost at all, and retrieve a condom from my purse. Then we're wrapped up in the blanket with our clothes in piles around us.

How is this so easy? So simple?

In a tornado of heat, skin, breathing together, I realize I've wanted this since the night he took me to the painted piano. I wanted another night under the stars. His forehead presses into my shoulder, his breath warm on my chest. I don't care that we're out in the open in the middle of nowhere and anyone could come along at any moment. I don't care that anyone else exists outside our picnic blanket and the starry sky above us.

His body stiffens beneath me, and I'm becoming part of that sky, a shooting star traveling light years across space, exploding and reforming again and again.

We lay silently in our blanket cocoon, side by side with our legs braided together. I watch his relaxed face. His eyes close. Strands of his dark hair splay around his forehead like roots. The tips of our noses nearly touch. I smile and place a gentle, playful kiss on his lips. He smiles back and kisses my cheek where the skin's just healed from the night we met. I sigh, and he trails soft kisses down my neck.

I watch the stars above us with my arms around his neck, wrapped in his heat. A whispering breeze ruffles my damp hair and I shiver, not really from cold, but from exhilaration. Happiness.

"You're right, we should come here more often."

He chuckles against my neck and winds an arm around my waist to pull me in closer. His hand slides up my spine and presses between my shoulder blades. He kisses my shoulder and bites playfully, raking his teeth on my skin. I close my eyes and smile.

Then the back of my neck prickles, like we're being watched.

When I open them again, I blink a few times to focus my eyes.

I see nothing. Am I imagining things?

I see only rocks, hulking shapes in the silver moonlight. Still, I think it's time to go.

I gasp softly when his hands go exploring again. My body's gearing up for round two and I can tell his is too, but something tells me we'll have to wait until we're somewhere more private.

"What's wrong?" Thiago asks, craning his neck to see where I'm looking.

"We should get dressed," I say, trying not to sound alarmed. "Before somebody sees us."

"Did you see someone?"

"No, I don't think so. I feel like there's someone nearby, though."

"Okay," he mumbles with his lips on my collarbone. He kisses me again, quickly, and pushes himself up, draping the blanket over me while he stands.

For just a moment, I forget all about the strange shadow. He's slim and lean, olive skin and smooth planes of his chest and stomach gleaming in the moonlight. I'm surprised how comfortable he seems standing naked outside. He hands me my clothes and I watch him slip on his jeans before I even think to put my own back on. I wriggle into my shorts and tee shirt under the blanket, stealing glimpses of Thiago as he dresses, thinking about what will happen when we get back to his apartment, or mine. A jolt of electricity shoots down my legs at the thought.

He gathers up the picnic while I fold the blanket. Hand in hand, we climb the hills to get back to the car, sneaking sideways smiles at each other like goofy children, but I still keep an eye on the open plain around us, watching for moving shadows and suspicious shapes. I see nothing, but my skin still tingles like we're being watched.

As we drive away, Thiago reaches over to put his hand on my leg, and I cover it with my own. I smile, glad my sudden urge to leave didn't completely ruin the mood. I weave my fingers into his and raise his hand to my lips before replacing it on my leg.

"I'm sorry," I tell him.

"For what?"

"For making us leave. I just thought I saw something."

He smiles and shrugs. "It's okay. You're probably right. We might have just scarred some poor hiker for life. The things they must have seen…"

I giggle. My body is still tingling.

"I had a really good time," I tell him.

He stares straight ahead at the road and smiles, his eyes twinkling in the moonlight streaming into the car. "Best night ever," he agrees.

"Strawberry Fields" plays softly over the car speakers. I reach forward to turn up the volume just a hair.

"I love this song," I tell him. I start to sing along.

I'm sure it was nothing. Awesome sex has a way of scrambling the brain. My heart is still thumping in my chest.

I run my fingers through my damp hair. I roll down the window, letting the cool air rush over my burning-hot face. I can't wait until we get back to one of our apartments. I tip my forehead onto the window to watch the stars, watch them fade from the brilliantly glittering sky to the smooth gray dome over the city.

22

Joan

The summer flows by in a blaze of heat, sun, iced lattes, open apartment windows, sangria, and steamy nights in Thiago's bed, making love with the fan on and Thiago glowing like a hot coal beside me all night.

Gabby tactfully spends lots of time in antique stores lately, usually with Luna in tow so Thiago and I have the apartment to ourselves.

Something in him has come alive, some side of him I never would have guessed was there. He still works hard, silently baking pan after pan of scones and croissants without a recipe, never wasting words, plowing through his day like a well-maintained machine, but there's a new brightness about him. His voice has lost that edge when he talks to his sisters. The lines between his eyebrows don't carve so deeply into his face.

Getting laid regularly will do that to a person, I suppose. I'm sure a few of my lines have disappeared too.

"I've never seen him this happy," she told me one day while we cleaned the espresso machine after closing. "He was singing at breakfast this morning." For Thiago, singing is akin to running down the street hugging strangers and twirling around lamp posts.

Something fluttered in my stomach as she told me that. I thought of two nights previous, him moving above me in the dark, gripping my thighs, the sheets rippling around me like waves. That night alone was enough to make anyone sing.

I'm relieved Gabby approves. I wonder how Luna feels about this new development, or if she's even noticed. Sometimes I wonder just how much of the present she Sees, if it's consistent or if it's like waking from a coma every hundred years or so.

Morning light creeps into Thiago's room after a particularly long night shift. I wake up in his bed with the sheets tangled around my legs. The ceiling fan whirls, blowing warm air around the room, ruffling my hair. My skin is sticky with sweat. The window is still open. I can hear people talking on the street, the rush of tires on pavement as cars drift by, and the call of pigeons on rooftops.

Thiago's gone. The covers on his side of the bed have been casually flipped over. The sheets and pillow on his side are rumpled. I still smell him, bread and sweat, even though I vaguely remember him kissing me and getting out of bed in the early hours of the morning.

Gulliver curls up on Thiago's pillow next to me, purring, with his back legs and tail swept over his face. I reach out to scratch his fuzzy ears.

It was nice of Thiago not to put me on the morning shift so I could sleep in. I'm not a morning person. I'm definitely the type who could stay up most of the night and sleep until noon, though I've learned to get up without much trouble through years of school and classes at seven a.m. I decide to stay in bed a while longer to relish the heat, the feel of the sheets, and the memory of the night before.

I curl up in the sheets and doze off again, slipping back into a dream.

I see Thiago downstairs, for some reason wearing a gray tee shirt instead of his usual white, mixing a giant bowl of muffin batter. It's like I'm standing right next to him. He zests a lemon into the batter, a little blizzard of yellow flakes drifting down in the bowl like snow. Then he picks up the bowl and uses a rubber spatula to fill the cups of several muffin tins neatly lined up on the counter. The creamy batter pours out, landing in graceful folds in the paper-lined cups before melting into itself and lying smooth. He turns away to put the trays in the oven. I then notice a plastic container of brightly-colored edible flowers on the counter; pink rose petals, bright orange nasturtiums. I can almost smell the lemon and the fresh coffee.

A swish of Gulliver's tail against my arm gently tugs me out of sleep. I reach out to scratch his ears again. He stretches on the pillow, rumbling with happy purrs.

Soon, the idea of iced coffee lures me out of bed. I sit up, head swimming from the heat. I slip back into my tee shirt and denim shorts from the night before and run my fingers through my hair. I catch a glimpse of myself in the bathroom mirror as I step into the hall. I look like Sonic the Hedgehog. My eyes are blurry from sleep. My cheeks are rosy and I need a haircut.

I go downstairs to the cafe, excited to see what Thiago's baked that morning and get an iced latte so big I could swim in it. The old floor creaks beneath my feet. I carefully step down the narrow staircase and let myself into the bright cafe kitchen.

Thiago takes something out of the oven. He turns to put a tray on the counter and smiles when he sees me. I smile back, butterflies in my stomach. I pause before I cross the kitchen to him, noticing his gray tee shirt, just like the one I'd imagined in my daydream. Strange. He usually wears white so the flour won't show.

He slips off his oven mitts and puts a hand on my hip as I approach, leaning in for a quick, subtle kiss.

"What are these?" I say, eyeing the golden muffins he's just taken out of the oven. They smell amazing. My stomach growls.

Then my eyes fall on the container of rose petals. Nasturtiums and rose petals. Exactly as I saw them in my imagination.

"Flowers?" I ask quietly.

"Yeah," Thiago says. I can hear that he's smiling. "I'm not sure about the rose, but I think the nasturtiums will be awesome. I've done a few test batches with petals in some of them, and I've also added—"

"Lemon zest?" I finish for him. My voice sounds weak.

"Yes, exactly," he says. He sticks a butter knife into the side of a muffin cup and pries one of the muffins out. Yellow flecks of lemon peel dot the golden dome of the muffin top. Some of the muffins have streaks of red or orange petals. Thiago peels the paper liner off the muffin and breaks off a chunk, which he offers to me.

I take it from him. He watches me expectantly, so I put it in my mouth.

"It's delicious," I say, forcing a smile. It's true. It is delicious, but...I knew he was using flowers and lemon zest before I came down here. I knew it. And the tee shirt.

"I thought you'd like this," he says, breaking off a chunk for himself and popping it in his mouth. He closes his eyes and smiles, pleased with himself.

"I want some!" Gabby comes up behind me and plucks the rest of the muffin from Thiago's hand, then bites straight into it. "Oh, wow," she says. "That's good, Thi. That's really good."

"I think I'm onto something with these flowers," he says. He picks a few nasturtium blossoms from the package and gently pokes them into the tops of some of the muffins. "Get the basket, Gabby. I'm setting these out."

I still have a piece of muffin in my hand, so I put it in my mouth, chewing thoughtfully.

Thiago looks over at me while he decorates muffins. "Are you okay?"

"I'm fine," I say immediately.

"No you're not," he says. "You get excited about things when you're okay. You don't look excited."

"I'm just groggy, that's all. I just woke up."

Thiago shakes his head. "You can talk to me, you know." He finishes the nasturtiums and starts laying rose petals onto some of the muffins. He lowers his voice, leaning in closer. "I had my head between your legs last night, so I think you can tell me if something's bothering you." A warm shiver runs down my body and my toes curl in my flip-flops. For a moment, I imagine shoving him onto the counter and taking him right there in his own kitchen, but that would be very bad for business.

His mouth curves in a wicked grin, like he can see my thoughts through my eyes. "You don't have much to hide," he goes on. "If something's wrong, I'd like to know about it."

He's right, but I also don't want to worry him with my weird déjà vu. He has enough to worry about.

I look to see if Gabby's within earshot, but she's gotten sidetracked. A customer points out the empty half and half jug, which she immediately refills. She then starts checking the other jugs.

"You don't have visions, right?" I say. Thiago jerks his head up and looks toward the seating area.

"No," he says quietly.

"So how do you know you're actually the present, like Gabby's the past and Luna's the future?"

He tilts his head. "I guess I don't," he says. "It just makes sense that I wouldn't. I'm here, in the present."

"But you're never anywhere else in the present?" I say. "You don't See anything else that's happening right now?"

"Nope. Here and now."

I nod. I'm not sure how to tell him. I'm not sure *if* I should tell him, at least not now. It might be a fluke, just a weird thing my brain did while I was skating on the edge of sleep.

And during my NASA presentation, when I saw my mom.

"Why do you ask?"

"Just curious," I say. "Just trying to figure this whole thing out, you know?"

"Uh-huh," he says. "You'd be a lot more direct if you were just trying to figure something out, but you don't want to tell me." He turns back to the muffins, his jaw set.

A pit forms in my stomach. I don't want to worry him. I want to tell him. I really do. And I don't want him to think I don't want to talk to him. This is going so well.

"I just had a really weird dream," I tell him. "It was really vivid and got me thinking about visions. About how Gabby and Luna See other times and places. I was just curious about what it's like." A half-truth. I'll spare him for now. If it happens again, I'll tell him. A one-time event means nothing. If it's repeated, justified, then I'll have something.

Besides, it probably was just a vivid dream. Brains do weird things sometimes. This is probably nothing.

He looks over at me, eyes searching. He knows there's more, but he's deciding not to push it. Finally, he shrugs. "I wouldn't know," he says. "Gabby could tell you, though. She'd be thrilled to talk about it."

He nudges the rest of the sample muffin toward me. My stomach is in knots, but I smile and take it anyway, tearing off another small piece and putting it in my mouth. I look at Gabby, who's done filling the jugs, watch Thiago finish popping muffins out of the tins, and Luna, who's been dusting the same shelf since I got down here.

I know they're involved in something bigger. They have a purpose, a mission. With their abilities, how could they not? I know I'll learn more about that mission in time.

Suddenly, I feel like I'm on fate's doorstep, about to walk into something bigger than me, maybe something too big for me to handle.

Whatever's coming for them, whatever they're meant to do, I'm feeling more and more that it's also my mission, that I'm a part of it too.

23

Gabby

I go through the motions of the cafe—taking money, brewing tea, making lattes without designs on them. Joan practically runs circles around me, expertly running the espresso machine and laughing with customers while she serves them. Sometimes she and Thiago exchange smiles. A few times, he touches her waist, or she brushes his arm when she reaches for a dishcloth. Sideways glances, conspiring grins.

I'm glad to see my brother happy. Something like joy blooms inside me. While I know it's there, I feel separate from it. It's like a flower in a glass case.

My mind is upstairs in my nightstand drawer with the pocket watch.

Thiago's in such a good mood that he allows me a full hour for lunch instead of fifteen minutes to scarf down a sandwich. I run upstairs and sit on my bed. Gulliver curls around my legs as I hold the watch in my cupped hands. It's not as talkative as it was when I first found it. The images appear to me slower now, blurry, but easier to stop and observe. I try to find the young woman I Saw and *spoke* to—Katherine, she said her name was Katherine—but I don't See her. I can't control where the images go. I can only hang on and go along for the ride.

I poke my thumbnail into the groove around the edge. I've been able to See a lot with the watch closed, but maybe I need to open it to get the full story.

I'm afraid. But I know sooner or later, I'll have to. It might as well be sooner. I take a deep breath, dig my thumb into the groove, and pry the watch open.

I barely glimpse the watch face before I'm thrown into a storm of images and sounds. I'm simultaneously climbing an endless flight of stairs, spinning, stepping through a landscape that changes instantly from city to open field to farmland to seashore. I catch flickers of faces, the blond woman, a powerfully built man with dark hair and a beard, a man with blazing red hair and black eyes.

A hooded figure in a red cloak. Somewhere, a clock ticks. It sounds like it's coming from the figure itself. Somewhere under the scarlet hood, an eye glints.

I shut my eyes and watch the images float by, snatching any meaning I can from garbled words and sounds. There's a woman humming again, the song Joan played on the piano outside the cafe. The one she composed.

Then there are screams. Lots of them. A man's screams, the one I assume to be the previous owner of the watch, and others. Bright light and heat.

The sounds and the images don't always match up. A man's fingers on piano keys accompanied by wails of anguish. The sound of wind whistling, clocks ticking, footsteps echoing.

Finally, I See her. Katherine. Her desperate face flashes in my mind. Her lips move silently.

I can't hear you, I try to tell her. I'm sure she can See me. Her blue eyes are wide and terrified. Blond hair floats around her face.

She's under water, I realize.

Her expression turns from desperate to terrified and her face wrenches in pain. Her mouth opens in a tortured, soundless scream, but I can't hear her. Her lips pull back from her teeth and her eyes squeeze shut. Her face fades from my view.

My head starts to throb like a giant hammer pounding a beat right behind my eyes, but I keep watching, concentrating. Black and white swirls in my mind.

Somewhere in the cacophony of centuries, a massive clock ticks. The powerful sound rattles my bones, coinciding with the faint tick of the watch I hold in my hand, somewhere far away. The giant clock isn't ticking steadily; the clicks are loud and then soft, a few close together followed by a few seconds of nothing. Like morse code. Like a faulty heart.

Overall, it seems to be slowing down.

I feel dizzy, sick from the overwhelming visions, but I strain to focus on that ticking. Through a mesh of pictures, ghostly images layered on top of each other like double-exposed film, I See a shape rising to a dark sky. My eyeballs throb. I feel like my head will explode.

It's a tower made of sooty black bricks, like it caught fire once but didn't burn down. I can't tell how tall it is, but it's at least as tall as the buildings in downtown Boston. There's a chunk taken from the side, the hole lined with jagged bricks like broken teeth around a gaping mouth. As I focus, the ticking gets louder, rattling my brain around in my skull. I drag my consciousness higher. On the top of the tower is a cracked, yellowed clock face. The second hand twitches, leaping from the three to the five, then stopping as if it has to rest before dragging itself around again. I can't See the ground beneath me, or the land around me, though a bright moon lights the night sky. It's as if the Clock Tower is in a world of its own.

A jolt of pain shoots through my head and I cry out. The images stop. For a moment, I only See bright flashes.

Then, nothing.

I gasp and open my eyes. The room swims. Colors swirl and bright lights flash at the corners of my vision.

Have I gone blind? I've fallen off the bed onto my hands and knees. The old brown carpet scratches my palms. I've dropped the watch. I grope blindly for it, just to know where it is even though I don't want to touch it again. I don't want to lose it.

Finally, the blurry outline of Luna's bed forms before my eyes. Something soft brushes my arm; Gulliver rubs against me. He sniffs at something on the floor before darting away in a scuffle of fur and claws, like the thing shocked him. The watch. I reach for the sock on the floor and use it to pick up the watch. I heave myself into a sitting position. Sweat plasters my hair to my scalp. My hand shakes as I turn the watch over, using the sock as a barrier.

This watch has crossed paths with Keepers before, maybe many times. The Clock Tower...I need to think about this. I need to know everything.

Then I get an idea.

Ice drops in my stomach, and immediately I know it's a bad idea. But what if it helps? This watch has somehow shaped our past, and I'm becoming more convinced it will shape our future. I want to know for sure. I want to know what we need to do. I can't talk to Thiago about this; he'll insist I get rid of it. Whatever power this thing has will be back in the ethers for anyone to get their hands on.

It's worth a try.

I amble to my feet, sway for a moment, and put one shaky foot in front of the other until I reach the kitchen, where Luna stares out the window as she dries a glass bowl with a dish towel. I notice the sink and counter are dry. If she washed the bowl, it was a long time ago, but she dries it anyway.

"Luna?" My voice comes out low and hoarse.

She doesn't turn, but she pauses her pointless task.

"Luna, could you do me a favor?"

She stops drying, but still doesn't turn around. Her shoulders tense ever so slightly.

"Luna, I need you to look at something for me." My stomach knots around itself. I hate myself for what I'm about to do. But it's the only way to know.

Cursing myself inside, I slowly lift the watch, gripped safely in the sock, and press its brass lid to Luna's bare shoulder.

Immediately, a shock ripples through Luna's body. She goes rigid like she's turning to stone from the inside out. I try to catch the bowl as it slips from her fingers, but it shatters on the floor around her bare feet. I squeeze in front of her, between her and the window, and grip her other shoulder with my free hand. Her mouth falls open and her eyes roll back in her head.

"Luna, what do you See?" I ask. I know she can't hear me, but some part of me hopes my question will echo through the future that flashes in front of her eyes, that she'll See and remember and find some way to relay it back to me.

But it just gets worse. She starts to convulse. Saliva streams from the corners of her mouth.

"Shit," I say and remove the watch from her arm, but she still shakes. "No, stop!" I fling the watch into the living room, where it plunks somewhere near the window. Luna's knees buckle. I try to catch her, but she's bigger than me and I can only grab her shoulders to stop her head from hitting the edge of the table. I hold onto her as she sinks to the floor. She convulses, only the bloodshot whites of her eyes showing.

"Luna, come back. I'm sorry, come back!" I cry.

Desperately, I pick up her head and massage her temples. She inhales and wails. Ice curls through my veins. I've never heard her vocalize before.

"Shhh, shhhhhh," I whisper pointlessly, my hands shaking as I struggle to hold her still.

She screams again and arches her back, digging her palms and heels into the floor. Broken glass slices into her skin. Crimson blood slowly spreads over the kitchen linoleum. Her head jerks back and her mouth opens, letting loose an inhuman howl.

Somewhere over her shrieking I hear pounding footsteps on the stairs. I look up from the floor to see Thiago appear in the doorway, face white as flour. Joan is right behind him, brown eyes wide in fear. I've never been so glad and yet terrified to see my brother. *Help her*, I plead with my eyes. *I'm sorry, I didn't mean to.*

"What did you do?!" Thiago demands, voice tight with terror. His eyes are wide, dark pits in his white face. He shoves the table out of the way, drops to his knees by Luna's side, and takes her face in his hands. Joan crouches by her side and takes of one her hands, enclosing it in both of hers.

Luna's shrieks fade to whimpering. Joan looks around and reaches for the dish towel on the oven handle, which she uses to wipe the saliva shining on Luna's mouth and chin.

"Should we get her to a hospital?" Joan asks quietly.

"No," Thiago and I say together.

"Is this a vision?" Joan asks.

"I think so," I admit, my voice cracking. Joan scrutinizes Luna's bloody hands and feet. Thiago looks up at me, dark eyes flat and dangerous. Thiago's eyes burn like a brand on my skin. I look away to brush Luna's hair from her face.

"I've never seen her have a vision like this," Thiago says. My face burns with shame. "Not since..." he doesn't finish his sentence. Out of the corner of my eye, I see he's still looking at me. The rest of his sentence lingers between us. *Since the day our parents were murdered. The day the power of the future passed to Luna.*

Luna falls silent and gradually stops shaking. Her blank eyes remain wide open. Her mouth opens in shock. A few minutes later, she relaxes. Though the color doesn't return to her face, her eyes and mouth finally close.

"Help me get her to bed," Thiago says quietly. I move to help him, but he holds up a hand. "Not you. Joan."

Joan looks from me to Thiago, then back to me, and gives a tiny nod that I return. She's not taking sides, but Luna needs to get to bed and Joan's stronger than I am anyway. Thiago doesn't look at me as he scoops Luna into his arms, aided by Joan.

"Find some tweezers and towels," Joan says to me, nodding at Luna's bloody feet.

I stand in the kitchen like a statue as they disappear into the hall with hushed voices. My hands start to shake.

What have I done?

My mind spins. My eyes fall on the pocket watch resting innocently on the floor under the living room window. I grab the dish towel Luna was using on my way out of the kitchen and tiptoe into the living room where I use the towel to grab the watch. I then shove it and the towel under the couch before darting down the hall to the bathroom. I yank the most convenient towels off the shelf and throw open the medicine cabinet to dig around for the tweezers.

I slip into the bedroom just in time to lay a towel under Luna's feet as they carefully lower her into her bed. Joan grabs the small garbage can by my nightstand and holds a hand out for the tweezers. I give them to her, and she kneels by the bed. Taking her phone from her pocket, she turns on the flashlight and shines it onto the soles of Luna's bloody feet. Glass shards glisten in Luna's calloused skin.

Thiago stands behind Joan with his arms crossed over his chest, glaring at me. I watch Joan carefully pick shards of glass out of my sister's feet and drop them into the garbage can.

"Living room," Thiago says to me. Joan looks up at me, then back to him. I hate to put her in the middle, so I nod my head, motioning for her to take care of Luna.

Thiago herds me out the door and into the living room, shutting the bedroom door behind him.

We stand on opposite sides of the coffee table. Thiago's eyes bore into me. Guilt and shame burn in my veins.

"Tell me what happened," he orders, his voice sharp and cold.

My voice catches in my throat, which is just as well because I don't know what to say anyway. "I..." I sputter.

"I've only seen her like this once," he says, holding up one long finger. "Something had to trigger a vision like this. What was it?"

My jaw stiffens. I hesitate. My mind desperately claws for an excuse or something to say. Thiago's eyes drill through me, then travel down to the floor.

Oh no.

"What is that?" he says, his voice low and dangerous. I turn to follow his gaze to the corner of the dish towel sticking out from under the couch, that I obviously, suspiciously, tried to hide. The blood in my veins freezes.

I jerk to stop him, but with unnerving speed, Thiago grabs the towel, throwing out an arm to keep me away. For a strange moment, I remember simpler days in our childhood when he'd pull that exact move to hold me off of him while he poked through my diary or seized one of my toys so he could hold it over my head and make me jump for it. Those times had been teasing, play; now my big brother holds me at bay while he pulls my deepest, darkest secret out from under the couch.

He stands with the towel open in his hand. The brass watch rests innocently inside it like an egg in a nest. Deep lines of fury carve into Thiago's forehead. His face turns angry red as his burning eyes shift from the watch to me.

I nearly crumble under that gaze, but I force myself to keep my feet planted, my face smooth.

"What…" he says slowly, his voice shaking with rage. "…is this?"

24

Luna

- See it again
      ages upon ages
      worlds upon worlds
ends upon ends
too many directions, pulling my fragile human mind to pieces
a tower of bone
a column of death and endless space
the tick tock of time slows
the tick tock of the thing pressed to my shoulder, a warning
he wants it
he searches for it
after all this time
time holds its breath
waiting for a decision
for a direction to flow
i See them all
every possibility
every direction
every option

all of them the end
a kaleidoscope of doom

25

Gabby

Thiago's eyes drill into me. I look from his furious red face to the pocket watch in his hand. I'm not sure which scares me more.

"Answer me," he growls. "What is this?"

"An antique," I whisper. The air crackles with his fury. Hot anger rises in my own chest, roiling like magma. Years of frustration. Years of hiding from him, delving into our parents' mysteries alone when he should have been the one person I could count on.

"What was it doing under the couch?" Thiago says. He looks at the watch, turning it over, then he presses his thumb to the groove in the lid...

"Don't open it," I say suddenly, jerking forward to reach for the watch. I stop myself and meet Thiago's burning glare.

"Why not?" He studies my face. I swear he must hear my heart pounding from six feet away. "This thing is dangerous, isn't it?" He looks at the watch, then back to me. "You touched Luna with this, didn't you? *Didn't you?*"

I scowl at him, standing my ground. I won't let him see how much I hate myself for what I did, but I remember why I did it. "That watch is important, and I'd Seen all I could from it. I wanted to see if Luna could See anything."

That vein in Thiago's forehead stands out like a root. My stomach sinks. I can't tell if he looks more terrified or furious. "Well, she definitely Saw something," he hisses.

The watch clutched in his fist, he strides into the kitchen, rips open the bottom junk drawer, and pulls out a hammer.

"What are you doing?" I demand, following him into the kitchen.

He lays the watch on the table, regarding it as if it were a slimy, diseased creature.

"What do you think I'm doing?" he says, holding up the hammer and squeezing it until his knuckles turn white. "You've been hiding it from me, Seeing with it. That's why you've been sneaking around behind my back. Don't think I haven't noticed you disappearing all the time!"

"You can't tell me what I can and can't do!" I snarl. "I wouldn't have to sneak around if you'd just let us figure out what we're supposed to do!" My hands bunch into fists at my sides. My face burns with rage. "We can't run away from what we are, Thiago. We can't hide from it."

"'What we are?' " he echoes, lowering the hammer. "What are we, Gabby?"

"We're Keepers, like our parents. They accepted it, but you won't!"

"We're *orphans*!" he roars. "That power got our parents killed. I don't want it anywhere near us."

"We have this power, whether you like it or not. We might as well be prepared."

"I don't care," he snarls. "You were a baby. You didn't see their dead bodies on the floor. You didn't see their faces. You didn't know Luna before she changed."

I narrow my eyes, my hands starting to shake. "You think I haven't Seen it?" Color drains from his furious face. Something twitches in his cheek. "You think I haven't looked into the past and Seen their deaths over and over? Not just when you walked in the door, but their actual deaths? I've Seen Mamá shove me and Luna into the closet and tell us to be quiet. I Saw that man waltz into our apartment and murder both of them when they wouldn't give him what he wanted. And that," I say, pointing at the watch. "I think that's what he wanted."

Thiago looks at the watch with disgust. "All the more reason to get rid of it." He lifts the hammer. Before I can think, I find my hand darting for the watch. I grab it off the table, towel and all, and stuff it down the front of my jeans.

The hammer twitches and surprised anger bursts on Thiago's face. I back away from him, out of the kitchen and into the living room. Thiago turns to me, his face turning red again, rolling his eyes.

"Real mature, Gabs," he growls. "Mamá and Papá would be very proud."

"We need this watch," I tell him. "Mamá and Papá wanted us to pick up where they left off."

Thiago's face darkens. "Don't tell me what they wanted," he hisses between his teeth. "You never knew them."

I blink, breathing in. "Just because I didn't grow up with them doesn't mean I don't know them," I say quietly. My voice doesn't sound like my own. "I've watched them in the past. I know them better than anyone. And I know about the letter."

He freezes, midstep. My stomach flip-flops, and I brace for the explosion. "Mamá told you something was coming, that someone was after this watch. She told you about a Clock Tower. They had a mission, and now that mission is ours."

A strange look passes over Thiago's face. "You've been through my things."

"Mamá's book isn't yours," I say.

"But the letter is. You had no right to read it. How long have you known?"

I stick my chin out. "Ten years." His face falls, and he shakes his head.

"I have to protect you," he says. "You and Luna."

"You can't," I whisper. It hurts to say it. He swallows hard. "This is happening whether you like it or not. Everything in her letter, it's happening. The watch. Joan," I motion to the bedroom door. I wouldn't be surprised if Joan were listening to everything we say, and I'm sure Thiago's thinking the same thing. Let her listen. This concerns her too.

Thiago shakes his head, then lurches across the room. I move to shield the watch from him. Instead, he sweeps past me and into his own bedroom. I hear shuffling, things being knocked over. I start toward the bedroom after him, but he comes back out with the familiar sheet of paper in one hand and a lighter in the other.

"I'm not doing this," he says. "I've worked too hard to protect this family."

"Thiago, no…" I say, starting toward him.

He holds up the letter and flicks the wheel of the lighter. A thin tongue of flame bursts from the lighter and he holds it to the corner of the paper. The letter catches.

"Don't!" I shriek, lunging for the letter. Thiago holds it out of my reach, hard triumph on his face. I grapple for the letter with both hands, but he stretches out his other arm to hold me back. That practiced movement again. I never dreamed he'd ever use that strength against me when it really mattered.

I watch Mamá's letter burn. My heart shreds to pieces in my chest.

When the flame comes close to licking his hand, he drops the letter in the sink.

My stomach turns to lead. I step forward as he turns the faucet on. The flame hisses out, and the letter is nothing but a black smudge in the kitchen sink.

"Mamá," I whisper, my voice hoarse. I had it memorized, but the tangible paper, the dried ink from her pen, gone. The molten rage in my core bubbles up. Moisture burns my eyes, but I force the tears back in my head.

"Mamá and Papá would be ashamed of you!" I shriek at Thiago. The words rip through my throat. My nails dig into my palms. "You're a coward and a fool!" Thiago doesn't flinch. He just glares at the pile of wet ash in the sink.

I turn and stomp into the living room, yanking the watch and towel out of my jeans. "You act like we have no purpose, but we do. We all do. Me, you, Luna, Joan, all of us. If we ignore it, we'll just be unprepared when it finds us. When *he* finds us."

Thiago stands in the kitchen doorway with his arms crossed, scowling. Deep lines cut across his forehead and between his eyes. I remember how those lines first started to form when we were teenagers bouncing around from foster home to foster home. I needed his protection then, but I don't now. I'm not a child anymore.

"You've read the letter." I fight to keep my voice calm. "You know about the signs, and that they're happening. You know about the Clock Tower and the one who's looking for it, and for this," I say, holding up the watch. "I've Seen the Clock Tower, Thi. It's broken. It's slowing down, just like Mamá said, and it's our job to fix it. What happens if the clock stops? What if time stops and it's our fault because we were too afraid to do our job?"

My hands shake, and I look down at the watch. It feels real to me now that I've said it out loud. The weight of it finally hits me—the job we have to do, the role of the Keepers—and the realization that my big brother will fight me every step of the way.

Somehow, that scares me more than the idea of finding and fixing an ancient clock with a murderer on our tail. We've always been together, and I thought we always would be.

"We can't let this divide us," I say quietly. "We have to do this, and we have to do it together. I think we'll need all of our powers."

Thiago stares at me, his stony expression unreadable. Finally, he shifts his weight. "I saw my family dead on the floor once," he says, all anger gone from his voice, replaced by something heavier, colder. "I will not do it again." Slowly, he turns, strides across the kitchen, his shoes crunching on the broken glass, and disappears down the staircase.

Finally, the tears spill over. I collapse onto the couch, the watch cradled in the towel in my lap, hot tears burning trails down my cheeks.

I glance toward my bedroom and see Joan standing in the doorway, arms at her sides, looking at me with a blank expression.

I swallow the lump in my throat. "You heard that, didn't you?"

She nods. "Every word."

I look at the watch while she slowly approaches me, leaving the bedroom door open. "How's Luna?" I ask.

"Asleep. I think I got all the glass out. We should clean the cuts."

I nod, glad she's here. "Okay." I get up, leaving the watch on the couch, and lead her into the bathroom, where I find a clean washcloth and some ointment. I hope Thiago comes around, but I know him. It's like throwing a stone into a pond. The ripples will eventually calm, but the stone is still in there. He'll hold onto that stone until it becomes part of him.

Something has broken between us. A fissure that's been forming for years has finally ruptured. I think I always knew it would, but inside, I still feel the pain of the break.

It hurts.

26

Thiago

etrayal. Everything I ever feared, and it's because Gabby did exactly what I've always warned her not to do.

I'm glad for the noisy cafe to drown out my thoughts. I load the dishwasher and make a ruckus. I need to make bread so I can slam a giant wad of dough on the counter over and over again to keep from actually breaking something. That's one of the reasons I learned to make bread in the first place: so I could have something productive to do, something to punch without actually causing any damage.

Tanya, one of my employees, handles the register and the espresso machine for now. I could really use Joan down here. Gabby too, if I'm honest, but I won't ask her to come down. She's the last person I want to see right now. I can't stand the way her chin sticks out when she thinks she's right. Besides, someone needs to stay up there with Luna.

I slam the dishwasher shut. Do I even trust Gabby with Luna anymore? She was alone with her just now, and look what happened. Her own sister.

Three more people come in the front door and I pull my phone from my pocket to call Joan down. As I open my speed dial, the back door opens.

Joan slips into the kitchen, apron still tied around her waist. Her honeyed brown eyes find me immediately. Reading me. She looks from me to the customers that just came in and immediately crosses the kitchen to help Tanya, glancing at me as she passes.

The roaring anger in my gut softens a little at the sight of her, but not much. I don't want to talk. Right now, I'm just doing everything I can to avoid thinking about how Gabby was right about one thing. I look at Joan, a dark pit growing in my stomach. Whatever is happening to us, Joan's a part of it. I'm sure she heard everything we said. We weren't exactly quiet and it would be just like Joan to listen at the door. Still, she needs to know everything. She's involved in this now and deserves to know what we know, even if it isn't much.

I look around for something else to clean, to throw around, anything. According to the one working clock on the wall, the milk jugs should have been refilled twenty minutes ago, so I tear open the fridge, load my arms up with half and half, skim, and two percent, and cross to the front to refill them.

I feel Joan watching me while she makes lattes. She and Gabby probably talked. I'll definitely have to talk to her, at least to diffuse whatever Gabby told her. There's nothing to worry about. Even as I think the words, though, I know it's a lie. I can't count how many nights I've lain awake, thinking about that letter. About what mother said: the Keepers, the Clock Tower, time stopping, and whoever was seeking the watch. Whoever killed them.

I finish filling the jugs before gathering up the milk to carry around the counter and put back in the fridge, a great deal more gently than I took them out. Joan crosses behind me with the dirty dish bucket from the seating area and starts transferring dishes into the sink.

Silence hangs between us like a heavy curtain. She catches my eye before looking away. I know that look. She wants to say something, but she isn't sure what.

"How's Luna?" I ask quietly, trying to keep a lid on my anger. My voice still sounds brittle. Clipped.

"Asleep," she answers without looking at me. "Gabby's not doing so hot though."

"She should have thought of that before she touched Luna with that thing," I mutter.

"You know she didn't mean to hurt her," she says, echoing the thoughts I don't want to admit. Gabby would never purposely hurt Luna, but that doesn't change the fact that she's been sneaking around behind my back, going through my stuff, and reading the letter Mamá wrote to *me*. She's been mucking around in the mess I've always tried to protect her from and she hurt Luna as a result, whether she meant to or not.

"I should go sweep up the glass," I say, trying to change the subject.

"Gabby took care of it," Joan says flatly, almost done emptying the bucket. "And I got all the shards out."

I wince, thinking of the sparkling flecks of glass studding Luna's arms and feet. "Thank you," I said. "I should have helped."

"Someone had to take care of things down here," she says. "You needed to cool off. You still do." The bucket's empty, so she picks it up and returns it to the seating area before starting another iced mocha.

We don't speak for hours. Joan and Tanya expertly cut through the evening rush while I keep the baskets well-stocked and the dishes clean. Gabby hasn't come back down, which is fine. I check my phone every once in a while to see if she has an update about Luna, or maybe an apology. Something. For hours, not a peep.

Finally, the rush slows down. Tanya leaves for the day and I thank her before she clocks out. It's a summer weekend evening, so there's a lull right around dinnertime while normal people are out at restaurants and bars. I make us each a cup of rooibos tea to sip while we wait for customers. I think about making an extra to run up to Gabby, but I stop myself. If she wants tea, she can get it herself.

I lean against the counter in the back of the kitchen, waiting for the tea to cool enough to drink. Joan leans next to me, our hips and elbows touching.

"I heard what you two said," she says. My spine stiffens. "I'm a part of this too?"

Dammit, Gabby. My anger flares again. I chew the inside of my lip.

Joan looks over at me, eyes gentle, but serious. I glance at her briefly before turning my eyes straight ahead again.

"Tell me. If I'm involved, I deserve to know how. And why."

I sigh. She's right, but I really don't want to talk about this right now. Or ever. If I avoid it, though, I know she'll pester me until she finds out anyway, or just ask Gabby. I'd rather she hear it from me.

I cross my arms tightly over my chest, looking at the customers to make sure no one is listening. There's no way they'd be able to hear us way back here anyway over the chatter and Gabby's stupid classical music she insists on playing over the cafe speakers.

"Mamá said there'd be signs," I start, everything inside me fighting each word that comes out of my mouth. "That I'd save a life and know she was one of us." I pause to fish out my sun pendant on the chain around my neck. Joan cocks her head, then understanding dawns on her face.

"Gabby has a star, and Luna has a crescent moon…" She tips her head down to examine her bracelet, fiddling with the charms. "This is how you knew?"

I nod. "I saw your bracelet that first night, and it was like seeing us all together. The sun, the moon, the star, and…"

"A rocket?" she finished, flicking the rocket charm with her thumb.

I nod again. "If that's not a sign, I don't know what is."

Joan sighs and takes a sip of her tea. "A few months ago, I would have thought you were crazy."

I shrug. I don't blame her.

"What else did it say?"

I clear my throat. "It said I'd meet you…then time would start moving faster. And that it meant we'd have to start looking for…"

"The Clock Tower," she supplies, eyes narrowing as her mind works to put things together. She was listening upstairs.

"…and that the other who seeks it is getting closer, and they want to stop the clock." I see my mother's handwritten words in my mind, and a sharp pang of guilt punches through my gut. I burned it. The letter I used to hide under my pillow when I had nightmares, that I'd read over and over with a flashlight under my blanket during the night. It's gone, destroyed in my rage.

Joan's brow furrows as she looks away. "So…now that I've showed up, you're supposed to find this Clock Tower because someone else is looking for it too. And I heard Gabby say something about…if the clock stops, time will stop. But that doesn't make sense. A Clock Tower that keeps time running? *Time?*" She looks at me incredulously. "But time is…time doesn't work like that. It's not possible."

"And people don't See the future. Or the past." I smirk. She rolls her eyes.

"Okay, so then this other person who's looking for the clock wants to stop it, and therefore stop time," she shakes her head. "Why would someone want to stop time?"

I shrug. "I have no idea."

"And if this is so important, why haven't you looked for it before? Why wait until you're racing against someone else?"

"My parents were looking for it," I say. "They only mentioned it a few times when they thought I couldn't hear, but…I don't think the clock stays in one place. Or one time."

I can almost hear her brain shorting out as she struggles to fit this in with what she knows, what she believes in her logical world where everything is orderly and governed by scientific law.

"A Clock Tower that travels through time and space?"

I nod stiffly. "I think so."

"So it could be anywhere. Any*when*." Her forehead wrinkles and she shakes her head, trying to knock the pieces into place. "*How?*"

I shrug again. "If it's holding time together, maybe it's because time was broken. From what I heard, my guess is that whoever built that clock…they were tampering with natural law. Twisting it somehow so that there had to be something to keep things moving in the right direction. Like a pin holding pieces of fabric together. The pin comes out, and…" I uncross my arms miming something falling to the ground. "Everything falls apart."

"This makes no sense at all," Joan says, squeezing her eyes shut and rubbing her temples. "I can hear Einstein spinning in his grave…"

"Join the club," I grumble. I take another sip of tea and nudge Joan's forgotten mug toward her. It's getting cold.

"That thing Gabby had…what was it?"

My stomach roils again, my hands tightening around my warm mug. "An old pocket watch."

Her brows knit again. "A family heirloom? Had you seen it before?"

"No. I don't know where it came from."

Joan's eyes narrow into her "thinking" expression. "I saw her with a watch when we went antiquing…" she says. "But she didn't buy it. She must have gone back for it."

I grind my teeth. I knew those antique shops would lead to no good.

"Where does the watch fit in?" Joan asks.

I shake my head and take another sip of tea. "No idea."

Joan picks up her mug and holds it near her chin, looking straight ahead, eyes clouded over with thought. "As crazy and impossible as it sounds, if it's real…this is a big deal, Thiago."

I heave a sigh. Not her too.

"If this is what your parents were doing…" she says tentatively, watching me. I don't look her in the eye. "If they've left it to you, to *us*…" A drop of soothing warmth flares in the writhing pit inside my stomach. "This is big. Gabby might be right, Thiago. I know you want to protect them, but this is bigger than us."

"Why are you taking Gabby's side?" I snip.

"I'm just telling you what I think," she says evenly. "Thiago, it might be safer to do what your mother said. If she Saw the future, she Saw this coming. She warned you. I think she wanted to protect you, not put you in danger."

My shoulders tighten. I take a deep breath, reining my urge to lash out. I glance at Joan. Her eyes are stern, but still kind and gentle. She's scared too. This must be insane to her, a student of logic and law now thrown into a world where time doesn't follow the rules.

"I don't want to hurt my sisters," I say quietly. "And I don't want to hurt you. I don't know what to do. I don't know where to start."

"You feel stuck," she says.

I sip my tea again, looking straight ahead as I take a long drink. "You could say that."

Joan nods and mirrors me, sipping her tea, then turns to plunk her mug down on the counter. "If I were you, I'd start with talking to Gabby. Make up with her, and we can put our heads together. She probably knows a lot more than she's letting on. Between the four of us, we can figure this out."

That writhing knot in my gut tightens. "I'm not talking to her."

Joan rolls her eyes. "Fine, ignore her. And we'll be screwed. Look, I have a feeling this is going to be challenging enough with all of us together, but if we're divided, it'll be impossible."

The door opens and a few customers come in. Without looking at me, Joan steps forward to prepare their orders. I stay where I am, leaning against the counter. Joan doesn't look at me as she preps their iced coffees. It's like I'm not there.

Damn her. Damn Gabby. And damn me too.

I'm not ready to talk to Gabby, mostly because I know she's right. I've always known, but still I've fought it with everything I have. I've protected my sisters, shielded them from this impossible task, this mission that claimed our parents' lives, that I swore I'd never let hurt my sisters. I'd hide them from it, from who we are.

As hard as I tried to prevent this day from coming, it's finally come. I can't ignore it any longer, no matter how much I want to.

It's found us anyway.

27

Arial

I sip my tea, watching them both in the back of the kitchen from my seat in the cafe. Every few minutes, I turn the page of the book I'm pretending to read, but keep my eyes on Joan and Thiago through the false lenses of my glasses, under the rim of the straw fedora I found in a shop two doors down. I've shaved since I was last here and taken to wearing hats and glasses and doing my best to avoid the gaze of Joan or the siblings.

It's been strange to observe these siblings. Twenty years ago when I killed their parents, I didn't give the children much thought. And I haven't since. At the time, I remember the fleeting thought that perhaps I should finish them too, but I'd never killed a child. They were innocent children, as I once was, but I'd just made them orphans. Would it be kinder to kill them as I had killed their parents, or to leave them alone in the world?

I've danced with nearly every possible conundrum in my long life, pondered nearly every philosophical question ever to plague mankind, but those questions never get easier. The answers change every time. I stopped believing in answers long ago.

I knew the girls were hiding in the closet. I stood outside that closet door for a few moments with my dripping knife, almost able to hear their shallow breathing. In the end, I didn't want the blood of children on my hands, so I selfishly left them to their orphanhood.

From time to time, I wondered if I'd made the right decision. But sparing them has led me back to my watch, so perhaps it was meant to be. Perhaps I'm being rewarded for my mercy.

In my visits to the cafe, I watch them and learn. They wear name tags, so I pick up their names quickly. The sisters have visions. I'd gleaned that much from watching Luna, the silver one, in the telling way her eyes dart back and forth as if watching a film. I know that expression well, the gaze of a Seer caught in another place and time.

From watching their conversations on their lips. I discover that Luna Sees the future. In fact, she doesn't seem to See much else.

The younger one, Gabby, Sees the past, I suppose. I've watched her tending her antiques in this cafe, her eyes glazing over sometimes when she touches them.

The brother, Thiago, doesn't seem to be special in any way, aside from a bit of talent in the kitchen.

Then there's the blond girl who plays piano, Joan. I haven't heard her play since that day, but I'd give anything to hear that song again, even if hearing it feels like a gunshot wound.

Today, it's just Thiago and Joan in the kitchen. I think there was some kind of conflict, because Thiago looks like a man restraining his anger. Joan composes her features with grace. Whatever happened, it wasn't between them.

I pretend to read, slanting my eyes sideways to watch the kitchen. I can't read the entire conversation on their lips, but I catch enough.

Visions. Pocket watch. The Clock Tower. Someone else is after it.

My grip on the hot mug tightens. They know about the Clock Tower and that I'm looking for it. I'm running out of time.

I've done terrible things, sometimes for terrible reasons and sometimes for just ones, but I'm not without virtue. Patience is certainly a virtue I've cultivated over time, sharpened it to a point like a clean, precise weapon that I'm eager to use.

233

28

Joan

I stay late to help Thiago close. Leaving doesn't feel right after what happened to Luna, when everyone's so scared. When I know Thiago's scared.

After locking the front door and turning off the lights in the seating area, I cross back into the kitchen to hang my apron on the hook and sign out. Thiago cleans counters with his eyes far away, wiping the same spot with the rag over and over.

I approach him from behind and reach out to rub his back. "Are you okay?"

He straightens, tossing the rag in the basket under the counter. "I'm fine," he murmurs. He turns to face me and leans against the counter. His hands find my hips, drawing me toward him, and I step closer to wrap my arms around his shoulders, pressing my cheek to his. "I'm sorry I got you tangled up in all of this," he says.

I kiss his cheek, inhaling his scent of bread and espresso. "I'm not."

His arms tighten around me. His chest heaves as he sighs.

"Will you stay tonight?" he asks almost sheepishly, almost like he's embarrassed. Though I know his anger hasn't receded completely, I understand; he doesn't want to be alone any more than I do.

I smile, tightening my arms around him. "Of course I will."

We don't see Gabby or Luna in the silent apartment when we go upstairs. I follow him into his bedroom, reading his exhaustion in the slump of his shoulders, his shuffling feet. He turns to sit on the bed I made for him that morning, kicks off his shoes, pulls his shirt off over his head, then collapses backward onto the mattress, his arms spread out.

I slip off my sandals, then sidle up beside him, resting my head on his shoulder. His skin is warm and smooth under my cheek. "We'll figure it out," I tell him.

Eyes closed, he curls his arms around me. We lay like that for a few minutes, folded together in the dark, saying nothing. I listen to his heart beating, resting one of my hands on his chest where he covers it with one of his own.

"You know," he says, his voice husky. "I didn't ask you to stay just to get into your pants."

"Bummer," I tell him. He doesn't open his eyes, but his lips curve in a smile. "I was kind of hoping I could get into yours." I mostly meant it as a joke, but his grip tightens on my shoulder. I tilt my head up, a wicked smile on my face, and nibble his ear before he turns his head to meet my mouth.

I gently part his lips with my own and slip my tongue inside, cupping his stubbled face in my hands. Then my hands slowly slide down the sleek planes of his torso, his skin hot and smooth under my palms, and grab the waist of his jeans to pull him on top of me.

Our lovemaking is slow, silent, and brief, but much needed. We don't say it, but I think we both wanted the feeling of skin on skin to ground us, bring us back to a place that feels safe and solid when so much around us right now is hazy and unsettled. We find comfort in the now-familiar landscape of each other's bodies, and I marvel at how, even though it's only been a few months, being with him feels like coming home after a long, hard day.

Afterward, we lie on our sides, nestled together like spoons. One of his arms drapes over me, his hand gently cupping my breast. The other wraps under my waist with his hand on my bare stomach. I feel his torso expand and contract against my back as he breathes, his warm breath on the back of my neck.

"I'm glad you're here," he whispers as he dozes off. I smile to myself. I'm glad too.

***

The familiar dream finds me.

I sit at the roughly hewn table in the room with one small, square window that looks out to a sparkling night sky. The familiar bearded man sits across from me as I write in my massive book. I look down at the blurry page, struggling to understand the language I'm writing. French? Italian? I'm not sure.

The man looks up at me from beneath a sheet of wavy dark hair, his green eyes sad and afraid. Something twists in my stomach—a deep and ugly fear.

I hear something I'd never noticed before. A steady rhythm, like a massive heartbeat. The ticking of a giant clock. For the first time in this dream, I look up, and I gasp.

For as far as I can see, gigantic gears and machinery grind together with huge metal teeth, turning each other, an insane mass of movement and metal and chaos.

I'm inside a titanic clock that seems to go on forever.

My eyes fly open.

For a moment I don't realize where I am. The room slowly comes into focus as my eyes adjust to the darkness. Thiago lies next to me, sprawled on his stomach with his loose hair splayed on the pillow. I place a hand on my sternum to steady my heart slamming in my chest.

I push myself up and tip my forehead into my hands, rubbing my temples with my thumbs. Cold sweat dampens my skin and hair. A fan blows over us, sending chills over my bare skin.

I think back over the many, many times I've dreamed of the man, the book, and the small room. Have I ever looked around? Ever looked up? I don't think so. I'm sure my brain is just processing the considerable information from the day, working it into my dreams, placing the familiar dream room inside a giant clock as a way of making sense of the impossible nonsense that is my life right now.

But Thiago said I'm a part of all of this somehow. Have I always been part of it? Have I been dreaming about it all my life without even knowing it?

I carefully flip the covers over and slide off the bed, slipping back into my underwear, shorts, and a tee shirt I find on the floor—Thiago's. I tiptoe to the door and open it quietly, careful not to wake him. On the way to the kitchen, I bump into a corner of the coffee table, hissing between my teeth, pausing to listen for anyone stirring. I take a glass from the drying rack and fill it in the sink. My heart starts to pound again as I remember the dream. I'm suddenly very aware of the ticking of the clock in the living room and my heart beating along with it.

I take my glass into the living room and sit on the couch, sinking into the worn cushions. Moonlight streams into the living room, washing out all color. I feel like I'm in a black and white movie with everything around me in shadow and shades of silver and gray.

Tick. tick. tick.

The ticking of the clock unnerves me. Each tick hits me like a slight shock, a tiny jump in my chest.

I feel dizzy, nauseous. A dull pounding builds behind my eyes. I close my eyes and instead of the blank darkness of my eyelids, I see stars. Am I still sitting down? Vertigo swells in my stomach and I worry I'll throw up. I feel like I'm up high, looking down over a vast expanse of nothing with only stars above and around me. The ticking grows louder, banging on my eardrums until I can't hear anything else. The ticking of the clock pushes blood through my veins, beats in my limbs, throbs behind my eyes and in my brain. A flash of gold fades into green. I'm moving, hurtling through space. I have no body, no idea if I'm still sitting on a couch in the room above the Clockwork Cafe.

Finally, I stop. Everything has gone white; the sky, the ground far below me, the horizon. I'm aware of cold, but I don't *feel* it. Everything just looks cold, a vast expanse of snow and ice in every direction. The clock still ticks and I'm still seemingly miles above the ground. I try to look down at my feet, but I have no body. Just a tall column of black stone.

I realize I'm on the top of a massive tower with a tick-tock pounding in my brain.

The Clock Tower. I'm in it. I *am* it.

Joan. I hear my name from far away, barely a whisper through the ticking that's taken over my mind.

"Joan."

The world sways. I'm moving. I'm shaking. The whiteness around me swirls and, suddenly, I'm back on a couch in the dark living room. Someone holds me, says my name. I blink. The clock on the wall swims into view, the ticking faded to a soft *hsh hsh hsh* as the interlocking circles turn on the face.

I slump over, limp, my cheek pressed into Thiago's bare chest. He holds me close with one of his hands in my hair with his chin resting on the top of my head, repeating my name over and over, softly calling me back.

"Thiago," I breathe. His arms tighten around me.

"Can you hear me?" he asks. He sounds far away. "Are you okay?"

I groan, crash landing back into my body. "I think so."

"What happened?"

I still feel dizzy and exhausted. I just want to go back to bed. "I don't know. I got up for a glass of water, then I must have fallen asleep again…"

"A dream?" he says. "Your eyes were going nuts under your eyelids."

I moan and rub my temples again. "It was so real."

"What did you dream about?"

"The Clock Tower," I wheeze. "I was on top of it. I WAS it. It was somewhere cold, in the snow…"

An ache swells in my head and I groan, pressing my face into his chest. His skin is surprisingly cool. He wears nothing but his boxer shorts. Marks from the bedsheets criss-cross his chest and stomach.

"You looked like you were having a vision. You looked the way Gabby does when she's Seeing something."

"What does it mean?" I ask.

I feel him kiss the top of my head. "I don't know," he murmurs against my hair.

We stay quiet for a moment, but my mind whirs.

Did I have a vision? A vision of the Clock Tower?

That brings my total of strange, vision-like blackouts to three. Three. I Saw Mom with the papers and Thiago with the edible flowers. And now the Clock Tower.

I'm starting to think this isn't a coincidence.

I stay still in Thiago's arms, listening to the ticking of his parents' clock. *Tick. Tick. Tick.* The ticking builds in my ears, synchronizing with my heartbeat. It's unsettling.

And then it happens again.

An image flashes on the screen of my eyelids again. The clock on the wall, like I'm standing right in front of it.

Then, *into* it. Through the outer housing, through the gears, into the center of the clock, to something that shouldn't be there.

I gasp and open my eyes.

Thiago jerks, startled. "What is it?"

I sit up. His arms slide off me, settling to rest on my thighs. I look around the room until my gaze lands on the clock. I push myself off the couch to cross the room, swaying a little with exhaustion and disorientation, then stop in front of the clock.

"Does this open?" I ask.

"The clock?"

"Yes. Does it open?"

Thiago pauses, confused. "I *can* open it. Why?"

I try to recall what I just saw, like remembering a dream. "There's something inside it. Something we need."

I almost feel Thiago tense up behind me. Finally, I hear him shuffle into the kitchen to open a drawer. He moves to my side, reaching up to carefully lift the clock off the wall. He places it on the floor.

"Can you get the light?" he asks. I flip the switch on the wall. The light stings my eyes, and we both blink to adjust.

Thiago inserts the tip of a screwdriver into the tiny screws that hold the housing of the clock together. I hold my breath as he removes the screws one by one, then lifts the back of the housing away.

Inside, small gears turn. Fine metal teeth lock together, turning each other in time to the ticking. I kneel beside the clock and peer inside, my head almost touching Thiago's as he looks in as well.

"What the hell..." he says, reaching into the back of the clock. He carefully fishes out a long, thin object about the thickness of his thumb, slightly curved and just barely longer than his hand. It's off-white, dull, parts of it darkened with age. It looks like...

"It's a bone," I breathe. "I...I think it's human." I touch my fingers to my forearm.

Thiago drops the bone on the floor as if it burned him. It thuds dully on the carpet. "A human bone?" He looks up at me, dark eyes narrowed with disgust. "What the hell is a human bone doing in my parents' clock?"

I shake my head, mouth slightly open. "I...I don't know."

"But you knew it was there," he adds. I nod. I did know. Why? Why is this important?

"I think we need it," I tell him. "I think we need it to fix the Clock Tower." It's like listening to someone else speak, because when the words leave my mouth, I feel just as shocked as Thiago appears.

He looks down at the bone. "How?" he says.

I shrug. "I don't know," I say again. "I just...I know we need it."

I stare at the bone and realize it's covered in tiny cracks crisscrossing over the dry surface. I squint to see closer, and I realize they're not cracks.

I pick the bone off the floor and immediately regret it. Holding it feels...wrong. I've never held a human bone before, but dread roils in the pit of my stomach. Far more than I'd expect.

I examine the bone closer, fighting the rising nausea and fear. Tiny symbols cover the entire surface of the bone, lines and circles, each symbol no larger than the tip of my little finger. I turn the bone over. Toward the end is a larger symbol carved deeper into the surface. Two nested circles with a vertical line cutting through them, like a line drawn through a target.

The door to Gabby and Luna's bedroom opens. We look up to see Gabby standing in the doorway, dark hair disheveled and eyes swollen, red-ringed. She looks tiny and doll-like in an old-fashioned nightgown that hangs to her knees.

"What's going on?" she asks sleepily.

Thiago pauses, then recoils. "Gabs, I'm in my underwear out here."

She rolls her eyes and steps out of the bedroom to crouch beside us. "Like I've never seen you in your underwear." Thiago still looks uncomfortable but doesn't retort. "What's that?" she asks, looking at the bone in my hand.

"It was in the clock," Thiago tells her. "Joan…Joan knew it was there."

Gabby looks at me, her dark eyebrows knitted together. "You knew? How?"

"I don't know," I say for what feels like the eightieth time in the past ten minutes. "I just saw it."

Gabby leans in to see it closer. "Oh my god…that's a human ulna. One of the forearm bones."

Of course Gabby would know. Those three semesters of pre-nursing school are coming in handy. Then, she voices the question I've been afraid to utter, and I'm sure Thiago is thinking too.

"Whose is it?"

None of us says anything. Gabby looks at me for a second longer before looking back to the bone. She seems to think about something for a few moments, then she reaches to pick up the bone.

"What are you doing?" Thiago says.

"I want to See," she says. "If I can See its past, maybe we can figure out what it is."

"I think we've had enough visions for one day," he snaps.

"Thiago," I say quietly. "She's right." He shoots me a glare, but I stare back. So does Gabby.

I look from Gabby to Thiago. They look so alike when they're mad. Their eyes are the same color, the same almond shape. The same arch of their eyebrows, with identical twin small cuts forming between them.

Gabby shoots me a grateful look before snatching up the bone, closing her small hand around it, and shutting her eyes. Thiago and I brace ourselves, expecting Gabby's eyes to clench shut, her body to tense. Nothing happens.

"Anything?" I ask.

Her brows furrow. She opens her eyes. "No," she says. "Nothing."

Thiago's shoulders relax. Gabby looks at the bone more closely, turning it over, seeing it from all angles.

"There…there are markings all over it," she says, turning the bone. She stops when she notices the larger symbol. Her hand trembles.

"I've seen this before," she says, just above a whisper.

"You have?" I say, my heart pounding. "Where?"

Gabby's face drains of color. "On the watch." Thiago's face darkens at the mention of it, but Gabby doesn't seem to notice.

"That symbol?" I say, my stomach churning. "That symbol right there? On the watch?"

"Do you want me to go get it?" she offers.

"No," Thiago barks. Gabby's eyes dart to him, shining briefly, but she straightens and looks back at me.

"I'd like to see it," I counter.

Thiago glances up at me, a flicker of irritation in his eyes, but then he sighs. Ignoring him completely, Gabby hands the bone back to me and disappears briefly into her room. Thiago turns pale.

"Why are you siding with her?" he says in a clipped voice.

My neck grows hot. "Because we need to know."

"That thing is dangerous."

"Knowledge is power. And safety."

Gabby slips out of her bedroom, keeping the door open just a crack behind her, holding the pocket watch wrapped in a dish towel. Thiago scowls at it. Gabby carefully holds it out to me and I take it. "I have to keep it wrapped up," she explains. "If I even brush it, I See like crazy. And it's not good."

Thiago looks like he's about to say something snarky, but miraculously holds back.

I sit with the bone in one hand, the watch in the other. The tarnished brass lid bears the same symbol. I look from one to the other. Finally, I touch the surface of the watch with my thumb. Gabby flinches like she expects the watch to explode, but nothing happens. Taking that as a good sign, I pop the watch open.

Gabby scoots away just a hair, her shoulders tensing. Thiago recoils. I stare at the tiny clock face with its motionless hands, transfixed.

Once I've opened the lid, the watch starts to tick.

It's not a regular clock face, but a nest of interlocking circles that turn around each other like an astronomical clock. No numbers. The watch ticks in my hand like a tiny heart, each tick growing louder, but then I realize it's only getting louder in my head, syncing with my heartbeat. In my head, each tick grows to the volume of a gong. I shut my eyes and for a moment, see that terrible face of the Clock Tower, see that massive pillar of stone surrounded by snow.

"The watch leads to the Clock Tower," I blurt. My eyes snap open. Gabby and Thiago both stare at me, wide-eyed, faces pale as milk.

"How do you know?" Thiago asks.

"I…" I start, but I realize I don't know how I know. "It ticks in time with the tower," I start, laying out the pieces I'm sure of one by one. "It leads to it because…"

"It's made from parts of the tower," Gabby finishes.

Thiago and I slowly turn to look at her. She shifts her weight uncomfortably, the definition of a deer caught in the headlights.

"And how the hell do you know that?" Thiago growls.

"How do you think?" she snaps, color rising in her cheeks. "Because I used it to See. I actually tried to solve this."

"And that's why someone is trying to get it back," I add, connecting the dots. I look to Gabby for confirmation. She nods. Gabby's face is white, sallow gray patches appearing below her eyes. I keep the watch open, examining the face. The circles on the tiny clock twitch, inching forward around each other as the seconds drag on. Each tick rips blood through my veins, something inside me leaping with every beat of my heart, every second on the Clock Tower. It feels like being startled over and over again.

A vein throbs in Thiago's neck. "We can't keep it here."

"But we need it to find the Clock Tower," Gabby presses. "We're totally blind without it."

"Screw the Clock Tower!" he shouts.

Gabby stiffens, preparing to shout back, but I interrupt.

"We're all really tired," I offer. My head throbs. "Let's talk about this in the morning. We're not going to get anywhere tonight." Unable to bear the relentless ticking any longer, I close the lid. Suddenly, I just want to go back to sleep.

Gabby looks at me and then nods, but doesn't relax her shoulders. "Yes. I think we're all tired," she says flatly. She holds her hand out for the watch. I wrap it back in the towel and hand it to her. For a moment, it looks like Thiago wants to protest, but he says nothing, though his eyes don't leave the watch.

Without looking back, Gabby steps into her room. Before she closes the door, I see Luna's silver eyes shining in the dark as she leans off her bed to see what we're doing. My blood runs cold. Gabby says something softly to her right before she closes the door.

Thiago pauses, still looking at the bone in my hand. I don't want to hold it anymore. I don't even want to look at it. Something about it just feels wrong. I put the bone on the floor. Thiago and I say nothing while he puts the clock back together. Neither of us know what to make of this.

A bone in a clock they'd carried around for twenty years. How did it get in the clock? Did their parents put it there? Why? I see the same questions passing behind his eyes like text on a teleprompter.

Finally, Thiago picks up the bone, pausing briefly with an expression of disgust, then stands and bends down to carefully guide me to my feet. I lean on him as we amble back to his bedroom. He picks up a clean-looking tee shirt off the floor and wraps the bone in it before crossing to the dresser and tucking the little bundle into his sock drawer.

I don't know if that's the best place for it, but I can't think of a better idea. My head hurts. I just want to sleep. I want to curl up with Thiago and pretend none of this is happening. When I crawl onto the mattress, I make sure to face Thiago, keeping my back turned on that menacing bone.

His eyes meet mine in the dark, shining like two furious jewels. I reach for him, my skin hissing along the sheets, but he jerks away, then shifts and rolls onto his other side, his back facing me like a wall.

I want to touch him, but I know it will make it worse. I wish he'd hold me, but I also wish he'd see reason.

Yes, the watch is dangerous. I'll give him that. But it's the only clue we have to prevent the collapse of time…and possibly the world.

The immediate danger blinds him to the ultimate danger that threatens all of us.

I don't remember falling asleep, but I do remember that Thiago's breath was still measured. I don't know if he slept any more that night.

29

Thiago

I approach the apartment door like I have so many times before. I don't want to open it. What will I find behind it this time? My parents, dead on the floor? My childhood home burned to the ground? An endless chasm waiting to swallow me?

The edges of my vision blur with dreamy evanescence. I don't want to open the door, but I know I will. I always do. I watch my hand reach for the doorknob as if it has a mind of its own. *No, no, no, no,* my mind repeats over and over.

I turn the knob and push the door open. It feels so much heavier than it actually was in reality. It creaks on its hinges like a rusted gate. Maybe it's because I don't want the door to open. Maybe my own mind is fighting against me.

As I step into the room, the twenty-year-old wound in my chest suddenly feels fresh and new like my heart was scooped out, leaving a jagged hole in its place.

I see Luna first, on her back with a puddle of blood blooming beneath her head, staining her hair crimson. Her empty silver eyes stare at the ceiling blankly, frozen in an expression of shock. One of her hands drapes loosely over her stomach.

Gabby lies next to her, flat on her stomach with her serene face turned toward me. Her dull, brown eyes lack their usual sparkling life. Blood spreads from underneath her, creeping across the floor from an invisible wound.

My hands shake. A suffocating pressure in my chest knocks the breath from my lungs. Even in the dream, that hole aches and contracts, as raw as it was two decades ago, never healed.

I'll kill him. Whoever did this, I'll kill him.

I wanted to keep my sisters safe, and that meant keeping them hidden. Now it's too late. There's nothing left to protect. I look from Gabby to Luna, knowing I can't help them. They're gone. I know it isn't real, but I picture this scene so often. This scene haunts my waking hours as if I truly saw it with my own eyes. My sisters, taken by the same fate that took my parents. A constant reminder of what could be.

Then I notice something different. Air rushes from my lungs.

No. *No.*

In the corner of the room lies Joan, spread on her back, blood leaking from her pale, slightly parted lips. A scarlet stain spreads over her chest and puddles beneath her, but I see no wound. Her usually honey eyes are flat and gray with death. I try to say her name, but it comes out as a strained moan. *No. Not her. Don't take her.*

Everyone I care about, dead at my feet.

It hasn't happened yet. I know this is only a dream, but I know it's my fault. *My fault. My fault.* My mind repeats the phrase over and over.

I scramble to Joan's lifeless body and drop to my knees so hard my kneecaps knock on the wooden floor. I shove my arm under her shoulders and haul her into my lap, cupping a hand around the back of her head.

"Joan…" I moan again.

Her pale eyes stare right through me. She's dead weight in my arms, no sign of the warmth and life that's *her*. I was mad at her because she took Gabby's side, and now she's gone. I never told her how I felt. Now I'll never get to. Grief crushes my lungs like a vise. My chest folds in on itself as all the oxygen in the room disappears. Somehow, I'm still breathing. Somehow, I'm still alive. But she isn't.

"It's a dream," I say out loud, trying to convince myself. "It's just a dream." I know it's a dream, but at the same time I feel her cold flesh, her limp weight in my arms, and it's just as real as if I were awake.

I wish I could wake up.

My mouth drops open, but no sound comes out. My hands shake. My fingers dig into her cold skin. My entire body wants to curl up like a dead leaf and blow away. I touch my forehead to hers, the tips of our noses meeting. My eyelashes brush against her eyebrow.

Joan is gone.

I plant a kiss to her marble-cold forehead, then look down to see blood staining my own clothes rusty red. So much blood. My mind doesn't want to connect it with her, that it's her blood, her life seeping out of her. I run a finger over her cheekbone, leaving a red streak.

Then her pupils snap to mine. Her pale lips part.

"Thiago," she rasps. My heart stops. "You can't run from it."

I freeze, still holding her stiff torso. I open my mouth to speak, but nothing comes out.

"You can't avoid it," she rasps. She speaks, but she's not alive. It's not her voice. The words are wind blowing through winter trees.

What does she mean? That I can't avoid this future? That I can't avoid their deaths? Or that I can't avoid what we are, our powers, and our parents' task?

My muddled mind struggles to form these questions into words, but I feel a tug somewhere in my head. I'm waking up.

Joan's eyes slide closed, and suddenly I'm lying in my bed, my heart thrashing in my chest. I gasp, sitting up to scan my bedroom. Everything looks exactly as it should, from my jeans tossed on the floor to the pictures on the wall.

Joan sleeps soundly beside me. Her skin is rosy and her lips are pink, not deathly white. Alive. Wonderfully alive and warm and breathing.

I wait for my heart to slow before rolling toward her and wrapping an arm around her shoulders to pull her closer. Her hand slides over my ribs and around to my back as her head tucks under my chin, tickling my neck with her short hair. Her shoulders expand as she breathes. Her exhales warm my chest. It's wonderful to feel her breathe.

Hours ago, I was furious that Joan sided with Gabby, but now I can't imagine being mad at her for anything.

Memories of a few hours ago rise to the surface of my hazy mind. The clock. The bone. The watch. Terror washes away any trace of anger. My sisters are in danger, just because of who they are. Because of their abilities and who our parents were. And Joan...Joan is in danger because she's with us. Some part of me knows that I'm in danger as well, but that hardly concerns me. I'm not worried about myself. I need to protect them, but I don't know if I can.

I close my eyes and breathe in the honey and rose scent of Joan's hair. I can't lose her. I can't lose Gabby or Luna either. In the dream, what did Joan—or the thing that looked like Joan—mean when she said I couldn't run away? Run away from our task or toward it? Which option saves the people I love, and which one will get them killed?

Or are we dead either way?

I've never felt so trapped. Not when we were bouncing around foster homes, struggling to stay together, not when I came home to find my parents dead on the kitchen floor. As it often does, my mother's letter echoes in my mind through the haze of fear and dread. *Trust your sisters. Listen to them.* I hear the words in my mother's soft, musical voice. So much like Gabby's voice. Maybe like Luna's voice if she had one.

Trust them.

The girls who can See the past, See the future, and who can understand the present. They're all braver than I am, and that makes them reckless.

They want to save the world, but I only want to save them.

I'm sorry, Mamá. I can't. I can't allow them to pursue this path. It'll kill us all. I saw what the watch did to Luna. Now that I know someone is looking for it, I can't let it stay in this house.

Carefully, I release Joan and slip out of the bed, pausing to pull on a pair of jeans. I'm going to find that watch and end this. It's somewhere in Gabby's room, but I'll find it.

I pad quietly to the door to avoid waking Joan—she needs sleep and I definitely don't need her getting in the way—and as I reach for the door, my heart almost jumps out of my chest when I hear it.

Slam. Slam. Slam.

I yank the door open and scramble into the living room. Pale blue light streams through the window from the nearing dawn, illuminating Luna kneeling on the floor, silver hair falling in her face and white-knuckled hands clutching a hammer.

Gears and metal shards litter the floor around her.

Behind me, Gabby's door flies open.

"Luna!" she gasps. "Where's Luna—" she staggers into the living room and freezes, taking in the wreckage before her. "Oh," she breathes, "Luna, what have you done?"

I hear scrambling footfalls and Joan flies into the room. "What happened?" she pants before her eyes fall on Luna.

The three of us stand like statues, realizing what we're looking at.

"The watch…" says Joan, breathless. "She destroyed it."

30

Gabby

lam. Slam. Slam.
 My eyes bolt open.
 My heart thrashes in my chest when I jolt awake to the sound of pounding. I jerk upright in bed, suddenly alert, and scan my bedroom.

Luna's bed is empty. My nightstand drawer is open.

The watch is gone.

A few moments later, we all stand in the living room around Luna and the scattered pieces of the watch, our only connection to the Clock Tower we must somehow fix to prevent time itself from stopping.

I kneel beside her, gazing helplessly at the broken clockwork.

There's no fixing it. Half the gears are snapped in two. The glass disc that shielded the face is now a shining pile of shards. I pick up a broken gear, wondering if the pieces are enough to help me See, but doubting it. Nothing happens. Something about the way the watch worked helped me See. As I feared, it was more than the sum of its parts.

Luna's hands shake. Tears roll down her face behind her veil of hair. I reach out to grip the hammer, then pry her fingers off the handle, one by one.

This is my fault. I never should have used Luna to See the watch's future. Of course she's afraid of it. Of course she'd want to destroy it.

Thiago moves to pick a throw blanket off the couch and drapes it around Luna's shaking shoulders. He coaxes her to her feet and guides her to the couch. She pulls the blanket tighter around her, curling into a ball on the couch with her face hidden. Is she ashamed? Scared? I can usually tell what Luna's feeling, but now, she's unreadable, even for me.

"The watch…" I say, to no one in particular. "It's gone…we needed it."

I look at my sister, huddled under the blanket. She must have seen me put it back last night when we went back to bed. I thought she was asleep. More than a few times, I've wondered if Luna Sees more of the present than she lets on. Now, I'm starting to think that's true.

I look to Thiago, then to Joan. Joan's mouth drops open in shock, but Thiago tries to hide a small smirk. I bite the inside of my lip. Of course. He's glad the watch is gone.

Joan sinks to her knees, staring blankly at the ruined gears.

I can't take the silence anymore. "So what do we do now?" I say.

"We do nothing," Thiago says. "It's gone. It's over."

"But what about the Clock Tower?" I press. "It's slowing down, and we can't just let time stop. It's our responsibility."

"Why?" Thiago shoots back. "Why is it our problem? Because Mamá and Papá said so?"

"Because we're Keepers! We have this power, and we have to use it! We're the only ones who can!"

"We're screwed," Joan says flatly. "We don't know when and where the Clock Tower will be. It could be on Neptune forty thousand years ago. Or thousands of light years away a million years in the future."

"But we know it will be on Earth soon, now," I say. "Or maybe it is already. Mamá's letter said so."

"She said it would be close. She didn't say where," Thiago sighs. "And let's say for a moment that we do decide to find this Clock Tower. We're just people. The planet's still a big place for us. We'd never find it before it's somewhere and somewhen else again."

"There has to be a way to find it," I insist.

"Why?" Thiago says sharply, looking up at me. "This isn't a fairytale. It's not a movie. Things don't have to turn out right just because we want them to. There's no way in hell we can find a damn tower that will be *somewhere* on the planet for…a few months maybe? Weeks? Even less?"

"Well we won't find it if we sit around lamenting about how impossible it is," I snap back. "The only way we'll have a chance is if we quit whining for a minute and actually think."

Thiago glares. "Okay, Pollyanna, how? And assuming we could find it, how in the hell would we fix it?"

"There has to be some way to track it down. The watch can't be the only thing."

"The bone, maybe?" Joan offers. "It has the same symbol as the watch. It might be connected to the Clock Tower too." She doesn't look convinced. "But I don't know how that would work. Do we play 'spin the bottle' with it and go where it points?"

I sigh and put my head in my hands. "Why, Luna?" I ask. I don't expect an answer, especially not from my sister. "Why would you destroy the one clue we have?"

A silent, uncomfortable moment. Then Joan speaks.

"Because she knows where the Clock Tower will be."

Thiago and I both look at Joan. Even Luna tenses ever so slightly.

"What?" says Thiago.

"She Saw it," Joan says, eyes wide in realization. "In her vision, I think she Saw the Clock Tower. She probably knows someone else is looking for it too."

"We're not using Luna to find the Clock Tower," Thiago snaps. "Absolutely not."

"That's not what I'm saying," Joan says calmly, though I know she's thinking the same thing I am: we probably don't have a choice. "I'm just saying that this is why she smashed the watch." Joan looks from Luna, to Thiago, to me. When her eyes meet mine, I know she agrees. Luna is our best hope.

As if she read my mind, Luna looks up at me. Really looks at me, her silver eyes focused on mine. It's like the world is standing still. It only happens for a moment, but suddenly it's clear.

Luna Saw it. She knows exactly where the Clock Tower will be, and then she destroyed the watch.

She's the only one who knows, and now she's made sure it will stay that way.

31

Arial

I feel it like a hammer to my sternum. Like a heart attack.

Then emptiness. Stillness. Like a part of me has disappeared. Pavement scratches my face. I only realize I've collapsed to the filthy ground of the deserted alley I'd slipped into for a smoke when the world is suddenly turned on its side. I can't move or breathe. My half-smoked cigarette smolders just a few centimeters from my face.

For just a moment, I think I'm dying. I smile and close my eyes, waiting for death to carry me away after all these centuries. But the pain sets in. My lungs scream for air and I suck in a ragged breath.

The watch has been destroyed. That gaping hole inside of me fills with oozing, existential panic. Thick, roiling fear heats into animal rage.

Then the wave hits. The power encased in the watch floods through my veins like a shot of adrenaline, rushing back to me after all these years. I gasp for air as blood rushes to my head and my heart races so fast I expect it to explode. Power tingles in my fingers, in my feet, along my scalp and down my spine.

All this in a matter of seconds.

The wave subsides. My heart slows. I forgot what this power felt like after centuries without it. The power to *travel*, to open a fissure, a Passage in space, and step through to somewhere else entirely. I sacrificed that power to make the watch, and now I feel more complete than I have in several lifetimes.

But the watch. The Clock Tower. That old, niggling doubt about connecting the Clock Tower to something so fragile flickers at the back of my mind. When I made the watch with the few pieces I had from the clock, I was half-mad with grief. I needed something small, easy to hide. I knew it was risky.

Now my connection to the Clock Tower is gone.

I roll onto my back to look at the column of hazy blue sky between the roofs of the buildings around me. My chest heaves with ragged breathing that gradually slows as I force my mind back into the safe corral of thought that allows me to maintain most of my sanity decade after decade.

Think.

My pulse settles back into its usual rhythm. The awful hollow inside me contracts back into its usual size. Finally, I haul myself into a sitting position.

There's another way.

I think of what I know about where the watch was, the cafe, the siblings, about who probably destroyed it, and why. The pieces click together neatly.

And now that I can travel…that changes everything.

I lumber to my feet and brush dust off my jacket. I should test the power, just to make sure. It's been so long. My hand twitches, and I realize I'm afraid. What if it doesn't work? What if the power is weak from decades upon decades of stagnation? Magic has a shelf life. It can't lie dormant for years without degrading like a battery.

I take a breath and lift my hand. The power shakes loose and slugs down my arm and into my fingers where it tingles like pins and needles. Slower than I remember, but at least it's working. I focus my mind on my destination, glad I investigated so thoroughly that I can easily picture it in my mind. I raise my hand to the height of my head and carefully pierce space to draw a Passage, a glowing, golden vertical line in midair.

My breath stops in my chest. A smile breaks across my face. It worked.

Unconsciously, I reach into my jacket to brush *Amica's* hilt and feel its reassuring weight. My boot crushes the remains of my cigarette as I reach into the line I've just drawn, part space like a curtain, and step through.

I can still find the Clock Tower. Just a slight change of plan, that's all.

I'll get the answer out of her, one way or the other.

***

I step from one alley to another and appear behind the Clockwork Cafe where, thankfully, no one has chosen that moment to take out the garbage and slip outside for an intimate moment. I grind my teeth at the thought of Joan and Thiago together, but push it from my mind. I have not a moment to waste.

I light another cigarette and casually stroll out of the alley and onto the street to glance through the window of the cafe. Thiago is distracted, filling pastry baskets with bread and bagels. Gabby helps customers along with another employee I've seen a few times. I don't see Luna, but she won't be far from her siblings. I wager that she's in the upstairs apartment. I also don't see Joan. Could she be upstairs with Luna? Possibly, but I can't be fussy. I have to act now.

I slip back into the alley. The door to the upstairs flat isn't even locked. Clutching *Amica* in my right hand, I carefully climb the stairs, stepping close to the wall to minimize the sound of my footsteps. No sense being seen or heard, but who's to say she doesn't already know

I'm coming?

I reach the top of the stairs and turn into a small, slightly cluttered kitchen. A round table with four chairs nearly fills the room. Four chairs. A family. I wonder where Joan sits when she eats with them.

Focus.

The living room is empty as well. A sleeping tabby cat curls on the couch. The cat raises his head and stares at me with nervous green eyes. He carefully gets up, ears turned backward and eyes wide, then jumps off the couch and runs behind it.

A narrow hallway off the living room leads to a closed door on each side and an open door to a bathroom at the end. I silently plant one foot in front of the other near the wall, testing my weight on each floorboard before committing to it entirely.

I hold still and listen. I know she's here, but I don't hear her. Which door?

I try the door on the left. I turn the knob silently and push it open.

Empty. And it's clearly not a female's room. I start to close the door, but my eyes fall on a pair of women's sandals poking out from under the bed. Joan's. Under his bed. My gut contracts, but I set my jaw and close the door.

That only leaves the door on the right. I lean in closer and hear the sound of breathing.

I open the door. Luna sits on a bed, staring at nothing. Then her head turns to me. Her eerie eyes are wide and terrified. Or are they? It's like she's not looking at me. Her pupils dart from side to side like she's watching a film.

"I'm so sorry, darling, but we need to talk."

I grab her arm. She doesn't make a sound. Doesn't fight back. This is going to be much easier than I expected.

I then summon the power again. It swells in me, untethered now that the watch is destroyed. Then, I raise a hand to open a Passage in time and space. I move my hand downward to draw a vertical, golden line through the air, like parting a curtain to another place entirely.

Then I hear a thud of wood on flesh. Pain explodes in my shoulder.

My mistake. I let myself get distracted.

Without letting go of the girl, I spin around just in time to see the end of a wooden baseball bat; I lean back just before it collides with my face.

Thiago's dark eyes blaze with fury and terror. The end of the bat flies back over his shoulder as he winds up to swing again.

Keeping a hold on Luna, I slip *Amica* from my coat in a practiced motion and swipe at his stomach. Surprisingly, he jerks back just in time, the blade barely catching his shirt, slicing cloth instead of skin.

I didn't expect his reflexes to be so quick, but he's off balance. I briefly release Luna to grab the bat as he brings it forward and efficiently jerk it out of his grasp. My knuckles whiten as I grip the cold wood and swing the handle back against his face. I hear something break as a stream of blood shoots from his nose.

He grunts and swings a fist that I dodge easily. The punch is hurried, unpracticed, but there's power behind it. For a moment, I admire his determination, even though it won't help him or his sister.

I think of Joan's sandals under his bed. Hot rage sizzles in my veins. I adjust my grip on *Amica,* contemplating whether I should slice his throat or plunge the blade into his gut.

In the two seconds since I dropped her, Luna scrambles back to her feet and lunges at me. Her hand closes on my ear and twists. Her wide silver eyes flick between me and her brother. My ear stings, but with a quick knock to her face with my elbow, she releases it. Her head jerks back in shock, but I've done no damage. She looks at Thiago, fear shining in her eyes.

He swings again. This time I grab his outstretched arm. His eyes widen as I twist the arm over itself. Bones pop as his shoulder dislocates. Thiago yells through gritted teeth and drops to his knees reflexively. For good measure, I aim a quick kick at his stomach. He grunts in pain and falls onto the floor, clutching his stomach with his good arm.

Someone will have heard him, and I don't want any more visitors. I consider slicing his throat and leaving him to bleed out on the floor like a pig, but I look at his sister's face and get a better idea.

"Time to go," I say hoarsely. With *Amica* still in my hand, I grab Luna's arm and shove her through the Passage, watching her stumble into the thin slice of light and disappear.

"No!" Thiago struggles to stand. Sweat shines on his arms and forehead. Color drains from his skin as he pants and groans in pain.

I reach down to grip his throat, slippery with sweat and blood. Gasping for air, he only struggles slightly as I drag him to his feet. The fingers of his good hand rake against my grip while his dislocated arm hangs limply at his side. I draw him closer until I can smell his sweat and the sharp tang of his fear.

"You know, you remind me of someone. Someone I hate," I tell him calmly. His brow wrinkles, but his eyes glitter with hatred in his bloody face, never leaving me, glaring up like shards of dark glass.

In his face, I see the ghost of his parents. He didn't see me that day, and I didn't see him. But he knows who I am. "Don't worry, I'll allow you to join your sister. We aren't finished yet."

There's no fear in his eyes. Just pained, simmering rage.

He doesn't protest as I drag him through the Passage, letting it seal behind us.

32

Joan

After my shift, I need to clear my head, go somewhere else to think and get answers.

I don't know what to do about the watch or the Clock Tower. None of us do. I'm positive Luna knows where the Clock Tower will be, but I wouldn't even know how to ask her, or if she could tell us. Besides, Thiago would put a stop to it immediately, especially after her vision yesterday.

So many questions in my head, but I think I might know where to find the answer to one of them.

I find the business card Marlene, the mother of the driver who almost splattered me all over the sidewalk, gave me when we met several months ago, and get on a bus. It's not far, just another part of Back Bay, but farther than I'd care to walk in the late summer heat.

I get off at my stop and walk down the shady street, scanning the metal number plates on the houses until I find the right one. It's painted a sunny yellow with white trim, two stories with a spacious porch and a small yard bursting with flowers.

When I see it, I take a deep breath. I need answers. I need to confirm what I've been suspecting for weeks now, but I'm afraid to hear it.

I walk up the path to the porch, climb the stone steps, and reach out and knock three times on the ornate wooden door before I can chicken out. A warm, ocean-scented breeze blows, rustling the spider plants in their pots. Wind chimes tinkle together, a set of delicate metal ones and a chunkier set of bamboo chimes that plunk together in a two-toned song.

I hear approaching footsteps and see a flutter of movement behind the glass inserts in the door. The knob clicks and the door swings open.

Marlene opens the door, dressed in an emerald green wrap dress with dangling bead earrings. Her glossy dark hair is twisted into a knot on top of her head. She reminds me of a geisha, unspeakably elegant, but her dark eyes look flat and tired.

"Hello," she says with a small smile. Her rich voice is slightly jagged, as if she hadn't slept much the night before. "Joan, isn't it?"

I nod. "Sorry to drop in on you, but I wanted to ask you a few things. About your son."

I expect the serene smile to fade, but it doesn't. She just blinks slowly and gives a tiny nod. "Come on in," she says, stepping back from the doorway and inviting me in with a sweep of her hand.

I nod my thanks and step inside. The house is warm, but not uncomfortable. The same breeze that swept across the porch moves through the front of the house from an open window. The walls are cream-colored with dark wood accents. A sitting room and an airy kitchen flank the entryway. A balding man in his fifties sits at the kitchen table, leaning over a newspaper spread in front of him and a steaming mug of tea in his hand.

"This is my husband, Everett," Marlene says. "Everett, this is Joan. From…the accident."

The man slowly turns his head. Three deep lines cut across his forehead. A shadow of stubble covers his pale chin and cheeks. His light blue eyes look empty, skin gray. He says nothing, but turns back to his paper.

Marlene, unfazed, directs me into the sitting room. "Sit down," she says politely.

I choose the maroon armchair, and she sinks onto the green loveseat directly across the coffee table from me, as if she's glad to sit down, like standing is too much with the gravity of her grief.

A pang of guilt jolts my stomach. I look from Marlene's beautiful, tired face to Everett hunching over his tea and newspaper. Two different people, grieving differently. The accident wasn't my fault, but I can't help but feel guilty. I walked away from that crash. Their son didn't. I wonder if Marlene's thinking the same thing.

A fat book lies on the coffee table facedown, with a tasseled bookmark hanging out the top about halfway through. Loaded bookshelves line the walls. The rows of books are broken up with the occasional horizontal stack, and some are even stacked on top of the neat rows. Somehow, it looks organized and neat, not a bit messy.

I shift my weight awkwardly. "I'm sorry again about your son."

Marlene looks at her toes in her leather sandals. "Thank you," she says quietly. "My husband is struggling." Her eyes flick toward the kitchen. I hear the sharp plunk of ceramic on wood. "I have to let him grieve in his own time."

"Aren't you?" I ask before I can stop myself. "I mean, wouldn't anyone struggle?"

She looks from the window to me. "I miss my son," she says. "I grieve for him, of course. But struggling? No. I'm not struggling."

I'm not sure what to say to that. She smiles, reading my confusion on my face.

"I don't believe he's really gone," she says, smiling. "I don't believe anyone is ever really gone. They're just somewhere else, behind a curtain where we can't see or hear them, waiting for us to join them.

This isn't good-bye; it's just a brief separation."

"Your husband doesn't think so?"

"No, he doesn't. But he's entitled to his beliefs, and so am I."

We sit in silence for a moment while this sinks in. I think I may have dropped in on a very strange woman. But I hang around with strange people these days.

"Anyway," I say, thinking of the best way to edge into my questions. "I wanted to talk about him, your son. Jason…"

"Jeremy," Marlene corrects me.

"Jeremy, sorry." My cheeks flush. "You told me he wasn't supposed to be driving."

Marlene crosses her legs and threads her fingers together over her knee. "He wasn't. He stole my husband's car that night. We still don't know why. He didn't say anything to either of us before he left. We didn't even realize he was gone until I went upstairs to check on him and saw his empty bed. Then Everett noticed the car was missing."

"Did he not have a license?"

"Not anymore. His license was revoked after his third DUI. He could have tried to get it back, but we all thought it best—safer for everyone—if he stopped driving altogether. She leans forward on her elbows. For the first time, her eyes sparkle. "You see, Jeremy was special. Psychic. Sometimes he Saw things, which of course would completely take his attention away from what he was doing. Naturally, we decided driving was a bad idea."

"Psychic?" I repeat.

"Yes," she says. "I know it sounds strange. Not many people believe in things they can't prove, but he was. He knew what was happening in other places, even if he'd never been there."

Visions. The fine hairs on my arms stand at attention.

"My mother had the gift too. Jeremy drank to keep the visions away, because sometimes he Saw horrible things. His abilities scared him…"

The scrape of wood on wood and three hard stomps. Everett appears in the doorway of the sitting room, his skin flushed red as he glares at his wife. A vein throbs in his forehead. "You shut up about that crap," he spits.

I tense in my chair, but Marlene appears relaxed and serene as ever.

"You hear me? I don't want to hear any of that psychic bullshit." His eyes are two burning-hot coals, glowing with pain and anger. They switch their focus from Marlene to me. I meet his gaze, but I wonder if I should look away. There's so much pain behind his eyes. "Jeremy had epilepsy," he says, his voice ringing with grief. "Since he was a child. Don't let her tell you otherwise."

"Medication, of course, was useless," Marlene continues. "Psychic abilities won't be suppressed by such measures…"

"He wasn't psychic!" Everett roars. "He stole the Mercedes, had a seizure, and got himself killed, and almost took this girl with him." He points at me, but he looks at his wife. She gazes back at him, completely unruffled.

"You're welcome to sit and talk with us if you'd like," she tells him gently. "I'm giving Joan my view of things because she asked, and you're welcome to do the same."

I feel like I've gotten a good idea of his view of things already, but I say nothing.

Everett presses his lips together and turns to wrench open the front door and slams it behind him. Through the window, Marlene watches him descend the front steps and start down the sidewalk, hands stuffed in his jeans pockets.

"As I was saying," Marlene continues, eyes turned down, "My husband is struggling."

"I don't blame him," I say. "I would be too."

"You don't believe in anything after this life, do you?"

I open my mouth to respond, but then close it. Not long ago, I would have responded "of course not" without hesitation. Now I'm not so sure. My worldview has been turned on its head in the space of a few months. If people can See the past, present, and future, what else is possible?

I wonder something though. "You said your mother also had visions. Where is she now?" I ask Marlene, anticipating the answer.

Marlene smiles. "She too has passed through the veil. Twenty years ago next month."

Goose bumps break out over my arms and legs. "When your mother died, was Jeremy with her?"

For the first time, Marlene looks surprised. Her eyes widen and don't quite settle back into her calm smile. "Yes," she says breathily. "Yes…he was." She turns her head to the side in a puzzled expression. "How did you know?"

"Just curious," I mumble.

She doesn't look convinced. My stomach flip-flops and I suddenly feel ill.

"And did…" I continue. "Did his abilities develop after that? After she died?"

Marlene studies me suspiciously. I force myself to sit up straight, to not shrink beneath her gaze. "I've never thought about that before…" she says slowly, eyes like obsidian. "But yes, come to think of it. I don't think he ever showed signs of psychic abilities before my mother passed."

The powers are passed through death.

I think I know what's happening to me now, why I've been having strange visions and intuitions.

Marlene looks at her open palms in her lap. For a moment, her eyes shine, but no tears fall. Two thin lines frame her mouth, but the rest of her face remains smooth. She must be in her early fifties, but she could easily pass for a woman much younger if she didn't project an air of maturity, of knowing. The word *ageless* comes to my mind.

"I miss my son very much," she says finally, without looking up. For the first time, her voice shakes. "But I take comfort in knowing that he's at peace now. But I'm still here. Without him."

I don't know what to say, either in confirmation or contrast. I have no idea where her son is. I've never believed in anything after death, anything I can't prove for sure. Lately, I'm not sure what I believe, but I see a woman clinging to her hope to shield herself from the pain of loss. I can understand that, and I will not take it from her. She could be right. She could be wrong. Either way, it doesn't matter.

"I'm sorry," I say. I mean it. "I can't imagine how difficult this is for you."

Marlene nods and looks up, out the window, down the street where Everett disappeared. She sniffs once, blinks, and her shoulders settle down away from her ears again as she regains her composure.

"I should be going," I say before standing. "Thank you for answering my questions."

"Any time, dear," Marlene says.

She rises from the couch and I follow her back into the entryway. She opens the front door for me and I step onto the porch. It's gotten hotter in the short time I've been inside.

"Thanks again."

Marlene smiles tightly, nods, and closes the door. It clicks shut louder than I expected.

I turn back to the street. A breeze blows, washing the scent of flowers and river over me. Gears spin in my mind. Connections form. Before the picture comes into full view, my phone vibrates in my pocket.

The last thing I want to do right now is talk to anyone else, but a jolt of fear knifes through my stomach when I feel the phone. Something's wrong. I know it. I hope I'm wrong, but my intuition is never wrong these days.

I slip the phone out of my pocket. Gabby's name flashes desperately on the screen. My heart drops.

"What's wrong?" I say immediately when I answer.

"Luna and Thiago…" she says, her voice tight with panic. "They're gone."

"Gone?"

"Our room is trashed, there's blood…I don't know how it happened. I was downstairs…I think someone took them. "

Dread burns in my stomach. My legs feel like lead.

"I'll be there in fifteen minutes. Call me if you find anything else." I end the call. There's no time to take the bus. I'll have to run.

I fly down Marlene's steps and take off sprinting in the direction of the cafe, my flip-flops snapping on the pavement.

I know what's happening to me now, and I'm about to put it to the test.

It might be the only thing that can save them.

33

Joan

I tear down the sidewalk, drenched in sweat with my heart racing wildly, both knees bloody from tripping twice over my flip-flops. My feet and knees shriek in pain. My lungs are full of razor blades, but I don't stop. I dart into the alley around the backside of the building and rip open the door to the apartment. My feet pound on the stairs as I take them two at a time.

Finally, I pause in the kitchen. The apartment feels wrong. Violated. Like someone else was there, and worse, like something's missing.

I lunge through the kitchen and into the hall. The door to Gabby and Luna's room stands open. My racing heart suddenly stops.

The covers are ripped off Luna's bed. The lamp on Gabby's nightstand lies in two pieces on the floor. The books that were stacked on top are sprawled over the floor, pages splayed and bent.

Gabby kneels in the middle of the wreckage, face pale and eyes squeezed shut, clutching a baseball bat in her lap with white knuckles.

"I can't See anything," she says in a high, pinched voice without opening her eyes. Her shoulders shake. Her grip on the bat tightens. "It hasn't settled in yet."

My eyes fall to a puddle of blood on the floor near the foot of Luna's bed. My muscles lock up.

The same power inside me that knew Gabby's phone call meant bad news knows this: it's Thiago's blood. I take in a rattling breath. Wherever he is, he's hurt. I don't allow myself to consider the possibility that he's dead.

Gabby curses and throws the bat to the floor with a thud. She shoots to her feet and cups her hands over her mouth and nose as she takes a deep breath. "I can't See anything," she says again. "Nothing. But I think whoever took them left from this room."

I pause, then understanding dawns on me.

There's only one way in and out of this apartment, and there was no blood in the kitchen or living room. None on the stairs. Only in here. Nothing outside the bedroom was disturbed.

I glance to the window above Gabby's bed just to make sure. Shut and locked from the inside, and no blood on the bed.

"How could they leave from this room?" I demand. "Did they just… disappear into thin air?"

Gabby drops her hands and looks at me, eyes glinting like volcanic glass. Her mouth sets in a thin line. "After everything you've learned, is that really so far-fetched?"

I swear under my breath. "But that doesn't help us. They could be anywhere." I want to beat the walls in fury, throw things through the window, and scream until my throat shreds, but that won't help us find Thiago and Luna. I take a deep breath, close my eyes, force myself to think logically. When I open my eyes, my gaze slides back to that puddle of blood on the floor.

"You can't See them," I breathe, "but maybe I can."

Gabby pauses, turning to look at me. "See them?" she asks. "Like…a vision?"

I reach out and touch the shining blood on the floor, then jerk my hand away. It's still warm. The coppery smell fills my nose.

"Gabby, I've been having visions…of the present."

Gabby freezes. All sound is sucked out of the room. "What?"

My skin chills. That's the first time I've said it out loud, that I've actually admitted my suspicions even to myself.

"It's been happening for a while. I'll have a daydream or something, or what seems like a daydream, but it's real. I Saw Thiago adding flowers to muffins right before I went downstairs the other day, and that's exactly what he was doing. Last night, I Saw the Clock Tower, where it is now. I Saw inside your parents' clock, and I knew something was inside. I was right. We found that bone."

Gabby's brow furrows as she processes.

"And when you called, I knew something was wrong. I can See the present, and I *know* the present."

Gabby looks at me like I've grown an extra head. "We always thought Thiago had the power of the present," she says. "But he doesn't have visions. He can't See anything past his big nose. I mean, he's intuitive. He can read people. He always knows when something's wrong or when we're in danger, but he's never had visions." Her dark eyes zero in on mine. "It's you? Has it always been you?"

I shake my head. "Just since I met you three."

"But the powers are passed through death. Someone would have had to die around you to pass the power on…" Her mouth drops open as she puts it together. "The driver!" She exclaims. "He died when he almost hit you. Do you think you got the power from him?"

I nod. "I just visited his mother. Turns out he was psychic, or at least she thought he was. He had visions of the present, just like his grandmother did. He was with her when she died, so he must have gotten the power from her. These powers get passed down and down from one person to another. Who knows where they started?"

"Oh my god," Gabby breathes. "No wonder Luna Saw you in our futures. No wonder Mamá wrote about you. You really are one of us."

Luna Saw me in their future? I take a short breath to marvel at that statement, but I shake my head.

I need to find Thiago and Luna. I know I have the power, but I've never felt more powerless. When she texted me, I hadn't had a plan. I just showed up and assumed I'd know what to do once I got here. Now that I'm here, I have no idea.

"So how does your power work?" Gabby asks, her eyes wild. "Do you have to touch objects like I do?"

My stomach turns. "I don't know…it just happens randomly. Mostly when I'm half asleep."

Gabby swears again. "Well, we don't have time for a nap. My brother and sister are in danger. You've got to get a handle on it, and you've got to do it *now*." Her voice takes on a tone of command I've never heard before, but something in it grounds me.

Figure it out, Joan.

I start brushing random objects with my fingers, pinching my eyes shut and hoping for something, anything.

"I have an idea," Gabby says. She grabs my wrist and pulls me across the hall into Thiago's room. "Try in here."

I don't understand. "What, should I just grab his dirty socks and sniff him out?"

"No stupid, think about him," Gabby growls. "If you have that mental connection with him, an emotional one, maybe you can See where he is."

I stare at her blankly.

She grabs my shoulders and looks me dead in the eye. I'm at least six inches taller than her, but she fixes me to the spot.

"Listen to me," she says very seriously. I can see the white all the way around her irises. "Visions are tied to emotions, from what I can tell. I pick up on the emotional signature left on an object. That's why I can only See from certain things. They must have been involved in an emotional event. I think Luna's emotions trigger her visions and vice-versa. So you just need to find that tether to whatever you're trying to See. If you have an emotional connection to someone or something, you might be able to find that and See them."

I nod, starting to understand. "Okay."

I sit on the bed and take a deep breath to slow my racing heart. I woke up here this morning. Everything was fine. A little weird maybe, stressful, trying to solve this issue of the Clock Tower, but that seems like a million years ago. Thiago and Luna were safe. Thiago was here, waking up next to me.

Thiago. He's always so warm when he sleeps. I picture him as he was this morning, sprawled on his back, long, dark eyelashes grazing the tops of his cheeks. How he always smells like freshly baked bread, herbs, and espresso. And every morning I think that despite everything, all the weirdness I've gotten sucked into, I'm always glad to wake up next to him.

I close my eyes, wonder if I'm supposed to, and open them again.

This is stupid. That freak could be torturing them right now and I'm here trying to find them with my feelings.

Gabby sighs. "Joan, do you love my brother?" she asks frankly.

I say nothing. Do I? Through the swirling fear and dread twisting in my stomach, something warm glows, like a drop of sunshine in a raging storm. I think of Thiago again, and the warm spot grows, flares brighter.

"Joan, get over it," Gabby snaps. "I know you do, but I want you to say it. Feel it. Connect with how you feel when you're with him. Say it."

I breathe deeply through my nose and let my eyes relax. It's not that I haven't thought about this before, it's just been so distracting with everything going on…and I tend to steer my thoughts away from this whenever the feeling swells inside of me.

"I love him," I say, finally. "I love Thiago."

Love is scary. Love is vulnerable. Love is illogical. But now that I say the words out loud, I know it's true.

"Good," Gabby says. "Think about him, and let it come."

My heart slams in my chest, but I breathe deeply. I remember that day eating ice cream by the river. Brushing against him in the cafe kitchen. Playing the painted piano for him late at night. That first time under the stars near the lighthouse. Blazing summer nights with him in this bed, making love or talking, or both, until we couldn't stay awake anymore.

Then I See him, like I'm looking through a telescope. Tied to a chair, slumping forward with his hair hiding his face. Bleeding. Still.

My heart stops.

"Oh my god," I breathe. "I See him. He's hurt."

"Where is he?" Gabby demands, her voice quavering. "Is Luna with him?"

I drag my sight away from him and instead look around. Craggy rock walls. Flickering firelight. Luna comes into view, tied to a chair on the other side of a small fire. Nothing to indicate where they might be. "Yes. They're in a cave somewhere..."

"Anywhere," Gabby says, exasperated.

I feel like I've seen this cave before, but I have no idea when. I don't know if I've ever been in a real cave. Have I seen it in a book? A documentary?

I squeeze my eyes shut. The farther I get from Thiago, the fuzzier the vision becomes. Finally, it fades completely and I pop my eyes open. Gabby's face swims before me and something pounds behind my eyes as she slowly comes into focus.

"Did you See anything else that might tell us where they are?" Gabby presses. "Did you See outside? Buildings? Plants? Was it night or day?"

I run my hands through my hair. My mind races in a spinning, panicked blur. Where, where did I just See them? Why did it feel so familiar? It felt so far away. It could take forever to get them, and who knows what could happen in the meantime. My throat tightens. Sweat breaks out on my palms and forehead.

"Joan, don't freak out on me," Gabby says, though I can tell from the tautness in her voice that she's fighting off her own panic. "We need to figure this out."

I feel sick. I stand, wobbling, feeling slightly unreal. Like I'm not all there. "We need to find them," I say. My voice feels like it's coming from somewhere else.

"I know," says Gabby. "We'll find them." Her eyes shine in her pale face. She doesn't look convinced.

Panic. Blind panic. We'll never get there in time. There has to be something faster.

There *is* something faster.

Something clicks inside my mind, in a place so deep I didn't even realize it was there.

Without thinking, I reach out to snatch Gabby's hand, which is just as sweaty as mine. She jerks in surprise, but grips my hand tightly.

Suddenly I feel like my feet aren't attached to my body. I fall forward, dragging Gabby with me, but I don't stop at the floor. We fall forward and forward, almost like a front flip in slow motion, though we're standing. Gabby's hand grows cold, tight around mine.

Finally, we fall face down on damp soil, twigs, and tiny rocks that dig into my palms. The air is cool, humid. I shiver in my tee shirt and shorts. Gabby groans beside me. I do a quick scan of my body. No serious pain. I don't think I'm hurt.

"Are you okay?" I whisper to Gabby.

"I think so," she whispers back. "What just happened? Where are we?"

Slowly, I rise to my feet and look around.

We're in a forest, surrounded by knobby trees dripping with moss and vines. Bright moonlight filters through the heavy canopy above. Something tells me we're close to Thiago and Luna, and that we're very, very far from home. The trees look familiar. The smell of dirt and wood and water nearby stirs something hidden deep in my memory.

"I think I've been here before," I say.

"Where's 'here'?"

I stare at the trees, slowly shaking my head. "I…I don't know."

34

Thiago

My arm screams. My head throbs. The muscles in my neck and stomach burn. Each breath I drag into my lungs feels like inhaling broken glass.

I must have passed out at some point, because I don't remember how I got here. I don't remember being tied to a wooden chair. It takes a moment for my eyes to adjust to the light of a small fire crackling on the dirt floor before me.

I'm in a small cave with rough stone walls. To my left is an opening to a dark, narrow tunnel. I can't see more than a few feet inside. I try to move, but the ropes cut into my skin.

On the other side of the fire, tied to an identical chair, is Luna. She slumps forward against her restraints. A curtain of silver hair hides her face.

"Luna…" I rasp. She doesn't stir.

I jerk against the ropes only to be rewarded with shards of shrieking pain in my arm. I grit my teeth and hiss, sucking in a ragged breath. The muggy air tastes of smoke and damp stone.

I look around, for *him*. Shadows dance on the opposite wall and I jerk my head toward the tunnel.

Footsteps.

The man appears in the mouth of the tunnel hauling an armful of cut wood. Immediately, his eyes shift to me, his face expressionless. He looks away, approaches the fire, and drops the wood in a pile next to Luna's chair.

"I apologize for my absence," he says. "We may be here a while, and I'll need light to see what I'm doing." His voice is tinged with a slight accent. British, I think.

I've heard that voice before. It takes a moment to place it, but then I remember.

The day Joan played the piano in front of the cafe. The man who listened to her play and left her first tip. I say nothing.

"I had a short talk with your sister while you were out," he continues, squatting by the wood pile and carefully feeding a few sticks into the fire.

No. I look at Luna, who's quiet and still, and scan for any signs of injury. Her hair and skin are dirty, but I see no blood or bruises. No sign that she's hurt.

"Don't worry," he goes on. "I didn't hurt her. She's not a talker, however, so I'm very glad you're here."

"What do you want?" I demand hoarsely.

The man stands, faces me, and smiles in a horrible way that doesn't reach his eyes. Chills trickle down my spine and I brace myself as he reaches into his black coat. To my surprise, he pulls a small leather canteen from an interior pocket, unscrews the top, and holds the end to my mouth.

"Drink," he says. "You sound terrible."

I glare. My throat screams for water, but I muster up all the saliva I can manage and spit on his shoes.

The man sighs and looks down at his feet, then shrugs and drinks from the canteen himself. "I see stubbornness runs in the family." He turns back to Luna. My stomach lurches as he reaches for her and I hiss at the shooting pain in my arm. He only taps her shoulder, then offers her the canteen.

Luna slowly lifts her head, her hair parting to reveal her face. I breathe a sigh of relief. Her eyes are unfocused, as usual, and she looks completely unharmed.

"Have a drink, darling," the man says gently. Without looking at him, or me, or anything, Luna's mouth drops open slightly. The man brings the spout of the canteen to her lips and pours some water inside. Luna gulps, taking several mouthfuls.

The canteen empties. The man puts the cap back on and slips it back into his coat. Then he lowers onto a rock near Luna's chair, leaning forward with his elbows on his knees. He watches Luna's blank face, eyes soft and almost sympathetic.

"Leave her alone," I hiss.

"Last chance, darling," he says to her, ignoring me. "I know it was you who destroyed my watch. That was a very special watch. But you knew that, didn't you? That's why you destroyed it." Luna stares straight ahead, showing no sign she heard him. She probably has no inkling of where she is or what's happening. I silently thank whatever god is listening for that.

"The Clock Tower will appear in this world soon," he continues. "Where will that be, and when?"

Luna, of course, says nothing.

The man sighs and tilts his head so he can see her face. "I'd really prefer to do this the easy way. Believe me, I can make things much harder for you. And your brother."

My stomach drops out. I strain at the ropes again, but the pain in my arm nearly blinds me.

"No? Nothing?"

My worst nightmare is happening before my eyes. I always worried that someone would try to use her or hurt her for her abilities. Many people would want to know the future. Many bad people would kill to know.

The man sighs again and reaches into his jacket. My aching stomach muscles clench when he pulls out a curved knife.

"No…" I say, yanking against my bonds, ignoring the pain. "Leave her alone!"

"I'm not a cruel man," he says softly, looking down at the floor. I'm not sure if he says it to me, Luna, or to himself. It doesn't matter. I struggle to inch my chair forward, my arm seizing with pain. "I want you to know I take no pleasure in this."

He twirls the knife in his fingers, seems to decide something, then holds it to the inside of her thigh.

I struggle, cursing, as he places the tip to her leg and pushes.

She quakes, her head lifting to face me. Her pupils contract. She gasps, whether from shock or pain, I'm not sure. The man drags the knife upward, slicing through her pants up the inside of her leg. Scarlet blood oozes from the cut, coating the end of the knife, soaking her jeans.

"Tell me," he says evenly. "Now."

Luna gasps again, and he pulls the knife from her leg.

"She can't tell you," I plead. "She can't speak. Please don't hurt her. Don't hurt her anymore…"

He looks over his shoulder to me, the fire dancing in his dark eyes. "She *can't* speak?"

"No…" I wheeze, desperate. I ignore the pain in my arm as I yank against the ropes, leaning as far forward as I can. "She hasn't spoken in more than twenty years." I hiss the last words through my teeth.

"Interesting," he says, rising to his feet to approach me. "Maybe she just needs proper motivation." I suck air into my lungs, my muscles tightening, steeling myself. "You know," he says, examining the bloody knife. "This knife has quite a long history. I wish I had time to tell you. It's served me well for centuries."

Centuries? How old *is* he? Or is he just insane? At the moment, I don't care which.

"This knife has done terrible things. Necessary things." He stops a few feet away, peering down at me, the knife still raised. "Like killing your parents."

For a moment, I completely forget the pain in my shoulder. I forget my terror.

His words resonate in my skull and my vision blurs as I'm hurled back into my memories, into my nightmares.

My parents lying in their own blood, blank eyes staring up at me. My family torn apart and my life changed forever.

"You killed my parents..." I stammer, my words slurring as I struggle to form the words.

The man's lips tighten. He doesn't flinch. "I'm afraid so," he says evenly. "I won't pretend I don't regret it."

I want to break my bonds, spring forward, and tear his throat out with my bare hands. "I'll kill you," I spit.

He nods, as if he expected that. "For what it's worth, I'm sorry for the pain it's caused your family. It was nothing personal."

Each breath burns my lungs. I watch him in horror, not believing what I'm hearing. "You're insane."

He nods again. "It's very possible." He twirls the knife lazily. A drop of Luna's blood falls from the knife and splats on the knees of my jeans.

"Among other things," he goes on, "this knife has helped me extract very valuable information. It has never failed. I've seen the invention and use of many different instruments of torture, but I find the simple knife to be the most effective and versatile tool."

He bends closer. I smell sweat, smoke, and the tang of blood. He smells like death, like cold stone and ruin. I can smell every terrible thing he's ever done. I tighten my jaw and stare back, unblinking.

"I'm not a cruel man," he says again. "But I might enjoy this just a little."

My heart pounds as he slowly moves the tip of the knife, lingering over different points on my body. My eye. My mouth. Nipples. Between my legs. Then he raises it back up, pointing it at my ear. His eyes narrow, head tilting.

"What on earth does she see in you?" he asks softly. He presses the knife into my earlobe.

White hot pain shoots down my neck and wraps around my head as he digs, slicing slowly. I grit my teeth, refusing to make a sound. Every muscle in my body strains against the knife.

"Tell me where the Clock Tower will be," he says over his shoulder to Luna, louder than before.

I feel the knife slicing my earlobe to ribbons. Every muscle in my body screams as the pain lances through my head and neck. My eyes burn and water. I hiss through my teeth and fight not to yell. His huge hand clamps around my head to hold it still. I can't breathe against the pain. I can't escape. The edges of my vision blur. The man's face slips out of focus, though I still see the fury burning in his eyes.

Finally, he releases my head and stops cutting. I suck in a breath, almost hyperventilating.

He turns to Luna. "Nothing?" He shakes his head and turns back to me. "It seems your sister doesn't care as much about you as you do about her. So sad."

"I told you, you shriveled son of a bitch," I groan. "She can't...speak." I look him dead in the eye, struggling to breathe evenly. "I'm going to kill you. For what you've done to my family. I swear to god, I'm going to kill you." I mean every word.

"Yes, yes, of course you are," he says with a condescending smirk.

He wipes the knife on my jeans and slips it back into his coat. Warm, sticky blood soaks the side of my face and neck.

"Let's try something new, shall we?" he says casually, turning to crouch by the fire. Sparks spray as he shifts sticks around and slides something out of the coals. "I've prepared a surprise for you, Thiago, in case your sister wasn't in a chatty mood."

My stomach drops as he lifts a long, red hot knife from the flames. "I don't use my good knife for this, of course." He grins wickedly.

For a split second, I drag my eyes from the glowing knife to look at Luna. Her eyes slip in and out of focus in the firelight, pupils contracting and dilating like the aperture of a camera. Her shoulders heave as she sucks in a breath, leaning forward against her bonds. Can she see me? I wonder briefly before the man lowers the knife to my chest.

"Any time you want to tell me something, darling, just give a holler," he calls to Luna, his eyes never leaving me. I grit my teeth and suck in a breath as he lowers the hot knife to my chest.

This time, I can't hold it in. I howl as he drags a line of white hot pain across my skin. Every muscle in my body locks up. I smell my own flesh cooking. My bellows echo off the stone walls until all the air is wrenched from my lungs.

The knife changes direction, digging and slicing toward my armpit, charring my skin. I try to gasp in another breath, but I can't. Red tinges the edges of my vision, but over his shoulder I see Luna, swaying in her chair, jaw slack. Her mouth opens and closes. She wants to talk. She's trying to.

A choked cry mingles with my gasping. At first, I don't realize the sound came from Luna. My fingers dig into the rough ropes, into my own palms, my knuckles about to burst from my skin.

The man releases the knife. My skin screams with each breath as my chest expands and contracts.

"Did you say something, love?" he turns around to look at Luna. I manage to shake my head at her behind his back, but her mouth still moves, emanating odd squeaks. "Now we're getting somewhere," he rises to walk around the fire to Luna's side. He bends down, leaning closer to hear her. "Don't be shy, now." The squeaking sounds stop. Only a dry hiss of air escapes her.

My head lolls back as I pant. The torn, fried muscles in my chest strain and burn. My skin bubbles like hot wax. I gather my strength, gritting my teeth, closing my eyes to steel myself. This isn't over…

I have to get us out of here. Somehow, I have to survive this. I force my breath to slow, to deepen, for my mind to clear. Joan's face swims into my mind's eye. Her smile, her eyes, her pale body stretched out on my bed. The way my name sounds on her lips. How strong I feel when she's with me. The only person outside my family I've ever trusted.

If I die here, I'll never see her again.

"Well that was progress," I hear the man say. I haul my head back up to see him stand. "Good news, Thiago. A miracle may occur today. After all these years, your dear sister may finally speak. Let's continue."

Joan. Joan. Joan.

"I'd prefer not to, but I can get really creative with this thing," he says, wagging the knife before dipping it into the fire, holding the blade in the flames. He pauses a moment, letting the blade heat again, then picks it up and crosses back to me. "Same game, same rules," he says to Luna. "Anything you'd like to tell me, I'm all ears."

Joan. I never told her how I feel. I never told her…

The knife flashes. Digging. Slicing. Burning. Skinning.

Pain explodes in my vision and I see white. My entire consciousness shrinks to the point of the burning blade. A horrible, guttural shout of pain echoes in the cavern, but it doesn't feel like it's coming from me. All I feel is fire. All I feel is the pain.

I *am* pain.

I hear his voice, somewhere far away. "You don't deserve her," he hisses. "You are nothing…"

Through the inferno of pain, I manage to speak. "What does that mean, pervert?" My voice doesn't sound like my own, like the voice of a demon.

He just smiles, and my vision flares red as he digs the knife deeper.

Somewhere through the blinding pain, I hear Joan. I feel her. I think he knows that, because the knife sinks even deeper, digging into the muscle. Through the shroud of pain, I see his face. Cold. Vicious. Satisfied.

Killing my parents wasn't personal, he'd said.

But this…*this* is personal.

Joan

Gabby pushes herself to her feet and looks around. Her shoulders heave as she takes deep breaths. "Joan," she says. "How did you bring us here?"

I exhale, letting all the air out of my lungs as it dawns on me what just happened. We were just in Gabby's bedroom. I can still smell the faint bready scent that permeates their apartment. But now we're here...and I have no idea where *here* is.

I just appeared somewhere else. Did I just...teleport? Or did it only feel instant? It could be days, months, years later. I have no idea where we are, what day it is, or how we got here. My hands shake. My breaths shorten, growing shallow and rapid as panic swells inside me like a balloon.

No, Joan. Don't give yourself to panic. We have to find them.

Under the fear and confusion, this forest still looks familiar. I don't think we're here randomly.

"I have no idea," I answer truthfully. "But I think this is where we need to be." I force myself to stand, turn, look in all directions. I can't see very far through the thick trees, even with the light of the full moon illuminating the forest. In my vision, Thiago and Luna were in a cave, not a forest. Where do we go from here?

It suddenly occurs to me that maybe I was wrong. Maybe it was all my imagination and I just happened to think of a cave for some reason. Or maybe I really did See Thiago and then just traveled somewhere else in my mind. How could this be real?

But I somehow took us from Boston to this forest in what felt like seconds. If I can do that, I can figure out exactly where they are and how to get to them.

"How…" Gabby starts, but I hold up a hand to silence her.

"I need to try Seeing them," I say. I close my eyes and try to pinpoint that same warm feeling I felt in Thiago's bedroom that led me to him like a trail of breadcrumbs. I struggle to swim through the panic and fear to find that pure feeling of clarity. I imagine Thiago in his kitchen, mixing dough, the concentration and sparkle in his eyes when he gets an idea. I think of how he protects his sisters. I spiral around and around this feeling until I find him again.

Far away, distorted, like looking through a lens, I See him. The same dark place. He's not moving. Then, the flash of a knife. Thiago's howls resonate in my bones.

I force my sight to pull away from him, backward, passing through walls and stone until I'm standing out in the forest, right where I am now. My stomach turns and my skin prickles, not just from the strain of the vision, but from Thiago's pain, confirming all my worst fears.

We're close, but we don't have much time. Thiago doesn't have much time.

I open my eyes, feeling vertigo for a moment before I settle back into myself. Gabby grabs my arm to steady me as I sway on my feet.

"It's disorienting, I know," she says kindly. I nod in agreement. I'm glad Gabby's here.

"This way," I tell her, and start moving as fast as I can over fallen trees and tangled ground cover. I feel like the needle of a compass pointing due north. Gabby tails me, taking several steps to each of mine to catch up.

My pulse outruns my feet, and I fight to keep it steady. *He's hurt. He's hurt.* I force myself to stay calm, because panic won't help me find them, but Thiago's shouts of pain feel like broken glass in my stomach and under my skin.

Within a few minutes, the trees become less dense, allowing patches of gray daylight to show through. The ground becomes rockier, sloping upward. Through the thinning canopy, a cliff of mossy gray stone looms in front of us, casting the woods in shadow. We clamber over loose rocks and boulders until we're close enough to touch the cold stone wall.

"Is the cave here?" Gabby asks. Her head whips from side to side as she searches for an opening.

I press my flat palm to the smooth, cool rock, and look to the left and right. An uninterrupted cliff face. No openings. "I think it's through here."

"What do you mean 'through here?'"

I brush my fingers over the stone, exploring cracks with my fingers until my thumb brushes a strange crack in the stone. I flinch as a tiny shock travels down my arm.

"What?" Gabby asks.

I gingerly brush the cracks again, leaning closer to see.

There, in the stone, are carved symbols in a long line, stretching in both directions over the stone as far as I can see, barely visible in the moonlight.

"Gabby, look at this."

She leans in, squinting to see the symbols. "Those look like the symbols on the watch. Like it's the same language."

"And the bone," I add. I shudder. I feel like I've been here. I know this place.

Focus. I turn my attention back to the rock. "I think this is the way in."

"I don't see an opening, or anything that looks like it could open."

"Just trust me," I say, trying to sound more confident than I feel. *This is stupid,* I think furiously. *They could be dying and I'm just standing in front of a stupid cliff.*

A weird feeling of calm washes over me. The same part of me that knew to open the clock, that knows this place, knows that this is how to find Thiago and Luna.

I turn to face the blank wall, grab Gabby's hand, and step forward. I feel Gabby tense up, but she follows. I close my eyes, ready to hit the wall, wondering what on earth I'm doing, but the impact never comes. Instead, the soft sounds of the forest fall away to echoing silence. The temperature drops at least ten degrees. The earthy green smell of the woods evaporates to be replaced by a damp mustiness.

I open my eyes to look around, but I'm surrounded by thick, inky blackness. I reach for my pocket and pull out my phone to turn on the flashlight.

When the small light turns on, it takes a moment for my eyes to adjust. We stand in the middle of a dark stone chamber with dripping walls.

I let out a shocked, hysterical laugh. Somehow, I got us inside.

"Oh my god," Gabby says, equal parts terrified and exhilarated. "Joan, who *are* you? How did you do that?"

"I don't know," I say again. So much I don't know. The urge to hyperventilate rises and I force it down. *Don't panic.* Whatever's going on with me, I'm willing to roll with it if it leads us to Thiago and Luna. I swallow hard.

"Where do we go now?" Gabby questions.

I look up at the ceiling, hanging with rotting vines, roots, and shreds of moss. Water drips into a puddle about three feet to my right, steady like the ticking of a clock. I wave the phone around to examine the rest of the room. Several tunnels branch off from the chamber, each completely dark.

Something flicks into my brain, a small mental tug to the smallest tunnel opening, the ceiling so low I might not be able to stand up straight inside. The blackness feels darker than the shadow of the other tunnels, almost like the darkness is a solid curtain instead of empty space. I've never seen darkness like this.

"I think we go this way," I say, pointing. I feel the mental tug again. Gabby looks to the tunnel. I can barely see her expression in the dark, but her face turns even more ghostly pale.

I take a step in the direction of the tunnel, then another. Gabby follows. We move forward until we're wrapped in the thickest darkness I've ever experienced, so heavy and damp it's like a wet black quilt. The air feels slimy as I inhale. I want to cough, but I force myself to hold it in, taking small breaths and stepping lightly. We don't want to be heard.

The darkness becomes so thick that even the light of my phone doesn't penetrate. Soon, we can't see a thing. I grope for Gabby's hand. Her thin, cold fingers wrap around mine. She's shaking, or I am, or we both are. I reach my other hand out in front of me, waving around blindly, both hoping to find something solid and dreading what I might touch. There's nothing but humid, stuffy darkness. The air presses on us. It's surprisingly warm, like we're walking through the breath of some sleeping animal. The musty smell of the earth's underbelly fades until there's nothing.

I realize I can't hear my footsteps anymore, or Gabby's. I can only feel her clammy hand gripping mine for dear life. Electricity buzzes through my limbs, tingling like the moment I touched the symbols on the rock. Then I know: this unnatural darkness is no simple absence of light. This darkness is…purposeful. Thiago and Luna could be standing right next to us and we'd never know.

Then I see something, a small pinprick of light. I charge toward it, dragging Gabby with me until I realize I'm not seeing it with my physical eyes, but with my mind.

The light expands. It's like the dreams about the room in the Clock Tower. It's like I'm back in the square room with the table, the long hair flowing around my face, falling to the elbows of my tunic. I See stars out the one small window. Across the table from me is the man, burly, bearded, with wavy hair falling into his green eyes, looking at me with something like remorse.

"I'm sorry," he says, his voice crackling with pain. I realize I've never heard him speak before. His voice is softer than I would have imagined, given his powerful frame. "I'm so, so sorry, Katherine."

I blink. The image cuts in and out with the darkness, then fades away completely.

I realize I'm leaning on Gabby. Her arm wraps around my waist to support me. "Are you okay?" she whispers, barely more than a breath. She sounds so far away.

"I think so," I whisper back. "We're close."

Gabby continues to support me, but I still feel disoriented. Her grip on my hand tightens and loosens, as if she's struggling to balance herself as well.

"Do you hear that?" she whispers. She's quiet, but her voice still bounces off the walls of the cave.

I pause and listen. A man's voice, so faint I'm not sure I heard it. I can't understand what he's saying, but my blood runs cold at the malice lacing each garbled word.

The voice stops.

With one hand in front of me and the other gripping Gabby's, I take a tentative step forward, reaching with my foot along the ground for anything I could trip over, or worse, fall into. I've heard stories of people getting lost in caves, falling into holes, and dying, broken on the floor of some cavern deep in the bowels of the earth. My lungs pump shallow breaths of fetid air as I fight to keep myself calm. Gabby's hand is clammy. So is mine. I hear her breathing steadily beside me, but I feel her strong pulse in her wrist. Or maybe it's my own pulse.

Finally, my hand finds cold, rough stone. I almost sink to my knees with relief. Gabby feels the wall too and lets out a choked moan as she collapses against it, mumbling something in Spanish.

Keeping my hand on the wall, we move forward, scooting one foot in front of the other.

A few times, my ears prick to a bigger kind of silence, like the room has become larger, or like we've passed other tunnels leading away, but I keep going straight, never letting my hand leave the wall.

Finally, a dim light. I'm almost shocked when I can see the rough rock walls bathed in warm yellow light, and the outline of an opening in front of me. No trees, nothing but open sky. We must be high up on the cliff somehow.

Except on this side, it's daytime. The opening frames a clear, periwinkle-blue sky.

When we appeared in the forest, the moon was high in the sky. How could it be daytime now? How long have we been here?

Gabby grips my hand, her arm shaking slightly. I can tell she's thinking the same thing.

The farther we step forward, the better I can see. I notice two shapes on the ground in the opening to the cave. At first, I think they're just rocks, but then I make out the shape of a shoulder, legs, a figure crumbled on the ground and another slumped against the wall of the tunnel.

The figure on the ground groans.

My heartbeat stalls. Breath catches in my chest. "Thiago…"

I drop Gabby's hand and run, my feet smacking a panicked rhythm on the stone floor. I hear a second set of footsteps as Gabby rushes forward as well.

Then a third figure steps away from the wall, between Thiago and Luna, feet planted firmly apart, silhouetted in the sunlight streaming through the opening of the cave. I can't see his face, but in his hand is a long knife.

Gabby and I both stop, about fifteen feet between us and the man.

This is a trap.

I look from Thiago to Luna to the man, my mind racing. How can we get them away from him?

"You can have them back in a moment," the man says in a familiar voice. The man's head tilts as he speaks. "But first, I need to talk to you, Joan."

36

Arial

might enjoy this a little.

Thiago roars as I drag the hot knife through his skin. Music to my ears. I think of him and Joan, that morning when she played her song on the painted piano. My stomach twists in revulsion, so I twist the knife in his chest, relishing how easily his skin slices and burns. I wrinkle my nose against the smell of burned flesh. The girl whimpers behind me, a tiny, pathetic sound underscoring Thiago's howls. She wants to tell me something, but I keep cutting. I still need a few moments.

I look down at my handiwork, the neat lines of burnt cuts on his chest. I've always found this method effective. Simple, yet highly painful with minimal blood, as the heat of the knife mostly cauterizes the wound as it cuts.

I examine the knife; it's time to heat it again. I could use a break anyway, and so could Thiago. I'd prefer that he remain conscious. I replace the knife in the fire. Silly me, I should have used several knives, but heating isn't good for the blades. I'd rather keep one just for this purpose.

I turn back to the girl.

"Did you say something, darling?" I ask. She looks up at me, her eerie silver eyes freezing the air in my lungs. I shiver despite the heat in the cave and the sweat coating my neck and forehead. I don't let her see how much she unsettles me with those strange eyes that never focus on the present. I've met many Seers, but I've never seen anything like her. Not even Katherine.

Her cracked lips move, only a hiss of air releasing. She strains against her bonds. Her face reddens as if the strain of focusing her eyes and attempting to form words is taxing. She's truly trying to speak, to save her brother. If it weren't for his relationship with Joan, I might consider sparing him.

Luna sucks in a breath, then emits a soft squeak that almost sounds like a word. My stomach jumps. Did she just say what I think she said?

I crouch down to hear her. "Could you repeat that please?"

Only a hiss of air, a hushed fricative, but not quite a word. She's definitely trying to say something. I watch her lips as she clumsily mouths a single word.

Snow.

I crouch on my heels, stunned. Now we're getting somewhere.

She looks almost as exhausted as her brother. Her head lolls on her shoulders. Sweat gleams on her face and arms. I don't know whether it's the strain of speaking or the effort to stay in the present that's draining her so severely.

"Anything else?" I ask.

Her chest heaves. Her head rolls back and her eyes stare blankly at the ceiling. I stand, looking down at her, deciding what to do next. "Snow" doesn't give me much, but it eliminates at least half the world and, more importantly, proves that she can be persuaded. She's willing to give me what I want.

"Well, Thiago," I say, turning back to him. His body tenses as I reach for the knife in the coals. "She speaks. I'm a miracle worker." He closes his eyes as I lift the knife. "I might need to work some more miracles, though." He inhales sharply, steeling himself.

I pause when I hear something. A woman's voice.

I turn back to Luna, thinking she's spoken audibly, but she still stares at the ceiling, shoulders slumped. Then I hear it again, a voice echoing in the tunnel. My brow wrinkles in confusion. I glance at Thiago, then replace the knife in the fire. "Don't go anywhere," I tell him, then cross to venture into the tunnel that leads deeper into the cave system, pausing every few steps to listen.

"Are you okay?" Comes a female voice. These caves are interesting; the voice sounds like its owner is just around the corner, but I know better. I know these caves, their disorienting darkness, and the strange way sound travels through them. The speaker is probably a ways off, but headed this way.

"I think so," a familiar voice answers. "We're close."

Joan. I'd know the sound of her voice anywhere. So much like Katherine's.

They're coming this way, and if I can hear them, there's a chance they can hear me.

An idea tickles my mind, something stirring deep inside me, a hope I've kept a lid on for centuries. I now allow it to lift its head and sniff the air.

Joan followed me here, where no one can follow. I almost laugh out loud. After all this time, her powers are at least somewhat intact. What about the rest of her? Is she still the same?

I pause a moment longer, then turn and step back down the tunnel to where I left Thiago and Luna.

"Change of plans," I say quietly, unsure of how much my voice will echo down the tunnel. "We'll have company soon."

I cut Thiago loose first, releasing him from the chair but keeping the rope that binds his hands behind his back. He's limp, teetering on the edge of consciousness. I let him fall forward over my shoulder. I slowly straighten my legs, lifting his weight into a fireman's carry, then I start down the tunnel.

Luna whimpers. "I'll be back for you, love, don't worry," I tell her, adjusting Thiago's weight. I hope he doesn't bleed all over my coat.

I carry him around the bend, another two turns until we reach one of the mouths of the cave. The tunnel opens onto a steep rock face, nothing but sheer cliff for hundreds of feet below. I carry him to the edge of the tunnel, consider throwing him off the cliff for a moment, but roughly dump him on the stone floor instead.

He grunts as he hits the ground, but doesn't move.

"Luna," he mumbles, clumsily trying to push himself off the floor. I give him a sharp kick to the gut. He cries out, then wretches on the floor, choking and gulping for air.

"If you move from that spot, I'll kick you off that cliff," I snarl, then start back down the tunnel for Luna.

When I reach her, I first kick some dirt onto the fire until it starts to dim. Before it's out completely, I cut her loose. I'm quite sure she can walk, but I throw her over my shoulder as well. She doesn't resist as I carry her down the tunnel, past two turns, until I can see the opening. Thiago still lays on the floor in a puddle of his own blood and vomit. He hasn't moved. Good boy.

He turns his head to look at me. "Don't hurt her..." he chokes. His chest and back heave with labored breath. I'm sure with the wounds on his chest, every breath burns. Good.

Carefully, I kneel and set Luna down into a sitting position where she can lean against the rock wall. Thiago watches every move. Luna doesn't seem to notice what's going on. She just rests against the wall, eyes unfocused and wandering. Off in another world.

What a fascinating girl. Pity I don't have the time to observe her more closely, to study how her power has affected her. I have more pressing matters to think about.

I move to the shadows, train my ears on the tunnel, and wait.

299

37

Joan

Panic swims through my blood. My eyes dart to the knife in the man's hand.

Thiago slumps on the floor, blood pooling beneath him. His shoulder looks strangely deflated. His breathing is labored. Blisters and angry red gashes crisscross his bare chest. I smell the tang of blood, the faint edge of burned skin and hair. My stomach roils, threatening to empty its contents on the cave floor.

My stomach jumps. I need to get Thiago and Luna out of here, but there's no way we could get to them in time with the man brandishing the knife. He could gut either of them or throw them off the cliff before we could reach them. Even if we can get to them, I'd have to get them both home, somehow. I don't even know how we got here, let alone how to get back out.

I can almost hear Gabby's mind whirring through a similar train of thought beside me. The light illuminates her face just enough for me to catch her sideways glance. We have no choice but to play along. To talk. At least until we can get him away from Thiago and Luna.

"Fine," I say. I feel Gabby tense up beside me. "I'm listening."

The man takes a small step forward. I fight to not take a step back.

My hands itch to wrap themselves around his thick neck. I want to plunge my fingers into his eye sockets, to rip out his throat. The only thing holding me back is the knowledge that Thiago or Luna would be dead before I could take two steps forward.

"Killed…our parents…" Thiago moans from the floor.

"It's rude to interrupt," the man says sharply. He kicks Thiago in the ribs. Gabby cries out and I jerk forward, but stop myself. Thiago moans.

"It was you, wasn't it?" Gabby hisses, her voice shaking with rage and terror. "You killed our parents!"

I shush her, but she ignores me. The last thing we want to do is piss him off. I force my feet to stay put.

"I'm very sorry," the man says. "I know I've caused your family great pain."

Thiago groans from the floor. He twitches as if he wants to rise and beat the man to a pulp, but he's too weak.

"It doesn't matter if you're sorry," Gabby snarls. "You killed them. For that damn watch, and they didn't even have it."

The man raises his head again. "No, they didn't. Unfortunately for everyone involved, I didn't learn that until after their deaths when I didn't find it anywhere in the flat. I don't expect you to forgive me. I know I can't be forgiven. But I want you to understand my purpose."

Gabby scoffs, and I shoot her a look. *Stay quiet. Let him talk.* It's the only way we might be able to save Thiago and Luna.

"My name is Arial," he begins. The name sends cold shivers over my skin, to know the name of the man who killed the Cardozas' parents. "My purpose for all of this, for seeking the watch, the Clock Tower, for killing for it, for everything I've done to find it." He takes a breath, as if he's getting a weight off his chest. "Is because I want to die."

The cave goes quiet. There's no sound except Thiago's pained breathing. Even my anger shrinks slightly to make room for my surprise.

"What?" I sputter.

"I've lived a very, very long life," Arial says, crossing his arms over his broad chest. "You can't understand what it's like to live, on and on, pointlessly, with no end in sight. And I've done terrible things in that long life. Your family weren't the only ones, or the worst ones.

"Before long, it became difficult, impossible to live with myself or my guilt. My existence became endless torture. I just want it to end. I'd do anything to make it end."

"That's why you want to stop the clock?" I snap. "To end your life? That's the stupidest thing I've ever heard." Now it's Gabby's turn to gape at me in horror.

Arial smirks. "Did you think I was on some evil crusade to put humanity out of its misery? That this is about ending the world? No, not at all. This is about ending *me*."

I shake my head. "Seriously? There's got to be another way to off yourself that doesn't involve destroying the whole world like a selfish asshole."

Arial chuckles and shakes his head. "I see your point. I really do. But believe me, I've tried everything. I've thrown myself off cliffs and buildings, tried to drown, suffocate, hang, burn. Knives, guns, poisons. Nothing works. Just pointless pain. And after so long…I don't care. I just want it to end, and I don't care who I have to take with me."

My mind spins. "You're even more insane than I expected."

Arial shrugs. "You think me a monster, but the world is going to end anyway. Simply stopping time is a far kinder way to end it than waiting for humanity to destroy itself, or waiting until the Clock Tower stops on its own and the world is ripped apart and thrown into darkness and chaos. After everything I've done, it might even be my only shot at redemption, to spare the world a great deal of suffering."

"What do you mean 'ripped apart'?" I ask, shifting my weight. My toes curl in my flip-flops. This is taking too long. Thiago doesn't look good, and Arial seems to be in no hurry. I don't know how to get them away from him. I can only buy time. I try to remember the way we came, the turns in the tunnel, but I'll never make it out of the dark.

Arial shifts his weight from foot to foot, mirroring me. He's watching. He knows I'm stalling.

"What do you know about the Clock Tower?" he counters.

I hesitate. I don't want to give away what we know. We don't want to lose our only weapon.

Arial sighs and continues. "The Clock Tower keeps time running in one direction," he says, pacing like a bored teacher in front of an inattentive class. "It's slowing, starting to break down. It's only going to get worse. Time is becoming more unreliable, working in stops and starts until the Clock Tower stops performing its function of holding time together. After that, anything can happen. You see, time was broken, very badly. It was shredded to bits from far too many experiments, too much meddling with the natural order. That's why it was built in the first place. It's just a patch for irreparable damage. I never expected it to last forever."

"You...broke time?" I ask. How is that possible? How could something as abstract as time be broken?

"*I* didn't," he says. "I was an accomplice, yes. A servant to a master. Along with my wife, Katherine."

The name strikes a chord in me, like a tuning fork humming in my mind. Like he's mentioning someone I know. I look at Gabby. Even in the dim light, I can see she's gone pale.

"Does that name feel familiar to you, Joan?" Arial asks, a smile in his voice.

"No," I lie, crossing my arms. "Should it?"

"In addition to being a magical and scientific genius, Katherine loved music. She composed a song. The song that was her soul in sound. I hadn't heard it in centuries until a few months ago. You played her song on that painted piano outside the cafe. That's when I knew…no one else on earth could know that song. No one. At first I thought I was finally losing my mind, but after meeting you, I realized it was you." I can almost see him smile in the darkness. "It's my Katherine, come back somehow."

I can't help it, but that part of me that does the wrong thing at the wrong time kicks in. I laugh.

Gabby gapes at me in horror. Arial's smile fades.

"Seriously?" I scoff. Gabby shoots daggers with her eyes. "You think I'm your dead wife? I thought your ending-time-to-end-your-miserable-life idea was stupid, but my god, you've outdone yourself."

Arial pauses, then reaches into his jacket. He takes something out, fiddles for a moment, then a small flame bursts to life in his hand. A lighter. He holds the flame higher, illuminating his face.

My laughter fades, and he grins. I've seen him before. Yes, he was in the cafe. I've made him coffee. He was there when I played the piano.

But I know him from somewhere else too.

The man in the dreams of the room in the Clock Tower.

My whole life, I've dreamed about him. A kidnapper. A stalker. A murderer. The thought makes me sick. I fight to keep an amused smirk on my face.

Arial smiles warmly. "You know me, don't you?"

My stomach squirms. "I know you've been following me," I say darkly. "You were at the cafe the first day I played the piano…"

He watches me intently. "Yes," he says. "I followed you. I wanted to be sure. I don't expect you to remember your former life perfectly, but you know it's true. I can see it on your face. You've never been a good liar."

I fight to keep my face blank. Arial continues. "You have, of course, retained your intelligence and kindness, your love of the stars, and your love of music. Your song survived and was reborn through you. You even look quite a bit like Katherine, once I looked closer. Of course your hair is chopped short, but it's the same color."

"What, are you talking about reincarnation?" I ask, trying to sound skeptical, but my voice wavers.

"I suppose you could call it that," he says. "Not all souls come back. Most don't, actually."

I don't want to believe it. Of all the crazy things I've come to believe in the past few months, this is the most insane.

But how do I explain the dreams? The waking dream of the Clock Tower that I just had in the tunnels? And why do I feel like I know him?

"What does Katherine have to do with the Clock Tower?" I ask. I'm not just stalling now. I really want to know.

Arial continues. "Katherine helped develop the magic that made its construction possible. We served our master as he meddled with time for his own purposes. The more he tampered with natural laws that were never meant to be broken, time became more and more fragile. He created the Clock Tower with him to patch up his mistakes, thinking we were doing the right thing. Until Katherine tried to stop him."

The hair on the back of my neck prickles. It's like listening to a story I heard long ago but forgot until now. Like remembering a horrible campfire story from my childhood.

"Katherine was executed. Our master's experiments caught up to him and he disappeared. And I was left alone with my immortality. Unfortunately, the Clock Tower was damaged in the process and became destabilized. But I managed to escape with some pieces from the clock and made my pocket watch, which kept me connected to the Clock Tower so I'd know when it came near again."

"So you could stop it," I finish for him.

He looks me in the eye, his cold gaze like a bucket of ice water. "Yes," he says simply. Then to my surprise, he turns his attention to Gabby. "Have you ever wondered where your powers come from?"

Her eyes widen. I'm sure she's wondered, that they all have. I certainly have.

"You could say that Katherine and I were the very first Keepers of Time. Katherine," he continues, "was a powerful Seer. When she was killed, her powers were scattered somehow. They attached to others, then were passed on through death over generations. This line of Seers called themselves the Keepers of Time. The unfortunate result"—he eyes Gabby, glances back to Thiago and Luna—"is you three."

Arial takes a few tentative steps forward. I recoil but stand my ground.

"I've been alone for hundreds of years, seeking death. Seeking the Clock Tower. He stops just a few feet away from me, the flame of the lighter flickering between us. I take a deep breath, jaw stiff. "But I might be willing to change my mind."

My stomach flips over again. My hands suddenly feel cold and clammy. A cool breeze runs over my sweaty neck from the mouth of the cave. I shiver.

"I will end my search for the Clock Tower and send them home," he nods to Gabby and over his shoulder at Thiago and Luna. "If you stay with me, Joan."

I take a breath and swallow. Arial's gaze stays soft, waiting with dangerous patience for my answer. "You don't have to answer right away," he adds. "But the boy needs medical attention, and soon." He gestures behind him. I look over his shoulder and notice that Thiago has inched away from the opening of the tunnel, is trying to push himself up into a crawling position with his good elbow, though his arms are still bound behind him. He looks up at Arial, his face dark and filthy, the side of his face caked in blood. His eyes burn. His lips curl in fury.

Arial sees my eyes shift and a hideous smile twists his face. To my horror, he turns back toward Thiago. "I told you not to move," he growls, stepping toward him.

This time, I can't hold back. As he steps toward my Thiago, Gabby and I both lunge for him.

We're not the only ones.

An inhuman screech rends the air and with a flash of silver hair, Luna flies out of nowhere, onto Arial's back. Her eyes are sharp.

Focused.

38

Gabby

I've never seen Luna—or anyone—move so fast.

I don't have time to grab her. Even Arial doesn't realize she's moved until she's on his back with her arms around his neck.

Luna screeches and bites at his ears, his shoulder, anything she can reach. Arial claws at her arms, scratching, cursing as Luna sinks her teeth into the back of his neck.

For a split second, Joan and I freeze. Joan's mouth drops open in shock. My eyes lock on Luna, biting and clawing the hell out of our parents' murderer. Then I see Thiago, still trying to push himself up.

Joan and I lunge at the same time. Joan dives for Thiago, and I rush toward Luna, grabbing her shoulders and trying to yank her off Arial before she gets hurt, all while hurling curses at Arial over his howls and Luna's shrieks.

Joan grips Thiago under the armpits and struggles to pull him to his feet to get him away from the edge.

Arial staggers closer to the mouth of the cave.

"Luna," Thiago groans. Joan has untied his hands, then she crouches, yanks one of his arms over her shoulders, and lifts with her legs to pull him to his feet. He struggles, trying to get to Luna.

I grab Luna's waist, but her foot flies back and lands squarely in my stomach. I stumble and fall right on my rear, coughing and curling over. I struggle to catch my breath.

She did that on *purpose*.

Luna clings to Arial like a monkey, clawing his face from behind and wrapping her other arm around his neck with her nails dug into his chest. He pulls his knife from his coat and stabs at her arm, but she shifts her grip just in time. The blade jabs into his own chest instead. He hisses like he's gotten a paper cut, but otherwise doesn't slow down even a bit.

Luna pulls herself forward on his shoulders and clamps her teeth on his ear. Arial swears loudly again. The slim muscles in her arms tighten and ripple as she squeezes his neck. She pinches his waist with her knees, holding firmly to his back. He jabs the knife over his shoulder again and again, trying to reach her face, but she always jerks it away just in time.

It's like she's one step ahead of him, like she knows what he's about to do.

She's anticipating his movements, I realize. Somewhere in my terror for her, I feel awe and a twinge of pride.

I scramble to my feet again and back against the wall. I don't know how to get Luna away from him. They're like a tornado of steel and thrashing limbs.

Arial turns, stumbling dangerously toward the edge of the cliff.

Joan has dragged Thiago a safe distance away, into a dark corner of the tunnel, and shoves him onto the ground because he's still trying to crawl to Luna. "Stay *here*," she orders.

My stomach turns when I realize her hands and clothes are covered in his blood. Except for the red gashes across his chest and the blood that smears his torso, his skin is blue-white, his lips pale. His face shines with sweat.

We need to get Luna and get out of here.

Joan sprints toward Luna and Arial, but Arial turns his back to a wall and bends his knees. Before he can ram her into the stone wall, Luna slides off his back and dodges a swipe of the knife in one smooth movement before landing an impressive roundhouse kick to his stomach. He doubles over, laughing.

Luna's sharp silver eyes lock on Joan for a split second, then she reaches out and shoves Joan away, hard. Joan stumbles backward. Her eyes are wide.

Luna turns to look at us. Instead of their normal unearthly silver, the whites of her eyes are turning red. A trickle of blood drops out of her nose. Luna sucks in a deep breath, her chest heaving, then her lips move.

"*Go*," she croaks, her voice low and raspy.

I freeze, every nerve in my body going numb.

My sister spoke. She *spoke*.

Arial backs off a few paces, gripping the knife and staring at Luna with a mixture of awe and fury. "I have no quarrel with you," he snarls. "You gave me what I wanted. Don't make me hurt you."

Luna bites her lip and smacks the bloody gash on the inside of her thigh. A pained hiss escapes through her teeth, but her eyes go wide, present. She does it once more before a calm, focused look settles over her face. I've never seen her focus like that before.

The pain grounds her to the present, I realize.

We can't leave her. I glance at Joan and we both spring to grab Luna as she dives for Arial again, but she's nothing but flying arms and swirling silver hair as she punches and claws. Joan grabs at her shoulder, but Luna dodges her just like she dodged Arial. I catch her arm, but she flings me off just as Arial's knife swipes in my direction. We can't get a grip on her and avoid Arial's knife at the same time. Luna seems to know exactly when he'll strike and where he'll step, using this both to attack and dodge his retaliation, and also when we'll grab for her. It's like she's in the present and the future at the same time. Arial's knife flashes again and again, each stroke a twang on my nerves as I wait for the blood, but it never comes.

All the while, Arial's booming laughter echoes off the cave walls.

Luna charges Arial, somehow dodging his jabs with the knife and punching him squarely in the face. He grabs at her with his free hand, and she dodges again, kicking him in the knee and hitting him again in the face. He moves with skill and precision, but she's always a second ahead.

"Amazing!" he exclaims. "You can See what I'm about to do, can't you? Even Katherine never managed that. You sly little minx." Instead of attacking, he takes a step back just as Luna takes a step forward. He steps sideways. Luna mirrors him, stepping to the other side like a fencer. It's a game to him now.

Now he stands between us and Luna. "It's not going to work, love," he says as he flicks the knife playfully. "They'll never leave without you."

For once, I agree with him. I won't leave here without my sister, and neither will Thiago, who's inching across the floor toward Luna, but he's still nowhere near us. I only hope Joan can get all of us home without Arial interfering.

Arial swings the knife at each of us if we get close, just to watch us dodge, like a cat toying with a mouse. Joan crouches to pick up a rock, then flings it hard at Arial. He holds up an arm to protect his face, and the rock bounces off harmlessly. Following her lead, I find a rock and hurl it lower, but he turns his hip just in time to block it from nailing him right in the groin.

Arial doesn't seem to mind fighting off three of us at once. Luna won't let us get close to her or him.

We just need to get out. All four of us. As we dance back and forth, I notice Arial is sidestepping, working his way between us and Thiago, forcing us back toward the cliff.

I remember how we got here, how Joan grabbed me and we just fell forward like a rollercoaster drop until we ended up here. She grabbed me. We just need to get close enough for her to grab all of us, then maybe we can leave.

Which means I need to get us all closer together.

Luna's eyes are losing their focus, now almost completely red. Her golden skin is growing ashen. Blood runs from her nose over her lips, and veins stand out on her pale forehead. The strain of staying in the present, of focusing on the task at hand, is draining her. She can't keep this up for long.

The space between us and the cliff shrinks. My window for weaving around Arial to Thiago has disappeared.

Luna looks from me to Thiago, noticing the same thing. For just a moment, Luna's eyes slide to me, the pupils sharp and clear. I pause, my breath catching in my chest. She's never looked at me like that before, like she's actually *seeing* me and not looking through me, at some future version of me. It's like looking at my sister for the first time. Luna gives me a small smile, and I smile back at her.

Then she slaps the inside of her leg again, shrieks, and charges Arial, arms extended and claws aimed at his face.

"NO!" Joan screams.

Luna reaches Arial, shoving him away from us to give us an opening. Suddenly, Arial stops laughing and the cave goes silent.

All the air and sound and cold is sucked out of the cave when I see Arial's knife plunge into Luna's heart.

"Luna . . ." I choke.

Her eyes go wide, then her face relaxes, utterly peaceful and expressionless.

Arial's eyes are wide too and he freezes, shocked.

Luna's eyes swivel to Joan, and a soft smile crosses her face before she stumbles backward, off the knife, and before either of us can grab her, out the mouth of the cave and over the cliff's edge.

All the feeling goes out of my legs.

Then I hear Thiago. Not a word, but a sound, an animal howl of rage and pain that grates on my nerves like a dull knife.

With a sudden burst of strength, he shoves himself to his feet. His dislocated arm hangs limply from his lopsided shoulder. He sways and starts to fall forward, but somehow manages to catch himself and run forward.

"Thiago, no!" Joan shouts. We both rush forward, grab him from either side. As weak and injured as he is, we struggle to hold him in place as he thrashes, shouting at Arial, spittle flying from his mouth.

"*¡Te voy a matar!*" he shrieks. "*¡Tú destruiste a mi familia! ¡Te mataré!*" Then his words are lost in garbled shouts. It's harder to keep him upright than to hold him back from Arial, as he is so unstable that he can barely keep his own feet underneath him.

If it weren't for my injured brother, my only family left, and the knowledge that Arial could easily rip him apart in this state, I'd attack Arial myself. I'd tear out his throat with my fingernails.

My insides feel like they're ripping themselves apart. Luna is gone. Thiago is teetering on the edge of sanity.

"Thiago, *stop*," Joan moans, somehow making herself heard over his furious howls. "He'll just kill you too."

"Don't . . . care," Thiago hisses through his bloody teeth, straining and fighting against us. Angry tears carve tracks down his filthy face.

My own face is wet, my eyes burning and blurring the horrible scene in front of me.

Luna can't be gone. She's just outside the cave somehow, completely fine and waiting for me to come get her so we can go home. She's waiting for me to brush her hair and put her to bed. She's not gone.

She's not…

Thiago's shoulders heave as he sucks in a sharp breath and then curls, arching his back and placing his head in his hands. A tortured yell rolls from him like a wave.

"We have to go," Joan says. She grips my arm so tightly it hurts, and with her other hand, grabs Thiago's shoulder. Joan squeezes her eyes shut and takes a deep breath. I wait for the strange sensation of falling forward through space.

But nothing happens.

Joan's eyes snap open again and all color drains from her face.

"You can't get back the way you came," Arial says quietly, still looking at the spot where Luna disappeared. "You can't travel out of these caves or the valley beyond them." He gestures to the sky outside the cave opening. "Not without a Passage."

Thiago goes slack in our arms, his strength gone, but he's shuddering, struggling to breathe through his sobs. I hold onto him, both to hold him up and to keep myself from falling apart.

He's all I have. The only family I have left.

Him and Joan.

"My offer still stands, Joan," Arial says. "I can send them home. Them for you."

Joan's eyes meet mine as we hold Thiago up, and I know exactly what she's thinking.

"Joan, no…" I moan. She looks from me, to Thiago, to Arial, her jaw stiff.

"You'll send them home and stop searching for the Clock Tower," she says, not looking him in the eye. "If I stay?"

Arial finally looks at her. "You have my word."

Joan chews the inside of her lip, her eyes shining. Finally, she looks at me. "I'll take care of Luna," she whispers to me. "I'll bury her."

"No…" I grab her arm, but she wrenches it out of my grip, stepping toward Arial.

"Fine. Send them home. Now."

Arial looks her up and down, but Joan only looks out the mouth of the cave, down at the landscape where somewhere, my sister lies, broken. My stomach heaves. Rage prickles my skin. Only Thiago's weight holds me back from sinking my fingernails into Arial's eyes or climbing down that cliff face to find Luna. He's all I have left, and I have to stay with him.

With a small nod, Arial lifts a hand and slowly drags it downward, creating a vertical line of golden light, almost as tall as me.

I stare at the floating golden line just for a moment, marveling, heart racing. But I can't stare for long.

"Go," Joan says to me, staring at the golden line. "Take care of him." She looks longingly at Thiago, then tears her eyes away to face Arial.

I can't leave my sister, but I have to save my brother. Everything in my body and mind fights against it, but I force my feet to move, taking Thiago with me. My eyes never leave Arial. I imagine peeling his skin off his face in strips.

"I'll see you again," I tell him. "And when I do, I will kill you." My voice sounds far away, even in my own head.

With my brother's ragged breathing in my ear, I step through the narrow slit of light, knowing it will take me home. Just before the cave disappears, I look at Joan. Her expression is alert, pointed. I give her a small nod and a final, promising glance at Arial before we step across the world, across who knows how much distance, leaving far too much behind.

39

Joan

The golden slit of light fades, growing dimmer until it disappears completely after Gabby and Thiago slip through. Leaving me alone with Arial.

I can't get the image of Luna toppling into the night out of my head. My heart slams in my chest. His presence makes my skin crawl.

He did this.

The first thing I'll do when I get a chance is find Luna's body and bury her. The second is hurt Arial as much as I possibly can. I know I can't kill him, but my mind runs through wild ways I can hurt or incapacitate him. Dismemberment, restraint, anything.

But he's strong. I doubt I can physically harm him at all, but I'll find a way to make him suffer like he's made the Cardozas suffer. I think of the seared red cuts across Thiago's chest, his beaten and bloody face. Rage storms inside me. It takes everything I have not to shout and lunge at him, biting and clawing and tearing at every bit of him I could reach, no matter how much he hurts me in return.

I might never see Thiago again. Or Gabby. And definitely not Luna.

Arial still looks to the mouth of the cave where Luna fell, his shoulders slumped and a faraway look in his eyes. It's strange to look at this man I've dreamed about for years, to see him with my waking eyes and hate him so much.

He sighs and then turns to me. I take a step back, but he doesn't approach.

"I'm sure you're thinking of shoving me out over that cliff right now," he says quietly. "I'd deserve it. You're welcome to try, but I'll be good as new in two minutes." He looks at the knife in his hand and then tucks it into his coat before approaching the opening of the cave, motioning for me to follow.

"I'm not going anywhere with you," I snarl.

"You will if you want our deal to stand," he responds. "The deal was you come with me, not that you stay here to wander these caves. You'll never find your way back out. So come along."

I suck in a deep breath, my heart still rattling. Finally, I take a few steps toward him. I'll go with him now, but I'll find a way out. I'll find a way back to them. I hope.

"I want to bury Luna," I tell him, crossing my arms over my chest. A cool breeze blows through the caves and I shiver.

Arial nods, as if he expected that. "You can bury the girl when we get to the bottom of the cliff, and then we'll go home."

That word, *home*, sends chills through my bones.

"You might even remember it when we get there," he adds. He stands at the cave entrance, looking down. He's right. I do want to shove him, just to watch him fall. Just to hear his bones break, even if they'll mend themselves in a few minutes. But the thought of him anywhere near Luna is revolting. I stuff my hands in my pockets to keep them from reaching out to push him over the side.

"We can't travel through this area," he goes on. "We can only travel in, like you traveled here, or in and out with a Passage, how your friends left. We'll have to go the slow way, but it's not far."

He turns to look back at me for the first time since Luna attacked him. I hold his gaze, glaring. I can't believe I'm staying with him. For the first time, my mind wanders to the implications.

At least Thiago and Gabby are safe. At least he's promised to stop looking for the Clock Tower. But how long would that promise hold?

The only thing I can do is cooperate and buy them time until the clock is safe. Until time is safe.

I step forward until I'm standing next to him, looking out over a valley carpeted with puffy green trees. A lake shines in the center of the valley, sunshine glinting off its glassy surface. I fix my eyes on the sky to keep from looking down. My gut twists inside me. Poor Luna.

"And forgive me if I forget to call you 'Joan,' sometimes," he says, looking sideways at me. "Old habits die hard." I glance at him and see him give me a shy, strangely childish smile that makes me want to turn and run deep into the caves, far away from him.

But I stay. I have to.

He reaches toward me. I jerk away. "Don't touch me," I snarl.

"It's very steep," he says calmly. "And you are still mortal."

For the first time, I let my eyes flick downward. The sheer cliff face stretches far below us, hundreds of feet high. I scan for Luna's body, but see nothing before dragging my eyes back to Arial. He's still offering his hand. I'd rather die than touch him, but if I fall, there's nothing stopping him from going after the Clock Tower and Gabby and Thiago.

Every cell in my body fights back as I reach out and take his hand.

40

Gabby

We don't speak. We have no words in the airless dome of our grief.

Thiago sits and stares at the wall for hours with hollow eyes. I try to clean him up, but he waves me off. He refuses to drink or eat, no matter how much I press.

The cafe sits closed and silent below. The apartment feels too big for two people, lifeless without Luna's quiet presence. Her things are still here, her clothes and a few childhood toys, but she's gone from this apartment. Even Gulliver twining around our legs, wondering why we aren't petting him, feels like a stranger.

I sit alone on my bed, staring at Luna's empty one. Made clumsily, with the covers pulled up crookedly and the mismatched throw pillows lying against each other like stones.

Luna will never sleep in that bed again.

I slowly stand, cross the two steps to Luna's bed, and shove the pillows to the floor before pushing down the blanket. A deep, unbearable ache seeps into the hollow inside me as I climb into Luna's bed, pulling her covers over me and resting my head on her pillow. The pillow smells like the jasmine-scented shampoo I used to wash her hair, like coffee from the cafe, and something else, some other animal scent that was distinctly Luna. Sweat from her night visions, maybe. I curl into the fetal position and pull the covers up to my eyes.

Something shiny on the pillow catches my attention. I reach up to grab a few strands of Luna's silver hair, the color of a newly minted nickel.

My chest tightens horribly, relentlessly. My heart is a lead weight pinning me to the spot, paralyzing me. I think of the moment at the top of a massive roller coaster right before you go over the edge, terrified, resisting, wishing for anything but to go over that drop, but you go down anyway. There's nothing you can do but hold on and plunge into your grief. Because it's going to swallow you anyway.

A sob shudders inside me and I cover my mouth, pinching Luna's hairs between my thumb and forefinger. I press my face into her pillow, letting the sobs rip through me in jagged waves.

My sister. My best friend. Luna. Never again will I share a room with her. I will never again fall asleep to the sound of her steady breathing. I'll never feel the comfort of her presence.

The sobs don't stop. A reservoir breaks over me. The hollow inside me fills with a contracting pain, like something's been removed from me and my body is trying to fill the space. I don't know how long I lie there, screaming into Luna's pillow, soaking the soft cotton with my tears and spit.

We couldn't even bring her home. We have no body to bury. The thought of my sister's body, dashed on the rocks and exposed to the elements, makes me sick. *I'll bury her*, Joan promised. I hope she does. I hope she can, with that monster around.

For the first time since we got home, I think of Joan. Joan is in danger. He thought she was his wife. Who knows what that filth will do to her.

I wish Joan were here to hold us together. I feel a twinge of anger that she stayed, leaving me to shoulder this alone, but I know she did it to save us, to save *everything*. But in this moment, I wish she hadn't.

I lie there all night, crying into the pillow until I feel empty. At some point, I feel the light pressure of Gulliver curling up in the crook of my legs.

***

When morning light streams into the bedroom, I finally roll onto my back, looking up at the wall above Luna's bed, covered with pictures and clippings from magazines that make no sense. Letters, faces, partial photographs, a hodge-podge I'd always found endearing. I always assumed she was trying to emulate my collages or something, or that the images triggered something for her.

Something catches my eye, and I sit up.

All the pieces, the images that I thought were random, form a word, I realize. How did I never notice this? I climb out of bed and look at the wall straight on, only to see a jumble of images. I lay back down and look up at the wall, and see it again. An image that can only be seen if you're lying down in the bed, where Luna would have been.

For the first time in what feels like forever, I smile. What if Luna knew what she was doing all along?

I know what Joan would want us to do now. What Mamá and Papá would want us to do. What Luna would want, if she could have told us. Maybe she *has* told us.

I know we can't mourn in stillness forever. Our grief will have to move us. There's more to do. I force myself to get up. Before I leave the bedroom, I tuck Luna's silver hairs into a tiny antique box I keep on my nightstand.

Thiago sits in the living room, staring at the silent television that isn't even turned on. Red rims his eyes, standing out like wounds on his pale face. His hair is tied hastily back in its bun, though loose tendrils fly wildly around his head. He hasn't cleaned his wounds, hasn't washed the dried blood from his face.

I have to break the silence. "Thiago…" He doesn't move. Doesn't even blink. "Thiago, we can't stay here. We have to find the Clock Tower."

"What Clock Tower?" he says mechanically.

"The one in Mamá's letter." His eyes flick to my face, full of pain, but he says nothing. Doesn't berate me for snooping. "That's what he was after."

"The clock can wait," he says tonelessly. "I'm going back to find him, kill him, and save Joan. Then we can worry about the clock."

"Joan's buying us time, you idiot!" I snap. "Even if we knew how to get her back, if we *could*, he'll go right after it again and we'll all be screwed. We need to find it and fix it so it can't be stopped."

"We don't know how to find it, or how to fix it," he says. "The only one who knew anything about it is gone."

"Luna knew what she was doing…"

"Don't say her name."

"She was my sister too!" I shout. My eyes grow hot with rage and loss. Luna. No more singing her to sleep on the ukulele. No more bringing home vintage magazines for her to cut up. "We'll find a way."

"We don't even know where to start."

"I think I know," I say quietly. "Come look at this."

Thiago looks up at me skeptically, then finally rises to his feet. I can still smell coppery blood on him, the musty smell of the stone room. My stomach twists.

I lead him into our room—*my* room—and stand facing the wall over Luna's bed.

"What?" Thiago says sharply, looking anywhere but at Luna's bed. "What are we doing in here?"

"Lie down and look up at the wall," I say.

Thiago squeezes his eyes shut for a moment before he finally crawls into the bed, lies on his back, and looks up. His jaw tightens and his eyes shine as they sweep over the collage. He frowns, but then his face releases into an expression of understanding.

"Oh," he says.

I know he sees it. The way the cut images slant together from that perspective, how even the glare on the glossy magazine pages comes together to form a word that can only be seen from where Luna's head would rest on her pillow: *Varanger.*

"What's 'Varanger'?" he asks.

"It's in Norway. I think that's where the Clock Tower is going to be. And it makes sense; look at the rest of her collage."

It all makes sense now. The pictures of snow, the northern lights, the written and numerical numbers of different sizes, arranged in a circle around the collage like a giant clock face. An article clipping catches my eye and I squint.

A National Geographic piece about the wildlife of the Varanger peninsula.

"She sent us a message," I say quietly. My eyes fill with tears. "She knew this whole time. What would happen, where and when it'll be. She's always known, and she was always trying to tell us. And…I think she knew she was going to die."

We're silent for a moment, taking in the emptiness of the room, looking over Luna's work on the wall.

"Can we fix it without her?" Thiago wonders aloud.

I shrug. "I don't know. Maybe she's left clues for that too, but right now we need to focus on finding it."

Thiago nods. After a pause, I lie down next to him on the bed, looking up at Luna's wall. We stay there for a while, transfixed. It's like Luna reaching out to us through time, leaving us a gift. My heart swells with a strange joy even though the rest of me is falling apart.

"But Joan . . ." he says.

"She'll be okay," I say quickly, trying to convince myself as well by saying it out loud. "Joan's smart. She knows what she's doing. As soon as we fix the clock, we'll get her back. If we try to find her now, though, none of us stands a chance. We can't fight him. She wanted to buy us time to get to the Clock Tower. She wanted us to find it."

Thiago's brow furrows. He stares up at the wall, eyes moving slowly over Luna's pictures. My heart thuds. I hope what I said was true. I hope Joan will be okay. She has to be. And we have to finish our parents' mission.

"All right," he says finally. "Let's go."

A weird mixture of relief and terror washes over me. Terror for us, for Joan. Relief that it might be over soon. We look up at the mandala of images, articles, words and numbers hastily cut and stuck to the wall. And I notice a picture of a clock tower, the picture of Big Ben that she cut a few months ago pointing to the twelve at the top, holding it all together like a pin.

At the center of it all, the last piece she added, the barn owl in flight, like it's leading the way.

I reach over and take my brother's hand, squeezing it, hoping he understands how big this is, how scared I am, but how much faith I have in Luna, in Joan, in all of us.

He squeezes back.

Acknowledgments

The list of people I could thank for the creation of this book is endless, but I'll start with my incredible writer's group. Jernae, Liesel, Mallary, and Wyatt, you are my support group, and I can't imagine trying to write a book without your incredible insights. Without you, I don't think I ever would have finished a book, let alone published it.

Thank you to my amazing family and their unending support of my writing. Thank you for always believing in me even when I don't. Mom, Dad, Chandler, Adam, Erianne, Kayci, Devin, you are the best family anyone could ask for. I love you all so much.

To my girl squad, Destinee and Lexi. You are the best cheerleaders and beta readers ever. Thank you for always celebrating my wins and picking me up after my losses, for believing in me, for being proud of me, and always, always being around for a pep talk, brainstorms, and for generally thinking I'm awesome. Your support is priceless.

Thank you to my incomparable editor, Suzanne, for giving my work that final polish, wrangling my rogue commas, and understanding the Chicago Manual of Style so I don't have to. Your words of support always give me the warm fuzzies.

To the long parade of teachers, authors, artists, and all-around amazing humans who have inspired me and offered nuggets of wisdom, encouragement, or insight along the way, thank you, from the bottom of my heart.

And to my readers who love these characters as much as I do and who choose to join them on their journey, thank you for supporting my work. Thank you for dedicating hours of your life to immerse yourself in the stories I create. Thank you, thank you, thank you, with all my heart.

Coming Soon!

Exclusive sneak peek at
Tower of Bone
Book 2 of the Keepers of Time Trilogy

Joan

I'm alone with a murderer.

I look out over the sunny valley, some part of me still wondering why it's daytime here when it was night outside the system of caves I wandered through, but I can barely think through the haze of rage and grief.

Luna's body lies far below on the rocks. I try not to look as I carefully descend, picking my way along the narrow ledge that serves as a path from the mouth of the caves to the ground, hundreds of feet below.

I hate that I took Arial's outstretched hand before that first heart-stopping step onto the ledge, but it was the only way to get down this cliff alive. He guides me down the path, pulls me back once or twice when I slip, sending showers of pebbles cascading down the cliff while my heart thrashes in my chest. But as soon as the path evens out, I throw his hand off. He simply shrugs as if to say, *suit yourself*.

Now he makes his way down, eight feet or so ahead of me. I watch his relaxed steps, his handholds, and follow him. He seems much more comfortable dangling hundreds of feet above the ground than I do. But of course, he can't die.

How am I supposed to get away if I can't kill him, can't even hurt him?

Should I even try?

After all, the only thing keeping him from looking for the Clock Tower, from stopping it and all of time with it, is me. I have to distract him until Gabby and Thiago can find it, fix it, and keep time safe forever.

Until then, I have to play nice. I'll have to get better at hiding my loathing for this insane, violent man who believes I'm the reincarnation of his dead wife.

Well, he's not wrong. I actually remember being her, a woman called Katherine, who lived hundreds of years ago. I know so little about her and the work they did. I don't think I want to know anything else just yet.

Right now, all I want to do is bury Luna.

My stomach clenches at the memory of Arial's knife protruding from her chest, her silver eyes flaring wide with shock and pain before she tumbled out of the open cave. My own heart stopping. Thiago's horrible howls of grief. Gabby's screams. The people I love most in more pain than I can ever imagine.

Thiago. My breath catches in my chest when I think of him, how weak he was, his blood-smeared face twisted in pain, the torn and burned flesh of his chest. It makes me want to lunge forward and shove Arial off the cliff just for the pleasure of watching him fall even though it wouldn't hurt him. I'd probably lose my own footing on the ledge and fall right along with him.

And I don't want him anywhere near Luna.

I take a deep breath and steel myself. *Thiago will be okay,* I tell myself. *Gabby will take care of him.*

For now, I'll bury Luna, protect the Clock Tower, and find a way to give this monster what he deserves. I calm my nerves on the way down the cliff by thinking of ways I could do it, a new method for each tentative step. Dismemberment, maybe. Cutting him into little pieces and scattering them over the earth. Sinking him to the bottom of the ocean. Encasing him in cement.

None of those things would kill him, of course, but death is too good for him anyway. Maybe a few thousand years in the bottom of the Mariana Trench would suffice.

After what seems like centuries, we reach the ground. My legs feel like jelly as they finally stumble onto actual soil. I feel dizzy from the descent. Arial watches me closely, his brow furrowed in concern. His hand twitches as if he wants to offer it to me again, but he decides against it.

Out of the corner of my eye, I see something colorful spread on the ground. Luna, her bright, mismatched clothes. Her blood. Finally, I allow myself to look.

About thirty feet away, Luna lies sprawled on her back on the rocks. Shimmering red blood still streams from the back of her head, soaking her silver hair, trickling over the rocks. Her shiny hair fans around her head and her arms spread to her sides. Her eyes are closed, her face serene. Aside from the blood, she looks like she could be sleeping.

Hot fury and pain bubbles up inside me. I bite the inside of my lip to hold back the shrieks of rage I want to unleash on the forest, on Arial. I stuff my hands in my pockets to keep from turning around and punching and clawing every bit of him I can reach.

"You wanted to bury the girl," he says softly.

The last thing I want to hear right now is his voice. I bite back my retort, choosing instead to say nothing.

"I'm guessing you don't want my help."

I shake my head, a quick jerk indicating a clear response: *Absolutely not.*

"I can fetch you a shovel."

"Just leave me alone."

I stare at a spot on the rocks just to the side of Luna's body, to avoid looking right at her. I don't want his help. I'll dig a grave with my bare hands if I have to.

"I'll return in a few hours," he says. "I have an errand. Don't get any ideas. You can't leave this valley without a Passage. And please don't try climbing back up that cliff and escaping. Even if you make it up, you'll never get out of the caves." Not just a warning, but genuine softness and concern in his voice. I clench my jaw until it aches.

He lifts a hand and draws the vertical golden line through the air again, as tall as he is—I think he called it a Passage—then steps through and disappears, leaving me alone at the bottom of the cliff.

My stomach sinks. I never expected him to leave me alone. I'm his prisoner, after all. Either he truly believes I can't escape, or he actually respects my wish to do this alone. Both options make me hate him more.

For a few moments, I stare blankly at the spot where he vanished, dreading what I have to do next. Finally, I turn to Luna's body and approach, my legs shaking with each step. A lump forms in my throat. Her golden skin is luminescent in the sunshine. Her hair, the color of moonlight, glistens against the pale granite, echoing the glittering specks of quartz sprinkled through the stone.

A scarlet bloodstain has bloomed on her chest, radiating outward from the small hole in the front of her shirt like the eye of a horrible flower. I try not to look at the blood from her head dripping steadily off one of the rocks.

Luna. Sweet, strange, brave Luna.

My own hand trembling, I reach out to take one of her hands. Blood smears her palm. Her fingernails are caked with it. For a moment, I wonder if it's Arial's or her own. I thread my fingers through her limp ones and hold her hand to my chest, resting my chin on our joined knuckles. Her hand is still surprisingly warm, her joints still pliable. No rigor mortis. I note that this is strange, but at the moment I don't care. She's still as stone, broken on the rocks. Lifeless.

"I'm sorry, Luna," I whisper. "I'm so sorry."

I watch her peaceful face. Somewhere in the forest, a bird chirps. The granite cliffs loom, crowned by a blue, cloudless sky. The trees stand silent; no breeze to ripple their leaves. Even the sun sits stationary in the sky, never progressing in its journey from one horizon to the other. Like no time is passing.

I see and hear no sign of Arial, or anyone else. Not even birdsong or the rustling of rodents in the grass. I'm completely alone.

A hot tear rolls out of my eye, stinging my cheek and dripping off my chin. I wipe it off and gently lay Luna's hand across her chest, covering the wound.

Time to get to work.

I wander along the edge of the woods, evaluating the ground, the quality of the shade, the wildflowers that grow at the base of the trees, until I find a spot of soft ground just inside the tree line tucked between two large aspens and surrounded by bluebells and little white flowers, the names of which I didn't know. Sunlight streams through the leafy canopy, speckling the ground. There's a small boulder dotted with green and orange moss, bathed in sunlight; a place I can imagine Luna sitting, watching endless futures before her and occasionally coming back to the present to enjoy the warmth of the sun on her face. She'd like it here.

I pause for a moment before returning to the expanse of rock below the cliffs, and find a wedge-shaped rock that fits my palm. When I return to the place I've chosen for Luna, I kneel between the two trees and drive the sharp edge of the rock into the soft ground. I stab at the earth over and over, tearing grass, chopping up the dirt, pounding until my arm aches, but I don't stop. It feels good to work like this, to feel my muscles burn and strain, to sweat and feel my heart pound from something other than terror. To hack at something with a rock.

I work for what could have been hours or days, never pausing as I break up the dirt and scoop handfuls out of the growing hole. I pound and scoop, pound and scoop until I have a hole about six feet long and a foot and a half deep, before I finally sit back on my heels and examine my work.

My chest heaves as I suck in breath, my heart thudding dully in my chest. Dirt and sweat streak my arms. Black soil rings my fingernails. I finally notice the blisters that have formed and popped on my right palm and fingers from holding the rock. My entire hand aches from gripping it for so long. I take a deep breath, filling my lungs slowly and letting them out, turning my face to the sky.

The sun shines at me through the same spot in the trees, beating down on me at the same angle as when I started. Sunlight spots the ground in the same places.

Has the sun moved at all?

What *is* this place?

While I note the strangeness, I'm too exhausted to investigate any further.

The grave is shallow, but I don't have the strength to deepen it, and I can't bear the thought of Luna lying in the open much longer.

My knees and back crack as I stand for the first time in what could have been hours or days. On wobbly legs I return to where I'd left Luna. Summoning my remaining strength, I crouch to grip Luna's arm and shoulder, and lift, rolling her up to a sitting position before she starts to bend over limply. Still no rigor mortis. Her skin still feels warm, but that might be from the sun beating down on us from its apparently permanent position in the sky. As she begins to lean over, I position myself beneath her, rolling her onto my own shoulders. My legs scream as I lift, hoisting her on my back, holding her arm with one hand and looping my other arm behind her knees until I'm supporting her in a clumsy fireman's carry. Then I straighten my aching legs. Though she's larger than Gabby, Luna is still smaller than me, which I'm grateful for as I adjust my footing, preparing to carry her to the grave I've prepared.

Her soft hair brushes back and forth over my arm as I walk, while the blood-soaked part hangs in tangles, soaking my clothes. I fight a wave of nausea as the warm liquid spreads. Too much blood. Luna's blood.

I progress slowly, hunched over with muscles straining to hold Luna in place on my shoulders and keep my footing on the sloped rock, to not trip on loose pebbles or plants when I step onto the soil.

Finally, we reach the grave. The sun shines cheerfully, illuminating the flowers in the little clearing. I swallow a lump in my throat as my eyes run over the grave. On the edge, I kneel near the bottom and carefully rest Luna's feet on the ground, then perform the lifting and rolling motion in reverse; setting her feet and legs down, then allowing her to slowly roll backward until she's lying down, catching her neck and gently resting her head on the soil.

I wipe my filthy hands on my shorts, then brush her hair off her forehead and arrange it around her face and shoulders. Finally, I place her hands over her chest, covering the wound.

I eye the mound of dirt next to the grave, but it's not time yet. I'm not ready.

I stand and walk around the clearing, picking handfuls of wildflowers, but never so many in one place that it leaves a bare spot. I kneel and tuck the flowers under her resting hands, arrange them on her chest to cover the blood, tuck a few into her hair.

I sit back, watching her. Peaceful. No sign of her violent death. Her skin still shines golden and luminous in the sun. Pale lips parted slightly. Eyes softly closed.

"Thank you for protecting us," I say. My eyes sting and the lump in my throat tightens. "Thank you for being my friend. For everything."

I sit in silence for a few moments, mulling something over. Finally, I ask one last thing.

"Did you know you were going to die?"

I know she won't answer, of course, but maybe if I say it out loud,

I'll understand.

I replay the awful scene in my mind, Arial toying with Luna, swiping the knife as she danced around him, always a step ahead. But then her pause, the expression of clarity that crossed her face before she told us to go. Goose bumps prickle on my skin as I remember the sound of that word on her lips, the only word I'd ever heard her speak. She was giving us a chance to leave. To throw Arial off enough for him to let us go.

I look over Luna's calm face. It was always something I'd wondered about Luna, if she'd seen her own death. There's so much I wondered about her, like how she stayed serene and gentle when she could see the horrors of the future, when she probably knew all of our fates. She was always sweet and kind despite what her abilities had done to her.

"You're the kindest person I've ever met," I go on. "I don't know how you did it, especially with your ass of a brother around all the time." I smile, but immediately take a breath. Thinking of Thiago is like a punch to the gut. His face flashes through my mind again, his pained shouting when he realized his sister had been killed, pain greater than what he'd already suffered at Arial's hands.

He should be the one to say goodbye to Luna now. Him and Gabby. Not me.

Do what you have to do, and everything will be alright, I tell myself. The thought calms me. I'll see them again. I'll see Thiago again, touch him again, be with him, but only if we can pull this off.

If.

I wish we'd had more time. I wish I'd had more time with all of them.

Grief rises inside me, the ache creeping higher and higher until I can't breathe through it. I lean against a tree, propping my elbows on my bent knees, and place my head in my hands. The heels of my palms press into my eyes, blocking out reality. Horrible spasms tear through my body, ripping through my muscles, clenching my insides with dry sobs.

It all bursts out of me in a howling shriek that rattles the trees and echoes in the empty forest, an inhuman wail that grates in my throat and lungs, scraping me raw on the inside. When I run out of breath, I scream again. And again. I scream until my throat burns and my mouth is dry as sand, until my chest aches I can't scream anymore.

With my eyes closed, I tip my head back against the tree and breathe deeply. The air stings in my lungs, but my head feels clearer. Quieter.

I look up again at that strange sun, still beaming at me through that same spot in the trees, then back down at Luna's face. Finally, I lean forward and plant a gentle kiss on her forehead and brush my fingers over her hands.

"Goodbye, Luna."

I grab a handful of dirt from the pile and sprinkle it over her clasped hands. Then another, and another. I scoop dirt back into the grave, over her body. It feels wrong. I wish I had a shroud or a sheet to lay over her, but there's nothing. So I keep scooping dirt until she's completely covered, a mound of freshly-turned earth between the two trees with the sun-warmed boulder at her head.

Because the grave is shallow, I return to the expanse of rock at the base of the cliff and bring back armloads of smaller rocks that I arrange over the mound, protecting it from the elements and any animals that might come along.

When the grave is completely covered in layers of stones, I gather a few handfuls of pebbles and arrange them in the shape of a waning crescent moon at Luna's head.

Then without turning around, I walk away, back to the place where Arial left me.

Covered in dirt, blood, and sweat, I find a rock to sit on, careful to position myself so that I can't see the massive bloodstain where Luna had fallen. My muscles twitch with exhaustion.

I don't know what will happen next. All I know is that I have to keep Arial away from the Clock Tower long enough for Thiago and Gabby to find and fix it, and until I can find a way to end him. Somehow.

For now, I wait.

The sun doesn't move as time passes. Or, maybe time doesn't pass at all.

Finally, I see movement in the trees, hear footsteps brushing through the grass.

Arial comes into view, his hands stuffed into his coat pockets. "Are you ready to go?" he asks, his face calm. No urgency to his question.

"Where are we?" I demand.

"Somewhere safe," he responds, meeting my accusing glare with an expression of patience that makes me want to punch him.

"We're in a time anomaly, aren't we?"

Now that Luna is put to rest and there's nothing ahead of me but lots of quality time with her murderer, with her parents' murderer, I want information. Anything I can use to hurt him or help Thiago and Gabby.

He looks at the sun, the corners of his mouth curving into an amused smile. "Very good," he says. "We're in a Timelock. I'm sure you noticed the symbols carved in the rock when you arrived outside the caves. Some of your best work, I'd say."

My stomach flip-flops. "Katherine made this?"

Arial nods, that stupid self-satisfied grin still plastered on his face. "Remarkable, isn't it? No time passes in this valley, or at least it passes so slowly that it's impossible to observe in a normal human lifespan. In the past few centuries, even I haven't noticed much of a change. It's been ten in the morning on June 5th for quite some time."

I look to the sun, dread growing in my gut. The sun never moves here. Night never falls.

That's why Luna was still warm. That's why rigor mortis hadn't set in.

This isn't how time works, my mind protests, but I've seen far too much to argue with him. If certain people can see through time, if I can somehow travel across the world in a split second, if the Clock Tower can keep time running after it's been torn apart by a deranged sorcerer, why not this?

A horrible thought hits me: If no time passes here, then how much time is passing in the outside world? How much time is passing for Gabby and Thiago?

"We can discuss this more later," Arial says. "For now, let's get you settled in."

I can't think of anything less appealing than getting "settled in," but I follow. *Play nice. Keep him busy. Get information.*

"Come on, now."

I follow him through the trees, hating him more with each step, the never-changing sun beating down as I wander deeper into this land where no time passes.

About the Author

M. N. Kinch is the author of *The Goblin's Daughter* (as M. K. Sawyer) and the *Keepers of Time* trilogy. She's been writing stories since elementary, often staying in from recess to sit in the school library and write.

When she isn't writing, M. is usually reading, painting, horseback riding, and eating inhuman amounts of dark chocolate.

M. lives in Utah.

You can connect with me on:

🌐 https://mnkinchbooks.com

Also by M.N. Kinch

The Goblin's Daughter (as M. K. Sawyer)

"I can honestly say that this is the best YA/NA fantasy I've read in quite a while."

-Suzanne Johnson, author of the award-winning Sentinels of New Orleans and Penton Legacy series (as Susannah Sandlin)